CAUSES OF CONSEQUENCES

CAUSES OF CONSEQUENCES

ALAN D. M. GARNER

Copyright © 2025 Alan D. M. Garner

The moral right of the author has been asserted.

Apart from any fair dealing for the purposes of research or private study, or criticism or review, as permitted under the Copyright, Designs and Patents Act 1988, this publication may only be reproduced, stored or transmitted, in any form or by any means, with the prior permission in writing of the publishers, or in the case of reprographic reproduction in accordance with the terms of licences issued by the Copyright Licensing Agency. Enquiries concerning reproduction outside those terms should be sent to the publishers.

The manufacturer's authorised representative in the EU for product safety is Authorised Rep Compliance Ltd,
71 Lower Baggot Street, Dublin D02 P593 Ireland (www.arccompliance.com)

This is a work of fiction. Names, characters, businesses, places, events and incidents are either the products of the author's imagination or used in a fictitious manner. Any resemblance to actual persons, living or dead, or actual events is purely coincidental.

Troubador Publishing Ltd
Unit E2 Airfield Business Park,
Harrison Road, Market Harborough,
Leicestershire. LE16 7UL
Tel: 0116 2792299
Email: books@troubador.co.uk
Web: www.troubador.co.uk

ISBN 978 1836282 198

British Library Cataloguing in Publication Data.
A catalogue record for this book is available from the British Library.

Printed and bound in Great Britain by 4edge Limited
Typeset in 11pt Adobe Garamond Pro by Troubador Publishing Ltd, Leicester, UK

To the resilience of the human spirit.

Suffering has been stronger than all other teaching, and has taught me to understand what your heart used to be. I have been bent and broken, but – I hope – into a better shape...

Charles Dickens

CHAPTER 1

In soft, amber sands, where for centuries camels had long been the main form of passage, three vehicles laboured along broken roads and through deep ravines. A formidable and unforgiving landscape at the end of ancient trade routes that once crossed the Sahara and ventured into the Sahel. These Arabic-named regions were christened when the West had little interest in a desert world where caravans slipped quietly across borders. Vehicle movement so far north was unusual, but the convoy drew no more attention than a few stone-throwing youths. In their attenuated faces, Owen recognised the same troubled gaze he saw on a blistering summer's day when he too joined in such a pastime.

Lowering the window, Moussa shouted greetings in perfectly nuanced Tamasheq to children running alongside.

"Did you have peace last night, my friends?"

Reaching out of the dust, they raised their palms in anticipation.

"No peace for us last night, or any night."

The noise jolted Owen out of the past and unceremoniously into the present.

Moussa looked across, shouting, his words drowned by the sound of engines and excited children.

"Shut the window," Owen said. "I can't hear what you're saying. And keep your eyes on the vehicle in front."

As the window closed on the outside world, a thin layer of the desert's dust settled across the inside of the vehicle's cabin. Some of the granules stuck to the wet surface of Owen's face, causing him to rub angrily to relieve the irritation. The rush of warm air was a reminder of the environment through which they travelled, many miles from the station in Bamako.

"At their age, I was underground mining gold with my father," Moussa said. Looking into receding taillights, his smile faded as he contemplated the memory. "The situation with mining that yellow metal isn't what it used to be. Many of the artisans of my father's time are now labelled criminals. *Qui profite? Pas mon people.*"

The occasional use of French was a formality Moussa used to remind colleagues of his country's past, regardless of their position within the organisation. Such ceremony was often dropped when they were alone or speaking as friends. On this occasion, Owen knew he was in for a lecture rather than the friendly chat he craved.

"I'll tell you who," Moussa said, speaking into the windscreen, "foreign corporations stripping this land of its resources, placing their own people into key positions. A continuing cycle of corruption…"

It was a story Owen had heard many times in a variety of forms.

An uncomfortable silence followed while Moussa searched for the reassurance of the taillights in the thick particles the vehicle in front was spewing into the air.

"They rush to take what remains. Do those children benefit, their families? This is what's left for them to inherit, heat and dust, these proud descendants of King Sundiata."

"What can we do about it today?" Owen asked, responding to Moussa's agitation. He had hoped to relieve the tension that had been building for some hours, but such an outcome seemed to have slipped away. "When we get back, we'll both go to the Ministry of Mines and make demands. You can stop working for the organisation and become minister for gold. Together, Moussa, we'll raise hell. Become the arbiters of our own destinies."

"Me and you together, yes," he said, smiling once again.

Both laughed hard at the inflated statement.

Mining gold in Mali shouldn't be our concern, Owen thought, conscious of the danger knowledge can bring.

Settling back into the journey, he continued to listen to Moussa's politicising because stories always occupied them during their expeditions.

The notion of antagonising one of the wealthiest men in government brought a wry smile to Moussa's aspect, encouraging his return to a more jovial character. But the awkwardness remained, something Owen seldom experienced in his friend's company. It was difficult to see how it had come to this, and now they were racing against the worst of the harmattan winds blowing up a storm. Convincing himself there were good reasons for his inertia was easy. The warning signs were there, but he chose to ignore them, those indicators he was trained to look for in a previous life. Aware time was no longer on his side, and only a short distance from Raz El Ma, Owen struggled to see the true purpose of their odyssey.

Everything is different between us now.

***

Moussa's comments prompted Owen to reflect on another mining dispute, a community struggle, not over yellow but black gold. For generations, Owen's family made a living nonchalantly taking coal from the earth. It was a way of life for the Morgan family. By the time of the coal miners' strike of the mid-eighties, three generations worked side by side in tunnels that stretched through the earth in all directions. His grandfather, Emri Morgan, relocated to South Yorkshire in 1982 to be closer to his daughter, Angharad. Navigating 180 miles to his new home in the north of England, a country unfamiliar to him, Emri listened to endless broadcasts dominating the airwaves that spring. A task force had been sent eight thousand miles into the South Atlantic to an obscure set of islands called the Falklands: *Las Malvinas* to Argentinians.

"No Owen, not off Scotland. The Antarctic, off Argentina," Emri said to his twelve-year-old grandson some days later.

The boy rushed upstairs to get the globe from his bedside table, a gift from his grandfather. Keen to demand answers, he sat on Emri's lap, calculating the distance using his mother's soft tape measure.

"One-inch equals roughly one thousand miles," Owen said, his cognitive cogs whirring loudly, shunted into action by the colossal distances involved.

Knowing what must have been going through his mind as he contemplated the enormity of the equation, Emri watched a quizzical expression spread across his grandson's face.

Owen had fond memories of this Welshman, who he often heard telling anyone willing to listen he moved from the valleys of South Wales "to teach the English how to mine coal." On the odd occasion, he heard great sadness in his grandfather's voice when he lamented about "the poor boys we far too often left underground." In such moments, Owen could sense the pain of his grandfather's sorrow.

During the early months of industrial action, Emri's main concern was keeping his family together, while some, divided by the side they took, were torn apart. To counter such a fate, the three men in the family met regularly, an attempt to maintain some form of solidarity within the household. It was on one such occasion, during a hot summer evening, Owen's grandfather, father and brother met in anticipation of one of the biggest gatherings the local colliery had seen since the start of strike action. A call had gone out for all available men to be on the picket line the next day.

Owen sat on the bottom step of the stairs across the hall, listening on the periphery, wanting all the details. As his mother passed, she placed a finger to her lips, gesturing with her eyes in the direction of the kitchen as if to say, *No noise, this one's important.* Before the kitchen door closed, Owen saw the three of them in their usual positions, cramped around the table, steaming mugs of tea resting on a recently ironed gingham tablecloth. In the middle sat a blue patterned willow plate, stacked with biscuits. If Owen had known it was going to be the last time the three would share the same space, perhaps he would have made more of an effort to hold them in a freeze frame, locking the memory inside his mind. Outside it was twenty-eight degrees, not warm enough to intimidate the neighbour's children Owen could hear running up and down the gennel. It was an activity that would infuriate his father. At any other time, he would have joined them, especially if Billy Johnson was among their number. But not today. The meeting was too important to miss.

"Thatcher has labelled us as the *enemy* within," Owen heard his father say some minutes into the gathering. "The coal we haul out of the ground day and night, that's what made this country great. Has the sneaky *bitch* conveniently forgotten that part of our history?"

"You know, Thomas, it used to be called black gold, but those days are finished," Emri said, measuring his son-in-law's response. "It's not gold anymore."

Thomas looked up, staring.

"The world's changing," Emri said, unperturbed. "Maybe it's time we accepted we're no longer mining a precious commodity."

"We're fighting for their future," Thomas said, pointing towards the kitchen door, knowing Owen was on the other side.

Early in the dispute, Emri had the same conversation with his grandson, but some months in, the futility of such ideas was obvious.

"He won't be following in your footsteps," Emri said. "That route's closed to the youth of this village, and there's not a lot we can do to prevent it anymore. This industry was lost long before our struggle to save it even started."

"I'm not sure I like where you're taking this," Thomas said. "We've been called an *enemy*. A provocative insult aimed at our comrades fighting for their livelihoods. Does that mean anything to you anymore?"

"Some would argue the fight has gone beyond what's reasonable," Emri said, knowing his words were pointless in Thomas's presence.

That's enough now, Grandad, Owen said to himself, mouthing the words inaudibly towards the door. Even at a young age, he knew his father's dispositions, a bully, a notion his mother never openly attested. It was one of the reasons Emri decided to relocate, to protect his child. Providing safeguards was the principle of good parenting, a belief adopted from his own father. When Jimmy was born, Anne and Thomas took him to Wales to introduce the child to his grandparents. A row broke out between them on the second day, raised voices coming from the garden. It was to do with Anne's insistence Jimmy carry the family name, Morgan, a throwback to their engagement, when Thomas supported his fiancée's wish. She and any children they had would use a double-barrelled surname, Morgan-Brown. All that changed. The bruise on her arm was an indication of what had taken place between them that day. "Inside, such men are really cowards," Emri told Anne some years later.

"If you don't want to join us on the picket line tomorrow, then stay here," Thomas said, raising his voice. "Jimmy and I will do what you no longer have an appetite for. But it surprises me, after everything your people have been through, you can't bring yourself to make them pay for such arrogance…"

Sitting opposite his father, Jimmy kept quiet. While he respected the man, he feared him too. For tonight, he would leave the arguing to his elders, there being more pressing issues weighing him down. What preoccupied him was not the value of coal, but rather an overwhelming sense of duty, one that came with a young wife and child in hard times. Jimmy wanted to reassure her everything was going to be alright. He had plans. A heavy burden of responsibility was keeping him awake at night, but he had no wish to share his concerns with either of them, not around the table. Waiting for his grandfather's response, Jimmy raised his eyes, observing Emri, trying to anticipate how the argument would progress.

Emri sighed, loud enough for Thomas to know he hit a raw nerve. *My people,* he thought. What did Thomas know about them? The tragedies they suffered.

"I'll be there," Emri said, breaking the uncomfortable silence, "not because this battle is winnable but because I want the best possible solution when it comes to the inevitable. My loyalties remain with the community, and I'll stand at its side, where I've always been."

"Be there, or not," Thomas said. "I no longer care. But keep in mind even Owen and his friend Billy will be in the vanguard to humiliate any *scab* daring to enter this village. Your own grandson."

It confused Owen that strike violators were labelled as scabs. He knew some of them. Went to school with their children. They were good people. How could an ugly dry crust be a label for such respected neighbours and friends?

"And that's where he should stay, on the edge of the village, away from the picket line. It's no place for a child. I hope you're listening to me, Owen. Stay in the vanguard," Emri said, raising his voice, knowing his grandson would be listening.

***

Later that evening, Emri took it on himself, as he often did with Owen, to explain the context behind the current unrest sweeping through the village. It was an opportunity for the boy to ask questions, exercise his fears. It was during such conversations Owen came to learn his grandfather was different from most adults, who would often lie, hiding the most important details.

"Grandad, will the scabs be punished for not supporting the strike?" Owen asked.

Emri always prepared a fresh pot of tea for them both, something that made Owen feel older than his years. It was like a religious procedure, mug first, then the paper bag from which Owen took two pear drops. One he immediately placed in his mouth. The other he stuck in his pocket for later.

"Once all this is over, Owen, those willing to cross the picket line will have to face the anger of their friends. In some cases, their own families. That'll be punishment enough. I suspect it'll be even worse for an unfortunate few. When we go back to work, and we will, those people, regardless of their reasons, will suffer a lasting humiliation. It'll take years for many to even start to forgive."

"Knowing Dad, humiliation won't be enough. He'll want more," Owen said, acknowledging the undertones of Emri's deduction.

"Don't worry, your father won't need to do anything. The shame will do its own work. I'm certain for some, exile will be more favourable than facing their community. Even worse tortures may follow."

"Like Judas Iscariot," Owen said, his intention to impress.

"Why do you say Judas?" Emri asked, concealing his emotions behind a forced smile.

"Because he's an example of the cost one pays for turning against those you once professed your love."

Owen had heard the quotation in a religious education lesson days earlier, regurgitated verbatim to promote what he hoped would be a positive response.

The notion strike violators could be labelled with such a dangerously pious meaning made Emri despair.

"The coaches you throw stones at," Emri asked, moving the conversation away from self-annihilation while looking gravely at him, "you do know they carry people, don't you?"

"Of course, I do. But Dad says not to worry because they're safe behind all the steel, watching from their cosy front-line seats. Like being in the cinema. Not that we ever see anyone at the windows anyway."

Owen's irreverent response failed to please Emri. Without the human aspect, his grandson would not be able to empathise with those inside the metal cages. His father was inept at generating such emotions, but in time, Emri hoped Owen would be able to transcend a world beyond his own ego. He considered telling the boy about the baton charges resulting in arrests, broken bones and pierced flesh. In the late hour, though, he decided such detail would be a lesson for another day.

"It's not a game on those picket lines," Emri said, instead.

"Grandad, I get it."

"I know your friends can't penetrate the metal coverings on those coaches with the stones you throw, but psychologically, Owen, that's a different matter. Your words will hit them where it hurts the most."

"Dad said—"

Recognising the emotion building in his grandfather's eyes, Owen chose not to finish his sentence.

"Remember, tomorrow, stay at the edge of the village in what your father calls the vanguard, with all the other children. And Owen, you and Billy, stay well away from the colliery and the police. They aren't your enemy."

With that last warning, he wished his grandson goodnight. There had been enough philosophising for one evening.

What did the boy know about the human cost on both sides?

It was a war of attrition, and the Iron Lady had all the hard power she needed to win. Walking the darkened streets back to his own house, Emri's sympathies were for those facing the anger of the strikers. They were the ones his grandson had been encouraged to throw stones at and shout obscenities. What Emri could never have foreseen was the context history would place on those events and the lasting impact it would have on his family.

CHAPTER 2

Throwing stones at passing scab coaches, as Owen and Billy called them, seemed grown-up to these two adolescents. The following morning, the two friends avoided the edge of the village, where they had been told to remain, finding a spot closer to the picket line. Owen chose a place from where they would have a stretch of road to themselves. One mile further along, following a route leading to the colliery, was where the striking miners waited. Many were bussed in for the day's events, ready to play their part at the business end, as Owen's father described it.

    Owen chose an abandoned railway station for his preparations. Other than the occasional high-speed train roaring through, the place had not seen passengers since steam was a method of propulsion. Older members of the community could still recall how those coal-eating engines whisked families off to east-coast resorts for fun and frolics. A footbridge connected its two platforms, the walkway long since boarded over. The once-white painted panels had turned a dull grey from age and steam damage caused by locomotives spewing out their excess gases as they passed underneath. Years of dried paint peeling from the woodwork hung flaccidly from its structure. The only people visiting the dying relic anymore were trespassers ignoring the sign nailed on the outside, advertising in red, six-inch letters the imperative, *Stay out*

– *DANGER*. In the old waiting room, where the village Romeos met their Juliets for a few minutes of pushing and shoving, the odd used condom decorated a greasy floor.

Billy looked attentively at an array of colours chalked onto the ageing concrete of the southern platform. Opposite was Owen, waiting for a response from his friend. With a facetious smile, Billy started proceedings, his wry comments aimed at distracting Owen from his serious demeanour.

"Where did you get all the chalk?"

"From school, of course. Where else would I get it?"

"You stole it?"

Owen hoped Billy was going to be grown-up about the day's events. Their role held national importance because they would be doing their bit for the cause. There was no room for error, Owen warned, and neither should they allow the demands of life to get in the way, including lunch and homework. Billy smirked at the mention of schoolwork because he never did any anyway unless his friend was helping.

Waking early, Owen allowed enough time to walk the route the coaches would take as they made their way through the village. Once the task was complete, he searched for the best position from where they could execute his ideas. The most suitable place to hide themselves was across the road from the station, among some bushes on Balaclava Street. Long before Billy arrived, Owen made some preparations, including the detailed drawing they were staring at on the floor of the platform.

"It's the map of the area I've chosen for our ambush site," Owen said.

"Ambush site?" Billy asked, fighting the urge to laugh.

Owen knew his friend was playing with him, trying to get a reaction.

"That's what we're calling it," Owen said. "So… does it all make sense?"

"You mean the drawing?"

"What else would I mean?" Owen asked, taking the bait.

"What's that?" Billy asked, nodding to an area on the chalked map before turning and pointing at a level crossing fewer than fifty metres up the steel tracks. "Are those two white lines supposed to be the crossing I can see over there?"

"You know they are," Owen said, annoyed at Billy's flippant responses.

"Why would you draw something I can see with my own eyes?" Billy asked in a hail of laughter. "Owen… please… explain."

Below the surface of his comedic guise, Billy was fascinated with the arrangement of colours and detail he saw in Owen's sketch. The visual aid made perfect sense, accentuating the topography in a way that suited his needs. He had no intention of admitting that to his friend.

Owen had to push his plan or risk losing Billy's attention.

"Let's assume the same tactics are used to deliver the scab coaches as they always use," Owen said. "Then we can expect a police escort, probably one car at the front and one at the back."

Producing some pebbles from his pocket, Owen placed them on the ground, representing six vehicles. He had chosen them some days ago: four large, all brown in colour and roughly the same size, and two smaller ones, immaculately white and shiny. The two white pebbles he placed at the front and rear of the brown ones.

"Absolutely nothing to be thrown at police cars. That's the two white stones. Understood?"

"Understood," Billy said.

"Anything in between these two is fair game."

"Fair game. Got it."

"Any questions so far?" Owen asked.

"I have some," Melanie Bancroft said, her voice echoing out of the shadows.

Both boys turned, surprised anyone had managed to follow them without being noticed. Owen glanced at Billy, raising his eyebrows, as if to say, *Well you were the last to arrive.*

Mel came from a part of the village they rarely frequented, an area where its residents owned their own homes in a spattering of venerable plots with wraparound gardens. Like many of the children from those more affluent areas, Mel went to the grammar school in town, unlike the boys, who were schooled in the village's comprehensive. She was different from the other children from her side, choosing to hang around the chip shop and youth club at weekends. A pastime that angered her parents. They had forbidden their daughter on numerous occasions from such gross entertainment. It was not unusual for them to drive across the divide and remove her from such places, much to the amusement of Mel's working-class friends. Mr Bancroft was a town councillor, and while his wife never seemed to be employed, there were rumours she once aspired to be a politician. They were the kind of contemptuous people who would be surprised, even offended, to learn Owen's grandfather owned a three-storey Victorian building back in his hometown of Pontypridd.

Striding out of the darkness, Mel walked up to the sketch. Her shadow fell across it, shielding Billy from the blinding sunlight.

His first thought was for her clothes, not suitable for an ambush at all. Mel was wearing white bell-bottom jeans with a matching denim waist-length jacket, a Bauhaus T-shirt and pure-white Converse All Stars on her feet. His second thought brought on a rush of guilt because he already had a girlfriend. Ruth would be with other children waiting for the scabs to arrive, where safety was sought in numbers.

Joining them, Mel crouched, adopting the same posture as the two boys before looking over the detail. Once she had the gist, she locked eyes with Owen, causing Billy to avert his gaze.

"Well, ready for questions?" she asked.

Owen held Mel's stare, determined not to be intimidated. Unlike Billy, his first thought was why this girl would be interested in his plan. Her father would be a million miles from the picket line, a Thatcherite to the core, as his own father would have said.

Boy and girl continued to look at each other, both in silent judgement.

"Okay, questions," Owen said, trying to make sense of the situation, pleased she was sharing his space.

"I have one," Billy said, before Mel could respond.

No, you don't, thought Owen, cringing with embarrassment.

Looking at his friend, he hoped it was going to make sense now they had an audience.

"Yes… Billy?"

"Well," Billy asked, his eyes darting between the two of them, "where did you get those two white stones, and did you find them polished or did you do it yourself?"

It was a serious question, the best he could come up with under the circumstances, obvious from the way it was asked, but a red herring, nonetheless. Out of respect, Owen managed to control his response. Had they been alone, he may well have reacted with a tirade of abusive banter, especially after the jocularity of the level-crossing comment. Mel, too, held her composure, wise enough to know she was the reason for Billy's response. Her respect for his question was the confirmation Owen needed. Not here to make fun, for which he was grateful.

That's just as well, Owen thought, because Billy's sunken eyes were evidence he had been arguing with his father. A relationship that took its toll on his friend.

He had a reputation: gambler, adulterer and fighter. "A man who uses his fists to communicate," Emri once told Owen, "is one who doesn't have a basic level of human intelligence. But sometimes, Owen… sometimes." Billy's father was reason enough not to shame him in front of the girl they both admired from a distance.

"I got these from school, like the chalk," Owen said, nodding sympathetically.

"Oh—"

"Next question?" Owen asked, addressing Mel to avoid further interruptions.

"I have a couple actually," she said, "but first I'd like to contribute to your model."

The two boys stared as she lifted her left hand to the area of her right breast pocket. Undoing a silver button, she released the denim flap, placing her fingers deep inside, before removing a pair of imitation pearl earrings. Leaning forward, she placed one on top of each white stone.

"There," she said, "now they have sirens."

Owen watched, transfixed, noting two things: one, she had a second pair of gold earrings in her perfectly formed ears, dangling in the afternoon's sun; and two, the flap of her pocket was still open, just enough for him to see the opening from where Mel had removed the pearls. He recalled later how he had an overwhelming desire to lean forward and secure the button back in place.

"Now for my questions," she said. "I know, by rite of passage, I shouldn't be here, my father being who he is, but I really want to support the cause and join the two of you today. If it's okay."

"We have no problem with that," Billy said, before Owen could consider the request.

Mel smiled her appreciation at both, revealing two perfectly formed dimples.

"Thank you for having me," she said.

"And your second?" Owen asked.

"Why is it you two stay away from the crowd?"

It was true, Owen always chose a spot away from interference, allowing him to make his own decisions, even if it went against his grandfather's direction.

"It's no fun following the masses," Owen said, "and this isn't a village fête."

"I get your point," she said, acknowledging with another knowing smile, this time much more open and friendly, reassuring even.

"We wait for the screaming of the crowd, and then we know they're on their way," Billy said, not wanting to appear as Owen's second. "It's better to hit the scab coaches after those amateurs have had their fun."

"There's no element of surprise with a crowd," Owen said, "and that bores me. Our way is more personal. When the coppers are free of the vanguard, we manage to surprise them one more time. A second pelting is even more embarrassing than the first. A little warm-up before the picket line."

"You hurl rocks at police," Mel said, her voice lifting in surprise. "Wow! That's brave of you both."

"No, we don't, we *never* go for them, *never*," Owen said.

"It's the three of us then," Billy said, as their attention returned to the sketch.

It was the first time Owen had spoken to the posh girl, and now they were sharing their day. The idea generated a warmth emanating from the depths of his stomach. He did have one concern, Billy's sudden change of character.

CHAPTER 3

"We wait on the bend, on the southern side of the railway crossing, where the pedestrian flyover crosses Balaclava Street," Owen said, aware the clock was ticking. "The incline will slow the coaches down, making them vulnerable. I'm fairly certain a gap will form once the police car reaches the lip of the hill."

"Only *fairly?*" Mel asked.

"They'll be in Granadas," Billy said, as if his statement held some discernible message.

"Ford Granada," Owen said, in response to Mel's confused expression. "A police car. It's petrol and fast, unlike the coaches, which are heavy and diesel."

"I know what a Ford Granada is and who drives them," Mel said. "But why accelerate away from the convoy? I don't get why the police would do that."

"I'm relying on probability, nothing more," Owen said. "I'm not saying they'll leave the convoy behind, just the gap will widen. In any case, even if they don't, the bend will shield us from the first car once it passes." Owen was starting to sweat, a consequence of the day's heat, or Mel's interrogation, maybe both. "We let the police car through and then strike the lead coach. It'll be moving much slower when you consider the hill and bend in quick succession."

"Surely the coaches will stop?" Mel asked. "When we've pelted them with stones."

"They won't," Owen said. "We can't penetrate the steel mesh over the windows anyway. A few stones will be the least of their worries today."

"And what if we're seen?"

"How many times have you done this?" Owen asked, starting to figure out why she was asking so many questions.

Mel looked at each of them, delaying her answer.

"Never," she said. "This is my first time. I'm a strike-day virgin."

Hearing her reply, Billy laughed so hard and sharp the other two jumped in response. He had never heard that word used by a girl before: *virgin*.

"No one will be looking out the windows," Owen said, ignoring Billy's sudden guffaw. "They want to remain anonymous. The stakes are too high to risk being identified. You won't be seen. I can guarantee it. Besides, we'll be gone before they even know we were there."

"I see," she said, looking at the map, her earlier confidence waning.

"Are you okay for me to continue, Mel?"

Then, as an afterthought, Owen looked across at Billy.

"Okay for me to go on?"

Billy raised his eyes, insult written all over his face. Having recovered from his laughing fit, he settled into impatient mode.

What was the problem? he thought.

The plan was laid out in all its colourful detail, right in front of her. The direction they would take across the road and the route once finished. It was all indicated on the sketch. Simple. Billy could see the browns and greens were bushes and small trees would shield them from sight. Owen had already placed small rocks and stones in preparation. Once under the pedestrian flyover, all they needed to do was slip inside the bushes, then they would be ready.

The best plan yet.

"Yes, continue," Mel said. "I'm starting to see how all this works."

Finally, thought Billy.

"To the rear of us is a small track," Owen said, "no more than a few feet wide. It's protected on both sides by a thick covering of thorns. A natural tunnel. Once we're done, we'll use it to get into the Cunard estate, and then we'll be finished."

"We'll be eating soggy chips with scraps from the chippy before you know it," Billy said. "Owen's treat."

In the distance, excited shouts erupted, a sure sign the convoy was about to enter the village. In response, Owen picked up one of the stones, throwing it at Billy.

"You lead us in," he said. "No more time to waste."

The excitement for Billy brought about a rush of adrenaline. Not because of the approaching scab coaches, he had confronted them before, but Mel's presence.

"You follow Billy," Owen said, "I'll bring up the rear."

Mel nodded, bit her lower lip, and started to run, trying to catch up with Billy, who had already made a start.

The three emerged out of the station onto a deserted street, Billy leading them under the flyover. It was a concrete giant, mockingly referred to by village satirists as 'that Stalinist structure'. The monstrosity had been erected to provide safe passage across what was normally a precarious road. On the far side, where its pillars sank deep into the earth, the three teens disappeared into contrasting greenery, returning Balaclava to its unusually serene state.

Once inside the makeshift den, both boys looked at each other, realising the spot was not chosen to house three teenagers.

"Billy, you squeeze up against the brambles on the left," Mel said, taking control. "Owen, you go to the right. I'll get in the middle."

The three settled into their positions, waiting, saying nothing, each facing back towards the road. In the near distance, the roar and whistle of diesel engines could be heard, challenging the silence of a hot summer's day. For a few more seconds, Balaclava Street was calm, the only movement a low shimmer as the sun's heat penetrated the asphalt.

Somewhere behind them, a dog could be heard barking. A reaction perhaps to the noise of approaching vehicles.

Each was preoccupied, trying to control their breathing, a result of Billy's mad dash across the road. Owen could feel the delicate rise and fall of Mel's body against his own. The idea Billy could also feel it brought on an abstract sting of jealousy.

Inside the undergrowth, between gaps in the branches, the sun's rays slipped through, sending shards of light cascading in, forming dust-balls dancing in and out of the shadows. For Owen, it was magical when mixed with the warmth of Mel's body against his own. The experience brought him back to her breast pocket and the two pearls she had presented.

"Mel, your earrings," Owen whispered, leaning into her, "you left them on the stones."

"I know," she said. "I'll go back when everything's calmed down. If it's safe to do so."

"It'll be safe, you'll see. We can go and get them together."

"Yes… let's," she said.

The awkwardness in her response was missed by Owen. All he heard in her soft voice was clarity and beauty. It would be some time before he understood the only thing he controlled that day was his own perspective. What he did notice, something that would never change, was the nape of her neck, exposed where Mel's collar had been pulled down. It was tanned like the rest of her visible skin, and Owen ached to see more. He saw her cheeks were smudged with dirt, and her hair had been given a light brushing of green leaves. Dampening the pure white of her jacket and jeans was a sprinkling of dust across her body. He was smitten. It was an image to be filed away in his mind, brought out in the privacy of his own space, to be played with when alone.

"It's my new look," she said, noticing his interest. "Your fault, choosing this filthy place to—"

She stopped speaking, staring at something over his shoulder.

Owen noted her pupils were dilated, a sure sign Mel's fight-or-flight mechanism had been triggered. Turning, he saw what she was looking at.

A police car with two constables inside was coming into view.

Now they had entered the village, both police officers were busy anticipating the violence of the picket line. The burning question they asked each other, over and over, was whether their colleagues could smash a safe route through the mass of men who meant to stop the convoy?

Had they not been preoccupied, maybe they would have worked it out.

Hill, bend, flyover.

The three assailants were primed and ready, stones held in each hand. Hearts racing, they watched the car drive over the crossing where the road became Balaclava Street. Approaching the bend, it slowed before drawing level with the bushes in which the pubescent teenagers hid. It seemed as if they could reach out and touch the force's polished logo embossed on the passenger door: a crown sitting atop a seven-pronged star and enclosed within, standing proud, the white rose of Yorkshire. Below all the pageantry was the slogan: *Justice with Courage.*

Billy's attention was drawn to the crown's tip, the cross pattée, a perfect point of aim. It dawned on him he had this one opportunity to prove himself in the presence of Melanie Bancroft.

Owen sensed Billy was moving, adjusting his body into a sitting position, readying himself to strike the police car.

Drawing his arm back, Billy started to count, "One, two—"

"Billy, no!" Owen said.

Before his traitorous friend reached three, Owen launched himself over Mel's body, staying Billy's arm.

Both boys stared, eyes wild and hot, a standoff unlike either had experienced during their friendship. Facing each other, their fists were clenched, shoulders tense, ready to fight, filled with boyish hatred.

The Ford Granada passed under the flyover, disappearing around the bend.

From that distance, if Billy had thrown his stone, he would have hit his target. Then the patrol car would surely have stopped. Had that scenario unfolded, it would have dragged the policemen out of the future and back into the present where they were needed.

"Both of you, stop it," Mel said, bringing the pair back from the brink. "Look… Crossing… Coach."

Time was moving too fast, adding to the tension and confusion in the confined space, preventing Mel from forming her sentences.

The last opportunity to change the day's events was unredeemable.

The first coach started to encroach on the scene, throwing a shadow across the street, shrouding the den in darkness. It seemed at any moment the scab coach would alter its course and bear down on them, turning the tables. Black diesel fumes billowed from its exhaust, spewing fog-like gases across the road. The change of light and choking particles made it difficult to focus on anything other than what was in their immediate vision, the coach's centre of mass.

Time was up.

In all the excitement, no one noticed two men above, hiding their presence behind the walls of the flyover. Even if, in those final seconds, someone had seen them lurking, it would have made no difference. They meant to stop the convoy, preventing the scabs from reaching the colliery.

To rescue Owen's plan, the teenagers had seconds. Speed

and teamwork was all that was left. Recent hostilities, any acts of mutiny, had to be pushed to one side.

Their eyes were fixed on the side of the coach. Nothing on the periphery mattered.

Each raised an arm, ready to strike.

But none of them released their missiles. Instead, they froze, incapable of action because of what they were seeing, bringing about a state of unplanned passivity.

Staring back was a young man, a scab. Through the grime sticking to the window, it was still possible to see the distorted image of the strike violator. His face was lean and haggard, exhausted-looking. In those features, they were witnessing what betrayal could do to the human psyche.

The surprise for Billy was immense.

For Owen, it was heart-breaking.

Looking back at them was Jimmy, smiling through the murky glass, just as surprised.

"You do know they carry people, don't you?" Emri had said. An appeal Owen finally understood.

All three held Jimmy's gaze, looking at him as if he were the focus in a surrealist painting displayed in a gallery they should never have entered.

Interrupting their concentration, breaking the spell, an object fell from above, coming out of nowhere. Hours later, at the police station, they learnt it was a three-hundred-pound slab of concrete placed on the pedestrian walkway in anticipation. Like Owen, two striking coal miners saw the potential of the hill and bend, targeting the vulnerability of the coach's soft roof.

The falling concrete sliced its way through with ease.

Between the crunching of metal and screaming passengers, there was a faint but definite thud, pleasant to the ear among the more violent sounds. The concrete continued its downward motion, crushing the driver and pinioning him in his seat. Death came instantly. Veering to the left, the coach slammed into the reinforced pillar closest to the den in which the three cowered. The ground under them shuddered, as if dancing to the melody of brutal noises echoing across the road.

Once the noise settled, Mel, wide-eyed, turned to Owen and whispered a retrospective statement, one he would never forget.

"Perhaps you should've let him throw his stone," she said.

CHAPTER 4

The potential for our kind to inflict such brutality is a lesson we all learn at some stage. That was the role of those hidden on the walkway, two men motivated by vengeance. There were other examples of violence outside the colliery. *Some of the worst clashes of the industrial action* was how the media reported it. If an accurate casualty list had been drawn up, then the three teenagers would have been on it. The injuries they sustained were the sort not seen with the naked eye. But it was 1984, who even discussed such human vulnerabilities?

There would be no more vanguard action for the infamous three, labelled by their peers as the Balaclava Street Ambushers. Once it was apparent they had no credible evidence, none that would lead to a conviction anyway, all three were cleared for release back to their families. Emri collected Owen and Billy from the police station, arriving from the picket line after hearing of their involvement.

The first thing he saw as he walked through the station's doors was Melanie Bancroft sitting alone in the waiting room.

"What are you doing here?" Emri said, his voice full of concern.

Looking up, Mel smiled, tears streaming down her face, recognising him. Emri had attended a poetry competition, a series of readings at the grammar, which she won in the originality section. She recalled his congratulations afterwards in the main hall as parents and guests drank complimentary tea and coffee.

Mel noticed he was holding a pamphlet the audience was given on arrival. It was open on the page containing her fifty-two lines of free verse, with numerous notes Emri had scribbled in the margin.

"I'm with them," she said, pointing towards Owen and Billy, who were receiving a lecture from a stoical-looking police sergeant in an adjacent glass-fronted office.

Emri insisted they remain by her side until her parents arrived, refusing to leave Mel on her own, even when the desk officer claimed he could look after the girl. It was dark by the time he saw them walking up the steps to collect their daughter. Emri sat watching, their faces featureless in the dying light. Then, as Mel was marched towards a waiting car, with no words of thanks, just suspicious glances in Emri's direction, he overheard her mother's lecturing of her husband. A man who far too often ran his fingers through his hair.

"What was she thinking?" Mel's mother said. "It's not our fight and certainly not Melanie's."

"Let's just get her home," he whispered back.

"What's it got to do with us?" she asked, raising her voice, as if directing her anger at anyone in earshot. "It's between the coal miners and the police. And *you*," she said, as Mel was pushed onto the back seat, "they're not your people."

Yes, Emri thought, *many hold the same view*.

A working-class dispute, a three-way fight between the miners, strike violators, and police. It was that simple to some. There was little that could be done to convince such folk otherwise, especially those who refused to accept their own fallibility.

Mel's mother knew where to put the blame.

Projecting her voice, in earshot of others, was a trait Mel hated, embarrassingly so. Her need to compete for the limelight. She was aware it horrified her father also, but he would never challenge such rudeness.

Emri walked Billy back to his home, but there was no one around to comfort the boy. He was certain Billy's father would be in the Working Men's Club, telling war stories and drinking ale with other likeminded souls, praising themselves for the role they played in the day's events. The self-preservation society was what Emri called it. There was no mother figure at home for Billy, having long since regained her independence from the man she married only weeks after leaving school. Emri decided it was best to take both boys to Angharad, where loving care would be waiting in abundance. Once delivered, and with a quick squeeze of his daughter's hand, Emri went in search of Jimmy with a newfound sense of urgency. Jimmy's decision to get on the coach sealed his fate, becoming one of the exiled, securing his name on the list of those eternally branded scabs. Emri had a plan for his oldest grandson, one he needed to action immediately, but it had to be done in secret, shared only with his daughter.

News of Jimmy's betrayal spread across the village, a place where everyone knew everyone, and personal business never remained private for long.

The shame almost broke Thomas.

The year-long strike came to an end. Its aim to prevent pit closures resulted in pit closures. There were no more myths of black gold buried deep beneath the earth. It returned to what it was: a sedimentary deposit.

***

Mel never went back to the railway station to retrieve her earrings, but Owen did.

"What do you mean they weren't there?" Billy asked.

"Someone beat me to it. Mel maybe?"

"Not a chance. You saw that mad woman when she left the police station. Mel's grounded, *forever*."

"Someone's been there. There were signs."

"Someone's always there. You know that."

"I mean a person interested in my sketch, not the other thing. They tried to scrub the map clean, wipe it from the platform."

"It's gone?"

"No, it's still there, but it looks like an abstract piece of art."

"Speak English, Owen," Billy said.

"It's just a mashed mess of colours. That's what I mean."

Returning to the railway station, it was obvious someone had tried to remove the sketch. At the time, he thought it looked like some artsy person's perspective of the carnage strewn across Balaclava Street. That was the point Owen wanted to impress on Billy. The approaching rains would eventually complete the task, washing the remaining tangle of colours from all existence.

"At least Mel's studs played a small part in your plan," Billy said, "before they were stolen."

It was a comment hitting an open wound with Owen, a reminder it was all his idea. Emri tried to reassure him on numerous occasions they were all willing participants.

"The studs, I get," Owen said, "but my stones?"

"Some dating couple. A gift for services provided…"

***

The three did their best to bury the experience, as is often done, by ignoring it. As they raced towards young adulthood, keen to be finished with the best years of their lives, the experience haunted their dreams, silently chipping away, demanding consequences. One such outcome, impossible to have foreseen, was the impact it had on Owen and Billy's relationship. They started to go through a period of letting each other go.

Inside those thorn bushes, everything changed between them.

As they grew, Billy was the first to escape into the world, choosing the army, leaving the village a couple of years before the other two managed to follow suit.

"Maybe it's for the best," Emri said at the time, "his father being the way he is. You too need to find another way. Your generation won't be following us into the industry. It's finished."

"Me, in the military, Grandad?"

"That's not what I meant. Far from it," Emri said, as if recalling some distant memory. "Your best asset is your brain, so use it. Those exams you have coming up, your mother says good results could get you into the grammar. That posh school in town."

"But we have a sixth form at the comp. I don't need to be travelling into town, *every day*."

It was a common topic between Emri and Anne, Owen's studies and his apathy towards them. She despaired at her son's distracted demeanour, blaming the school for failing to engage him academically. The proof she argued was in his IQ, 135, a test Emri insisted he take. The number meant nothing to her, but her father said it was close to the best.

"Knowledge is power, Owen, stick with your education. Take the chances I didn't get. It'll be your ticket out of here," his grandfather said.

Emri's persistence was a sustained attack, a continuous verbal assault to prevent Owen from floundering. Billy was not joining the army because of any romantic notions or multicoloured uniforms and shiny trinkets. For him, it was much simpler. It was the only way forward he could see, but it was different for Owen.

"You should go and see him before it's too late," Emri advised weeks before Billy's departure. "From what I hear, he won't be around for much longer."

"He's at Ruth's most of the time," Owen said. "Why would they want me bothering them with so little time left together?"

"Go Owen. You'll only regret it if you don't."

***

Standing on Ruth's doorstep, the two boys caught up on trivialities: Rovers' miserable season, the state of all things school, and girls, the ones Owen was carelessly chasing.

"I can't believe you didn't tell me," Owen said, getting to the point. "Such a big decision."

"I don't run everything past you before making my choices," Billy said, behind a serious smile.

"You used to."

"All that changed some time ago."

Unsure if he understood the statement, Owen took it to mean Billy's defiance when faced with the police car, taking matters into his own hands, deviating far from the plan.

"It did change," Owen said, "but you had your reasons, and I respect them."

"Anyway, I'm going. Getting out of this miserable place. Thank God."

"When?"

"After exams. Went into town last week to be attested."

"You're not even going to wait for results?"

"We both know what they'll be like. Disastrous. I can't get you to sit them for me. It's not homework."

"But I would if I could. You know that, don't you?"

"Ruth has promised to write to me," Billy said, avoiding the question.

"I never thought you two would last."

"Yet, we did."

"What did your dad say?"

"It's none of his business what Ruth and I get up to," Billy said, a patent smile creeping across his face.

It was a glimpse of the friend Owen once knew. He tried to respond with something equally entertaining, but words failed him.

"I'm surprised he's letting you go so early."

"He *doesn't know*, and I don't want him to *know*," Billy said, emphasising his words to avoid any chance of misinterpretation.

"How could you possibly join without his permission?"

Billy looked at Owen, encouraging him to work it out for himself.

"If your dad didn't sign the papers, who did?"

"He's never sober enough to sign anything," Billy said.

"You signed them, didn't you?"

***

True to his word, Billy was gone post-exams. His predictions proved accurate. Disastrous. Mel sailed into the sixth form of the private school where her mother had sent her, away from distractions. "There'll be no more trespassing into their side of the village," was her justification. Owen was top boy at the comprehensive, securing a place at the grammar, the same establishment where Melanie Bancroft was once educated. A name one day they would proudly claim as one of their own.

"You've made family history," Emri congratulated. "Now go and make more."

Within two years, Owen secured results worthy of a university place, another Morgan family first. York was his chosen destination to read international relations.

"My grandson, international relations," Emri preached to anyone willing to listen. He was so euphoric it almost came to fists when someone in the Labour Club questioned the subject's worth.

Some days later, Emri asked, "Owen, what exactly is international relations?"

"It's about seeing the bigger picture in the world, those global ideas," Owen said, enthusiasm flowing out of him. "I want to see what makes this world tick and be part of that ticking."

"I'm not a man of the world," Emri said, "but what I do know is you shouldn't always expect it to be in sync. Use hard lessons wisely."

"I've taken some knocks from this place, but there's nothing for me here anymore, for anyone. I've also learnt a lot from you. Lessons I'll never forget, Granddad."

Emri welcomed Owen's words, even though they conjured deep emotions. He fought the tears because men never cried openly in the world he came from. There were very few lessons left he could teach the boy now he was a man, a notion he accepted as being the way of the world. Owen would have to navigate his own route, one taking him far from the influential sphere of family. Losing their special relationship brought Emri to an emotional low. Life at some stage will try to break us all, he knew that, but every experience, good or bad, was all part of living. It was a mantra he had long since come to respect.

It was during this time Owen started to notice his grandfather's vulnerability, a frailness creeping in, evident in his thinning frame. Such observations evoked bouts of guilt, knowing he would soon be leaving behind his guardianship.

"There are plenty who'll be sorry to see you go in this village," Emri told Owen some days before he left for York. "Make sure you do the rounds."

Owen laughed.

"I'm only going to the north of the county."

"It'll be a very different world from this," Emri said.

"Talking about farewells, it would've been good to see Jimmy before I left."

"I'll say your goodbyes—"

"You know where he is?"

"I do, but let me worry about him. He's safe, getting back to his usual self. It'll take a long time to heal this community. For now, Jimmy's better away from it. I'll pass on your well wishes to your brother."

"Surely, he'll want to speak to me. It's been four years."

"He doesn't want to speak to anyone. Believe me, my priorities are your mother and the two of you."

Owen noted the omission of Thomas, who, as far as the Morgan family was concerned, had also become an outcast, an emotionally illegitimate one.

"Have you heard anything from Billy?" Emri asked, welcoming the change in subject.

"I don't know why, but I never hear from him. Ruth keeps me up to date on his movements. The best she can anyway. Right now, he's in Northern Ireland, so even she's not seeing much of him. Only eighteen and already scrapping with the Irish. I can't help feeling left behind."

"Your adventure is about to start," Emri said, prodding Owen on the shoulder, "so don't feel left out of anything. Don't regret. It'll only consume you. Focus on what you're doing and create a life for yourself." Then, with a knowing wink, he said, "No one comes out well from a scrap with the Irish. I'd rather wrestle Satan."

"He did leave a message for me with Ruth," Owen said, "when she told him I was going to university."

"You see, he hasn't forgotten. What did he have to say?" Emri asked, eager to hear something positive about Owen's childhood friend.

"It was just a short personal message, Grandad," Owen said, playing with Emri's expectations.

"And… that was?"

"Tell the *wanker* to get a real job."

Both howled with laughter.

"Did you know Melanie is back for a few days, before she heads off to academia?" Emri asked, once they had recovered.

***

A light drizzle fell on Mel's umbrella, under which they both huddled. They chose the lake in the country park bordering the northern edge of the village, away from prying eyes. Even though she was eighteen, legally an adult, Mel's mother still tried her best to be vigilant, but she was no match for her increasingly rebellious daughter. The only witnesses to the rendezvous were wild geese feeding at the water's edge, having arrived early from their summer breeding grounds. Over the years, Mel grew out of her Bauhaus look, choosing a more thespian aspect, what she called her moody poetic character. She was wearing a long woollen jumper, two sizes too big, with baggy jeans and a pair of Doc Martens, ones that squelched in and out of the muddy puddles.

"You don't look much like a politician to me," Owen said, hearing Mel had secured a place at Oxford to read political science.

"Thank God. I'd much sooner be reading Elliot any day than *The Path to Power*. That's what my mother bought me as a leaving gift. She truly believes I'll be the next female prime minister. As if the first hasn't fucked things up enough. We'll see. What my mother wants isn't necessarily what she's going to get, allowance or not."

Owen listened, happy to be taken along in her company, enveloped in his obsession. They had spoken on the odd occasion she managed to outwit her mother's machinations over the years, usually in town, random meetings, nothing prolonged. Even so, she was shocked to see how serious he had become, and she was supposed to be the poetry lover.

How ironic, she thought.

Once they completed a full circle of the lake, Mel stopped walking, realising who had been doing all the talking.

"*Well*, Owen," she said, "have you got anything to say? I've got a train to catch, remember."

"Can you recall what you said that day?"

There was no warning, no build-up to his question. He just blurted it out, and there was no need for clarification.

Mel knew what he was referring to.

"Listen, they were just words. In life-and-death situations people say all sorts of rubbish. Use humour in the darkest of moments, which is what happened. That's what I was trying to do."

"You told me I should've let him throw his stone."

"Please listen to me carefully. It just came out. There was no meaningful reason. It was an understatement that didn't match the brutality of what we'd just witnessed. But I won't lie, since then, I've wondered, what if?"

"If what?"

"If you hadn't stopped him. I'm not trying to proportion blame. It's just a logical thought process. No value attached to it."

"But someone died. Where does the responsibility lie?"

"Someone was going to die anyway. There wasn't anything any of us could've done to prevent it. It could've been one of those policemen, *both*, even one of us, but it wasn't. The responsibility lies with those who shoved the concrete block over the side. Those two sick fucks playing judge and jury. No, it was bigger than that. Another example of collective insanity, way beyond our control. We were just children caught up in it all."

"You don't blame me?"

Had he been looking at her, rather than a gaggle of geese flying in formation above, he would have seen Mel's frown, registering her despair at where the conversation had been taken.

"You mean for someone dying? Of course not! Oh, Owen… no! Now stop talking nonsense and let's have a real leaving conversation," she said. "Nothing so heavy."

He wanted to ask if she agreed that Billy was trying to show off, in her presence, looking for praise, from her, but he got the message and said nothing further on the subject.

Had someone seen the two of them leaning into each other, deep in conversation, they may have thought the pair were inseparable, but within hours they went their separate ways.

CHAPTER 5

"It's a possibility," Owen said into Miranda's ear, competing with the noise of a local band's version of Deep Purple's *Black Night*.

"What's a possibility?" she asked, her expression suggesting she had not been listening.

"Working for a non-governmental organisation this summer," he said. "Food for All. Six weeks in Tanzania. Pay attention and keep up."

Miranda put a finger to her ear, then pointed at the stage where the band was finishing a thrashing of what they both considered a classic track, now ruined.

"At least it's their last song," he said.

Miranda waited for the noise to subside before continuing.

"I'm going to give you my professional advice. No charge."

"That's good of you," he said, trying his best to look serious.

"To quote Freud, it's the fear of having a small penis that motivates young males like yourself to work for an NGO."

Owen screamed back, unable to control his laughter.

"Is that based on your own observations?"

"Seriously, it's a well-known fact. That sense of feeling deficient."

"But I don't feel anything," he said, knowing he was being mocked and enjoying it.

"I know," she said, laughing into her pint glass.

"I don't get it."

"Of course you don't."

"What I mean is, how's it got anything to do with working for an NGO?" he asked, trying to sound more serious than he was capable.

Miranda leaned into him, eager to clarify, spilling lager over the crotch of his jeans.

"Oops. Looks like you've gone and pissed yourself."

"Now look what you've done!"

"Calm down and listen to the point I'm trying to make."

"Go on," he said, rubbing his jeans, waiting for the climactic conclusion.

"It's because it replaces your smallness with a gas-guzzling four-by-four."

"You'd better explain your hypothesis."

"It's phallic," she said, giggling drunkenly at her own joke.

"Are you seriously comparing a car to my cock?" he asked.

Pointing towards the stage, she said, "It's a little like them. They turn the sound of their instruments up to compensate for the vocalist's inability to sing. In fact, they're crap. Remind me why we came here?"

"But what about all the female NGOs?" he asked, trying to hold his concentration.

"They love big shiny trucks too," she said, "but a pair of expensive sunglasses seals the deal. Straight out of *Vogue*. Wandering across the face of the Earth sporting a pair of Ray-Bans, saving the world from itself."

"Wait, just wait a moment," he said, taking hold of Miranda's arm, steadying himself. "So, you're suggesting, no, saying, people choose to work for an NGO so they can drive around in shiny new trucks with others of the same ilk wearing expensive sunglasses, and that's it?"

"They also get to throw large sums of money at economic predators for mediocre humanitarian projects," she said. "The more they spend, the bigger the promotion."

"Now you're getting all political on me and a little jealous," he said. "But I'm convinced. Shiny car, expensive sunglasses, money to throw away. Where do I apply?"

Miranda turned to face him, square on, then, pushing herself into him, she placed one hand between his legs, saying, "It doesn't seem you're qualified."

Owen watched as she walked across the room to find the bathroom, howling as she went.

It was early in the second semester of his first year when Owen met Miranda, a psychology student. They started speaking in the student bar as they waited to be served. After discussing everything from the student union's ineffectiveness to who was responsible for the downing of Pan Am Flight 103 weeks earlier, they continued the momentum by moving from one drinking establishment to another.

"Harry's Bar on Micklegate, best place for music and beer," Miranda said late into the evening.

On their initial night, when they found themselves crammed into the back room of Harry's, feet sticking to the carpet, listening to a convincing cover of *Lucifer Sam* by Pink Floyd, they became short-term lovers. It was a relationship that lasted to the end of the academic year.

"Don't become too attached," Miranda said, "because when I'm finished here, and that's soon, I'm leaving for good."

It was mutually decided Harry's would be a fitting venue for their final night before Miranda left for London. The live bands suited both their tastes, heavy and loud. Planning to finish her studies in the capital, her long-term ambition was to settle somewhere central, marry into money and open her own practice. The order in which it was to happen remained flexible. When Owen pointed out most people aspired to find someone they could love, she told him to check national divorce rates. Miranda used two loaded words to support her argument: abstract and fleeting.

"I'm not letting anyone, or anything, distract me from my plan," she often insisted.

Miranda also told him he could not possibly fulfil the role because he lacked the security she was searching for, but in the future, if his circumstances were to change, he should get in touch.

During his first year at York, she was the only real friend he made.

While he relished the academic independence and intellectual freedom of an undergrad, he struggled to connect with other students on his course. During seminars, he was dismissive of their ideas, as if they were inferior, which, intellectually, most were. Even some of his lecturers found him challenging. Argumentative had been used to describe his contributions. In a short space of time, he became skilful at manoeuvring the thought processes of others when entwined in academic debate, not in a supportive way, more disruptive, another attribute his masters used to describe him. Justifying his social inadequacies, Owen convinced himself he had no interest in the cliques he saw forming as the year progressed.

"The problem, Owen," Miranda said one afternoon as they were eating beef burgers and fries while sneaking vodka into their extra-large cokes, "is you consider yourself cleverer than all those others, which is true, but arrogant."

"And then there are the societal differences," Owen said, in mitigation.

"You mean because their parents weren't coal miners? Where does that leave me?"

"That's not what I meant," Owen said, with the slightest hesitation.

"But it's what you implied."

"Can't you just humour me for once?"

"Look, you need them more than they need you," Miranda

said. "It's their world you're trying to enter, not the other way around. On your course, what careers are they chasing?"

"Ones following whatever their parents were into," Owen said, yawning artificially, parodying the narcoleptic.

"The diplomatic service, United Nations and a whole host of non-governmental organisations," Miranda said, answering for him. "That's why they're here, to get a piece of paper that'll open the right doors."

"And your point is?" Owen asked.

"Because that's what you'll be looking at when you've finished here. Am I right?"

"Something like that," Owen said.

"Do you know what it is *they* have you don't?"

"No, but I know you're going to tell me."

"An established network of friends and family, all embedded in those organisations. Agreed, that's nepotism, but that's the way it is and the way it'll remain. They have something you need. Tap into it. Go and listen to their amusing anecdotes of a colonial lifestyle when Mummy and Daddy travelled the third world. Political tourism they call it. Make those contacts while there's still time. It's a bit late in the year, but at least try. If you don't, if you continue to alienate yourself, then I fear you won't want to return next year. Maybe it'll be your own choice, but maybe that choice will be made for you, which would be a great shame."

"Thank you for your prognosis," Owen said, accepting her opinion.

"Oh, shut up, you son of an unemployed coal miner. Now pour more vodka in that," Miranda said, removing the plastic lid and pushing her paper cup across the table.

She was right. He recognised the gap widening with his peers, one driven by his own reluctance to accept his fellow students as equals. If there was a class barrier, then it was one he created. He was starting to sound like his father, a theory he withheld from Miranda.

Having left Harry's for the last time, they decided the night would be spent in Owen's room. As they walked back to campus, he told her about a summons he received that morning. A handwritten message in his pigeonhole, requesting he attend a meeting with the head of faculty.

"Written personally by Professor Smyths," Owen said, trying to convince Miranda.

"Professor Annabel Smyths has personally written to you?" she asked.

"Yes, but it's more like an order."

"She has a secretary for such trivial matters."

"I recognise the handwriting from marked papers. She also posted one of her published articles, asking for my feedback."

"Then I don't like the sound of it. Some kind of test, perhaps. Trying to catch you out. Maybe she's heard you're struggling to fit in and decided to act?"

"Her feedback's always been positive. Consistently top marks."

"I don't mean academically, you fool," Miranda said. "Let's hope it's nothing serious."

Arriving at his room, they made love for the last time with an erotic intensity. After, they slept through to the following afternoon.

While Owen was aware of Professor Smyths's reputation, of all his lecturers she was the one he held in reverence. Her talks on East-West relations were inspirational, bringing in theories and notions he considered well before their time. He knew others felt the same, but he also noted there were a fair number on his course who demonstrated frustration at her style. He heard some of the uninitiated when speaking in the student bar, their bravery matched only by their drinking, criticising her abrupt manner. But from Owen's perspective, she was one of the few academics who encouraged them to think and argue for themselves. "A good pass on this course is all about rigour." To some, that meant work, effort and persistence, not necessarily the reason they decided to come to university in the first place. They simply followed tradition. When in her presence, Owen knew he was where he was meant to be. There were rumours this petite, yet ferocious lady had powerful friends, but he disregarded such exaggerations. She dressed in a nondescript manner, her attire grey, like her hair, someone no one would notice in a crowd. Her wedding finger was bare, a derogatory observation used by some to attack her choice to live alone. She had written five books, three of which sat on the shelves in the library: one about the tribulations of European nation-building, another on the flawed aspects of communism, and the third explored the failings of democracy. Owen searched them out, finding them fascinating and enlightening, having identified a thread running through each one: distrust everything.

He never got to discuss their meeting because days later, as the academic year was coming to an end, he accompanied Miranda to the train station for her final journey out of York. There had been some edifying months together, ones neither would ever forget. Owen found it difficult to steer the relationship in a way he wanted, not without Miranda cracking some joke, making fun of his seriousness. His affliction, as she often jested, was her way of deflecting difficult conversations. It was one of her attractions, an infectiously high-spirited nature, never serious, unless dishing out personal advice.

"I know how you must be feeling, darling," Miranda said, as they walked towards the waiting train, "but be brave for both of us, and let's get this done with the minimum of fuss."

They loaded her luggage with seconds to spare, leaving no time to make a fuss anyway. As he exited the train onto a busy platform, Miranda gave him one last piece of advice.

"If Smyths offers you help, take it. Remember, September is a fresh start."

"Enjoy London," he managed to say before the engine started to drag its body along the tracks, slowly at first but picking up momentum as it left the station.

"Goodbye, Owen," he heard her shout above all the commotion.

As she watched him becoming ever smaller, then losing him in the crowd, Miranda fought the urge to admit there was something tragic about the way he looked. Penelope observing Odysseus's sail as it disappeared over the horizon came to mind, just in reverse, she told herself. That was fine with Miranda, happy to be on her way, continuing with her own journey.

CHAPTER 6

With only minutes to spare, Owen rushed up the steps of Heslington Hall, a grade two listed building housing many of the faculty offices. Shrouded in darkness, the odd light burnt through the casements, penetrating the fading light. It was reassuring there would be others in the place, the late hour adding to the strangeness of the summons. Entering, he was faced with an imposing wooden staircase, large enough to walk three abreast. Ascending the steps two at a time, he turned right at the top, entering a corridor with doors on either side, knowing the office was halfway down.

There were voices on another floor. A small gathering, he assumed.

Earlier in the day, Owen read and annotated Professor Smyths's article, *Fragmentation of a Communist Empire*, dated June 1985, published in a right-leaning academic journal. Having absorbed its premise, he penned a response, one that was critical and, in places, negative too. Anyone could applaud for the sake of vanity.

Owen took a moment in front of her office door, its woodwork a montage of wrought patterns carved out of solid oak. A third of the way from the top was a brass plaque embossed with black letters informing the unaware this was the office of Professor Annabel Smyths, head of international studies. The door was ajar, no more than half an inch, but enough to send a shard of light cascading across the corridor, illuminating a section of the wall opposite. It was decorated with sepia-coloured photographs of uniformed students, all of them male.

Fist clenched, Owen readied himself to knock, but before he could, the professor beckoned him to enter.

He found her sitting behind a desk, a cigarette in one hand and a mug in the other. Gold-rimmed spectacles, ones Owen had seen her wearing in lectures, were resting on top of some papers. The high ceiling and oversized desk made her look out of proportion and much too delicate, as if everything around her was exaggerated. In the lecture halls, this ageing academic projected her voice with such strength she commanded authority, an image contrasting with the setting.

Indicating with a slight nod for him to sit and pointing to a mug on his side, Annabel said, "I hope you like coffee." Then, taking a silver flask from a drawer, she unscrewed its lid, putting a splash into her own drink. "A little whisky improves the taste," she said, leaning forward in anticipation.

"Thank you," Owen said, surprised at the informality of her greeting.

Lifting the mug, he took a small sip, tasting the bitterness of the coffee. Mixed with the spirit, it warmed his insides, helping him relax.

There was a third mug steaming away on the windowsill.

"I must apologise for the timing," Annabel said. "I wouldn't normally meet students so late in the day, but I was going to be on the premises anyway. I've wanted to arrange a meeting for some time, just sorry it's come so late in the year."

"I appreciate your time," Owen said.

"I must warn you, fifteen minutes is all we have. A little gathering of colleagues. Usual Friday shenanigans before the holidays. If I don't return soon, they'll classify me as missing and come looking."

It surprised Owen a social gathering was keeping her on campus. Marking papers, sifting through struggling dissertations from desperate third-year undergrads demanding extensions, perhaps, but not late-night drinking.

"It's an honour to meet you personally, Owen," she said, "and a pleasure not sharing you with your peers. Having read several of your submissions this year, I'm starting to see we finally have someone in our midst with remarkable potential." With a nod towards the article, she said, "Well, your thoughts."

"Hmm," he said, shifting in his chair, calming his nerves. "If you don't mind me saying, you made some sweeping predictions. With the state of relations between East and West being as positive and promising as they are right now, some of your arguments just don't add up."

"I don't mind at all," she said. "That's why I wanted someone like you to look at it, knowing you'd tear it apart with your criticism. I'd be disappointed if you'd taken any other approach. Tell me, which predictions?"

Taking a long drink, Annabel settled into her chair, keen to hear his ideas.

"Most sweeping of all are your comments on the total collapse of the Soviet Union within the next decade and your argument it'll lead to wide-scale instability well beyond the Eastern Bloc."

"And you can't see that happening because?" she asked.

"To demonstrate, Professor, Gorbachev is now the general secretary of the Soviet Union, and he's talking openly with the US, unprecedented in recent years. He's also brought in key policies reforming the Communist Party. In the Soviet Union at least. From my reading of the situation, we're on track for more stability, yet your article is predicting widespread instability…"

There was a pause in which he waited for her to respond. In that space, he tried to read her expressionless face, but there was nothing.

"The Soviets have withdrawn from Afghanistan," she said, "and the buffer countries between East and West are rattling their swords, making unchallenged comments about independence from Moscow. Two huge humiliations. Potentially, the ripple effect will reach well beyond Eastern Europe."

As she was speaking, Owen noticed a misty condensation forming on the window's flat surface, due to vapour from the incongruously placed third mug of coffee. As it turned to water, the vapour started to widen and spread across a small section of glass. Such symbolism demonstrated Professor Smyths's point perfectly.

"Who is the driving force behind such colossal changes?" she asked.

"The West," Owen said.

"And it's the West that'll be picking up the pieces for years to come. Now tell me why you think I wrote the article. Please be succinct because we're running out of time, and I'm hoping to get to the real reason we're here."

"I'm assuming you wrote it to shine a lens on global events and their consequences," Owen said, contemplating what she meant by 'real reason'.

"It's a mediocre piece, 8,000 words at most, of what I'd expect someone of your calibre to write in one evening. I wrote it because I'm a university lecturer. Publishing is my job. It's expected. I found an angle fitting the journal's political agenda. Plus, the revenue such writing produces comes in useful."

"Even so," Owen said, "it drew some attention from several broadsheets at the time. Some important media people listened to what you had to say. Took your comments seriously. I've read their responses."

She looked down at her desk, deep in thought, as if seeing something there for the first time.

"When you're trained to do so, it's easy to see through someone's façade. The way they talk, their facial expressions, how they sweat, their gestures, etcetera. Such indicators can give a person's real intentions away. Likewise, it's possible to counter such observations. Ask a poker player. They're experts. Do you get what I'm saying, Owen?"

As if going through some long equation, he considered her question.

"I'm here to discuss more than just your article," he said.

As he spoke, Owen heard Miranda's advice echoing through his reasoning.

"I must admit the article is of some importance. My publishers want it updated as we race towards the end of the decade. I'm searching for something to add that'll make it current. Drag it into the modern world."

"Then you're disappointed with my suggestions?" Owen asked.

"Not at all. I'm flattered you've taken time to research the paper and respond to it."

Owen looked at it, realising that for now it was no longer needed. Picking up his mug, he took a long drink, matching the professor's.

"A friend of mine warned me against my apathy and for being too aloof. At first, I didn't blame myself, but now I see her point. If I'm honest, I'm starting to feel estranged here. Brought about by my own actions, of course."

"Oh," Annabel said, surprised at the honesty of his disclosure. "Admittedly, what you say hasn't gone unnoticed, but I hadn't realised it'd become such an issue for you. I have something in mind that could help, starting tonight. The big question, now you've brought the matter to my attention, is do you want to be here? In this university?"

"My grandfather said, 'Go and break the family mould', and that's what I'm here to do. Due to my experiences so far, I'm starting to see world events as interconnected, more than I ever have, and it *excites* me. Global history unfolding in front of my eyes. Seeing my place within it is fascinating. If half of what your article predicts comes to fruition, then we'll experience history in the making. Such global changes are too frightening for many to perceive. Some people I know, including ones on this course, remain in the past where history is already fixed, making them feel safe. But I chose international relations to learn how the global cogs work and recognise what makes those same cogs break. Future history doesn't frighten me, Professor. It thrills me to think we are history makers. So yes, I want to stay. But a part of me was ready to walk away, the arrogant part. That's why I'm here, isn't it, to save myself from self-destruction?"

"History comes at a price," Annabel said. "I've been around long enough to witness that."

"I have some experience there too," Owen said.

"Yes, I know. But it's your intelligence that's gotten you noticed, well beyond the walls of this university, not perceived social inadequacies. Your writing demonstrates a high level of reasoning and mental representation, not normally seen in the average person we get on this course. You think deeply and reflect widely about the issues raised across the globe, showing a heightened intellect. That's why you're here, tonight."

"But I don't fit in," Owen said, the awkwardness in his voice proving he was missing her point.

"What does that even mean, *fit in?*" Annabel asked, a look of amusement giving away her surprise at his revelation. "Some of the most interesting people I know wouldn't be considered mainstream normal. Academically, you're exceptional. With the intervention of that trainee psychiatrist, you've identified there are wider issues to transcend, but that's not my concern."

"Miranda, you mean?"

"I've taken some interest in your extracurricular activities. Most of those you rub shoulders with aren't gifted like you. Identifying difference, which is what you've done, isn't a weakness, it's a strength. From what you're saying, it seems you haven't used it to your advantage. Many students on this course are destined to follow preordained paths. One or two will make something of themselves, become big players out there in the world. Having a network of friends can be turned into a serious advantage. With *our* guidance, *your* intelligence can be put to good use. We can get you into special employment, where you can continue to break that mould you mentioned. Before you arrived in York, I already knew the extent of your potential."

"Potential for what? Learning—"

"That's a starting point," Annabel said, cutting him off. "When I was your age, my university professor recruited me for something rather specific. Maybe he too was drawn to my intelligence, the high-quality papers I submitted. My lack of attachment even. Along the way, some didn't share his confidence in me, but that's to be expected. By the time I arrived in West Germany to take up my first post, espionage was common practice. At first, I spent time behind a desk, analysing, highlighting things I didn't understand, wasn't meant to. Little more than a grocery clerk, until I wasn't. Very exciting for a young girl. Lurid machinations that'd make your toes curl. It was a man's world then, still is, but I outperformed most of them."

"Is that what you're doing now, *recruiting me?*" Owen asked.

"Times change, methods too, and expectations," she said, analysing some distant experience. "When I was your age, post-war, fewer people went to university, and now look at it. University for me was where it all started. It took me to other countries. The world was much bigger then, and it felt like I was entering far-off places. I started spending much of my time in the East, where a wall was being built to separate two opposing ideologies that feared each other.

"About eighteen months ago, I spoke to your grandfather when he was looking for the right place for you to study. We had a long chat in this office as you wandered the campus with your mother. He told me you come from a line of coal miners, generations in fact. The mining dispute fascinated me, as did your grandfather's perspective. He had a very different view on the union's leadership at the time. Unlike your father. Yet they stood side by side. Speaking to him was truly captivating. Blood really is thicker than water."

"My grandfather didn't stand by my father because of family loyalties," Owen said. "He did it for his community. And my brother was a strike violator, so blood, water, and the whole family thing doesn't necessarily work. Not when applied to my family anyway."

"Families are like microcosms," Annabel said, "mirroring the fragile state of our social structures. Yours is the perfect example."

"Really—" Owen started to say, concerned his past was being opened for inspection and comment.

"To illustrate, your father is the old order. His ideology is finished. He can't control his satellite states anymore, that's your brother. The choices he made changed everything, breaking far from expectation. A new order is needed. That's you."

"An amusing anecdote," Owen said. "We were just another dysfunctional family. One of many during those times."

"Far from it. Your family is no different from millions of others. But your grandfather, he's different. When I met him, I knew I was in the presence of an exceptional person. I can see where you get it from."

"And my friends, where do they fit into your hypothesis?" Owen asked.

"You and your two friends are society's collateral damage, as was the driver. To witness such violence… Unfortunately, it doesn't make you unique. If you want, I can get you some help. We have people here working on the effects of trauma."

"Not necessary," Owen said.

"Your inability to forge relationships with fellow students, not being able to cope with change, it could all be linked to what you experienced. Mental stability is as important as knowledge and skills. You'd do well to keep that in mind."

"It's all in the past now."

"That may be," Annabel said, looking at her watch, "but don't allow it to fester. For now, I've given you all the time I can. We'll speak again soon if you'd like. There are others keen to meet with you. People who see your potential as an asset."

"So, you are recruiting me," Owen said, pushing for an answer.

"Only if it's what you want. In time, certain opportunities will be presented to you. At any stage, you can walk away. Absolutely no pressure."

Before Owen could respond, footsteps were heard in the corridor.

"We have a *visitor?*"

"You do, not me. The third mug of coffee you've been staring at," Annabel said, rising in anticipation. "Good evening, Roland, please come in."

As Roland entered, Owen stood to face a tall, athletic-looking figure, papers in one hand and a pen and highlighters in the other.

Professor Smyths walked around the desk, pausing to pat Roland on the arm.

Considering her small stature, Owen imagined how she had slain a few Goliaths in her time.

"Owen, this is Roland Roden-West, a second-year student," Annabel said. "The paper he's carrying is my article. You two have all night to debate the pros and cons of the *Fragmentation of a Communist Empire*. Enjoy. The whisky is in the top-left drawer should you wish to water down the coffee. With your opposing views in mind, I'm expecting some well-thought-out additions. Let's say on my desk midday Monday. Good luck with the weekend, you two. And Roland, take special care of him."

"I will," Roland said.

"And Owen," Annabel shouted from the corridor, "Roland's father was once the British ambassador to the FRG."

"The Federal Republic of Germany," Roland said, sizing up the opposition.

"I know what FRG stands for," Owen said.

"I'd prefer Rod if that's OK, but please, never in front of my parents, particularly my father. He's looking forward to meeting you."

They fell silent, listening to Annabel's hurried footfalls, as she made her way to a social gathering somewhere in the building.

To Roland, it was obvious why she asked him to chaperone this first-year undergrad. He had no intention of expending any more energy, effort or time than was needed. Things would be done the Roland way. Once Annabel's footsteps faded, he sauntered over to the window, opened it, and threw the coffee into the night. Then, sitting in her chair, he opened the drawer, took out her whisky and poured himself a drink. Rolling the article into a baton and placing the highlighters into his pocket, he looked at Owen, as if expecting an answer to a question never asked.

"It's ten-thirty," he said, tapping the article on the desk, "and I have no intention of reading whatever's in this paper. I'm assuming you get the gist of it?"

"Yes, I know the gist, *Rod*," Owen said.

"Then send me the main bullet points so I get the idea too. No more than five. Anything more on a weekend would be too much. I suspect Annabel Machiavelli Smyths will question me on the detail."

"I can do that," Owen said.

Roland relaxed into Annabel's chair, placing his feet on the table.

"What we're going to do now," he said, with an annoying presumptuousness, "is make our way to the student bar, where some untalented music students are mimicking an untalented sixties band. Not the best venue for a Friday night, but thanks to your appointment, there's little time for anything else. Our main concern is to get you seen in my company."

"Your company," Owen said, trying to reason why the conversation was taking such an unexpected turn.

"I have a bit of a reputation," Roland said, waving his hands in the air, "as something of a socialite, which is why old Smyths chose me to look after you. That and my father wanting to keep me occupied."

"Why would he want her to do that?" Owen asked.

"Because I'd get myself into trouble if I wasn't constructively entertained. They go way back, Smyths and my father."

"Did he study here?" Owen asked.

"God no. Arthur Roden-West is a thoroughbred. Cambridge. They met in Bonn during the height of the Cold War. Tenacious old woman, but she has an eye for talent, *apparently*. I heard my father speaking to her once while I was spying outside his office. 'Remember Annabel, a bored Roland is a dangerous one', which I must admit is true. Told her he wanted to divert any embarrassing situations away from family."

Owen heard anger in his voice, or maybe it was pain.

"Looking after potentials like you is one of the responsibilities she throws my way," Roland said. "I'm not here because of academic ability, more to do with breeding. Nothing fancy like eugenics. Smyths wouldn't have anything to do with such beliefs, unlike me. I'd take anything giving me an advantage. Learned that from my father. Always attack from a position of strength."

Roland's father came from a well-connected family, one that had served the country in a variety of ways, usually, but not exclusively, via diplomatic routes. Arthur followed suit, working his way through the military to the Intelligence Services, before joining the Foreign and Commonwealth Office, where he made his way up the diplomatic chain. In retirement, he took up consultancy for the FCO, headhunting potential talent for the UK's intelligence community. Owen had come to his attention because Annabel passed his details to Arthur's team of analysts for scrutiny. Even before Owen's portfolio was dispatched, she knew

Arthur would be interested in her prodigy. Annabel and Arthur had been through tough times together during the height of Cold War tensions. It could be said she owed him a debt for keeping her safe during the darkest moments of those unpredictable times. Keeping a watchful eye on his son was only a small gesture of her gratitude, caring for the blackest of sheep.

As they rushed back across campus, Roland dumped Annabel's article in the first rubbish bin he came across. She had seen it in his hand, and that was enough. In any case, her latest puppet would fill him in on the details.

CHAPTER 7

Owen spent his last days of his first year at York in various states of intoxication, paraded by Roland from one social gathering to another. He was introduced to Juan, a flamboyant second-year student who had come to England from Catalonia to read history. Roland and Juan were social magnets, their lavish and loud conduct attracting audiences eager to be part of their revelling. It was evident to Owen neither wanted him around, but they got him meeting and mixing exceptionally quickly, and in no time, he became strangely popular.

During his final morning, before departing York for the summer, Owen was recovering in a local café on the periphery of the university. A place known for its inexpensive breakfasts. Drinking strong tea, waiting for his morning remedy to arrive, Owen was recuperating from one of Roland's all-night extravaganzas. To pass the time, he gazed out the window at a spattering of oaks decorating the avenue opposite. It was a bright, sun-drenched day, full of promise. As he was about to slip two more painkillers into his mouth, Juan emerged out of the trees, striding with confidence and purpose, heading straight for the café's double doors. He was wearing a chequered woollen three-piece suit, with a large polka-dot handkerchief hanging out of his breast pocket matching his shirt, and a pair of round sunglasses with reflective lenses. Juan's style was one of a modern foppish dandy, a fashion he aimed to emulate. That morning, he had the look precisely where he wanted it.

Owen appreciated what Juan had in common with Roland: self-belief and bags of confidence.

Believing he was about to be lured into another day of partying and having no escape, despair descended over his whole being, evidence of which was a sinking sensation in his stomach, all the way down to his already rumbling bowels.

Juan made a grand entrance, melodramatically flinging the double doors open. Then, scanning the interior, he catwalked over to Owen's table. Towering over him, he extended his arm, presenting a pristine white envelope.

The juxtaposition between the two was striking: Owen in flip-flops, shorts and a soiled T-shirt.

Peering into the mirrored glasses of the immaculately dressed and manicured Latin figure standing in front of him, Owen spoke with as much candour as he could muster.

"Yes, Juan?" he asked.

"For you, my friend, from Rod. *Disfruta la fiesta.*"

Before Owen could respond, Juan spun on a sixpence, disappearing through the doors and into bright sunshine. Because it was the end of the academic year, and to Owen's relief, only a few stragglers were sitting in the café to witness the spectacle. All stared at Owen with curious expressions. Then their attention turned to the much more appealing and finely dressed figure of the Spaniard walking elegantly away. The waitress, idly waiting for the next order, listlessly walked over to the doors and slammed them shut.

"Was your friend born in a barn?" she asked, shouting in Owen's direction.

Owen stared at the envelope lying flat on the table. Square in shape, his name was written in thick black print across the front. Taking a breakfast knife, he sliced it open. Inside were two things:

a square piece of white card matching the envelope's shape and a separate handwritten message on a small slip of expensive paper. The card, elaborately decorated with a medieval shield and golden crown sitting atop, was Owen's formal invitation to Frimley House.

Mr Arthur Roden-West CBE and Mrs Elizabeth Ashely Roden-West invite Mr Owen Morgan to a Garden Party, Saturday, 21st June, from 6pm to 10pm.

The note was a personal message from Arthur, insisting he come for the weekend, accommodation provided, and Roland would be in residence.

***

Sitting in the Labour Club, Emri's choice of venue, Owen presented the invite for his grandfather's perusal.

"But you don't have any connections to their world."

"Maybe his father wants to thank me for the good impression I made on his son," Owen said.

"Maybe," Emri said, recognising his grandson's curt response.

"Or maybe it's the lasting impression you had on Professor Smyths."

"It's Annabel to me," Emri said, bringing a smile to both their faces.

There was no mention of his conversation with the professor or the communication he received before departing for the summer, explaining he should expect such an invite.

"It's more of a job interview, so treat it like one," she advised.

Owen told his grandfather about Miranda. Not every detail, but enough for him to understand the lasting impression she made. Of all the tales he had told since arriving home, it was their relationship he found most disappointing. Even more than

Owen's recounts of his overindulgent days spent frolicking in and around York's city centre with Roland and Juan.

"I've always thought you had a thing for Melanie," Emri said, picking up on Owen's rising intonations.

"Her mother did a good job making sure nothing would come of it. Since we left for university, we've drifted even further apart. I haven't heard anything from her. Wouldn't know how to get in touch even if I wanted."

A frown of displeasure spread across Emri's face.

"How could you lose contact with such a lovely girl?" he asked. "She speaks to me regularly on the phone."

"Mel phones you… *regularly?*" Owen asked.

"Your mum says it was the bond we formed, waiting for her to be collected that day. The police station," he said, as if it needed clarification. "She says I'm like a surrogate father to the girl. A safe person where she can offload her worries, seek advice. Melanie often sends me her poetry for feedback. Like I know what I'm talking about."

"*Regularly*, though," Owen said.

"Well… just the odd call on random weekends," Emri said. "Maybe not so regular. Your mother would appreciate the same from you now your father's not on the scene anymore."

"How is he?" Owen asked, already considering his next Melanie question.

"He never really recovered from that crushing defeat. It's continued to eat away at him. Not that there was anything he was able to do about it. I tried to prepare him, but he wouldn't listen. Never has. Then the government's plans to privatise what was left of the coal industry finished him off. Your father, I'm sorry to say, is like water, he follows the easiest route. For him, that was taking his anger out on your mother. I couldn't allow that."

Owen knew the rest. Anne beat a hasty retreat, taking refuge in the sanctuary provided by her father's house.

"Let's not allow him to ruin our day, Grandad," Owen said,

hoping for a return to their previous conversation. "What do you say to giving me Mel's number?"

"I can't just give it you. That'd be a breach of trust," Emri said.

"Grandad, it's the twentieth century, chivalry went out of fashion in the Dark Ages."

"She's been through a lot lately, and that's not up for discussion either. The best I can offer is giving her a call when we get home. I'll ask if it's okay first."

"If you insist, but you're only delaying the inevitable."

Deflecting further discussion on the issue, Emri asked, "One more for the road?"

"Okay, and then we go home and make the call," Owen said, unwilling to yield.

While Emri wandered off, Owen looked around, reminiscing about the old place. He had fond memories of the Labour Club, once the centre of the village's community. It had seen better times. The place smelt of hops and tobacco, and an ever-present mist hung in the air, yellowing the light fitments and polystyrene ceiling tiles. From what Owen had seen since his return, something was lost across the whole village, not just in the club. A far cry from May Day parades when brass bands marched with their banners proudly flying, culminating on the playing fields across the road. In those days, the village knew how to honour its workers. Such ceremonies were followed by jubilant celebrations, making the walls of the building vibrate with the sound of merriment. The nostalgic pull was powerful, a yearning for a life lost. The few customers sitting at the bar stared into the bottom of the misty remains of their pint glasses as if they had witnessed some Pied Piper charming the good times away.

"The things you have me doing," Emri said, returning with drinks.

"What's the problem now?" Owen asked, eager to hear what was irritating his grandfather.

"Bloody *snakebite* and *black*, that's what's wrong. Embarrassing. I told the poor girl to mix beer with cider and then add some blackcurrant," he said. "Here, take it. I don't want anyone saying I drink that rubbish."

The two laughed, huddled together like old friends.

Arriving home, Emri rang Mel, while Owen waited in the background, trying to calm himself for the anticipated conversation. Once finished, and to Owen's shocked surprise, he hung up.

"Sorry," he said, "but she's busy. Can't speak right now. She asked if you could call in a couple of weeks. Like I said, the poor girl has taken on too much."

"But she's just spent twenty minutes on the phone with you."

"A couple of weeks, that's all," Emri said, sensing his grandson's disappointment.

***

In the first weeks of summer, Owen spent much of his time hiking or jogging in the surrounding countryside. Pushing himself to the limits of his physical ability became an activity he found exhilarating, allowing him to empty his head of everything except the physical pain of endurance.

Jogging into the village along Balaclava Street, he ran under the pedestrian flyover. Owen stopped and looked up into its structure. The original was weakened beyond repair and replaced with a more modern footbridge, including a reinforced glass roof and sides. The surrounding area was different too. Gone was the constant buzz of cars zipping back and forth, another sign the village's heartbeat had slowed. It seemed to Owen the bridge was no longer necessary because pedestrians could walk safely across the road if they wished. The shrubbery and bushes were gone, replaced by a mud bank covered in grey shale, matching the colour of the bridge. Had the architect purposely implemented the colour scheme to suit the village's personality, or was it just another of life's circumstantial oddities? It was where their childhoods abruptly ended. No plaque, just thousands of drab stones.

Across the road, the old station was still standing, looking much more derelict than he remembered. A six-foot fence, with barbed wire laced along the top, had been put in place to deter intruders from gaining access. From where he stood, it looked impenetrable. Plastic signs were attached at regular intervals, informing anyone who took the time to read the notices that the station would soon be demolished. Owen walked the perimeter, finding a hole where someone had cut the wire. Squeezing through, he made his way to the platform. All the windows and doors to the buildings were secured with thick metal sheets, giving the impression the place was under siege. The rudimentary defences on the outside of the old waiting room had been vandalised by someone desperate to gain access to its dark interior. There were huge dents in the solid material and bolts securing it to the wall were covered in deep scratches, as if some metal-taloned creature had tried to rip them from their housings. It was impossible to tell if this was the work of a single trespasser or a concerted effort by many.

The defences remained intact.

Moving to the edge of the platform, before it fell away to the tracks below, Owen looked left and into infinity, where they disappeared over the horizon, on towards an endless number of scenarios. To his right was the level crossing, its gates replaced by automatic red-and-white barriers with flashing lights. Owen reminisced, recalling Billy's mocking: "Are those two white lines supposed to be that crossing?" In his mind's eye, he imagined his friend pointing and laughing on that wonderfully hot day. The ghosts of his youth lingered, keen to remind him of those happy moments before everything changed. It was the last time they had really been friends.

Owen let go, allowing tears to flow. There was no one to witness his emotional response. No Melanie Bancroft lurking in the shadows. If a passerby had noticed him standing close to the track, then the Samaritans would surely have gotten a call.

Recovering his composure, he left the station to its fate, never to return. Within weeks it would face its own annihilation.

***

"Sorry Owen, it's been a roller-coaster of a year," Mel said some weeks later. "So much has changed since we last spoke."

Mel was no longer reading political science but English literature, which she referred to as her passion. Even more surprising was that it had all been arranged against her mother's wishes. The enormity of such defiance shocked Owen, as it did anyone who knew her mother's venomous potential. Emri often joked, "It may be her father that's a bigwig in the council, but it's her mother who dictates the agenda for any council business."

"Fuck me!" Owen said, hearing her news.

"I know. That's what I said when Mum threatened to cut me off from all things family, including my allowance."

"You said what?"

"Mother, rather than screaming at me, go home and make love to yourself. You never know, you might enjoy it."

Owen laughed so loud that Anne, in another room, jumped out of her seat in panic at such an alien sound.

"You know what though," Mel said, "I've learnt an important lesson about our village."

"And what's that?" Owen asked.

"Exile removes all traces of a person's history. It's a cruel tool used on both sides, not only mine, but yours as well."

Owen made the obvious connection.

"You can't go home?" he asked.

"It's a small price to pay for my freedom," she said.

Owen considered the pattern forming within his small circle of friends, privileged to have his mother and grandfather for support.

"We should meet," he said, "compare stories. Really catch up."

"I'd love to, but it's a working summer for me."

"Doing what?"

"I'm writing reviews for my college's literary magazine, plus some independent work for a local newspaper. It keeps me busy."

"But we don't start back until September," Owen said, trying and failing to hide his disappointment.

"I'm working right through, Owen. It's the only way I can support myself."

"Then I'll come to you."

"I'm flying to Paris on the 22nd, out of Heathrow. A series of lectures on Baudelaire I've been asked to attend and review. Then on to Rome, something similar."

"Wow!" Owen said. "You really are making an impression."

"The travel is great, and being chosen to write for the magazine is a real honour. The work, though, isn't so exciting."

"Then let's meet at the airport," Owen said. "We can share a pot of tea before you depart. I'm in Surrey all that weekend. I'll take a train."

"That'd work," Mel said. "What's in the home counties for a lad from the north?"

"Nothing special. Bit of a duty really. I'll fill you in on the details when we meet."

After putting the phone down, the melancholy that had been present since visiting the station started to lift. It was only an hour they would have together, but it was a rendezvous he aimed to keep. The most important event of the summer.

***

"All I need now," Owen told Anne, "to make this summer complete, is to track down Billy."

"Then you'd need to go to Germany," she said.

"He's on holiday?" Owen asked, surprised Billy was also travelling.

"No," Anne said, "he's stationed out there. Loving it from what I'm told."

"Then I'll arrange to see Ruth. She can fill me in on the details no one else is *bothering* to tell me. You never know, she might even give me his number if it's not such a big problem for her," Owen said, his brutal sarcasm intentional.

"Sorry to be the bearer of such shocking news about your friends getting on with their lives," Anne said, "but Ruth's in Germany with him."

"*What?*"

"They were married. A small affair, and quick, by all accounts. The registry office in town."

The widening distance between his childhood friends brought on a deep-down sense of sadness. Having arranged to meet Mel kept him from sinking even further. There was potential to rekindle their friendship, and while he told himself not to be too optimistic, he had enough money left in his savings for a flight to Paris or Rome.

Hope, when mixed with yearning, can trick the mind into believing anything is possible.

CHAPTER 8

When Owen saw the woman from a distance, walking through the car park outside Camberley station, she reminded him of Sophia Loren, a favourite of his grandfather's, a sixties icon. It was the resemblance, not her potential, that drew his attention. She was too far away to make any personal judgements. Her bouffant hairstyle with signature white-framed sunglasses pushed high on her head and a blood-red raincoat gave the game away. What else was he supposed to do while he waited, other than people watch? 7pm he was told a car would be waiting. Forty-five minutes later, still no sign.

Then he noticed she had noticed him looking.

Miranda gave it a name, explaining how insulting it was for women: the male gaze.

"I don't mind you desiring me, but don't ever let me catch you objectifying me," he recalled her saying, laughing hoarsely.

Before he could look away, Sophia Loren locked eyes with him, and like a homing pigeon recognising its cage, she changed direction, heading for what he anticipated was going to be a tricky confrontation.

Christ's sake, that's all I need, Owen thought.

The lookalike casually strolled over, coming uncomfortably close, so much so he was sure he could smell garlic on her breath.

"You've got to be Owen Morgan?" she asked, to his surprise.

"And you are?" Owen said with relief, not grasping the meaning of such an uncanny encounter.

"Roland's sister, Penelope… Penny," she said. "I'm your ride."

It was all he could do to repeat her words.

"Roland's sister?"

"I'm assuming from your response, he's never mentioned me."

"Oh, okay," Owen said, sticking out his hand. "Lovely to meet you."

She ignored the gesture.

"In Roland's absence, I've been ordered by Daddy to pick you up and deliver you safely to Frimley House," Penny said, smiling, exposing a perfect set of straight white teeth.

The only similarity she had with Sophia Loren, he realised, was her clothes. As an immediate afterthought, he admitted to himself he was no Charlton Heston either. Maybe the expensive outfit was fogging his judgement, but he could not decide if she was attractive.

"Yours?" Penny said, looking down.

Sitting next to him was a large suitcase, borrowed from his grandfather. The few possessions Owen brought with him lay crumpled somewhere inside. Penny picked it up before he could object, lifting it like a dumbbell, emphasising how light it was for its size.

"Are you planning on murdering someone?" she asked, before indicating he should follow.

He was about to tell her he could manage, but she was off, leaving no option but to follow in her wake. Having waited for almost an hour, he wondered why she was in such a rush. Reaching their destination, it all became clear as she opened the boot of a battered Ford Fiesta parked in a no-waiting zone. She threw the case inside, filling the small void.

Climbing into the passenger seat, Owen noticed a black suit wrapped in clear plastic on the back seat.

"That's yours for tomorrow night," Penny said. "Had to pick it up from the cleaners, hence why I'm so late. Another of Daddy's demands."

Three days earlier, Owen received a call from a man claiming to be in Arthur's employ, with three pieces of information: "You'll be picked up at the station, and the dress code for Saturday is formal. We can provide if necessary." Where else would Owen secure a dinner jacket with only days to spare.

Speeding through Camberley, as if she owned the roads, and into the suburbs of Frimley, Penny shouted through the windscreen at anyone who dared to slow her progress.

"Daddy won't be home until morning," she said, "possibly even later. Something unexpected has kept him in London, but you never know with him. My brother and Elizabeth are home, though. Don't worry, I have plans to keep us both entertained. We don't want to be stuck in the house with those two."

"I thought you said Roland wasn't home," Owen said, using his full Christian name just in case.

"Not *Roland*, my younger brother, *Benjamin*. He's Elizabeth's, and Daddy's, of course."

Owen knew little of the Roden-West family tree and had no wish to garner anything regarding the complexities of the ex-ambassador's affairs, other than what was offered.

"Will he be attending the party?" Owen asked.

There was an obvious pause in which Penny seemed to be composing herself. When she answered, her voice had lost its animation.

"Until three days ago, Roland was in Barcelona. Daddy brought him home. Or rather, Jake did, Daddy's Mr Do Whatever I'm Asked. You'll meet him tomorrow, I'm sure. Where Roland is now, I'm not certain, but he'll be somewhere safe, where Daddy can have him cared for."

Owen waited for her to say more.

As Penny moved up and down the gears, he sensed her

concentration. Having just been introduced to her driving, he was convinced her focus had nothing to do with the road's hazards.

"If you know my brother, then I'm assuming you know Juan?" she asked.

"I can't say I know either of them well, but yes, I'm acquainted with Juan."

"He was stabbed and killed in a bar in Barcelona a week ago…"

Once again, Owen waited for her to say more, but when nothing was forthcoming, he said, "No way!"

"My brother was there. Standing right next to him."

"I don't know what to say."

"I'm told you're leaving us Sunday morning," Penny said, changing tack, as if responding to his statement. "You'll be missing one of Elizabeth's famous Sunday lunches."

Owen was in shock, having been in Juan's company only weeks earlier. The news made him uncomfortable. A sensation we experience when confronted with someone else's tragedy. There was something else, Juan's death, a person he barely knew, touching him in a way he would never have anticipated.

"Yes," he said, grabbing the distraction, "I need to be on the 7am train to London. Meeting a friend at Heathrow."

"A girlfriend?"

"A girl, but not girlfriend, if that's what you mean."

"She must be important if you expect to catch a morning train after a Roden-West party."

"It won't be a problem with a 10pm finish."

Penny looked at him in mock seriousness before laughing loudly at his assumptions.

For the remainder of the journey, Owen listened to Penny talking, taking a mental note of her life. Having just finished three years at Warwick, she was hoping to start a post-graduate course. "That's the long-term plan anyway," she said, with no mention of a timeline. Penny's mother died when she was young, leaving an absent father to bring up two children. "Elizabeth stepped into the breach," as Penny put it, entering their lives, giving her father a third child. Owen could hear disappointment in her voice as she recalled that part of her life. He was already starting to learn something telling about her: she talked a lot, and freely, especially about family. For some reason, she never questioned Owen about his familial history. Maybe she already knew everything from Roland, or perhaps she just had no interest.

As they sped through Frimley Green, Penny pointed out the King's Head, the establishment, she told him, where they would be spending the evening. Pulling into Frimley House, they were confronted with a hive of activity. An events company was preparing the gardens for the next day's party.

The Roden-West residence sat at the top of a small hill, a substantial Georgian building with a gravel driveway in a half-moon shape, one way in and one out. Bringing her car to a jolting halt, Penny skidded, spewing gravel onto concrete steps leading up to an imposing set of double doors. The positioning of her Fiesta played havoc with the symmetry of the architecture, but she had few concerns for such aesthetic appreciations. Exiting the car and surprising Owen yet again with her need to rush, Penny jogged up the steps shouting to him over her shoulder.

"Leave your things in the boot. I'll arrange for someone to bring them upstairs."

There was a fleeting introduction to Elizabeth and Benjamin, who had come into an opulent entrance hall to meet him. Owen noted Elizabeth's striking beauty and guessed at her age. Probably mid-to-late forties was his rough calculation. She had a soft voice, generating a sense of serenity, the opposite of her stepdaughter. The few questions she asked were non-invasive: York's appeal, his studies and his journey being the ones he recalled. She looked angelic with her son obediently at her side.

When in her company, he felt apprehensive, choosing his words carefully, desperately wanting to please.

After their brief introduction, in which Penny waited for such niceties to be over, she took him to his room. Looking over his shoulder as he climbed the stairs, he saw Elizabeth exiting the hall, heading for the garden across the gravel drive where trucks were still arriving, offloading their cargo. Once inside the bedroom, Penny pointed out a secret door behind which was the bathroom. Knowing he had an en-suite calmed his nerves. Having to toilet quietly in someone else's home was a phobia Owen had recently acquired.

"See you downstairs in thirty minutes, ready to go," Penny said, as she dashed off once again.

Wandering over to the window, Owen looked out across palatial gardens. Among all the activity, he saw Elizabeth chatting with workers, pointing in various directions while referring to a plan she held in her hand. In the absence of her husband, it was obvious who was at the helm, readying the place for the party that would be underway in fewer than twenty-four hours. As he watched, paying little interest to the changing shape of the grounds, there was a small tap at the door.

"Penelope asked me to deliver these," Benjamin said, holding Owen's suitcase in one hand and a dinner jacket in the other. Beads of sweat on his forehead were an indication of how he must have struggled with such huge deliveries for a slight child.

Uncomfortable he had not carried them himself, Owen blushed with embarrassment. He expected some suited employee would have delivered his possessions, not Penny's younger brother. But then he had no recollection of any servant types loitering in the background. Had Penny directed the child to deliver the items out of spite, or was it a ploy to embarrass her guest? Both seemed the most viable answer.

Any fears he had of entertaining Penny for a few hours in the Red Lion were dispelled. It seemed she was something of a celebrity among the locals. Maybe that was the rush, her desire to be with her disciples. While she preached, Owen ordered food: there was chargrilled this and chargrilled that, so he ordered chicken, chargrilled, realising how famished he was after his day. Feeling abandoned, Owen struck up an interesting conversation with the landlady. Just as he was starting to enjoy her banter, Penny returned, telling him it was time to leave.

"I'm assuming we're walking?" Owen asked, as they exited the pub into the cooling breeze of the night.

"Not bloody likely," Penny said, offended. "That's like, two miles."

"You've had too much to drink," Owen said, knowing changing her mind would be beyond his persuasive skills.

"How do you know how much I've had?" she asked. "You were the one propping up the bar all night."

"I saw," Owen said.

"You've been spying on me," she said, teasing him. "I don't know whether to be offended or flattered. I'm going to choose flattered. Yes, flattered it is."

"Concerned is what you should be," Owen said, flattery far from his mind.

"Are you getting in or not?" Penny asked, opening the door.

Her driving was just as aggressive as their earlier dash through the suburbs. Penny's Fiesta seemed to know its own way home. The law of the land had evidently been expelled from its memory, just like Penny's. Their conversation focused on Owen's plans for Sunday, particularly his reasons for travelling all the way to Heathrow for such a short meet-up.

He withheld his ulterior motive for fear of being crucified.

"Well?" she said, looking at him, as they crunched to a halt once more on the gravel drive.

"You don't seriously expect me to congratulate you?"

"Yes, I do, Owen," Penny said, placing her hand on his thigh, as if it would sway him.

"Then thank you for delivering us safely," Owen said, pushing the sarcasm.

She led him through the darkened house to the door of his

room, where she kissed him on the cheek before thanking him for what she said had been the perfect evening… When she released, Penny exhaled, taking a small step back. Maybe because of the alcohol, maybe because of her exotic perfume, or maybe because he wanted to fulfil some primeval need, Owen leaned forward with the intention of continuing what he considered a passionate moment. But before he could act on impulse, Penny distracted him with a kind of snorting sound, a little like a child imitating a pig. Drunken laughter, he surmised. Taking a handkerchief from her glittering purse, she soaked one end with her mouth's wetness and stroked Owen's rouge cheek before presenting the darkened silk for inspection.

"What would your *very* special literature student say if you turned up covered in me?" Penny asked, grinning contemptuously as she continued to remove all traces of the encounter from his skin.

Owen laughed, not at Penny's teasing, but at the sexual connotations of being covered in her sexuality.

"I'm sure," she said, "a poorly rhymed sentimental ode would be penned, musing on lost chances and lost love."

"That's not fair," he said, regretting having mentioned Mel at all.

"Let's continue this tomorrow," she said, before walking into the corridor's darkness.

With an animalistic pang of disappointment, Owen watched her go, realising there was something he admired about Penny after all. The heft of her rear. It was an image he expected to entertain him into what was going to be a lonely night.

Once inside, he heard a door being slammed somewhere above and imagined Penny arriving triumphantly to her bedroom. Then, a few seconds later, he heard another closing, this time much quieter and closer, somewhere on his floor. Standing in the middle of the room, Owen tilted his head to one side, listening. Light footsteps, he was sure, walking away, along the corridor towards the stairs. The noise subsided as the owner of those delicate footfalls descended to the ground floor.

When everything fell silent, Owen opened the secret door. Entering the bathroom, he manoeuvred himself past the lavatory and commode and on towards the nearest of two sinks. Then, with Penny's mocking laughter echoing in his mind, he took a long and satisfying piss into the nearest one.

CHAPTER 9

A note requesting Owen's presence in Arthur's office was lying on the floor when he woke, pushed under the door. It was written in a cursive style in flowing black ink, unlike the one Juan presented in the café. The writer had taken great pride in its presentation, and in his delicate state, he welcomed any form of comfort, however much imagined. An after-note informed him it would be best to arrive dressed ready for the party.

Owen showered, cleaned the sink, and headed for the gardens with the hope some fresh air would clear his head.

Meandering through an oasis of white roses decking the pathways, he heard a quiet and assured voice coming from behind.

"Did you manage to find breakfast?"

"Not yet," he said, turning to see Elizabeth.

"When you've finished here," she said, "kitchen, at the back of the house, it's all laid out. Just help yourself. We don't usually gather for breakfast, so you'll have the room to yourself."

"Thank you. Appreciate it," he said, realising the awkwardness of his response.

"Walk with me first. I could do with a second opinion."

Owen noticed something odd in her last sentence, a simple vowel sound, only slight, but it was there. Her *i* sounded more like *ee*. Not English then. European for sure, but more eastern than western. A throwback to Arthur's diplomatic times, perhaps.

As they toured the grounds, her charm seemed boundless, evident in the way she veritably communicated her gratitude for the efforts of the few workers making last-minute changes. Owen was sure any one of the tradesmen would work their fingers to the bone for this lady.

Walking back towards the house, their tour complete, Elizabeth placed her hand gently on his elbow, bringing Owen to her side.

"How was your night with Penelope?" she asked.

"Nothing special. You know, the Red Lion."

"No, I don't know, but one day, I'll get around to visiting."

"Not such a late one," Owen said, with no idea what late was for Elizabeth.

"I hope you didn't allow her to make all the decisions. Penelope tends to do that."

Imagining the footsteps he heard descending to the ground floor were Elizabeth's and struggling to find a suitable answer, Owen said, "I can look after myself."

Once it was out, he regretted his short retort.

"Do we have enough flowers decorating the approach?" Elizabeth asked, with no sign of disappointment in her voice.

Before he could answer, a grey four-by-four pulled onto the drive. After crunching across the gravel, it came to a stop at the bottom of the steps, dead centre and in sync with the house's symmetry.

"Finally, my husband," Elizabeth said, the joy in her voice unmistakable. "Good luck today," she added, abandoning him as she rushed towards the idling car.

Owen was unsure whether she was referring to the interview or something that had to do with Penny.

"With Arthur, I mean," Elizabeth shouted over her shoulder as she glided up the path, realising the ambiguity of her statement.

Watching her go, Owen decided her appearance was indeed angelic.

Elizabeth rushed on, meeting Arthur as he climbed out of the passenger seat. From a distance, Owen calculated he was a good two inches taller than his wife, who was not short by any means. While Elizabeth wrapped herself around her husband, the front door opened, and Benjamin came rushing down the steps, overjoyed to be greeting his father. Any prior prejudices Owen held about the Roden-Wests never applied to these three.

Elizabeth whispered something into her husband's ear, prompting him to look in Owen's direction before waving.

He waved back, noting there was no sign of Penny.

After breakfast, Owen spent the remainder of his time repeatedly trying on his evening wear, the clothes being as alien to him as his stay in the opulence of his surroundings. With the arrival of Arthur, his time had come, as it does with us all, to start making those big decisions.

***

Arriving early, Owen was met by a squat, muscular gentleman, athletic-looking, in a heavy lifting sense, leaning against the wall outside Arthur's office. He too was dressed in black-tie, prompting Owen to think they had been double booked.

"Take a seat," Jake said, pointing to the middle chair of three, as if the others were out-of-bounds. "Mr Roden-West will be ready for you soon."

As he approached, Owen asked, "This one?"

After a couple of minutes, Jake opened the door, leaned into the room, and said, "Sir, your appointment." Then, jerking his head in a controlled movement, he directed Owen to stand.

Inside the office, Arthur and Annabel were sitting on the far side of a wooden table.

The walls were decorated with pictures celebrating Arthur's

life. One included him sitting astride the gun barrel of a tank while soldiers gathered at the base of the colossal vehicle, spellbound by what their saviour was preaching. Another, and perhaps the most striking, was of him riding a white horse up the steps of what looked like a grand Georgian building. Owen could see Arthur's drawn sword with shards of light bouncing inconsistently off the blade's fuller and edge. The photograph that most amused him was Arthur posing with the Iron Lady, an image that would turn his father into a willing Abraham if he knew the company his son was keeping. It took pride of place on a low table where its silver frame sat next to a decorated cavalry helmet resting on a hat stand. Sitting just as boldly on the same table was a rack of military medals, presumably won by the owner of the headgear. Did such a presentation make Arthur a narcissist, or was he reminding those who sat across from him who he was and where he came from?

"Finally, Owen, we meet," Arthur said, with genuine pleasure. "Annabel has brought me up to date on all I need to know for now. The time I'd allocated for this weekend is no longer my own, for which I must apologise. Thankfully Elizabeth was here to coordinate events, who I know you've met."

Owen compared the two: the one-time head of the British station in Bonn and the university lecturer from York. He knew from his own research they were only years apart in age. While not young, Arthur still looked strong and healthy, with only a few telltale flecks of grey. The same could not be said of Annabel. Owen could only guess what had weathered this revered academic in such a cruel way. A pair of crystal glasses sat resting on the table, one in front of each of them. The ice cubes in Arthur's floated in amber liquid, while Annabel's was already empty.

Nothing was offered to Owen.

"First question," Arthur said, discarding formalities. "Why did I invite you to Frimley House?"

"It's clear to me Professor Smyths passed my details to you for consideration," Owen said, uneasy how fast business had started.

"Consideration for what?" Arthur asked.

"I'm not exactly sure, but I can make a good guess."

"Please do," Arthur said.

Taking some ice from a small bucket sitting on the table, he placed it in Annabel's glass before replenishing her drink from a crystal decanter, all the while focusing on Owen.

"My grandfather wondered why someone like me would be invited into your home," Owen said. "He couldn't see the connection, but after I'd done my research, I could. An ex-ambassador and an academic spending time in each other's company may seem odd. But then I found you were both in West Germany during the sixties and seventies, with long periods in the allied sector of Berlin. I also see each of you led one delegation or another long before you became ambassador. Such information is well documented. It's the mundane nature of those delegations I found interesting and strange for two exceptional people. A fascinating period, the Cold War, with the FRG and GDR being on the front line. My assumption is you were both involved in maintaining East-West cross-border relations. A euphemism, but of course I'll never be privy to such information. Over the years, in Annabel's retirement, she's become well-placed to serve your recruitment interests."

While Owen was speaking, Arthur turned in Annabel's direction, giving her a slight nod, a gesture of affirmation, indicating they had shared something important.

"As for inviting me for the weekend," Owen said, "I'm assuming you had some plan to fill my time constructively. Whatever that may have been was interrupted. Hence your daughter's hospitality and my evening in the Red Lion."

"True, I was hoping to spend more time with you," Arthur said, "but matters more personal to me got in the way."

"A robbery gone wrong, perhaps?" Owen asked.

Something flickered across Arthur's face, a nuance demonstrating he was deep in thought or annoyed at Owen's inference.

"Not everything is as it seems, but an unfortunate affair all the same. Sometimes, rather than accept the truth about oneself, we choose to cover it up," Arthur said.

Owen was not sure if he was being addressed.

Before he could respond, there was a small tap at the door.

"Sir, dignitaries waiting," Jake said, leaning into the room.

Noticing Owen looking at him, Jake winked, flashing a wry smile before withdrawing back into the corridor. Perhaps an indication he understood Owen's jest about the middle chair.

"We know you are intelligent, exceptional even," Arthur said, "with an IQ placing you in the highly gifted bracket. With such talent, there's no doubt you'd make a good analyst, sifting through mountains of information the service receives every day."

"*Analyst?*" Owen asked. "If you've brought me all this way to tell me you'd like me to sit at a desk and *sift*, then I'm surprised, even disappointed."

"I'm making a point," Arthur said. "Your intelligence alone isn't that useful, as impressive as it may be. Based on Annabel's recommendation, I'm keen to get you on a pathway where your progress can be monitored appropriately. One that'll demand more than just an IQ."

"A pathway?" Owen asked.

"It'll allow you to finish your studies before moving on to a short career in the army. A short-term commission, let's say. That's if you continue to meet our expectations."

"I've never considered myself the military type," Owen said.

While he expected some guidance, having a career mapped out so precisely was surprising.

"There is no type," Arthur said. "Consider a year at Sandhurst a continuation of your education. Then, assuming all goes well, some form of specific duties. An opportunity to build your character. It'll allow us to see our investment grow. If you agree, in return, we'll sponsor you all the way, through university and the academy."

"It seems like a long path," Owen said, trying to absorb the offer.

"We take our investments seriously, carefully tracking them all the way to maturity. The ones that perform get our protection and a job offer," Arthur said. "It's an exciting opportunity we're offering, one in which the onus is on *you*, not *us*. We'll simply observe from a distance."

Owen knew what his grandfather would say, a military career, as short as it may be. But Emri told him to go out into the world, make a life for himself. An offer from Arthur should have been expected after Annabel's advice, but the army...

"We must insist on one thing, Owen," Annabel said, "and we can't compromise on this one aspect. Discretion. Everything we discuss, now and in the future, and everything we do, is always to be kept secret. Nothing is up for discussion except with those we allow."

"Assuming you continue to meet our needs," Arthur said, "then potentially you could be offered an interesting position working for your country. Exactly where you'd be placed is a conversation for the future, not tonight. But I can promise you our full support along the way, as long as you keep performing to the standards we set."

"Sir, you're needed downstairs," Jake said, looking into the room with no introduction this time.

"One moment," Arthur said.

"You're needed now," Jake said, with an air of urgency.

"I'll leave you with Annabel, duty calls. Then I must return to London. If you want to work in a unique environment, then we insist on self-drive and independence, along with your sharp intellect."

Rising, Arthur kissed Annabel's cheek before whispering something in her ear, making her smile.

Before leaving the office, he shook Owen's hand, holding it in a firm grip.

"How you live your life will determine the difference between you and the rest. I want your answer today, before you leave this room."

Once the door closed and they were alone, Annabel slid Arthur's glass to Owen.

"Take it. It'll help," she said.

Owen took her offer, lifting the heavy crystal to his lips.

"A little dramatic of him, I know," Annabel said, "but this business with Roland is drawing out his vengeful mood. Believe me, I know what that looks like."

"Under the circumstances..." Owen said.

There was a moment of silence between the two before Annabel broke his train of concentration.

"Well, your answer?"

"I'd like to take what's on offer," he said.

Annabel rose from her seat and walked around the table, placing her hand on his shoulder.

"The choices we make can cause serious consequences, but you know this, so I won't dwell on such matters," she said, with a widening smile.

"I'm eager to get started."

"Your enthusiasm is commendable, but first you study, and I'll be watching. Say hello to your grandfather for me when you get back up north. I'll see *you* in York. Now go and enjoy the party."

"I'll walk you down," Owen said.

"There's no place I'd less like to be tonight," Annabel said, sounding tired, "but before I go, one last piece of advice. Relish the sweetness of your youth because it won't last long."

Having spoken her last wise words, Annabel left, leaving Owen in the silence of the room. The ice in her glass had melted, leaving only redundant water. Owen considered her dependence on alcohol, having witnessed it twice. There was a darkening around her eyes, shadows not there before. He could only guess what history had thrown at her over the years. Arthur knew about the forces that had wearied the ageing academic and the cost of her conduct of secrecy. Their special relationship was obvious from the way he looked at her, touched her, and whispered tenderly into her ear.

I, of all people, understand.

Alone, among the artefacts of Arthur's life, it felt like an anticlimax. But what did he expect, fireworks? Owen had a sudden urge to be with his mother and grandfather, to share his news and take their counselling, but such a wish was not an option. As well as funding for his studies, Owen had just been given something many of us strive most of our lives to find: a sense of purpose.

Remaining at the table, Owen drank Arthur's whisky. After all, when would he get the opportunity to drink from the man's glass again?

From the gardens below came the low thrum of music.

CHAPTER 10

"Drink," Penny said, sticking a champagne flute into his hand. "It's the only worthy activity among this lot."

Taking the glass, Owen drank, eager to celebrate the security he had just been given. The first hour of the function was spent wandering and chatting with guests who seemed interested in only one thing, his credentials for such a gathering. Because Penny had no interest in his social standing, he saw her as his best option for a respite from such tedium.

"I'm assuming all went well with Daddy?" she asked.

"As well as expected," Owen said, remaining vague.

"Don't worry, I'm under the strictest orders never to pry into Daddy's business. Cheers anyway," she said, tapping her glass against Owen's, producing an audible clink. "I don't suppose you know who ate all the breakfast cheese this morning?" she asked, smiling above the rim of her glass.

Owen welcomed her playful banter, knowing he was the one responsible.

"I'm guessing it was that muscle in a tux I met outside your father's office," he said.

"You mean the illustrious Jake?" Penny asked.

"We bonded with our long and meaningfully deep conversations."

"I doubt it," she said, laughing at Owen's outrageous statement. "Let's get out of here. We won't be disturbed down by the pond."

Leaving the constant hum of chatter behind, they walked down a small embankment, at the bottom of which was an expanse of water, not what Owen would call a pond, more like a small lake. On the far side, in the direction they were heading, was a cluster of fir trees, tall enough to hide a six-foot wall encircling the Roden-West ancestral home. Inside the privacy of the canopy, a blanket had already been placed on the ground, cool box resting to one side.

"You've been busy," Owen said, surveying the preparations.

"Not necessarily. I just gave the orders," Penny said.

Of course, he thought, hoping such an effort had not involved Benjamin.

Looking across the pond, the house stood in all its splendour, reflecting mirror-like on the water's surface. The only disturbance was two swans gliding across, distorting the façade of the building's reflected image. It was hard to imagine, in the relative tranquillity of their surroundings, that beyond the brick wall was the sprawling urban commuter belt of Surrey. If one listened, there was a constant rumble, a result of the spread of urbanisation outwards from the capital, challenging any suggestion the house was a country residence, as many in the area still insisted on calling their homes.

Taking off his jacket, Owen sat, waiting for Penny to uncork the first of the bottles.

"To my newfound friend," she said, proposing a toast. "May your relationship with Daddy be *safe* and prosperous."

Owen recognised the reasoning in such a tribute, wondering how many potentials Penny had seen come through Frimley House.

"Before we get started," Owen said, "remember my early start."

"Don't worry, I have it covered," Penny said.

"Covered?" Owen asked.

"You can go on the train if you wish, but I'm taking Jake to Heathrow in the morning anyway. Hitch a free ride with us if you want. I'll give you a knock. Jake won't allow me to sleep in."

"Jake's still here?"

"Daddy's ordered him back to Barcelona first thing in the morning."

"Barcelona?"

"*Roland* silly. Obviously, something requires Jake's expertise out in Spain."

"Okay, makes sense," Owen said. "I suppose a car is more dependable than a Sunday-morning train."

"For sure," Penny said, "and cheers," she added, passing him another bottle to uncork.

By the time the sun dropped behind the pines, they had emptied two bottles, both of which rested idly to one side, half-submerged in fallen pine needles. The chatter of guests wafting across the lake continued late into the night, dismissing a 10pm finish. An absurdity, as Penny had alluded.

Under the waning of a crescent moon, and after much rolling around, Owen removed Penny's pants, then, after a short period of foreplay, the two-backed monster performed for the watching swans. Once finished, Owen stood, walking half-naked to the water's edge, sweat seeming to drip from every pore. Unceremoniously, he removed the sheath, throwing it into the black void where it floated on the surface. As if in protest at such a grotesque act, the swans trumpeted their complaint before rising from their daytime resting place, flying into darkening skies.

***

Next morning, much later than Penny promised to wake him, Owen dressed before rushing downstairs, heading for the kitchen where he could hear voices. Bursting into the room, he was faced with Elizabeth and her son.

"Where's Penny!" he said, no longer concerned with his conduct in front of Arthur's wife, her seraphic beauty forgotten.

He searched the room for the one person he was hoping to find.

Penny's absence moved his stomach with extreme disappointment.

Having listened to Owen's desperate explanation about why he needed to be at the airport in less than thirty minutes, Elizabeth attempted to calm him before explaining Penelope had already left with Jake. The most disturbing piece of information was by car or train, he would never make it in time.

Owen took a taxi to Camberley, arriving about the same time Mel's flight was due to depart. Defeated, he purchased a ticket to take him home. It all seemed ironic, considering what had been secured in Arthur's office the day before. Recalling Annabel's words, Owen considered the pleasure of revenge.

Arriving at King's Cross, he decided to call Penny, the words 'vengeful mood' playing on his mind, taunting him.

After a couple of rings, Elizabeth picked up.

"Is she there?" Owen asked.

"I tried to warn you," she said, before putting him on hold.

Minutes later, Penny was on the receiver.

"Owen, you left. I thought after last night, I'd allow you to sleep."

"I have a question for you. Do you mind?"

"Of course not. Then I'll come and get you."

"Have you ever been invited into your father's office for the same reason as me?"

"That's a strange thing to ask, but no, I haven't."

"Do you know why?"

"No..." she said, pausing to absorb such a random inquiry.

"Because your father knows what real talent looks like."

Not waiting for an answer, Owen hung up.

Collecting his grandfather's suitcase, he walked towards his waiting train.

There was no rush of sweet revenge, only a saddening sense he tried and failed to punish her. In a self-indulgent way, the self-pity delighted him.

Owen paid a high price for his lakeside indiscretion. It would be many years before he was alone with Melanie Bancroft. His disappointment at missing their rendezvous was like a child realising their favourite fantastical figure is only make-believe.

***

After the summer of eighty-nine, Owen returned to York. To no one's surprise, he worked his way to a first-class honours degree, meeting the first of Arthur's conditions. Unaware of Annabel's role, Emri demonstrated his displeasure and then anger, pointing out that going in the army was not breaking the family mould.

Owen's great uncle had been killed in Korea in fifty-one.

"I'll be in and out before you know it," Owen said, attempting to appease his grandfather's frustrations.

"My brother lasted less than eighteen months before paying the ultimate price while holding the line at Imjin," Emri said, trying to turn the poignancy of his statement into an argument-winning tool.

Postgraduate study, even something in education, where his intellect could be put to good use, were alternatives put forward to deter Owen from making a huge mistake. His grandfather's proposals were a wasted effort. The moment had arrived when his influence started to diminish, what some call the downward journey. For the first time in their relationship, long silences started to come between the two.

There was good news for Thomas during Owen's final year at York. The Iron Lady's grip on power came to an end. The Thatcher experiment was finished, ousted by her own kind. Owen heard of his father's euphoria, but it was only fleeting. The dismantling of the coal industry was well underway, and like the death of a tragic hero, it was unstoppable.

About the same time Owen walked through the gates of the officer academy, to fulfil Arthur's second condition, the Eastern Bloc was disintegrating under Mikhail Gorbachev's leadership. One of the catastrophic consequences was the start of unrest in the former Yugoslavian states, to which the West's weak response looked like apathy. It seemed, to the newly commissioned Owen, Annabel's predictions were becoming a stark reality.

Dying peacefully in her bed in the autumn of ninety-one, Annabel witnessed many of her prophecies come true. Arthur, who remained at her side during those last moments, was grateful the word peaceful could be used to describe her passing. One of the highlights of her final years was seeing the Berlin Wall torn down, behind which she mastered her tradecraft. It was an event signposting the beginning of a new world order, one that was becoming increasingly fragmented and uncontrolled.

***

In the same week he became Second Lieutenant Owen Morgan, the IRA detonated a 1000 kg bomb at an army checkpoint outside the border town of Newry, in South Armagh. It destroyed the base, killing one soldier and injuring twenty-three others. It was to this dirty war that Arthur sent the young officer on his third and most trying test.

CHAPTER 11

Cillian O'Brian was a name Owen became familiar with during the time he spent in and out of republican neighbourhoods in the heart of West Belfast. When he first arrived, he was told that O'Brian was the classic example of how a nobody can be turned into a somebody, a dissident paramilitary, terrorist to many.

To Cillian, the notion he was labelled in such a way was absurd. He came from a long line of republicans who wanted a unified Ireland. He also considered the struggle for unification a just war, nullifying the label terrorist. As a young boy, he was enthralled by the many stories, now embedded in Irish folklore, about the early struggle for freedom. In 1921, Cillian's great-grandfather was living in Belfast with his family when Ireland was partitioned, finding themselves on the wrong side of the border. Fifty years later, Cillian's father lectured in the pubs and clubs off the Falls Road on the discrimination suffered by the Catholic population in the north. Cillian's mother, early in the Troubles, tried to shield her children from the violence sweeping across the sectarian divide. Her efforts were frustrated in seventy-one when her husband was interned without trial, leaving her to bring up two riotous boys. At the beginning of seventy-two, Cillian's older brother was shot dead by the Royal Ulster Constabulary while joyriding in a stolen car. Then, in seventy-five, shortly after being released, Cillian's father was assassinated on the Falls Road. Cillian was fifteen at the time and witnessed the shooting by so-called loyalists. Left alone with his mother, the event was the final chapter in Cillian's transition to becoming a Provo.

Driving the streets of the Ballymurphy estate, where the O'Brian family lived, Owen was reminded of the community's unwavering republicanism. Irish tricolours flew on every corner, informing those patrolling its thoroughfares to go back to their own land. Murals decorating the gable ends of terraced houses were another colourful and defiant reminder of the sacrifices made by the Catholic community, documenting and paying homage to their martyred.

"You've been summoned to army headquarters in Lisburn," Scott said, after bringing Owen up to date on the few details he was able to offer. "O'Brian is one thing, but so many others going off radar at the same time is putting us under pressure for answers. It's not difficult to work out something's in the planning."

"Why me though?"

"Probably because everyone's busy, so we're having to scrape the bottom of the barrel."

"Of course, let's send the new boy."

"Honestly, I don't know, but you've been asked for personally."

Scott was a white Zimbabwean who came to the UK to study engineering. Deciding to stay, he joined the army rather than head back to the family farm. "It's a privilege to serve the mother country," he often jested. With a fine head of golden hair and strong features, his friends said he should be surfing rather than serving. He had an exceptional mind, able to remain calm in fast-moving situations, and when time allowed, he could plan deeply and methodically. As the operations officer, there were few better at dealing with the amount of information coming across his desk.

Owen took to him from the moment they met, placing complete trust in his capabilities.

Arriving at RAF Aldergrove, northwest of Belfast, Owen was assigned to lead a covert team responsible for an area in the west of the city. During his first weeks, he familiarised himself with the network of roads crisscrossing the dangerous neighbourhoods, infamous for their history of violent paramilitary activity. Throughout his acclimatisation, he tried to become the chameleon because the people with whom he found himself moving amongst gave no second chances to the complacent. Owen respected the resilience of the nationalist community, especially the tenaciousness of those volunteers taking up the struggle.

He was aware of Cillian O'Brian's reputation and his position within the Provisional Irish Republican Army.

***

The room to which Owen was shown was windowless and plain. For a while, he was the only occupant. The dreariness of his surroundings was broken by maps decorating the walls, geographical in nature, defining sectarian boundaries in unimaginative colours: orange and green. In the centre of the room was a table on which sat two further maps. Leaning forward, he placed an index finger on each, pinioning them to the surface. The one on his left showed the environs of the Falls, Springfield, and Whiterock Roads. Changing his attention to the map on his right, Owen noted it was the border crossing linking the towns of Newry in the north to Dundalk in the south. Both were arterial, leading into the beating heart of Belfast. Owen's analytical mind was already making deductions, eyes moving back and forth in quick succession as he started to put the pieces of the puzzle together. It was on the second map his eyes rested. An area unfamiliar to him. The road came out of the northern mountains of County Louth as it crossed the border before descending into the open plain of South Armagh, dominated by the Flagstaff ridgeline to the east and Slieve Gullion to the west.

His concentration was broken when the door opened and

three men walked in. The leading figure was someone Owen recognised, a squat-looking individual who filled his jacket with a sinewy muscular shape. His face was what some, to their cost, called ugly, pocked with the scars of acne. Now in his mid-forties, he still resembled a savage dog waiting to be unleashed.

"Owen, I see you've managed to find a seat," Jake said, before introducing his two companions.

"This is Giles Bratton, Northern Ireland Office. Needs two minutes of your time before we make a start."

Bratton nodded his acknowledgement, as did Owen.

"And this well-manicured specimen is Ross Shepard, RUC Special Branch. Here to observe."

Ross walked over, shook Owen's hand, then positioned himself opposite.

"Jake's told me all about you," he said.

Bratton remained where he was, rooted to the spot.

A career politician, Bratton had a permanent good-natured grin on his face, concealing his anxiety. He was some months into a two-year placement, rarely taking any assignments requiring movement beyond the safety of his department. During such times, he comforted himself by imagining family scenarios, ones he intended to turn into reality upon return. He longed for the comfortable normality of commuting daily into London from his Kent home, a life in waiting. Before arriving in Northern Ireland, the last time he experienced such stress was when he tried and failed to impress his parents during examinations. It was a sensation he never expected to experience again, but here he was. Back then, he was culpable, but he told himself he was not going to share such liability while in this northern province. It had ruined too many careers for his liking. Bratton had ventured out because he was directed, ordered even, to deliver a few simple words that would take seconds to convey. Once the task was complete, he intended to rush back and phone his wife. It was something he did religiously each time he returned from such excursions.

Looking at Owen, he struggled to know why this young man was willing to place himself in harm's way. It was as far as his sympathies extended. Bratton was not the kind of person who wasted time contemplating the realism of the situation. Owen only mattered in a political sense, and today's message had political substance, so much so that he recognised the potential.

Owen poured himself some water from a jug placed in the centre of the table, waiting to hear what Bratton had to say. The last thing he expected when summoned was a lecture from a career politician. But all Bratton was capable of when lecturing were short bursts of nonsense. Owen had met visiting dignitaries before, ones he gave little to no attention. Some saw such an approach as arrogance, but he still had much to learn about influential figures. Had O'Brian not been an adversary, then he could have learnt a lot from him, not least the inseparable connection between politics and the use of lethal force.

Bratton was well acquainted with the relationship between the two. He was also aware that tactical mistakes led to strategic weaknesses and embarrassing questions for his kind. "I have enemies," he admitted to his wife before leaving for what was viewed as a career-enhancing position. She knew he was capable of self-pity, which privately disgusted her. But to Bratton, self-pity was addictive, not a feature in himself he even tried to control. Standing in an insipid room, observing Owen, a young man he refused to acknowledge or care for, his self-pity was overwhelming.

"This is your choice for one of the routes?" Bratton asked, addressing Jake, while acknowledging to himself Owen was no older than his mid-twenties.

"Yes, sir, and his team. Lots of experience between them," Jake said, interpreting Bratton's irritating nuances. "The Dundalk crossing."

Jake threw a sympathetic and knowing glance at Owen, acknowledging he was aware of such judgements.

Owen was dressed for the environs of the Falls, scruffy jeans and loose jumper. Not the attire for a meeting with someone from the NIO. Bratton had his standards, formulated in the offices of his father's company and, more recently, on campaign trails. He never managed to adapt such simple principles to the business in which he found himself. Owen saw the necessity to adjust as a matter of survival, a reality someone like Bratton was not willing or capable of grasping.

"I'm sure you're asking yourself why we've brought you down to Lisburn," he said.

"Looking at these maps, I assume something is heading north, coming from Dundalk. Something important enough to bring you all here to speak to me personally." Placing his finger on the map showing the environs of the Falls Road, he added, "And it's heading for here."

Bratton nodded at Jake, who returned the gesture before placing a leather briefcase on the table. Once the combination was aligned, Jake opened it, removing a brown envelope before placing it on the table.

Owen recognised the thick red cross at the top, denoting the sensitivity of what was inside. Secured to the envelope was a rectangular piece of paper, a simple system for tracking who opened the envelope at any given time. Owen could make out only one signature, presumably Jake's. A small piece of string was attached to the top flap and tied to the lower, which Jake removed before taking out four large photographs.

Owen saw the envelope contained other documents, but they remained inside.

Once the photographs were all on the table, Bratton continued.

"I'm here to tell you the importance of what's about to be discussed. I'm sure I don't need to tell you about the successes the IRA is having with their sniper operations in South Armagh—"

"No, you don't," Owen said, perusing the four images.

"—since the beginning of the year. It seems *your* O'Brian is down in Dundalk being trained in the same tactics and weapons we're seeing employed successfully and more regularly on the border."

There it is, Owen thought, *the political body swerve.*

It slid off Bratton's tongue with no effort, 'your O'Brian'. For a moment, he looked up at Jake and then back at the photos.

Owen recognised three of the four men.

"We can't allow them to deny us ground in Belfast," Bratton said. "Not the way they're doing in the south of the province. People need to walk confidently on our streets. Politically damaging event… can't be allowed… I hope that's clear."

Owen considered Bratton's words and what he meant by 'our streets'. He kept such subversive thoughts to himself, confident Jake would not want any controversial icebreakers.

"Politically damaging," Owen said. "But what event, exactly?"

"Jake will bring you up to date. To make it clear, he'll be reporting directly to my office on progress."

"Your office. Understood," Owen said, recognising the intended warning.

"I'll leave you all to make a start on what's needed," Bratton said, readying himself to leave.

A long silence followed as they watched him go. No goodbyes, no pleasantries, he just left, relieved to have completed business.

Once gone, Owen asked the obvious question.

"How do we know all this?"

Jake turned to Ross for the answer.

"An informer. One who knows when O'Brian and his team will be heading back to Belfast. We have the time, the place, and the crossing."

"Other than O'Brian, what do you know about the others?" Jake asked, nodding towards the faces on the table.

"Dessie Gallagher and Sean Kelly," Owen said, fingering each image, "but the younger one, never seen him before."

"That's Hugh McKelvey," Ross said. "Made a name for himself in County Fermanagh. An exceptional shot with a long-barrelled rifle. We're told he's O'Brian's first choice for pulling the trigger. His family provides funds to any republican grouping willing to permit them freedom of movement across the border unhindered. Not because of any sympathies for the cause. More to do with lucrative smuggling operations. Unlike the other three, his family lives in Southern Ireland. Mainly in the coastal towns and villages around Donegal. There's nothing to suggest they're even aware of their son's involvement in paramilitary activity."

"And Gallagher and Kelly?" Jake asked.

"Gallagher's a callous bastard from what I know," Owen said. "Takes pleasure striking out across the divide. Reprisal killings. Mainly targeting random civilians. Kelly, we see him often, coming out of the Rock Bar on the Falls. Out of his head most days. A button presser, or was. Must be coming up in the world if he's joining O'Brian."

"Kelly and Gallagher went to school with him," Ross said. "Don't underestimate Kelly. He's aware of his dispositions. Able to put the drink aside when the situation requires. Unlike O'Brian, they were both born into a family of Provos. Gallagher's father is buried in Milltown Cemetery, lying next to other IRA volunteers. Kelly's has spent much of his adult life imprisoned in the Maze."

"Wasn't O'Brian's father executed on the Falls?" Owen asked.

"He was guilty by association," Ross said. "Never a paramilitary."

If there was a chance of an honest answer, Owen would have asked why O'Brian's father was imprisoned at all.

"What we need from you are his movements tracking," Jake said. "If the information proves to be accurate, and he does cross, then it'll validate the informant's worth. Once confirmed, the emphasis will shift to stopping his team, denying them the successes they aspire towards."

Owen knew the potential of having someone close to O'Brian, someone willing to provide information. What had turned them against their own kind: money, the promise of a better life, security for the family, or all three?

"If you have access to such a person, what else do you know?"

"If I were to tell you O'Brian will cross just after midday tomorrow," Jake said, "and we know the vehicle he'll be travelling in, what would you say?"

"We'd better get moving."

"Once you have confirmation he's back on this side," Jake said, "then we want him kept under surveillance. If that's something we can achieve, it'll give us a tactical advantage."

Jake retrieved the four photos from the table, placing them on top of each other before he squared them off, as if putting away a pack of cards. As he opened the mouth of the envelope, Owen glanced at the contents. What he saw were other documents and photographs. All he could manage to identify was a name, *Erebus*. It was written in black upper-case letters in the top centre of a document.

As Jake was resealing, Owen looked up to see Ross watching.

"What about the other three?" Owen asked, ignoring Ross's quiet scrutiny.

"Other routes, other teams," Jake said. "You focus on O'Brian. Report directly to your operations in Aldergrove, who'll report to us. We'll keep Bratton updated. He's of no matter to you."

"I don't envy you having to deal with such pricks," Owen said.

"We all have strings," Ross said, "even men like Bratton."

"Still a lot to learn," Jake said, "but it's the reason you're here. Right?"

"Long term," Owen said, "O'Brian and the others, what's the long-term plan?"

"If all goes well," Jake said, "we'll remove the lot of them. If we don't, then you know the alternative. For now, let's get him this side of the border. We'll be waiting for confirmation from you, midday tomorrow."

Whatever impression Jake made on Owen all those years ago

had faded into the past. What he saw standing in front of him was an intelligent man, one demanding tangible results. It made sense Arthur would dispatch him to Barcelona to get answers and act upon them. Jake walked in the room with Bratton, two very different types, but Bratton needed Jake, as Arthur did. The difference between Arthur and Bratton was Jake's actions were not lost on him, he knew the consequences, while Bratton had no idea, knew nothing of any use to anyone.

Relationships between life's protagonists and antagonists intrigued Owen at that time, but right then, there was no clear definition between each.

Before leaving, Jake looked at Owen, remembering some distant memory.

"You do know it's not good for the planet?"

"What?" Owen asked.

"Rubber in water. Takes fifty to eighty years to decompose."

"Fuck off, Jake!" Owen said, realising the joke was on him.

Jake glanced back as the door's pneumatic closer took the pressure, allowing him to see an ever-decreasing image of Owen pawing over maps, deep in concentration.

CHAPTER 12

By the time Cillian received his route for a return to Belfast, he was already restless, a state becoming more acute the longer he was away. He was never comfortable leaving his family for such long periods, having learnt how those you love can be taken in less than a moment. Training in the south dragged on much longer than expected due to the intricacies of the covert way in which they worked. Before leaving for Dundalk, he promised Saoirse they would all go to midnight mass, the first time together at Christmas for a long time. No longer a believer, Cillian lost faith some time ago, viewing Christianity, in any form, as a religion of fear. The enormity of his sins kept Saoirse awake at night, especially when he was away. Should something happen in a place where a priest would not be able to get to him in those last moments frightened her. Saoirse's parents pleaded with her not to marry him. While they had republican sympathies, they found his family history vulgar to their own sensibilities. Had they known he was an active volunteer, then they would have had their daughter shipped off to wealthy relatives in Boston. Saoirse knew from the beginning. "I'll be as open and honest with you as I can," Cillian told her, "but what I don't tell you will always be for your own protection." To his wife, family, and close friends outside the Provos, he was a reasonable and kind man, putting community first. In that way, he took after his father. As a young boy, he always considered himself boring, unlike his older brother. Had he gotten into the car with him, then the consequences for his mother would have been dire.

"You chicken shit," were the last words Cillian's brother said to him before roaring off into oblivion.

***

Owen positioned himself in a small passing place on Flagstaff, an area of high ground from where he could see a wide section of the route Jake said O'Brian would use. Manoeuvring his vehicle up against a dry-stone wall, he lowered his window, allowing a view to the south and west.

The biting December air rushing in helped to heighten his senses, something he welcomed.

As the twelve-thirty deadline came and went with no sign O'Brian had crossed, Scott ordered his teams to stay in place. Remaining so far south for such long periods was dangerous, something Owen had hoped to avoid. He was also conscious of how difficult identifying O'Brian would be after dark. It would mean someone getting much closer for a positive identification.

Stepping out of his vehicle, Owen completed a three-sixty of his location. If not for the Troubles, he could imagine hiking along the ridgeline dominating the Flagstaff Massif.

From his eyrie, he could see the A1, cutting its way through a patchwork of fields and farms. It was a strip of outstanding beauty stretching all the way to the horizon, where three other cars waited for O'Brian. Looking further south, Owen noticed the clouds darkening, a sure sign daylight was retreating rapidly, stealing his advantage. Out towards the border, he saw the silhouette of an army watchtower, a vantage point from where to observe the comings and goings in this troubled section of land. A reminder of the precariousness of his surroundings. Watching the ghostly silhouette start to fade, merging with the late-afternoon's colours, he thought of Billy. Maybe he was out there, patrolling across those darkening velvet fields. It struck him that stopping O'Brian would make Billy safer, but then he recognised the simplicity of such an idea.

With the last of the day's light almost gone, Owen's earpiece broke the serenity provided by the natural world.

"We have eyes on him, heading north."

Erupting out of the airwaves, the words dragged Owen away from the comfort of his setting. The tension returned, spreading throughout his body, a much more appropriate response to the task ahead.

Owen's plan swung into action as his mobile teams started to report on O'Brian's progress. Pulling onto the A1 to join the chase, Owen looked up at the ridge. There was something strange about that remote place, a lingering he was part of, if only in a small way. Such romantic notions evaporated with a light spattering of snowflakes smearing the windscreen as he pressed the accelerator and sped northwards.

Early in training, Owen was taught a crucial lesson: plans, however deliberate, rarely survive contact with the enemy. It was an instruction he was reminded of when, at the M1 interchange on the Lisburn roundabout, O'Brian pulled into the services. Parking his car, he walked into a Christmas crowd, entering the indoor plaza.

"Someone needs to go in," Scott said when Owen informed him of the development.

"I'll go," Selena said over the radio, with no evidence of hesitation in her voice.

Selena had the experience, with more hours of surveillance to her name than any other member of Owen's team. She told him when they started working together to always expect the unexpected. She was from the northeast of England, having grown up in Hendon. "The toughest suburb in Sunderland," she often said with pride. When she was nineteen, Selena joined the navy. At twenty-eight, with one failed marriage to her name, she decided filing secrets from shore-based stations was no longer a viable option. She volunteered for covert duties, surpassing everything thrown at her. According to circulating rumours, she had ice flowing through her veins, not blood, a compliment aimed at her cool and instinctive decision-making. She respected and responded to strong people, and for that reason, Cillian O'Brian elicited her reverence.

Ignoring her request, Owen informed his team to manoeuvre their cars to cover all entrances because he would be the one following O'Brian inside.

Positioning her vehicle with a view of the front, a tremor of irritation flowed through Selena as she watched her young boss walk up the steps and into the building.

Sitting next to her was Phil, who had worked with Selena for over a year. During that time, he came to know her as well as anybody. He sensed the primitive rage rushing through her veins at being refused.

"Next time…" he said.

"Go fuck yourself. He's just made his first big mistake."

With a nervous move of his hand, Phil gingerly felt for the comfort of the Heckler & Koch placed neatly between his seat and door, knowing fear was alien to the woman sitting next to him. The cold of the rifle's steel went some way in calming his nerves.

Phil was from Skegness, on the east coast of England. A working-class holiday destination. The seaside town had an underlying vicious temper and an anything-goes atmosphere. As a teenager, in the summer months, he worked the rides on the seafront for a few pounds a night, and in winter, when any form of work was hard to come by, he watched the roaring sea eating away at the fragile coastline. He often wished the crashing waves would speed up their destruction because he doubted how much more he could take of the decaying town. As a schoolboy, Phil witnessed his drunken father lashing out at his mother. In such moments of heightened frustration, his father would scream over and over, "This place is killing me!" The absurdity was not lost on Phil because his mother was the one having the life drained out of her. Shortly after his eighteenth birthday, an age when the law said he could make his own decisions, he broke away and joined the army, promising his mother he would come back for her one day. He was now thirty-two and still promising, long after she had given up on such an illusion.

Owen had no clear plan other than to verify O'Brian was inside.

A deep uncertainty swept over him, as if something was eating away internally. Fighting the urge to glance over his shoulder, desperate to know his team was behind him, he walked up the steps. It was a surprise to see people coming and going indifferently, a phenomenon he found difficult to compute. He was playing a dangerous game in their midst, and they knew nothing about it. Reaching the entrance, a girl held the door open, smiling as he passed. Entering, he noticed a small shop to his left full of travellers happily buying miscellaneous assortments for their journey. To his right were the bathrooms, signposted by black gender symbols embellished on white plastic backgrounds. In the entrance was a Christmas tree, decorated with lights and baubles, with an angel sitting on top surveying all who entered. Did those coming and going identify with its Catholic or Protestant spirit?

There was no sign of O'Brian.

He moved on towards the food court, noticing a vending machine to his right. Strolling over, he forced himself to concentrate on the contents, seeing but not acknowledging what he was looking at. Taking some coins from his pocket, he pushed them into the slot, listening to the metallic sound scratching and clattering down the sides of the metal tube. Behind him, he could hear a constant chatter as people continued to come and go, their day no different from any other. Fumbling with the numbers, he pressed to extract something, anything to give him a reason for being there. Releasing his finger from the last digit, a small bottle of water was pushed forward. It balanced on the edge of the precipice before falling into a dark tray below.

Having retrieved his purchase, Owen forced himself to turn and face the crowds.

The food counters made a circular shape around a large seating area, not unlike an amphitheatre. Owen scanned the waiting crowds queueing for their fast-food meals. Then, looking across the tables, he searched for his target.

There was nothing.

Taking a seat, Owen played with the bottle, attempting to settle his nerves. From a central position, he was able to observe the food counters, the open frontage to the shop, and the door to the men's room. Unnerving Owen, the atmosphere remained just like any other service station. Even though he searched for oddities, something out of place on the three-sixty-degree canvas, there was nothing.

If O'Brian was not in the bathroom, then he was gone.

It was a planned stop for Cillian. All part of his counter-surveillance, prearranged so he could change the Dundalk car. The vehicle was already on its way back south when he emerged from the bathroom. Having sat in a cubicle, giving his contact time to get away, he knew that if he had been followed, then the surveyors would be caught up in the confusion of an unknown driving back towards the border.

Exiting the men's room, he made a cursory and instinctive glance across the tables, noticing something unusual. The young man, the one sitting on his own, playing with a water bottle, opening and closing it repeatedly, no food, no company, just people-watching.

For the layperson, such an observation would not necessarily be out of place. But to Cillian, on his way back from Dundalk, it was a cause for concern.

Owen had seen O'Brian appear from the toilets, watched him as he paused motionless in the shadow of the Christmas tree. To his disbelief, not only did he start to walk in his direction, but he was looking straight at him, forcing Owen to contemplate his vulnerability. He considered his lines of defence now that he was faced with the possibility of a confrontation: he had a pistol in the back of his jeans, a radio sewn into the lining of his jacket, and his cover story. Even with these options, he was numb and indecisive. Although he was fighting it, fear was taking over, a state he acknowledged as perspiration started to spread across his body.

Cillian sauntered over to Owen's table and pulled out one of the seats.

"May I?" he politely asked.

Owen glanced at the other empty tables to his left and right, trying to point out the obvious.

O'Brian sat anyway.

"Please do," Owen said, once he was settled.

"English then?" Cillian asked.

"Half-Welsh, on my mother's side," Owen said, aware his cover hinged on as much truth as possible.

"What brings a half-Welshman to the north of Ireland?"

Owen had seen O'Brian at a distance before, but sitting across from him was different. Feeling his heightened heart rate, he hoped O'Brian could not sense that primal human emotion, fear.

"Study..." Owen said, "...student at Queen's."

Cillian had witnessed such fight-or-flight reactions in his adversaries over the years. It was an emotion in himself he was able to control. Surprise gives a fundamental lead over your rivals, which is why he decided to approach the young man sitting on an isolated table. A simple check, nothing more, before moving on.

"You've come a long way to study in someone else's land," Cillian said.

The softness in his voice, a tone welcoming and friendly, surprised Owen, but the undertones of those words kept him in the realms of reality.

"Not such a long way," Owen said. "Queen's has a reputation for political journalism."

"Are you alone?" Cillian asked, scanning the other tables and their occupants. "Surely a young man like you should be heading back to England for the holidays."

"Looks like I've been stood up," Owen said.

"If it's a local girl you're waiting for, she'd do well to stay away from a Brit. Perhaps not a girl?" Cillian asked, a cynical grin spreading across his face.

"Tomorrow. City airport into Bristol. Then home to the Welsh valleys for Christmas."

"I can see the interest in political journalism, particularly here," Cillian said. "Many have turned such opportunities into profit-making ventures. Plenty of horror stories on our streets that sell papers. A few journalists here speak absolute shite, and some of those have paid a high price for their tall tales."

Cillian leaned forward, placing both hands on the table, waiting for an answer.

"My interests are political journalism only, so no, if all goes well, I won't be reporting on the Troubles. I chose Northern Ireland because of its politics, nothing else."

"Then let me give you something to write about and perhaps educate you on the relationship between politics and the struggle. First lesson, you're studying in the north of Ireland. I suggest you get your geography right. There are people here you could anger with such imperialistic rhetoric. Second, my da always told me the British won't come to the political table unless they're forced. The two are inseparable."

Owen glanced over O'Brian's shoulder, averting his eyes before answering.

"It seems we have something in common then."

Cillian turned to see what had drawn Owen's attention.

"Just looking for my date," Owen said.

"Perhaps she's seen you have a better offer?"

"Perhaps," Owen said.

"*Common?* What could you and I possibly have in *common?*" Cillian asked.

"My family was involved in the miners' strike in the mid-eighties. It tore them apart. My Welsh grandfather told me how prosperous Englishmen stripped his homeland of its natural resources. My family knows what expansionism looks like."

"Hmm…" Cillian said, contemplating. "My da was interned. Picked up in the early hours of the morning by paratroopers. With two young children and a wife in the house, what could he do against such odds? Your newspapers seem to have conveniently forgotten that piece of our history."

"Why interned?" Owen asked, his interest piqued.

"He paid dearly for daring to speak freely. It seems to me your comparison has its limitations. The coal miners of the eighties were ineffectual reactionaries achieving nothing. Like your family, giving up the fight so easily. What price did they pay for their feeble efforts? They were divided and then defeated because of their weakness," Cillian said, pushing for a reaction.

"No jobs, no prospects, a fragmented community, a way of life taken away. They paid a high price, alright," Owen said.

"When he was eventually released, my da was summarily executed," Cillian said, "on the Falls Road by unionist paramilitaries claiming loyalty to *your* crown. Do you know the reason they gave for his murder?"

"No?" Owen said, shaken but no less intrigued.

"He was Catholic. Hated for what he was. Nothing more."

"I see," Owen said.

He recognised the irony, the short-sightedness of such bigotry, and the tragedy.

"He never lifted a violent hand against anyone," Cillian said.

"But he did want his people to have a future, an inclusive one. Not necessarily unity. But one that was equal. He spoke out, made his voice heard. Had he turned to violence to achieve his vision, then surely his actions would've been viewed by any rational person as political. Likewise, if I, having seen him slaughtered like a wild animal in the street, turned to violence, it would be a political decision too. Would you agree?"

"I see your point," Owen said.

"That wasn't my question."

"Yes... I agree."

"It surprises me a student studying political journalism at Queen's chooses to differentiate between politics and the violent struggle."

"In Wales we don't have a crown, only a puppet prince," Owen said.

The comment seemed to amuse Cillian, turning his smirk into a smile.

Rising from his seat, he paused, as if giving Owen's last comment serious consideration.

With O'Brian towering above, nerves taut, Owen readied himself for what was to come...

During what turned into a prolonged silence, Owen wondered if O'Brian was considering the validity of the cover story or whether there was some connection regarding Owen's last comment. It made no difference because his next remark demonstrated, with biting clarity, his future intentions.

"If I ever see you again, it'll be the last time anyone does. Understood?"

"Yes, but—"

"No! No buts!" Cillian said, eyes locked on Owen's face.

The change in his features, from calm complacency to sheer ferocity, panicked Owen. He saw a deep, suspicious hatred, a loathing not evident in his earlier, sedate pretence.

Owen watched him walk into the festive crowds, mingling once again with his own kind.

Waiting for O'Brian to leave, Selena stood holding two coffees. She remained out of O'Brian's line of sight, where Owen could see she was nearby. Even though he ordered her to remain outside, her presence went some way in calming his nerves.

"You made a right dog's arse of that," she said, handing him a cup. "A puppet prince. Where did you get that idea from?"

"We'd better get moving or we'll lose him," Owen said.

"Drink your coffee. There's no rush now. O'Brian outmanoeuvred us and split our efforts. We've lost two cars, both following some unknown back south. We've been ordered back to Aldergrove anyway."

Owen considered what Jake's reaction would look like.

"Nothing you can do now," Selena said, reading his mind. "For the moment just empty your head and get a grip on your sphincter."

Going over events, Owen thought guilt must have been written all over his face. Yet it seemed O'Brian accepted the story. Taking responsibility for having lost him, Owen was keen to claw back the advantage, but he had already been booked on a flight back to England.

Emri was in hospital.

The message he received from his mother was to expect the worst.

CHAPTER 13

Standing around the grave in a small cemetery in Pontypridd stood ex-colleagues who worked with Emri in the colliery. These were self-reliant men who recalled the hardships of life in the Welsh coal mines. Earlier they stood waiting and chatting, recounting Emri's reputation for strong leadership, under and above ground. Others had travelled down from Yorkshire to pay their respects, including Thomas. He remained on the opposite side of the family, who were grouped tightly on the graveside. Had Owen's father made the journey because of some strange sense of duty, or had it taken his grandfather's death for Thomas to learn the nature of the man that was Emri Morgan?

Anne paid little attention to her husband's presence. She was here to bury her father.

Standing on either side of her, Owen and Jimmy held their mother in her grief, like sentinels guarding Rhodri's queen, that Welsh noblewoman from whom she took her name. Next to Jimmy stood his wife, providing the reassurance needed since the day he got on that fated coach. Leaning into her was their son, taking comfort from his mother's warmth on a chilly January morning. He was distressed because he feared what might be inside the wooden box resting above a dark hole in the ground.

***

When Owen arrived from Northern Ireland, his mother told him of Emri's condition, aortic valve disease. She explained how he insisted no one was to be told. Following her father's instructions, she packed clothes and toiletries, expecting him to stay no more than a few days. Emri anticipated the new lease of life the operation promised, an energy he intended to direct at his great-grandson. He had been seeing more of the child, giving him the purpose missing since Owen finished his studies. Before Anne left the ward, he told her of a holiday he was planning.

"For all of us," he said, with great enthusiasm and feigned strength.

The bright lights hanging above the operating table reminded Emri of the first signs of daylight as the winding gear heaved him up from those dark depths of the mine's shaft. In the early days, before moving to Pontypridd, he would walk home from the Lewis Merthyr Colliery, not fifteen minutes from his mid-terraced home in Trehafod, eager to spend as much time as possible with his wife and child. His last thoughts, before he gave in to the anaesthetic, were for those simple days they spent walking through the hills of South Wales, its fresh, crisp air filling their lungs.

It was to those hills and mountains Anne referred when she started speaking at the graveside.

"I'm going to begin by telling you a story of a lifelong guide, one who took me to the Black Mountain, over those hills you can see to your north…" she said, pausing to compose herself. The silence she could hear all around threatened to overwhelm her. "On my twelfth birthday, Dad dropped a map at my feet and told me to find my own way back. I didn't take his comments seriously, not until he got in the car and drove off, leaving me standing in the wind all alone. You see, my father was the perfect guide. He gave you the tools and told you to find your own way, forcing you to take responsibility for planning your own route. I spent the day navigating through valleys, around lakes, and up and down rivers. Not a simple task for someone so young…"

She paused again, savouring the memory, one special enough to mention at a funeral. It was a valuable lesson to those willing to listen. Anne was now in her late forties, she had been a mother, daughter, and wife, but by her father's graveside she felt like a vulnerable child, not the brave lady her name suggested.

"I remember arriving home just after dark, my father in the kitchen, mug of tea in hand, and Mum looking anxiously out the window. As I entered the house, by the back door, always the back, I saw his walking boots on the doorstep covered in Welsh mud. It was some years later, Mum told me how Dad shadowed me all day, taking the high ground to see my every move, never interfering, even when it seemed I was going the wrong way. You see, he was always there, ready to act if action was needed. For me, he's always been there and always will be, observing from a safe distance. He's been there for many of you," she said, gazing over the crowd, "and even when you didn't follow his directions, he was still by your side just in case. All you ever had to do was ask, and he would willingly secure your steps."

Before continuing, Anne squeezed the hands of her boys, knowing they had experienced those words.

"Now he lies in this decaying graveyard. Not the most beautiful of places." Releasing her hand from Jimmy's grip, she pointed to the furthest gravestones. "Over there," she said, "are my grandparents, his mother and father, and beyond, through those green pines, his brother. And now, Dad, you join Mum. You see, I wanted to bring him home, to be among those from whom he came. To be with you," she said, looking over the coffin at those gathered opposite, "because this is where it all began."

***

Owen travelled with his mother from Yorkshire, driving south on the A470, cutting its way through the Brecon Beacons. Anne asked he follow this route so she could point out various hilltops she wandered as a child with her father and mother. From the road, they could see frozen peaks on that crisp January day. The wind was blowing hard against the white tops, throwing a showering of snow up into the infinitely blue sky. When the wind eased its erratic gusts, Anne shouted with an almost childish glee as she spotted some knoll or gully that brought back childhood memories. Stopping at Storey Arms, now an outdoor education centre, they parked. They planned to walk to the top of Corn Du, a couple hours of strenuous walking for the hardened trekker.

From the boot of the car, Owen pulled out a daypack and map, but to his surprise, his mother insisted no map was needed.

"I'd know the way even if you blindfolded me," she said.

She worked her son hard, setting a brisk pace as she strode out along the side of a forest above the car park and into open wilderness. Apart from one gully, the route took them up with no respite in the ascent. At the foot of Corn Du, Anne pointed out a concrete obelisk, a memorial built in remembrance of a young boy who wandered from his farm, caught out on the side of a wild mountain, dying alone in the unforgiving wilderness. It was a poignant reminder of nature's power, one threatening to ruin their enthusiasm for the climb. But neither allowed anything to get in the way of their time together. Anne was engrossed in her nostalgic excursion, while Owen soaked up the special moment they were sharing.

Once on top, she had to shout to be heard above the howling wind.

"Down there, Owen, that's where your grandfather would bring me and Mum to swim."

She was standing precariously close to the edge, looking over, snow at her feet, the wind lifting freezing flakes from the rocky outcrop into their faces. Owen had never seen his mother like this before, so carefree, so happy, so animated. He crept to the edge peering into a perfectly formed emerald lake, hanging at the end of a deep valley.

Owen was in awe of the sight before him.

When the spell broke, his mother was standing at his side, not looking into the pool but into her son's piercing green eyes, laughing as the wind threw her hair in all directions. What she saw in his face was her father.

"Can you feel it, Owen?" she shouted.

And he could, no explanation needed. It was the same sensation he experienced on Flagstaff but could not explain, as if the landscape was saying look no further, it's right here in front of your eyes.

It was okay to be burying Emri. He was simply coming home.

Neither could claim, as they climbed back into the car to continue their journey, they felt the same self-confidence as they did while balancing and peering over the edge of a craggy outcrop. They fell silent, continuing the journey, contemplating, remembering.

Entering the outskirts of Pontypridd, Anne requested one more diversion.

"The Memorial Park," she said. "Let's go there. Someone you need to meet."

Standing in front of a low wall, both stared at a name. Private David Morgan. It was carved into Welsh slate, and like many of the other names on the monument, the engraving was filled with a white enamel, contrasting with the grey.

"Your great-uncle Dei is the reason your grandfather was angry," Anne said. "He really didn't want to see your name on such a thing. I hope you understand?"

"Yes, Mum… I do," Owen said, in a low voice.

"Promise me you won't end up on this wall."

"Mum—"

"Promise me."

"I promise," he said, as if a whisper could hide a lie, grateful she was oblivious to his recent activities.

***

By the time Mel stepped forward to recite the poem Anne requested, Owen had already spent some time observing from afar. She looked well and healthy, beautiful too, wrapped in her long, trimmed faux fur coat protecting her slight body against the biting cold. The handsome man at her arm gave a helping hand, a show of moral support.

Mel continued to surprise all those who knew her. After completing her course at Oxford, great things were expected. To everyone's disbelief, she became a journalist with a local newspaper, choosing to remain in the village.

"Why that paper, Mum?" Owen asked, stunned at her choice.

"Something about protecting the vulnerable," Anne said. "That's what she told your grandfather."

"But the local rag. She's an Oxford graduate."

"She's already turned it into a popular read, upsetting a few people along the way. It's a start."

"And her parents?"

"What an evening that was, round our place, when her mother heard. She came banging and shouting, screaming really."

"Mel's mum… at our house?" Owen asked.

"Your grandfather was like a second father to the girl by this time, having been disowned by her mother. Her own father's just as useless. Never was able to stand up to his wife. Not even for his daughter. That's why she came to stay with us, for a while."

"Can't imagine what it must've taken for her mum to come anywhere near our side of the village," Owen said.

"Like a crazy woman, yelling obscenities through the letterbox. The whole street could hear. 'Over my dead body', she howled, over and over, until Mel answered. Your grandad offered to speak to the poor woman on her behalf, but Mel wasn't having it. She opened the door, pointed to a shovel lying in the garden, and calmly said, 'If you don't piss off, I'll bury you with that. Consider it my first exclusive'. Then she slammed the door. Your grandfather walked the unfortunate woman home. Terrible state she was in."

Within touching distance of Emri's coffin, Mel stared across at Anne, who nodded her approval. She read *Elegy for the Miner*, with its reference to the Rhondda, a familiar piece that brought poignant smiles to many of the mourners' faces. Some had lived the context of those words. Emri's passing, like the industry itself, was the end of something special, not beautiful in the aesthetic sense, but something with depth, touching others in a physical way. It was in those deep coal seams where Emri had toiled, like thousands of others now relegated to a historical past, making it an apt poem to be read for such a man's farewell.

After Mel's reading, Jimmy planned to speak, but the blow of losing his grandfather was too much. The nervous disposition he suffered was a consequence of what he witnessed inside that coach, close enough to touch the remains. It still followed him, encroaching into his life at every opportunity, even family funerals. Realising his brother was unable to move, let alone speak, Owen stepped forward as Mel took a small step back, guided in her movements by her companion. They smiled across the divide and nodded knowingly, like the reunion of old friends in a crowded room who once shared a special moment.

Owen composed himself before starting...

"How can I do justice to this man?" Owen said, his voice hoarse with emotion. "In truth, I can't, but I can speak with fond memories of my grandfather." Behind him, he could hear his mother weeping. "I've heard stories from some of you today, ones I was oblivious to. Tales of a man who had courage, moral and physical. The kind few of us can claim. My grandfather pulled men out of the rubble in fifty-seven. He never told me of his actions that day, but that was the man, quiet and reserved, unless you really angered him. Those of you who joined him underground know how his efforts, and yours, kept this country running. That black gold, as I've often heard him refer to it, may be going out of fashion, but in its time, it kept power stations running and the home fires burning. Coal from the Rhondda even fuelled the Titanic. All those luxuries we took for granted meant our nation was self-sufficient because of his kind, *your kind*, something we can no longer claim. The scars ripping open this landscape, the ones tearing gaping holes in the mountainsides, the ones you see as you drive through these valleys, are like the scars my grandfather carried. I saw them with my own eyes, even counted them on his back when he taught Jimmy and me to swim. Thankfully, he never threw us in the deep end like he did Mum." A few sorrowful laughs gave Owen some relief. "I have early memories of Pontypridd, in the big house where he moved after Trehafod. My brother and I would sledge down these freezing hills before throwing ourselves in front of a roaring fire, one Granddad stoked in anticipation. That's where Jimmy now lives. It makes me happy, knowing someone is here, close by…"

Owen paused, looking at the coffin, before concluding.

"I could go on, as could we all. If I were to ask anything of you, it would be to keep telling the stories, saying his name, for as long as you can."

Once finished, Owen rejoined his mother as Emri was lowered into the ground and flowers were thrown as remembrances. The mourners wandered off, whispering to each other as if their voices could offend those who slept in the Welsh soil. The graveyard returned to its quiet state, disturbed only by gravediggers backfilling the earth. Perhaps, once the task was complete, and the crows returned to their nests, and the wind died, and the day started to fade, just perhaps, the ghosts gathered and welcomed Emri home.

CHAPTER 14

"A lot going on," Phil said, greeting Owen off the plane, "and Scott's waiting."

"A quiet Christmas then?" Owen asked, keen to know how the festive ceasefire had been received.

"Didn't make much difference," Phil said. "Three days, nothing more than a propaganda stunt."

"Perhaps they wanted to give you the holidays off," Owen said. "Allow the love light to shine between us all."

"Difficult to see the real intention behind it, but the bullets and bombs stopped for a few days. I suppose winning the propaganda war gives them a game-winning advantage."

"So where are we going?" Owen asked.

"Everywhere west of the Westlink," Phil said, uncomfortable he was the one breaking the news.

The Westlink, a dual carriageway separating the Falls from the city, a kind of no man's land. An inner border that, once crossed, has an uncanny way of sharpening the mind's focus.

A lingering sense of anxiety, one Owen had experienced since leaving his mother and Jimmy in Pontypridd, intensified. The recent ceasefire reminded him of the odious conversation in the service station. A lesson in how easily one's vulnerability can be compromised. As unsettling as it was, what O'Brian had to say was captivating: the links between politics and violence and the right to self-rule. His journey into insurgency was textbook, a lesson it seemed the security forces had yet to learn. And now a ceasefire, even if it was only three days, going some way to proving the point O'Brian made.

Listening to Phil, as they drove the short distance to the military side of the airfield, Owen tried to maintain a calm composure, while on the inside he was already anticipating what the immediate future would look like. Emri once told him that during the most difficult of times, we need to stand up to reality. His grandfather was gone, and O'Brian was still out there.

That was the reality.

Entering the operations room, everything was familiar, a sensation he found relaxing. Scott was sat in the same chair where Owen had last seen him. The flight ticket he had been holding was replaced with a radio handset, used for coordinating the movements of surveillance teams on the ground. The room was like a submarine: no windows and a forced air flow, with the constant humming of electric fans.

"Multiple shots were fired at New Barnsley RUC station two days ago," Scott said, as Owen entered, "and we're being told it was likely O'Brian's doing."

"Happy New Year to you too," Owen said.

Scott smiled in greeting, keen to get on with business.

Owen nodded in acknowledgement towards Selena, noticing she was dressed ready for the streets. She smiled back, confirming they were members of the same club. It was odd, but he wanted to reach out and touch her, craving reassurance that everything was going to be just fine. It was a mistake ignoring her offer of assistance when O'Brian caught him off-guard. Placing herself close by, where he could see her, ignoring his order, helped him hold his nerve while expecting the worst.

New Barnsley RUC station was well situated to gain quick

access into the labyrinth of streets that led to the centre of the Ballymurphy estate. Pockmarked with bullet holes, it resembled a medieval outpost rather than the community police station it was meant to be. The comings and goings of armoured Land Rovers, with their heavily wired grills and bulletproof windows, was a sign of how concerned the police and army were when leaving the relative safety of their bases. The estate's central point, aptly named the Bullring, appeared like a dropped pebble in a pond, with the outward ripples forming the streets in ever-increasing circles. For those aware of its hazards, it was like entering Daedalus's labyrinth. It was where O'Brian resided, and like the homes of other paramilitaries, his doors were reinforced within steel cages because even he could not claim immunity should a doorstep killer come calling from across the divide.

"Not the modus operandi of the man we know," Phil said, looking at the others for support.

"I agree," Selena said. "Sounds like fuckery to me. Why would he waste such a high volume of ammunition?"

"Maybe zeroing their weapons," Scott said. "Not an easy task here in the north."

"Still—"

"Then who," Scott asked, "and why?"

"Frustration a target didn't present itself," Selena said. "We've seen it before."

"The area was out of bounds at the time," Scott said. "No movement allowed by uniformed army or police for thirty-six hours prior to the shooting. Someone obviously tipped off the intelligence community."

"There's your answer then," Selena said. "They waited for a patrol to exit the station, and it never materialised, thanks to the tip-off. Rather than collapse the whole operation, they decided to fire anyway. Like dogs pissing against a wall, marking their territory. And that's why it wasn't O'Brian."

"What did research have to say about it?" Owen asked.

Having entered the conversation, small as it was, his recent troubles started to slip into the background, allowing him to focus on the present.

"They don't know anything," Scott said.

Always secrets and dangers, thought Owen, his exasperation unspoken. As if revealing nothing would keep anyone safe.

"If it was an informer, then my guess is he or she is run by RUC Special Branch or MI5, possibly both," Selena said. "Perhaps it's the same tout who informed on O'Brian's movements when he crossed the border?"

Having experienced the rivalries between the various intelligence units, including military, Selena was aware the relationship verged on paranoia. Any one of those agencies would go to extraordinary lengths when it came to protecting their sources. What they all knew was gathering effective human intelligence relied on exploiting and manipulating weakness, and everyone had something exploitable.

"Those two who briefed me in Lisburn were MI5 and Special Branch," Owen said, nodding in Selena's direction.

"Then it's unlikely we'll be trusted with such information," she said, "but whoever it is, if they have access to O'Brian, they're embedded deeper than Roman shit north of Hadrian's Wall."

They all laughed at the crude metaphor while subliminally lodging the message just below the threshold of their conscious minds.

"What about Erebus?" Owen asked. "Ever heard that name mentioned before?"

"I've heard rumours," she said. "Bit of a myth, nothing more."

"It's a name I saw in a secret document when I was in Lisburn. One I wasn't supposed to see."

"Maybe a code for a person or an operation," Selena said.

"Could the informer be O'Brian himself?" Scott asked, testing the water.

Owen raised his head, looking around the room, searching

their faces to see if Selena and Phil saw the absurdity in such a suggestion.

"O'Brian... an informer," he said.

"Why not?" Scott asked, leaning back in his seat.

"Why would he?"

"Why do any of them?"

"Does it even matter who it is?" Phil asked.

"It matters because if it's within his unit, then he's even more vulnerable than we expected," Scott said. "If it's from outside, someone higher up, then the only way we'll have a shot at him is if he decides to take on more ambitious jobs, bringing in other volunteers, increasing the chances of a compromise. But New Barnsley, I agree, not O'Brian. Too sloppy," he said. "He'll go for isolated targets, emulating those who trained him in the south. They'll want to create a similar effect. A kind of psychological warfare. When it comes to informers, he knows the constraints within which he operates, and he'll take action to avoid such threats, even from his closest allies."

And on they went, trying to fathom what they did not know.

Perhaps they thought what they were doing was for some greater good, a principle they had in common with O'Brian. Another shared commonality was both sides would try and shape the situation for their own purposes. But all Owen had to go on was a name in an envelope. Despite the continued efforts of the intelligence community, O'Brian started to operate with impunity, maintaining the strictest security and discipline within and beyond his team.

When a breakthrough came, it felt more like a reckoning.

CHAPTER 15

Cillian had been busy during Owen's absence, drawing up plans for attacks against security forces across Belfast. The weapons his team used in Dundalk were now in the north, stashed in hides. "Only those responsible for logistics are to know their location," Cillian instructed, "and until I give the order, it'll remain that way." The arrangement was for couriers to deliver what they needed, handing over the ordinance at the last safe moment.

Reducing the risk of a compromise in whatever form was born out of fear and suspicion.

"We've learnt the hard way," he told anyone who questioned his tactics.

To Cillian, the three-day ceasefire was more than a formality or a propaganda coup, but a sign of goodwill authorised by the IRA's Army Council. By the early nineties, those sitting at the top were becoming involved in politics, holding behind-the-scenes discussions with the British. "It's a sign the struggle is finally bearing fruit," Cillian announced jubilantly to Saoirse. The Troubles had lasted twenty-four years with few visible results, justifying Cillian's belief in violence for political means. He decided not to tell Saoirse about his meeting with the student from Queen's, but when a temporary ceasefire was announced, he recalled the young man. The lesson he tried to teach while sharing a table was now self-evident. But to many within the republican movement, talks with the British were a seditious act.

"Fucking surrender, that's what it is," Sean said to anyone willing to listen to his drunken rants. "Call themselves Fenians. Traitors more like. Next, they'll be sitting round the table with loyalists from the Shankill."

The day after the New Barnsley shooting, Cillian received a call from the proprietor of the Rock Bar, informing him Sean was making a nuisance of himself, a euphemism, meaning come and get him before someone else does. It was an agreement he had with the landlord, ensuring he was called first, fearing others might decide to act on Sean's loose talk.

The bartender nodded towards one of the booths from where Sean's voice could be heard above the rebel songs playing on the jukebox. He was holding court with a couple of youths Cillian recognised, both listening to every word the Provo was saying.

With a slight nod, Cillian gestured they leave before lowering himself into a seat next to his friend, an activity becoming common practice.

"I hope you're here to tell me we have a job planned," Sean said, raising his voice above the music, speaking to an audience rather than Cillian. "It should've been us firing those shots at New Barnsley."

"Shut up, Sean!" Cillian said.

His response was immediate. Not out of fear, but respect for the man that was Cillian O'Brian. Devotion verging on worship.

While the Rock Bar was as republican as they came, frequented by sympathisers and activists proud of their rebel reputation, suspicion was still in the forefront of Cillian's mind. "I'm a realist, not an idealist," he told Belfast Command when trying to convince them secrecy, at all levels, was the only way he could guarantee success.

"I'm just trying to manage my darkness," was Sean's usual response.

"It's blackout drinking," Dessie told Cillian. "His way of coping. If he's not careful, one day we'll find him in an alley with a bullet in his head."

To hear such talk sickened Cillian because Dessie was the kind of man to be called for such a task. It suited his inclination.

Cillian pushed Sean into the back of a black taxi ordered to wait on the Falls, jumping in with him to stop any more talk. Not fifty metres away was where his father was gunned down. He was willing, for now, to absorb such pain for the safety of his friend.

Sean was one of four children born into a family who were no strangers to the privations suffered by those on the republican side of the peace line. Growing up, he was denied the same luck as his siblings, missing opportunities to go south of the border or head across the Atlantic in search of something better. His mother put those missed chances down to his character: a shy and relatively unnoticed youth. In time, he was spotted by the Provos, attracted by his grey personality. "Come and tell us, Sean, as soon as you see a patrol enter the estate." Such simple responsibilities led to more serious obligations. It was his complete loyalty and hard work that paid off, becoming a trusted courier and scout, then an active member of an armed service unit. IEDs became his speciality, maiming and killing soldiers, even civilians caught up in the indiscriminate nature of such random devices. Cillian was certain it was a tortuous guilt that turned him into the drunk he had become, marooning himself in his misery. A sober Sean would have seen the recent attack as a cowboy shoot, achieving nothing more than putting splat holes in reinforced concrete.

What Cillian had in mind was far more sophisticated, something that would send shivers down the spines of all who dared to patrol in the shadow of the tricolour. His vision was to have a unit whose deadly accuracy and audacious actions would match those of their South Armagh partners. He refused to allow any of his team to compromise those plans, and loose talk, like Sean's, was likely to find its way into the shadows.

The notion that informers were embedded within the Provisionals was a common paranoia Cillian and others like him lived with daily. Even within his own unit, their loyalties were questionable. "To believe otherwise is at best complacent, but at worst it's plain dangerous," he argued with his superiors. It was sanctioned at the highest levels that any details of planned attacks would be withheld until the last possible moment, including his own men.

To secure such freedom, Cillian promised results.

Those results were slow in coming, but in May of ninety-three, when others were losing faith, Hugh, on Cillian's order, fired his first shot at an army foot patrol in the Ardoyne, wounding a soldier. The next day, another attack before the security forces had time to recoil from the first. A police officer responding to a hoax bomb warning on Divis Street was shot dead. In just two days, Cillian had everyone's attention. Their successes continued into ninety-four, killing and maiming right across the city, while the intelligence community struggled to make any progress in thwarting what appeared to be a new offensive.

During this time, rumours of a permanent ceasefire gained momentum.

It was the absolution Cillian needed.

***

"We need more warning!" Dessie demanded, after the tempo of the first tranche of shootings.

Ignoring his request, Cillian continued in his own way, telling the other three he was happy to leave any one of them behind if they threatened his expectations. In Dessie's mind, Cillian's warning was a personal insult, heightening an antagonism that had always been present. To men like Dessie, enmity was only skin deep, and insults, however slight, could not be allowed to go unchecked.

"I have other duties, ones of tactical importance to the

movement," Dessie said, confronting Cillian on his doorstep. "The way you run operations is damaging to those responsibilities. It can't be allowed to continue. Not like this."

Cillian was aware of what Dessie was referring to: punishment beatings, reprisal killings, and interrogations, dirty tasks men of his expertise were called upon to execute in the name of the cause. For men like Dessie, being judge and executioner was a climactic experience. Cillian accepted that such extremes, in the direst circumstances, were needed, but he took no hedonic pleasure from those levels of brutality. For Dessie, though, those acts were what motivated him, a frightening and nefarious attribute a certain type of person feeds upon.

"I'm not standing in the way of those responsibilities," Cillian said, "but I'm not prepared to compromise the momentum we've gained."

"I'm not asking for anything more than a simple warning. A couple of days. Keeping the other two in the dark I get, but me," Dessie said.

"I must insist you keep the two separate."

"I have friends at the top too. You'd do well to remember that."

Cillian had seen that look in him before, a frozen concentration lacking any sign of warmth.

"We have them beaten," Cillian said, making one last appeal.

"It's disrespectful."

"Operational security only. Nothing personal," Cillian said, resigned to the fact he had lost his petition.

"You're saying no then?"

"You know the rules."

Dessie's response was immediate and full of intent.

"There are no fucking rules," he said, before sauntering off, laughing to himself.

It was all Cillian could do to hope for an outcome not edging on recklessness, a result often seen after such a narcissistic defeat.

***

By the beginning of ninety-four, it seemed news of a permanent ceasefire was responsible for a surge in violence, much like panic. Many feared being accused of capitulation when the time came, taking the opportunity to improve their legacy before it was too late. Such vanity never failed to amuse Cillian, like those striving for dominance for no other reason than to feed their own ego. There are countless examples where such primitiveness has led to tragic consequences. In the closing days of February, when the new year seemed to be ushering in glimpses of victory, Cillian was summoned to a priority meeting in a safe house in the New Lodge.

Since his argument with Dessie, Cillian sensed his authority slipping, an assumption confirmed when he arrived. Davy O'Carroll, commander of the Belfast Brigade, was waiting, a powerful figure within the Belfast Provisionals. Next in hierarchal order was Loki Walsh, commander of the Ballymurphy Battalion, a polar opposite to Davy. A man who struggled to maintain any sense of order with those under his command. Sitting next to Loki was Dessie, appearing like an untethered horse recently freed from its constraints.

Davy's opening remarks confirmed Cillian's fears.

"Overall command for your next operation will be with Loki," he said, "and Cillian, he has my authority throughout."

It sounded like an excuse when Davy told them he had been ordered to give the Brits something big to consider, for fear they would leave the table if pressure was not maintained.

"We need a spectacular," he said.

Even though he was speaking to all three, he was informing Cillian what the other two already knew, a notion confirmed in his closing remarks.

"Your team will play a crucial role in supporting what we've come up with," Davy ordered.

We, thought Cillian, *Loki, and Dessie more like.*

The proposal, a spectacular as it had been called, was submitted behind his back, then sanctioned from above. Cillian knew he would never be allowed to approach whoever gave the final seal of approval. Not only did Dessie have the irreverence to come calling unannounced, bringing business into his home, but he had also openly defied him in pursuit of self-importance.

Arguing his case would have been pointless because Davy already knew how he preferred to operate. They had exchanged opinions on the subject many times.

And now they were bringing in others.

The frustration was stifling, like being in a dream, wanting to scream. How easy it must have been for Dessie to have convinced Loki, the least astute of the pair. Even the venue was symbolic. The preferred location for interrogations, punishments, and executions. Dessie and Loki had decided the fates of suspected informers and petty criminals in that very space. The roles of plastic sheeting stored in the adjoining room were evidence of how swiftly punishment was dealt out in their kangaroo courts. Volunteers to the cause like these two were dangerous, never doubting for an instant their own actions or words, incapable of self-reflection. It was a combination that frightened Cillian, but he refused to be panicked.

CHAPTER 16

Most things about military life suited Billy, but the separation from his growing family was becoming more difficult to bear. Ruth proved to be the stability lacking under the autocratic wing of his father. Their son was born while he sweated in the desert of Saudi Arabia waiting to cross into Kuwait, where coalition forces would expel Iraqi invaders in ninety-one. On February 24th, he moved through the breach while Owen was still at York. By the time Billy returned from the desert, his child was already walking. Prior to being sent to the Gulf, he had completed one tour of Belfast, aged eighteen, still a boy, an observation Ruth would one day scream at Owen. What was supposed to be a short-term answer to a troubled home life, turned into a career, one in which, after eight years, he was excelling.

By the time O'Brian had been ordered to the New Lodge, Billy was once again in Belfast. The third in command of his unit's observation platoon, he monitored static targets, building a picture of the comings and goings of paramilitaries on both sides of the divide. In the middle of March, he was charged with taking three teams of four men in two armoured vehicles to Grosvenor Road RUC station.

Supporting other assets as needed, was one of the few details he was given.

Navigating his way westwards, Billy considered the little he knew. A liaison officer from military intelligence would be waiting to update him when he arrived, unusual but not unheard of. Odd too was the amount of equipment they would be taking, enough to conduct vehicle and foot patrols for up to forty-eight hours. He questioned those details because rarely did his teams find themselves deployed on such routine duties. Observing through long-range binoculars, staring at monitors, reporting movements in and around trouble spots was what routine looked like. Billy considered the last time he patrolled the area, what some called the triangle: an urban sprawl enclosed within the Falls, Springfield, and Whiterock Roads. His memories of the place evoked wistful flashbacks. A sensitivity he learnt to live with. He often imagined he could taste it, something like blood, metal, or both.

As his two vehicles pulled onto Grosvenor Road, Billy ordered two men from each to provide overwatch from the metal hatches cut out of the roofs of their armoured Land Rovers. Grosvenor Road led to Springfield Road, where it continued westward, crossing the Falls. Turning to enter the station, he glanced in that direction, giving the place his respect before the sensation changed to one of fear. The crossroad was the meeting place of major arteries. It was in those thoroughfares that he learnt the potential of his enemy. There was a resistance, something physical he could sense, an entity that could not be stopped by force alone, only slowed.

Many within the security forces experienced the insidious nature of that crossroad, extending its hatred for people like Billy in all directions.

It was where he witnessed his second violent death. A colleague caught in a deadly explosion. The injured soldier was moved to Billy's vehicle for protection from gathering crowds. He watched his friend's life slip away on the cold floor, never reaching the treatment he needed. The experience left a void, one he filled with a loathing for those hindering their efforts. It was an education forged in blood, a realisation that the actions of ordinary people can be malevolent. In those early days, Billy still had to learn they viewed his presence in the same way. All he could do afterwards, until he returned to Ruth, was to keep putting one foot in front of the other, not knowing if his turn would come next, expecting one day he too would walk into the molten confetti of a hidden device.

Ruth tried to purge her husband of the hatred he brought back. It was when she first noticed a twitching in Billy's hand, only slight, but it was there.

They came to a stop in front of reinforced gates designed to protect against unauthorised entrance into the RUC station, not unlike a portcullis. It was while they waited to enter when Billy's teams were most vulnerable. After considering his options, he radioed the rear vehicle's commander to keep his top cover up, maintaining a three-hundred-and-sixty-degree coverage with their rifles. Even with such precautions in place, their anxiety levels increased each second the gate remained closed.

Billy's radio crackled into life.

"What's the hold up?" asked an intense voice.

The call came from John, one of Billy's team commanders. At twenty, he already knew the dangers of long-range shoots against troops presenting themselves in such a way. As they waited, he peered through bulletproof glass, its green tint making it seem like an alien world on the other side. Looking west, there was nothing of significance moving, but like Billy, he was aware the place never remained still for long.

"Should I bring the top cover down?" John asked, expecting an answer confirming his proposal.

"Keep them up," ordered Billy, knowing his answer would cause further angst.

Everything was a gamble, and while bringing his men into the protective metal of the armour would lessen the chance of a shoot against them, it would heighten their vulnerability to other forms of attack.

"Fucking RUC. Urgency non-existent," Billy whispered as they continued to wait.

Unlike his first time in Northern Ireland, he had the added responsibility of leadership. Making popular decisions was not going to keep anyone alive. The only witness to his indignation was his driver, who knew Billy well enough to appreciate this usually calm individual's concerns were for the wellbeing of his men. He had been working with him long enough to know he was focused in the moment, trying to anticipate, wanting to do the right thing, not for his chain of command but for those with him. Their safety relied on intuition, experience, and, of course, luck.

Once the gates opened, the vehicles rolled inside.

There was little movement in the open spaces of the station because its residents remained in the safety of their offices encased in reinforced concrete, just in case something deadly was lobbed over the wall. In the entrance stood an RUC constable, directing Billy towards a gap between two blast walls with space to park his vehicles.

"Ethan Moore, Headquarters Mobile Support Unit," the constable said, extending his hand. "I'll be working with you for the duration."

Billy was aware of HMSU's reputation. Normally used in support of RUC Special Branch, what some described as their uniformed back-up, willing to strike with speed and aggression when needed.

"I was under the impression someone from military intelligence would be waiting for us," Billy said, considering the officer's presence. It was his first tangible indication that whatever they were about to get involved in was going to be different.

"There's a lot happening behind the scenes," Ethan said.

"Like what?" Billy asked, hoping he could offer something useful, other than his presence.

"We'll just have to sit tight and wait for your man to turn up."

Billy guessed he was in his early to mid-forties, but in fact he was only thirty-five, the anguished lines spreading from the corners of his eyes giving the impression. When he spoke, he did so with speed, as if a sense of urgency was necessary.

"All I can say for certain is we're heading for New Barnsley. We'll be taking over patrols in the area, supporting intelligence assets in the Ballymurphy."

"Anything else?" Billy asked, acknowledging how little he was being told.

"That's all I know," Ethan said.

His expression was a look Billy had experienced many times, a sign Ethan was reluctant to share anything further. The spurious nature of the information was still something he could work with, bringing on a realisation of the officer's deep lack of trust. It gave him some reassurance, being able to acknowledge the nuances to himself so obviously. Looking like any other neighbourhood police officer in this troubled place, Ethan carried a six-shot pistol and a short rifle, but leaning against a black holdall at his feet was a shotgun, dispelling the intended appearance.

"Just a little extra for night patrols," Ethan said, noticing Billy's interest. "No one will know the difference in the dark."

As they spoke, a nondescript car entered the station, its driver scanning the interior, looking for the patrol he had come to meet. Seeing the little gathering, he pulled over, parking alongside Billy's Land Rover before lifting his hand in a welcome gesture. While the greeting was intended for all, he focused on the army sergeant standing next to the policeman.

Pushing the car door open, Owen's quizzical expression changed to one of recognition.

***

They had been in the operations room for some time, and Scott was winding it down, summarising the main points because much still needed to be achieved before they would be ready.

"You'll control rear of house," Scott said, "everything from New Barnsley, up to but not including Springfield Avenue, where the target house is located."

"If needed," asked Owen, "can we cross that line?"

"Categorically no movement beyond it unless I get clearance from above. There's also a one hundred metre exclusion zone around number twenty-three, where we expect O'Brian to set up."

The restrictions were put in place by Jake, but he chose not to share the reason for such measures: concern for Owen's lack of instinctiveness for vengeance.

"What if—" Selena started to say.

"Even if," Scott said. "It's reserved for executive operators only. No point asking."

"Executive operators," Selena said, shifting her position.

She considered the enormity of the betrayal. An obsessive Judas, perhaps. While she was aware of the duplicitous nature of the dirty war, this was unlike anything she had experienced, bringing on a surprising sensation of retribution.

"We've been told Belfast Provisionals have been ordered to deliver something big," Scott said, "before a ceasefire kicks in. Ballymurphy command wants it on home soil."

"What does that look like?" Owen asked.

"O'Brian's team inside number twenty-three," Scott said.

"Another shoot then?" Owen asked.

"Yes, but with a difference. They'll be using IEDs in support. Take out any troops reacting to shots fired. Slow them down to allow O'Brian's team to get away. We're being told they want to take on as many targets as possible. Finish on a high."

"A shoot to draw them in and secondary devices against their reaction…" Owen said, pausing to absorb what he was hearing.

"That's ambitious, even for O'Brian," Selena said.

"We know the location of each secondary position," Scott said.

"And do we know when?" Owen asked.

"Not exactly, but we aim to control that aspect by drawing O'Brian and his team out. Finally take back the initiative. It's been confirmed they're waiting for an opportunity to present itself. IEDs wired and ready, but not manned. Three in total, but they'll be immobilised before they get chance to use them. That's why nothing's been in or out of New Barnsley in the past twelve hours."

"That's going to look unusual," Owen said. "Surely, they'll know we're up to something. Maybe they'll do what they did last time, empty their magazines into the station's wall."

"That's why patrols will resume into the Ballymurphy at six in the morning."

"Uniformed army and police will continue patrolling even though we know they're being set up?" Owen asked.

"Right now," Scott said, "a three-team patrol is driving towards Grosvenor Road station to be briefed by you. They'll come under our command for the next twenty-four to forty-eight hours. With them is an RUC constable from HMSU. It'll seem like any other patrol. Army in support of police. I'm told the policeman is aware of the finer details, exactly how much, who knows. Two mobile teams of HMSU will be in Springfield Road RUC station, waiting, ready to respond. They'll take over once O'Brian's team has been neutralised. When we make contact and shots are fired, they'll move in to secure the area."

"We lure them out by sending patrols in?" Selena asked.

"In its most basic form, yes," Scott said. "The intention is to give the Provisionals an opportunity they won't want to miss. An army patrol right where they want it to be."

"Fucking hell!" Owen said. "We're sending the foxes in to draw out the hounds."

"That's why special teams have been chosen, for their expertise," Scott said, aiming to reassure them everything had been planned down to the smallest details. "The sergeant in charge, I'm told, knows the area well…"

There was a long private silence as they considered what Scott had said.

The first to speak was Phil.

"If we don't shape this operation very carefully, it won't matter how well he knows the place."

Scott ignored Phil's comment, grasping the intended meaning.

"Owen, you need to leave now to brief those teams personally."

"And if it all goes wrong?" Owen asked.

It was Scott's turn to move uncomfortably in his chair, a frown creasing his face as he looked about the room.

"We have your teams in the west of the estate, others on the periphery, executive operators in the middle, HMSU on call, and green troop quick reaction forces from Fort Whiterock and North Howard Street."

"Like I said, what *if* it all goes wrong?" Owen said, believing it sacrilegious to be tempting O'Brian with human bait.

"We've had nothing over the past twelve months, and now this," Scott said. "We saturate the area, keep the target in the middle, and then, *finally*, we have him and his team. After all this time. All of them in the same place, others too. We get to choose the time, giving us something we can control. What matters now is how we respond."

Scott could have told them he had been briefed hours earlier by Jake, impressing on him a sense of urgency and at what level the operation was being monitored. He decided not to include that added dimension, wishing only to demonstrate his own confidence in the plan and their ability to work within it.

"Everything we do from this moment," Jake told Scott, "is focused on ensuring we get to O'Brian. Nothing else should be allowed to get in the way. Follow the instructions you've been given. No deviations. This is our one chance to permanently close down that fucking Ballymurphy gun club."

Scott understood the order and the power Jake wielded, like a servant recognising the superiority of his master.

Jake had his pundits, too, and this time it was a transient politician.

***

Owen had other friends at school, but none he bonded with like Billy. A form of mutual dependency. He imagined his friend would forever be the closest to him. After all, it was Billy who courted his attention, constantly looking for approval and recognition. Since their teenage days, Owen wondered if it was the other way around. In truth, they needed each other, a workable relationship until they witnessed a savage murder on a hot summer's day. Such shared tragedies can negatively affect close friendships, demonstrated when the distance between them widened into a progressive nothingness. Now in their mid-twenties, Owen and Billy had not been close since they were fourteen.

If they had known how little of their innocence was remaining, maybe they would have been more appreciative of those preadolescent times.

Excuses are often made when old friends meet after a period of extended time, a wedding or funeral being the most popular of human gatherings, when trite justifications are plentiful. For the two boys, it was an unspoken agreement, dictating they would not discuss their shared experience. Making a pact, communicated through silence, was much easier than dealing with the pain. It was a slab of concrete, crushing flesh, that brought their fleeting childhood to an abrupt end. The scale of the tragedy became too difficult for either of them to circumnavigate.

There was no open show of affection as they locked eyes, just a surprised recognition. Part of the shock for Owen was how much older he looked. None of Billy's colleagues noticed the exchange, but Ethan had. The policeman saw something, but never came close to the truth in his assumptions.

Owen called them together, placing a map on the bonnet of

one of the Land Rovers, getting proceedings started. It reminded Billy of the times spent listening to his detailed plots during their childish games. There was no immediate warmth for the man he saw standing in front of him. Maybe it was because those standing around, listening to Owen, were his men. Or perhaps there was something much deeper, locked away in his unconscious mind. Unlike Billy's questioning all those years ago, the interruptions this time came from young soldiers eager for answers, interrogating Owen as he spoke, while Billy observed, fighting the urge to compete for his old friend's attention.

Ethan remained quiet, already aware of the bigger picture. His main concern was the sergeant leading the patrol. When it came to it, he would do what was required. What he was told must be done.

Owen gave enough detail to get patrolling started, leaving out the fox and hounds scenario. "We need the estate dominating to provide a safe space to conduct sensitive operations," was the closest he came to giving the full picture.

There was no mention of O'Brian.

Handing a marked map to Billy, one with a thick red line drawn across it, Owen told him there was to be no movement beyond the boundary, echoing Scott's words. Billy passed it to John and Stew, his team commanders, giving them time to draw the same marker on their own maps.

Ethan nodded in acknowledgement.

Then Owen gave Billy a schematic showing patrol times and tasks. Nothing too complex.

"How you approach this is up to you," he said, "but not the timings. They remain rigid."

Once the briefing was complete, the soldiers broke away, readying themselves to leave. As final preparations were being made, Owen gestured for Billy to join him, walking him towards a quiet space.

"Sorry to hear about your grandfather," Billy said. "If I could've been there—"

"—I understand."

"He'll be missed. A real character. The likes that village will never see again."

"Thank you," Owen said, appreciating his sympathies.

"And you, *you wanker*, the village won't miss your sorry arse."

"Who would ever have guessed? The two of us, here, together…"

Each considered what to say next.

"So, what's really happening?" Billy asked, taking the lead.

"Good skills and drills, that's what's needed. No shortcuts."

"What would you know about skills and drills? I bet you've never put a uniform on since you left the factory."

"Err on the side of caution and check the ground every time you stop," Owen said, not wishing to respond with humour.

"Really?" Billy said, trying to hide his shock.

"I'm just saying. You know what these people are like. Have all your bases covered."

"I know what they're like."

"Six in the morning. Your first patrol."

"Will you be there?"

"I'll be nearby, and so will others," Owen said, with what he hoped was a reassuring smile.

"They're my men. My responsibility."

"Yes, of course."

Billy knew each of them: their interests, their concerns, and their aspirations, made it his business to know everything. It was valuable knowledge because within hours they would be stepping into a situation proving to be elusive, and after Owen's veiled warning, dangerous too. It was obvious he was holding back, due to a lack of trust or fear his team would somehow compromise whatever it was they were really doing in the Ballymurphy. To the intelligence community, they were boots on the ground, nothing more.

Even if Billy got on his hands and knees, searching for some form of truth, he knew he would find nothing.

"What about him?" Billy asked, nodding towards Ethan.

"Never met him before, but he's here for a reason."

"He seems to have some idea of what's going on."

"Has he mentioned anything about Erebus?"

"Why?" Billy asked, taking his opportunity to hold back, while exploring Owen's reaction for signs of collusion.

CHAPTER 17

Having left in the early hours, Cillian pulled the thick collar of his jacket around his exposed skin, the cold night starting to bite. Heading in the direction of Springfield Avenue, he was confident Hugh would already be inside. From the rooftops, he could hear the familiar fluttering of flags, those colourful symbols of defiance. Opening his pace, he thought of his children, reassuring himself that what he was about to do was for their future. Had he been able to see deep into the dark shadows, where much of this dirty war was conducted, Cillian may have seen the eyes of those monitoring his movements.

Some hours later, Dessie delivered a rifle to the front door of number twenty-three, where Cillian took possession before passing it to Hugh. Carefully, the two built a firm firing position from where they could see a stretch of road below, at a point where it curved sharply. They worked in silence, the one seeming to know what the other was thinking. Then they waited, hoping the patrol would once again enter the estate.

The relationship between Cillian and Hugh was not easy at first, but after their initial jobs together, he learnt the young man could be trusted in a way the other two could not. The sniper from County Fermanagh arrived with a name for himself, one extending beyond his deadly ability to hit targets at great distances. When he turned up in Belfast, he brought a young wife with him, a girl who had never been outside County Donegal. Cillian took Hugh under his wing after learning he was the kind of person who looked elsewhere for intimacy, something, as it turned out, he did at every opportunity. While Cillian made no attempt to save Hugh from himself, he did convince him to set his wife free.

"If this really is who you are," Cillian said, "then show some compassion and let her go."

There was no attempt to try and change him, and neither did Cillian judge his weaknesses, but he did see the girl as vulnerable and confused. Protecting such people, not just from themselves but others too, was a principle innate in him.

As they were finishing their preparations, with the rifle resting on top of a table and mattress, the sun rose above the horizon, its soft glow appearing above the rooftops.

"From here, moving or static, I can take one easily," whispered Hugh, as they looked across unkempt gardens towards the road.

Cillian smiled, demonstrating his confidence in Hugh's capabilities.

"I know you can… but two this time… it must be two," he said.

Leaving Hugh upstairs, Cillian positioned himself in the kitchen, where he planned to remain with the owner. The old man sat at a table drinking tea from a white mug decorated with a four-leaf clover, a gift his grandson brought back from a recent trip to the south. He knew very well who Cillian O'Brian was, and while he was republican in his own leanings, he wished these people would stop dirtying their own doorsteps. At the slightest sound of movement from above, his eyes darted between Cillian, the pistol resting on the table, and the ceiling, knowing what was in the back bedroom. Even though the Provo sitting opposite meant him no harm, he still felt helpless, like being caught doing something shameful. These were strong feelings, ones he had been unable to shake since answering the door to a masked man demanding entrance on behalf of the Provisional Irish Republican Army, pistol in hand, pointing it at his chest.

***

For the fifth time in less than twenty-four hours, Billy's three teams were ready to go back into the estate. Huddled together, they listened to his orders as he readied them for their next patrol. The road separating the police station from the Ballymurphy needed to be crossed with speed, minimising the risk of becoming easy targets. The first two teams would have to sprint, not slowing until they reached the first row of houses on Divismore Park, where walls and parked vehicles offered some form of protection behind which to lean or kneel.

"John, once across, take your team south," Billy said, "and Stew, you go north. I don't need to remind you to cross quickly."

"Yet you just did," John said, keen to get started.

They all laughed, the merriment a welcome distraction from the anticipation of the task ahead.

With the tip of a pencil, Billy pointed on his map where he wanted them to go while illuminating its surface with torchlight.

"Two of my team will cover you across," Billy said, "one in each of the front sangers."

He was referring to square concrete boxes with small firing ports to observe through, not unlike the pillboxes we see on our shores, once used to defend from foreign invaders. If needed, rifles could be fired through loopholes cut into the structures. The reassurance it gave, knowing someone would be covering, was invaluable to the psyche of those relying on such crude inventions.

"We've been tasked to set up a vehicle checkpoint in this area here," Billy said, pointing to a section of the Ballymurphy Road.

As he spoke, Ethan, who normally remained on the edge of the group for such briefings, leaned forward, looking at the map, appearing more roused, even interested in what Billy was saying.

"Can I make a suggestion?" he asked.

They all turned in the policeman's direction, surprised he had something to contribute. During their time together, Ethan remained detached from the group, pacing up and down or whispering into his radio.

"Of course," Billy said.

"I suggest the bend in the road. For the VCP."

Leaning forward, his gloved finger pressed the map's surface, causing a small indentation. The black leather blotted out the Bullring, seeming to remove it from existence, leaving an area of the Ballymurphy Road visible at a point where it changed direction.

"Here," Ethan said.

Billy looked closer, noting there was a gap between houses on both sides of the road.

"Why there?" Billy asked.

"Because it's on the bend. I'll be able to see what's approaching from either direction. It'll be me speaking to the occupants of any vehicles coming through."

Billy weighed up his options, wanting to give Ethan what he asked, but concerned for the exposed location.

"One hundred metres south of there, best I can do," Billy said. "If I had an extra team, with no constraints, then the bend would be fine, but as it is, further along is where we'll set up."

"Okay," Ethan said, shrugging his acknowledgement.

Leaving Billy to finish organising the exit of his teams, he wandered off into the station's main building. Unlike Billy, he was aware of movement in the estate, people of interest coming and going. Ethan had followed the sergeant's direction this far, but the situation was changing, and it was happening fast. Speaking into his radio, he looked through the murky glass of a window, watching them, knowing they were ignorant of the conversation he was having.

Through his earpiece, Billy received the order.

"Change of plan. Set the vehicle checkpoint outside number forty-seven Ballymurphy Road."

Before he looked at his map, he knew forty-seven would be where Ethan suggested. Seconds later, he watched the constable saunter back, parodying the nonchalant bystander. Taking up a position by the gates, Ethan waited for the order to exit, leaning against a blast wall, saying nothing further.

What could Billy do? He was a soldier grounded in commands.

Leaving the protection of New Barnsley, Billy's team walked across the A55, confident that John and Stew were already in the first streets. It was early morning, and daylight was starting to overtake the dispersing darkness, revealing a few grey clouds hovering in the sky, reflecting Billy's mood. Such sensitivity had nothing to do with the weather. It was his past coming back to haunt him, brought about by Owen's profound warning: "Check the ground every time you stop." As they entered the estate, Billy confirmed the positioning of his men, secure in their abilities. They had fanned out into a staggered rectangle, leaving enough space between each to lessen the possibility of more than one being caught in a shoot or explosion.

Ethan remained close to Billy, only dropping back to speak into his radio. With so many possibilities ahead of them, the pervasive power of those streets taunted him with their superiority. An arrogance he longed to break. With each step, he was moving closer to that ambition, knowing O'Brian had taken the bait.

***

Sean watched as John's four-man team stopped at the Junction of Whitecliff Drive, kneeling behind whatever cover was available. The closest soldier to him positioned himself behind the protective cover of a car, his back resting on the wheel arch. Once settled, he lifted his rifle to scan the area, looking for potential threats. Above him was Sean, standing behind a net curtain, observing, holding a switch. Protruding from it were two wires placed through a small hole drilled through the window frame. The wires, hidden behind a downpipe, led to the ground where they disappeared into dirt. Buried in the earth, they ran across the garden and through the privet, that well-established boundary marker, before being pushed and camouflaged into the cracks of the paving. Numerous people had stepped over them, oblivious of the wires under their feet, inches from an IED. Emerging from the base of the curb, the wires continued out into the road and underneath the car where the soldier was leaning. Changing direction, they rose upwards from the ground into the vehicle's body, woven through plastic and metal towards their intended resting place, the engine, before being connected to the IED's trigger and fuse.

Lowering his rifle, the young soldier considered the morning with its earthy smell, caused by dew rolling off grass and into the dirt, nudging at his nostalgia. He recognised the sweet, pungent odour of privet, evoking early morning paper deliveries. Had he looked closer, he may have noticed the disturbance, where the consistency of grass to soil was fresh and disturbed. A telltale sign he was trained to spot, but on this occasion, the most important moment of his short life, he missed.

***

"I know how you must feel," Cillian said, "and believe me, I argued against it."

"Loki's decision? Nothing you could or can do?" Sean asked.

"He has Davy's backing."

"Davy? I suppose he's too fucking busy securing a political career to care."

"Careful, Sean," Cillian said, knowing he was already under the microscope. "You wouldn't want to attract Davy's attention."

"I'm back to pressing buttons then. Maiming and killing our own people. Or is that too sensitive a topic to mention?"

"We both know Loki wants the glory—"

"—and he'll get it by replacing me?" Sean asked.

"Three IEDs, in the locations he wants them. Just do your job and keep off the drink until all this is finished."

Sean looked at him in shocked annoyance.

"And that's coming from me," Cillian said. "No one else."

The antagonism was palpable, not unknown, but rare when Sean was sober. He no longer knew what it meant to do his job. The final betrayal after all he had given to the cause. His father in jail, the family dispersed, yet he was still willing to take the chances, even with the possibility his mother would be left with no one. Sean placed the devices, three of them as directed, but only two where Loki ordered. The third, the one Sean was ready to detonate, finger on switch, was placed with his own conclusions of how the situation would unfold.

Fuck Loki, he thought, as he looked down to where the soldier's head was visible.

***

"Executive operators still not in place but on their way," Scott radioed to Owen's team. "A couple more minutes…"

Owen was on foot, inside the estate, while Phil and Selena remained close in a covert vehicle. In his jacket pocket, his thumb hovered over his radio's switch, waiting for Scott to finish talking, concerned everyone was still not in place.

"It's going to be tight," Owen said, knowing his team would be listening and anticipating. "Get me permission and we'll move closer to number twenty-three."

"Wait, I'll ask," Scott said.

Trying to second guess the reply, Owen's heartbeat increased, a powerful reminder his senses were heightened.

As he walked down Divismore Park, he noticed the back of Stew's team just ahead, the rear man watching him with suspicion, not realising they had met only yesterday.

If Billy's satellite teams have progressed this far, thought Owen, *then he won't be far behind.*

After what seemed an age, the silence was broken.

"Request denied. You remain outside the exclusion zone," Scott said.

"Then they'd better get a move on," Owen said, radioing back. "No need to put those teams in unnecessary danger."

Picking up pace, Owen considered his options.

"Selena, move in closer," he ordered, calculating they had minutes before things would start to happen.

"Executive operators now on Springfield Avenue," Scott said. "They're reporting two cars parked outside twenty-three. Walsh in one, Gallagher in the other."

"And O'Brian?" Selena asked.

The airwaves went quiet. Another silent moment, acting like a nervous tremor.

"Wait," Scott said.

"No time for more fucking delays," Selena said, addressing Phil in the driver's seat.

Reacting to her frustrations, Phil pressed hard on the accelerator, at the same time reaching for his pistol, placing it between his legs. Like Selena, he knew if executive operators were outside the front of twenty-three, then it would be seconds before the shooting started.

The silence extended beyond what seemed real as they waited for Scott's reply, becoming more intense the longer they listened to the hiss of static.

Time pushed on with its relentless ticking, remaining impartial, propelling everything and everyone forward. The quiet calm of the morning added to the anxiety as the patrol continued to move through, unaware of what was about to unfold. To the early morning bird, soaring high above, they must have looked like ants in a warren, using different tunnels but heading for the same location, as if something was drawing them in.

When Owen reached Ballymurphy Crescent, he saw Billy's team crossing a T-junction two hundred metres short of the bend. Owen calculated that by the time he reached that spot, Billy would already be in position.

"No point waiting for an answer," came Selena's voice across the airwaves. "If Cillian's inside then we need to slow the patrol down. No need for a VCP now," she shouted into the radio.

As Owen arrived at the junction, he saw the futility of her suggestion. Billy was already in place, giving out his orders.

Ethan was where he wanted to be, on the bend with a view of the rear, hoping to get a shot at whatever came out the door. Having waited a long time for this, it brought out an unexplainable excitement. An anticipation that was unbearable, climactic even. The morning was still and mute as he stood in the road, yet, behind it all, he was aware everything was sprinting towards a conclusion.

Fewer than one hundred metres away, Owen could see Billy starting to crouch on the corner of an end of terrace.

Leaning into the wall, Billy felt the texture of the render digging into his shoulder, its rough surface uncomfortable, but he pushed harder, regardless, stabilising his firing position. Peering through the rifle's scope, he scanned the back row of houses opposite, the ones on Springfield Avenue. A low fence, with overgrown weeds creeping up its decaying wood and an unmanaged hedgerow of greenery, obscured his view of the ground floors. Looking upwards, at the first-floor windows, he tried to identify anything out of place.

All seemed normal, less the solitude oozing out of his whole being.

In his peripheral vision, contrasting with the green, was a child's toy, a sun-bleached red bus with a seat and pedels for its owner to propel themselves around the garden, a sign life existed in this unusually quiet place. Turning, he checked the positioning of his men, concerned for their vulnerabilities. He noticed Ethan, standing in the road, raising his arm to stop a vehicle speeding towards him.

At least it'll give him something to do, Billy thought.

Senses alert, he refocused his efforts on the upper windows. There was movement, a curtain twitching. Staring at the space, trying to penetrate the darkness of the interior, nothing further could be seen.

Billy sighed, his breath evaporating into the cold morning air.

CHAPTER 18

Hugh breathed slowly, his chest rising and falling in perfect rhythm. His right hand gripped the pistol grip, index finger taking the first pressure off the trigger, while his left held the rifle's magazine, steadying his firing position. Looking through the weapon's telescopic sight, the crosshairs moved up with each inhale and down with every exhale, splitting the shape of the police constable's body in perfect symmetry. Although he was two hundred metres away, looking through the scope gave the impression he could reach out and touch the man. His warm breath dulled the cold steel of the rifle, evaporating as it condensed against the colder surface. Weapon and man became one, merging like the statue of the Four Tetrarchs. Hugh stopped breathing, allowing the crosshairs to settle on the centre of mass. A millisecond later he pulled against the resistance of the trigger's second pressure.

Ethan was hit just below the neck, the bullet striking his clavicle, forcing the high-velocity round downwards through his chest before exiting just below his right armpit. The force of the impact turned him violently, sending the constable reeling against a low wall, where he lay, his facial expression startled in death. Blood spurted from his neck, mixing with the dark green of his uniform, while some, smearing his face, contrasted with his paling skin.

Having released the first shot, Hugh pulled the bolt of the rifle back, extracting the empty case, the force flinging it across the room where it clattered against a wall. Then he pushed forward, pressing hard against a small, bulbous knob of steel with the palm of his right hand. There was resistance as another bullet was taken from the magazine, forcing it into the rifle's chamber. Looking over the scope, he saw Billy's head and shoulders peering around the corner of a house, pointing his rifle, ready to return fire. Placing the crosshairs in the middle of the soldier's face, Hugh once again took up the first pressure of the trigger.

In the same fleeting moment of the same second that he squeezed, Billy turned.

***

Hearing the first shot, Sean pressed the button, sending an electrical pulse down the wire. The soldier was engulfed in a yellow flash as steel ball bearings and nails passed through his soft and exposed skin. When John got to him, he was still breathing, but there was nothing to be done, other than hold his hand and wait. Across the road, another of his team lay whimpering on the pavement, having been caught in the kinetic energy of the blast.

Dropping the switch, Sean knew the soldier was dead or dying. More importantly, the whole team was removed from any further action, forcing them to deal with the chaos and carnage strewn across everything within a fifty-metre radius.

Having done his duty, Sean walked casually towards Whiterock Road, listening to the intense gunfire erupting deeper within the estate. It increased in volume, rising to a savage crescendo, echoing across the rooftops. They all knew sacrifices were a necessary consequence, but such a defeat would be hard to bear. When the firing stopped, he was already mixing with the rush-hour crowds on the Falls.

***

Across the breakfast table, Saoirse stared in shock at Cillian's mother, her eyes acknowledging the implications of the violent noises invading the morning. If he was caught up in that hail of bullets, there was nothing her beliefs could do now. Years earlier, on the eve of their marriage, Cillian told her, "Marrying me is the bravest thing you'll ever do." It was true, it took all her courage, not because she defied her parents, but because he was a man who dared to act when others accepted their servility. Seconds earlier, her children were taunting each other over breakfast, unaware their father had already left.

***

Billy turned, recognising Owen's voice, shouting his name, just as the bullet cracked past his head, embedding itself in the wall of a house across the road. Impulsively, he spun around, facing the direction from where he heard the thump of the weapon. In quick succession, he fired three shots into a window, where only moments before he had searched for movement.

The bullets missed Hugh by some inches, causing nothing more than a distraction for the volunteer now pushing a third cartridge into a hot chamber. As he placed his eye against the scope, the house erupted with a deafening noise, reverberating through the walls. It was a consequence of bullets shattering glass and ripping through metal as concentrated gunfire passed through the two vehicles parked at the front. Gallagher and Walsh died in the first seconds. Killed in their seats. Once business was concluded outside, the fury that had been unleashed diverted its interest to the house, impatient to enter, knowing who and what was inside.

By the time Hugh had the third round in the breech, he knew it was all over. The walls of the buildings all around refracted with the sound of gunfire, bouncing its deafening noise in all directions.

In response, he froze.

With nervous clarity, it dawned on him there was nowhere to go and only seconds to react. Taking his finger off the trigger, he placed the rifle on the ground before stepping to one side. His last conscious act was to raise his hands, demonstrating he was no longer a threat.

The thudding of boots on carpeted stairs and the smashing of wood as the bedroom door imploded were mixed with a different sound, a metallic scraping. He was familiar with the noise, having made it himself only moments before. Hugh's last thought, before those sent to execute him entered the room, was for the woman he sent back to Donegal, who came to this strange place because of him. She was an idealist, someone who saw love as the only thing that mattered.

***

The lock on the front door gave Cillian the slightest of advantages, enough to make a dash for the back, where, if luck was on his side, he would be able to escape using the path running between Springfield Avenue and Ballymurphy Road. It was the only option his senses gave, knowing a malevolent force was about to come crashing in.

It was anger he felt in those last moments, not fear.

Brushing past Billy, Owen crossed the garden, moving towards the hedgerow. It was obscuring his view to the back of twenty-three and needed to be overcome. To get in close, he entered the exclusion zone. With arms outstretched, pistol pointing forward, he reached the garden's boundary as Cillian appeared in the doorway. For the briefest of moments, they locked eyes, long enough for Owen to see what he later convinced himself was recognition, evident in the smallest of hesitations.

Then Owen fired, twice.

***

Scott swivelled his chair through a hundred-and-eighty degrees, placing his back to the wall of maps on which he had recorded every detail.

Jake was sitting behind him, observing, only speaking when needed, allowing Scott to monitor what was happening on the ground.

"HMSU and uniformed soldiers are now in control," Scott said.

"And Owen?" Jake asked.

"On his way back."

Rising from his seat, Jake walked over to where Scott was sitting, placing a bottle on the table next to him.

"For Owen and his team. A little something to celebrate."

"I'm not sure they'll want a celebration," Scott said. "We lost people out there too."

"Blood will have blood if that's what it takes, and in this case, that's what it took to get business done."

"And the old man?" Scott asked.

"Collateral damage. Are they asking themselves the same question?" he said, a little too aggressively for Scott's liking.

"And now?"

Before answering, Jake placed an envelope next to the bottle, balancing it against the glass.

"This is for Owen's eyes only."

"What happens now?" Scott asked, unwilling to surrender to Jake's frustrations.

"I phone the NIO. Report the news Bratton's been waiting a long time to receive."

"Before you do, I have a question that's bothering me."

"And what would that be?" Jake asked.

"Erebus… is he real?"

"We don't need to worry ourselves with him anymore," Jake said. "But yes, he was real."

"Past tense then."

"He's dead, Scott, killed out there, on those streets, and that's more than I should be telling you…"

Scott walked it through his mind, unable to make the connections because it made no sense.

"You're saying we killed our own tout?" he asked.

"The common betrayals of men are nothing when compared to their potential for wartime treachery," Jake said. "That's a lesson we've learnt many times in this place. You know that."

Walking over to the secure phone, readying himself for a conversation with a politician who was weeks from completing his fleeting stay in the province, Jake picked up the receiver.

"And Kelly, do we pick him up?"

"Pick him up, for what?" Jake asked. "There won't be anything in that house to link him to the device. He's too professional to leave any trace, but we'll look, on the off chance. Seems to me he did his own thing. The other button pressers were where we'd been told they'd be. Kelly was lucky, but he won't survive long without O'Brian. His own kind will do the job for us. After today, they won't be able to resist."

Scott looked questioningly at Jake.

"Fear and suspicion, it'll get the better of them," Jake said, giving Scott the clarification he seemed to need.

He knew it was futile trying to tie anything to Kelly, and neither did he care. The operation had been a huge success. Jake was unwavering in his belief that the decisions made, those quick and instinctive actions, were just and necessary. Being magnanimous in victory was stuff of fiction, not reality. For men like Jake, who dealt in clandestine subversion, such abstract notions were a sign of weakness, and that, with Owen in mind, worried him.

***

After today's events, it may seem like a murky business, but for those who can see clearly, the rewards are obvious. The third and final condition completed... speak soon,

Jake

That phrase, *murky business*, prompted Owen to consider Billy's loss: one man killed and another injured.

Right about now, he thought, *the next of kin will be getting the news.*

With the envelope tossed to one side, he reached for the bottle, not as a celebration, but to forget, even if only for a moment. For as long as he could, he would continue to hide from such memories.

About the same time Owen was drinking himself into oblivion, Billy was at the bedside of his wounded colleague, trying to put the pieces of the day together. His conclusion was obvious.

Like bear baiting, his men represented the chained and bloodied beast.

Before the drink and exhaustion took him, Owen told himself that the island of Ireland was a land where we had no reason to be. Perhaps it was the alcohol talking, the day's events catching up on him, or maybe it was what he believed.

***

Having completed the third condition, Owen left the army. He had every intention of using the change to separate himself from his time in Northern Ireland. Jake once told him freedom was found in not caring too much. But who was capable of such self-deception? Not Owen.

CHAPTER 19

Mel wrote her breakout article in the spring of ninety-seven when she published *Srebrenica, The Failings of Western Power*. It took months to research, write, and then secure publication in a mainstream Sunday newspaper. Its recognition led to a job offer from a London magazine, *Eyes Across the Country*. It was a news and public affairs publication, renowned for holding power to account. "Let's go and get these bastards together," the editor reportedly told her. An offer she could not refuse. Overnight, she became a local celebrity and an investigative journalist. What Mel could never have foreseen was the upset her subject matter would cause Billy or the ugly confrontation it ignited. The extent of his anger, for those who witnessed it, was an unveiling of the trauma-induced condition he was suffering from. Until their confrontation, such episodes were something only Ruth witnessed. All that was before his violent outburst in front of guests at a leaving party in a country hotel, where friends and colleagues gathered to say their farewells to Melanie Bancroft.

"You have an invite sitting here, Owen," Anne said during one of her routine calls. "Mel's being dined out by colleagues from the *Village News* before she heads to London. Me, Ruth and Billy are all going. Your brother's decided not to attend. Refuses to come anywhere near this place."

"Can't blame him, Mum. Some of those people."

"Bigoted is the word you're looking for. Anyway, can you remember Mr and Mrs Robinson? They own the local rag Mel worked for. Paying for everything."

"I remember that pair," Owen said. "I used to deliver newspapers for them. Modern-day slave drivers."

"Hmm," Anne said, not wishing to taint her positive news. "They want Mel to have the best possible send-off. It's the least they could do after she transformed their weekly into a daily. It's sold right across the county now. I've accepted for you. No need to reply."

"Can't make it. Sorry."

"You can. It's Mel," Anne said, irritated neither of her sons would be by her side.

"The move. We're getting the keys. Remember?"

Owen was in Paris, working out of the British embassy on his first diplomatic posting. It was during this time he met his first serious girlfriend, Catina, assistant to the ambassador's private secretary. At twenty-two, she was straight out of university and an office favourite. They planned to be busy over the weekend of Mel's function, moving into a single-bed apartment on Rue Jeanne d'Arc.

"Two firsts," Catina boasted to her girlfriends, "new job and our own place."

Making Owen's apologies, Anne told Mel he was experimenting living with a woman for the first time. What he chose not to share was Catina's pregnancy, the deciding factor in their cohabitation experiment. The only person Owen confided in was Jimmy. He also told him, in a fit of self-deprecation, that Paris was becoming something of a prison cell. What he really meant was moving in with a woman for the first time was making him feel that way.

"The mundane has finally trapped you," Jimmy said, half-joking.

***

It was about a week after Mel's farewell when an email titled *Urgent* pinged on his computer. Still at the office, Owen was working late, having been given a last-minute task.

"An administrative oversight by someone," Owen said to Catina. "I'm providing nothing more than a travel agency service. A few more hours, then I'll be home."

She had gone ahead to ready herself for an evening they planned to spend with friends on the Left Bank, a *Nuit Blanche*.

The head of chancery, Fabian Chowdry, informed Owen late into the afternoon that a group of Senegalese dignitaries was flying in on Sunday, and he wanted Owen to personally arrange their stay. "I don't need to remind you of London's interest in keeping them on side," Fabian told him. Even before a rushed briefing to bring everyone up to date, Owen was aware of the growing importance of Dakar, its airport once again going through a feasibility check as a potential staging post. Tensions were building in one of the UK's former colonies, nine hundred miles south of Senegal, and statesmanship, on the grounds of self-interest, was needed.

"Call the embassy in Dakar," Fabian said. "Your opposite will give you details of who to expect. And Owen, you have freedom to make your own choices on this one, just ensure they're settled for the night. I want them fresh and ready in the conference room Monday morning. Look at it as a chance to practise your French."

Freedom, more like a cheap trick to cajole him into taking a task no one else wanted. During his short time as a junior diplomat, Owen learnt diplomacy was not necessarily a question-asking exercise.

Fabian Chowdry, known for being averse to risk, finally found the courage to allow Owen to start making the simplest of decisions. Since his arrival, he tried to ignore the ex-soldier, a profession that privately repulsed him, as did the notion Owen would be around for some time. Fabian let it be known at the highest levels that the sooner these military types were moved into intelligence and out of politics, the better. Such spooks were unnecessary anyway because

Fabian had been lying and manipulating for the sake of the British government for over twenty-five years. Interviewing Owen, when he first arrived, the career diplomat saw no suggestion this young man would be any better at turning untruths into realities for the sake of the state.

It was a mutual lack of respect because Owen despised Fabian Chowdry's circumspect character. On occasions they needed to speak, during morning briefing, passing in the corridor, or at a function at the residency, Owen always maintained a steel expression, a poker face, giving nothing away.

Not being able to read him irritated the career diplomat.

Letting the email sit in his inbox, Owen fought the urge to press open, having watched it flash like a Faustian conscience. It was late by the time he had everything in place for the Senegalese representatives: meet and greet, transfers, hotel, restaurant, and a plan to get them to the embassy on time. About to turn off his computer, with the evening's events still salvageable, the good angel whispered into his ear: *Your mother's email.*

Leaving her messages unread for a few days was not unusual, and while Anne's liberal use of urgent should mean something, he was aware of her loose use of the term: urgent, don't forget your brother's birthday, urgent, remember we're meeting for lunch. Those were the types of urgencies Anne considered worthy of the term. When he was a child, she told him many times the story of the boy who cried wolf, yet it seemed she chose to ignore the fable's lesson. The paperclip, the one between the end of the email's title and date, a little grey squiggle, was unusual for Anne, a first even. That small detail hooked him. When had his mother learnt to attach a document? Looking at his watch, then back at the screen, Owen decided five more minutes would do no harm.

Left-clicking, he opened her message.

The attachment was a copy of Mel's damning article, a shaming analysis of the UK government's part in withholding air strikes against Bosnian Serb forces in the Srebrenica area. According to his mother's email, it was the reason for Billy's confrontation with the newly promoted Mel.

Just humiliating! Her special night. In front of her colleagues and friends, Anne had written.

Prior to ringing Ruth, he called Catina, knowing he was going to disappoint, their evening ruined.

***

In the summer of ninety-five, while Owen was being discharged from the military, Billy was promoted and attached to a Dutch army unit headquartered in Potocari in Bosnia, Srebrenica. A UN safe zone. It was during this time Ruth witnessed a significant change in his character, one she was unable to explain until she saw the news coming out of the besieged enclave. Billy developed an apathy, a trait not seen in him before. Ruth would recall how she witnessed his emasculation, a process brought about by Billy's sense of abandonment and a powerlessness experienced in the encircled town.

"How could anyone witness what he saw and come out sane?" Ruth asked Owen after one of Billy's episodes. "Savagery, on that scale. Too much for him. For anyone. He feels betrayed, and I do too. Treated like fucking human jetsam washed up on the shore."

She sent Owen a copy of an extract from Billy's diary, her attempt to solicit his support. He was aware of what had taken place in Srebrenica, but not Billy's part in it. *The worst mass killings on European soil since WWII* was how it was reported. As if being on home ground made it worse. On the first page, Billy had drawn a montage of kneeling people, all male from what Owen could tell. Around the images, he scribbled a variety of words and phrases. It was evident to Owen he was describing executions on a grand scale: *screaming, glazed eyes, young men, old men.*

There were many more such lists in his jotter.

***

After reading his mother's explanation, Owen opened the attachment, reading it in its entirety. Although he tried to be as objective as possible, there was nothing suggesting the blame lay with those who were there, the likes of Billy. It was more a smear aimed at a collective failure at the highest levels to defend the safe zone, even though troops on the ground begged for support. It was beyond Owen why such a piece would cause a rift between these two erstwhile friends. Maybe he was biased, swayed by an acute sense that was pleasant and painful at the same time. It was a reaction to reading the byline: Melanie Bancroft.

"It's not really the article," Ruth said. "I've read it myself and tried to discuss it with him. It's Billy's state of mind. His aggression. His drinking. He's not the person we once knew. That man's gone."

It was the early hours of Saturday morning when Owen arrived back at the apartment, exhausted with all the night had thrown at him. After speaking to Ruth, he booked a flight for the following weekend, knowing something had to be done. Arranging to see Billy would at least be a start.

***

Billy stared at the title of the document lying on the table, trying to fathom why it was there at all. It was an unnecessary formality, put on display for guests to read. Mel allowed the organisers the freedom to be creative, knowing how much preparation had gone into the party on her behalf.

The hotel was chosen for its rural location, usually the preferred venue for weddings due to its opulence and sweeping vistas across the country park, seen from the hotel's manicured grounds. It was possible, from the lawned gardens, to see the lake around which Mel and Owen walked all those years before. In the near distance, tall trees hid the fringe of the village from view. On the other side of the old mining community, winding wheels from the colliery stood above the canopy, emerging out of the trees like ageing sentinels. A reminder of another age. The setting matched the excitement of the day, suiting the occasion because all those present had come to give their local hero a memorable send-off.

Ruth knew something was wrong, cutting Anne off in mid-conversation, interrupting her description of Owen's role in Her Majesty's Diplomatic Service, a title she was eager to repeat as many times as possible.

"Everything okay, Billy?" she asked, noticing his hand trembling and sweat forming on his brow, both telltale signs she recognised.

"That!" he said, pointing to the title.

"The article she wrote," Anne said, pleased to be discussing Mel's newfound fame. "Such a bright future in front of her. Destined for bigger things than this village could ever offer."

"I suppose she sees it as my fault!" Billy said, with unrecognisable intensity.

The change in him was profound, but it was the speed of transformation Anne found most shocking. Looking between the two, she never knew who to address first.

"What's your fault?" she asked.

Anne had seen it before, experienced it with Jimmy, an anxiety brought on by traumatic memories, triggered by the simplest of reminders.

For Billy, it was the headline that brought graphic images flashing back. It threw him into the grip of a waking dream, invading his senses, regurgitating unimaginable cruelty.

"Billy, listen to me," Ruth said.

Paying no attention to her pleading, he stood, looking around the room for the author.

"Perhaps I've missed something or said something unintentionally?" Anne asked.

"You didn't say anything. This is what he's become."

"I don't understand," Anne said. "Has something happened to him?"

To Ruth the question was ridiculous. How could she, after Jimmy, Owen even, not know? In response, all Ruth could manage was to look at her in a way that said, *You of all people.*

"Tell me, Ruth. Perhaps I can help."

"It's like the earth is pressing down on me," Ruth said, "its weight crushing. Like in those coal mines. Like fucking coal! I no longer know what to do or which way to turn."

"I see," Anne said, nervously smiling, as if she needed to apologise.

She knew all about self-blame. How it's possible to assume too much about the role we may or may not have played. Anne delayed informing Owen, preferring first to provide the support no one else was giving. It would give her time to gauge if the situation was as bad as it seemed.

One week later, she sent the email.

What Owen experienced as he spoke to Ruth that evening was a deep empathy with his friend, not just because of shared tragedies, but because of a special bond they formed long before their stone-throwing days had begun.

***

Flying into London, Owen gave in to the powerful pull of nostalgia, smiling to himself as he remembered. He recalled when a new history teacher, a Mr Cox, *the penis* as he became known among the more astute members of H3, was introducing a new unit based on one of England's most famous monarchs, Henry V. The previous day, in anticipation of what was to come, Owen informed Billy about the two-fingered victory sign used by English archers to taunt the French at the Battle of Agincourt. Just as Cox was explaining how the English longbow helped to steal victory from the jaws of overwhelming odds, Billy, who normally kept his eyes down, fearful a question might be thrown his way, turned to Owen, smirking in acknowledgement. Owen flashed the reversed victory sign to his friend. While he was being evicted from the classroom, Billy laughed so loud that seconds later he too was removed into the calm of a quiet corridor. Up and down the two patrolled in gleeful anticipation of the chaos they were about to unleash, like the English king's army eager for victory. The two-fingered gesture they gave through each window they encountered caused disruption on an unprecedented scale. Mr Cox, in an instant, turned the two friends into schoolyard celebrities.

CHAPTER 20

Owen was far from equipped to deal with what Billy was going through, including the uncontrollable terrors visiting in the night and the shame following him into his working day. Within the circles he moved, few recognised Billy's illness, a taboo subject back in the nineties. Like others he worked with, Billy fled into his own dark pit, hiding rather than seeking the help he needed. Any psychiatrist will tell you if the preferred option is to conceal your suffering, then crucial warning signs can be difficult to recognise, if not impossible. Ruth had seen it, so had Anne, but neither knew what *it* was. For Owen, the choices he made had nothing to do with knowledge of his friend's affliction, more a sense of duty, born out of a shared ignorance.

"I'm in London for a few days. Thought we could catch up. Have a beer. I'll come to you."

Travelling by train to the Wiltshire town of Amesbury, a few miles from where Billy lived with Ruth and their son, Owen was occupied by his life in France, particularly Catina and the direction in which they were heading. The recent late nights shielded him from the practicalities of their shared life. Her morning sickness came and went, largely unnoticed by Owen. On the occasions he considered their future together, building a family was not in the forefront of his mind. Rather, he longed for a return to the excitement of their first months together when they wandered the bars and clubs of the city, looking for new experiences.

"Now it's going to be three of you, all that's over," Jimmy said, teasing his brother.

"It was a mistake. The pregnancy," Owen said. "Not what we wanted or planned."

"I know," Jimmy said, trying to give the reassurances of an older sibling. "No magic wand, I'm afraid. Only reality, to quote Grandad."

Owen knew what he wanted but never dared to share, not even with Jimmy. Many of us at some stage in our lives will experience a shameful moment, stumbling through those early experiences, trying to make sense of the world. But a child on its way. It frightened him. The time will come when ignorance is crushed. For Owen it was Catina's pregnancy that brought with it his moment.

Such concerns evaporated when he caught sight of Billy sitting at the bar.

Taking a stool next to him, Owen spoke first, his voice competing with the noise of a television mounted on the wall broadcasting a round-up of the week's sporting events.

"Same again?" Owen asked.

Billy was caught unawares, staring into the bottom of an empty glass, with a deep-down look that was immediately disturbing. It was striking how much weight he had lost, apparent in the lines extending down both cheeks, like crevasses scarring his skin. Owen wondered what had happened to the confident soldier he last saw in Belfast. The one after Owen pulled the trigger stood at his side, sounding more like a father figure than a subordinate.

"You can lower your weapon now. It's over," Billy said.

Arms stretched, hands steadying his pistol, Owen continued to point his weapon at the lifeless figure of Cillian O'Brian.

"Lower it!" Billy said, a second time, realising executive

operators, their appetites wetted, were about to come through the back door.

Placing a hand on Owen's wrists, he pushed them down.

"It's done," he said, reverting to a softer tone.

During their first hour in the pub, they relived their collective memories. Like the time they spent all night moving milk bottles from one neighbour's doorstep to another, right across the village. Inside glass bottles were tokens informing the milkman of the household's order. No doorstep went untouched as they giggled away mischievously, like the young boys they were. The prank started at midnight, with the last bottle shuffle completed when the sun started to rise. By the time the milkman was delivering to houses at one end of the village, the formidable pair were already finishing the task at the other, moving stealthily through the streets.

"A time when people still put tokens in glass bottles in return for milk. Delivered by a man in an electric cart," Billy said, roaring into the face of the barmaid.

"Why would you do that?" she asked.

"So one house got the other's milk," Billy said, failing to see why she was struggling to grasp such a simplistic concept.

"Oh, I see…" she said, before moving off to serve another customer.

She returned as they were finishing another tall tale. This time involving black boot polish and the door handle of the school's staffroom.

"Environmentally friendly," she said, imposing herself on the two.

They were arguing which teacher turned the handle immediately post-smearing of the waxy substance, before falling silent to listen to her delayed reaction.

"Electric carts and glass bottles," she shouted above the crowd starting to fill the place. "Saving the planet. Really cute."

Both watched her retreating figure, perplexed, as she wandered off towards the next waiting customer.

"They were the best of times," Owen said, breaking an extended silence.

"What really brings you to Amesbury?" Billy asked. "I'm guessing my argument with Mel."

"And concerns regarding your reasons for such an outburst. People are worried about you."

"I was there, she wasn't. Surely, of all people, I'm allowed an opinion?"

"Yes, of course—"

"Anyway, it's all been sorted," Billy said. "I've read it in the vein Mel intended, and I agree, not related to my experience. Just a moment of frustration on my part."

"You've discussed it with her personally?"

"We've had a chat. She's asked me to help her write a follow-up based on what really happened, by those who were there."

"And you've agreed?"

"It's a great idea. Get the facts out there. Finally put some ghosts to bed. Then I'm done with it."

"Do you want to talk about it, with me?"

"What's the point living it over and over? It doesn't help. I'm fine. Let's just drink. We have enough of our own shared experiences anyway."

"You mean the Ballymurphy?"

"To name one," Billy said. "You were lucky to have that woman on your side. Seemed a formidable character from where I was standing."

"You mean Selena."

"If that's her name, then yes," Billy said, doubt written across his face. "The way she took control. Impressive. Rushing to your side when she could've been mistaken for one of them. That took balls."

As Billy was coaxing him to lower his weapon, Selena came alongside, having sprinted from the car, while Phil focused on the dead policeman. Taking Owen's identification card from a chain around his neck, she rested it on the surface of his jacket for all to see he was military. Owen recalled her soft voice and how it sounded out of sync with her usually forthright character. "Place your weapon on the ground. We don't want to be mistaken for nasties." With seconds to spare, she raised her own card high in the air.

"I lost a good man," Billy said, staring across the room.

"Maybe we should just drink," Owen said, averting his gaze, uncomfortable with where the conversation was taking them.

It was the closest these two would ever come to saving each other, an opportunity, the slimmest of chances, gone forever. If we were to search for an example of how the past can impede the present, a way of learning and reconciling, ready to face the future, then there it was. In their shared moment, Billy fought back tears, ashamed of himself, a reaction encroaching on his demeanour far too often.

"Top shelf. You decide," Owen said.

Two taxis were waiting in the October drizzle when the pair exited the pub onto a dimly lit street, rain soaking everything it touched. The low lighting emitting from Victorian streetlamps bounced off the wet surfaces, giving an impression of a reflective mirror. The night was still busy with the comings and goings of a Saturday crowd, but neither noticed as they stood on the pavement engrossed in each other's company. One taxi was booked for the train station, while the other would take Billy to Bulford Garrison, skirting the edge of Salisbury Plain.

Earlier, Owen received a text from Catina, forgiving him for abandoning her over two consecutive Fridays. She offered to pick him up at the airport, but he declined, preferring to make his own way, giving him the opportunity, if he wished, for a diversion.

"Thanks for coming," Billy said. "I know you didn't have to. While I thought I'd never get the opportunity to say this, it was fucking good to see you."

Owen stuck out his hand, which Billy took before wrapping his other around his friend's shoulder. The two hugged, holding the embrace. Attention was drawn to their outward show of affection, but neither noticed.

Billy absorbed the security, wishing it to remain.

For Owen, it symbolised fresh possibilities.

"Paris, in two months. Don't forget," Owen said. "Ruth will love the Christmas lights."

"You're right, she'll love them. I'll tell her as soon as I get home."

"Oh, before I go," Owen said, trying to make it sound like an afterthought, "how's Mel?"

"Meaning?"

"Is she happy?" Owen asked.

During the evening, he openly discussed his recent history, mainly Catina and the state of their relationship, presenting a whole host of his lusts and anxieties in one fell swoop of alcohol-induced conversation. But, other than the article, there had been little talk of Mel.

"We finally get there."

"Where?" Owen said, waiting for the punchline.

"Your lifelong infatuation," Billy said. "She's happy and in a relationship. He's a total tosser as far as I'm concerned."

"Why?" Owen asked.

"Why what?" Billy said, playing with Owen.

"Why's he a tosser?"

"Figure of speech, I suppose. Like you're a wanker. Some poetry type she met while at Oxford. That's the problem with you educated types, think life is like those books you read. Anyway, he's that type of guy. Head so far up his arse he can't see what's real. I suppose that's why all his poems are about shitty fucking darkness."

"It'd be good for the three of us to get back together sometime. A reunion perhaps?"

"Be careful, Owen. I've seen the modern Mel. If she ever found out about O'Brian, you'd be her next scoop. Now there's an idea."

Both became silent again at the mention of his name, the warmth of their embrace fading as the dampness of the night started to take hold.

"Have you ever heard of the butterfly effect?" Billy asked.

"Of course. Why?"

"Well… I'm not educated like the two of you, but the opposite happened, underneath the flyover."

"I don't get it."

"I tried to flap my wings, and you stopped me. That's why we're standing here in this rain, right now."

"Go on," Owen said, replaying Billy's words.

"Because *you* changed history, *our* histories. From then on, Mel was destined to write her article."

Billy took a few steps towards his taxi, the evening's alcohol catching up with him.

"What happened to us?" Owen asked, into Billy's back.

Opening the rear door, he half-turned to face Owen.

"You did," Billy said.

Since exiting the bar, Owen had given no attention to the change in weather, his only focus being his friend. But after Billy's comment, the coldness of the rain broke through, sheets of it. Everything was wet and warped, a world distorted through a covering of water. The night was heavy, incomparably so.

"I did?" Owen asked, his heart sinking.

"If you'd let me throw my stone, I'd have hit that fucking miserable-looking police car. No way I'd have missed."

Owen's confusion was evident in the uncertainty creeping across his face.

"Your point?" he asked.

"You couldn't let me have my moment."

"We'd have been arrested, Billy."

"Finally, you get it."

"I'm not sure I do."

"Yes," Billy said, his voice rising, "you do. You just said it yourself. A criminal record for us all, especially in that environment. Sons of coal miners. No army, not for you or me, and Mel's article would never have mattered."

"Oh, I see."

"Everything would've been different," Billy said, opening the taxi's door to its full extent. "*Everything.*"

He slid into the rear seat before Owen could respond, slamming its door shut, placing a barrier once more between the two of them.

Standing in the rain, Owen watched the cab crawling along Amesbury Street, its rear brake lights flashing, matching the chaos of the town's late hour, before turning right onto High Street. Owen tried to get a last glimpse of him, but the rain streaking down the taxi's windows obscured his view.

What he failed to see was his friend looking back at him.

The multiple personalities we all carry inside can often be hidden behind the one prevailing self, all fighting for dominance. For Billy, post-Srebrenica, the controlling self was becoming ever weaker. He never got to see Paris. Billy hanged himself two weeks after their reunion. The letter he left said many things. Taking responsibility for his own actions and no longer being able to endure the pain of living were deemed the two most important according to the coroner, but Ruth had her own ideas about that.

CHAPTER 21

"He must have remained rational because in his last moments of despair the only option visible to him was death," Ruth told Owen as they waited in the front room for the hearse to arrive. "You see," she said, arguing, trying to convince herself, "he planned it, right down to the last detail. Typical of him. The idea was already in his head, long before the two of you met in Amesbury. Fully thought out and processed. You know he phoned the police?" she asked, not waiting for a response. "Explained I was out shopping. Even told them where I'd be in Salisbury. The last thing he said, before he pushed away the chair, was our address and what he was about to do. He didn't want me finding him. Didn't want his son to see *that*... so you can see, rational."

Owen was following his mother's advice to listen and not argue.

"The article reflected his paranoia," Ruth said, her anger rising. "That fucking bitch, Melanie! Your ex-girlfriend! Bringing it all back. I hope she's proud of herself. Making a living out of the suffering of others."

It was as if her statement made him implicit in some way, enticing Owen to shout back, *not an ex-girlfriend*, but he held his silence.

"Until Anne, I dealt with his distorted perceptions alone. Thank God she was at the send-off. Someone else finally seeing. Not having to deal with it on my own anymore. He was grieving, Owen. Angry too. All that guilt building up. It made him incapable of caring for me, even his son, and that hurts because he was the best father, husband. He no longer felt anything. This must stop, suppressing one's feelings. For what, a false bravado? Stress, grief, these are real emotions."

Ruth stopped speaking, staring at the handkerchief in her hand, wet with tears and mucus, her expression softening, as if remembering something forgotten.

"He left you this," she said, leaning over the side of her chair to retrieve a shoebox.

"For me?" Owen asked.

"He must have prepared it some time ago because it's weathered badly."

Leaning forward, she passed it to him, exposing its damaged corners, smudged with mould. What caught Owen's attention more than anything was the stencilling on the lid. An expletive he stared at for some time.

Wanker.

"It's a term of endearment," Ruth said, in mitigation. "You know he always meant it in the best possible way."

"I'll open it when I get home," he said, eyes fixed on Billy's mystery box.

"I'd like you to open it now," Ruth said. "If you don't mind."

Working the lid loose, he removed the tape securing it shut before peering inside.

What he saw solved the riddle, after all those years.

Sitting on a cotton wool bundle were six stones: two white, their shiny surfaces long since faded, and a further four, all large and brown. Owen touched each of them, as if he feared damaging their impenetrable hardness with his soft fingers. Then he lifted one of the white ones, raising it to his nose, sniffing across its circumference, trying to call something back from the past. Lying next to the precious artefacts was a red envelope, like you would expect to house a greeting card. Owen took it from its resting place, disturbing something inside. Two objects fell from the unsealed interior, landing on the cotton wool.

On closer inspection, Owen saw what they were. Mel's stud earrings.

"What is it?" Ruth asked.

"Just a game we used to play."

"I hope it brings you some comfort."

"It does," he said. "Truly, it does."

The weight of his grief was unbearable.

***

After the funeral, Owen returned to France, longing for stability and comfort, but weeks after burying his friend, Catina miscarried. Her parents pleaded with her to return home to convalesce, a suggestion Owen wholeheartedly supported. In her absence, he comforted himself in other relationships, trying to recapture his early experience of the city. "Let's toast to the promiscuity of Parisian women," one of his colleagues proposed when Owen admitted his relationship was over, an announcement, until that night, not shared with anyone, including Catina. On that inaugural evening, a middle-aged prostitute walked him across the Rue Cuvier and into the labyrinth of the Jardin des Plantes, guiding him to the Gloriette de Buffon, where she more than matched his instincts for the survival of the species with her animalism, right up against the cold iron of Buffon's Gazebo.

Some weeks later, Owen explained her absence was difficult for him too, but time apart, and he hoped she agreed, was what they needed. It was easy to convince himself that what he was doing was no different from the multitudes of other people who seek their desires. The Left Bank became his narcotic, an escape from responsibility. "You forget," Catina said, "colleagues talk, and you're the main topic. You and your fucking French whores." It was an outburst releasing him from any further obligations, allowing him to put the phone down for the sake of his own comfort. Until then, he had never deceived a woman like that.

In her final correspondence, Catina told him how she once considered him as her best friend and that she would never return to the job she loved while he remained.

It was too painful for Owen to spend Christmas in Paris, not because he would be alone, but because he should have been sharing the city's festive lights with Billy and Ruth. A sense of foreboding, a constant presence, followed him into the new year, heightened by the promise of a permanent return to peace in Northern Ireland. Every television screen seemed to be broadcasting the story. In the embassy, it was the main topic of conversation, important enough to make the morning briefing.

For Owen, it brought back weighted memories.

"It seems you made quite a commotion over there," Fabian said, having called Owen to his office.

Lying open on the head of chancery's desk was his personal file.

"Mine?" Owen asked, wondering why they were necessary.

"A peace process," Fabian said. "One that's finally looking like it'll deliver. Are you aware a document is being prepared? One aimed at sealing a lasting ceasefire."

"Our final repentance," Owen said, trying for the witty response. In truth, he spent a lot of time considering what a lasting peace would look like and the possibilities it would bring.

Fabian fell silent, contemplating.

Owen could not decide if he was going to laugh or order him out of the office.

"All a bit of a rush, I'm told," Fabian said. "They want it completed in time for the deadline, in a way that appeases all factions. Good luck with that, I say. Probably Clinton's visit in ninety-five that did it, not forgetting Hillary's contribution, of course. Remember it well. Lots of talking from soapboxes. All plain sailing from there. But that was before those gross fellating accusations came to light."

"I wouldn't say plain sailing. There's been a lot of violence since then," Owen said, choosing to ignore the comment about another philandering politician.

From Owen's perspective, Fabian's certainty was eroded somewhat because of a few words uttered by an American president talking about dreams becoming reality. He was sure some of those realities would have to be compartmentalised, pushed into some dark corner among all the other silence. Perhaps it is the role of those who fight for their nation or for a cause, not just to give their lives but to carry the guilt so everyone else can move on.

"Not exactly an Easter uprising," Fabian said. "Anyway, a call has gone out to European missions for any spare hands to assist with what they're calling document checking. With your experience, the ambassador thinks you'd be perfect. You're booked in with him straight after me."

"I'm returning to England—"

"—and you won't be coming back to the French Mission," Fabian said. "Your time in Paris is over. London, I'm told, will arrange your next posting."

With a smile and a slight nod of solemnity, the ambassador gestured that the five minutes he allocated was over. "You should look at the move as an opportunity. You'll be helping to make British history. Not many diplomats can say that." It seemed to Owen, Catina was right about people talking, and while the reason for the move had never been linked to what his life in Paris had become, he had his doubts. Such suspicions were fuelled further by the triumphant smile on the face of the ambassador's personal secretary as he left the office.

As always, his mother remained positive, seeing his role as a great responsibility, even though he explained he was little more than a well-paid clerk shuffling paper around a desk, with few references to any agreement.

***

Some months after Owen's relocation to London, the Good Friday Agreement was signed. During a thirty-year period, more than 3,600 people lost their lives, including Cillian O'Brian, that erstwhile terrorist. His name was added to an official list of the dead, laid with full honours next to other former volunteers. There was no such honourable resting place for William (Billy) Johnson. It was as if his service equated to nothing more than a delaying action. For Billy's kind, the agreement was viewed as pure sophistry, due in part to their exclusion from its pages.

Owen knew Billy was a haunted soul long before they met in Amesbury. Not because of what Anne and Ruth told him, but because he knew it about himself too. Although there was no Srebrenica for Owen, there was Cillian O'Brian and a lump of concrete pushed over a bridge. Losing his friend reminded him of what an aging lecturer once said during his college days about the events leading to the death of an established fictional character. "He had to pay with his life. It's the way it had to be because this is the classical approach, authentic tragedy. I'm not saying it should be that way. Not at all. Not now or in the future. Indeed, I'm saying the opposite." Such theorising was lost on most of his classmates, but for Owen, the medieval prince was way ahead of his time. "There are lessons to be learnt by sending messages from the past into the present, ones with the potential to better our lives in the future," Owen recalled the teacher saying.

His mother said something similar on the day of Billy's funeral, but Owen was too wrapped in his own grieving to listen. "Think about that, Owen," she said, referring to the professional help Billy never received. Her remark resurfaced from the back of his mind, where it had been stored, waiting for its moment, bringing with it an aroma of inevitable sadness.

After some searching, a name flashed up in the list of possibles. The one he narrowed it down to was in London, where she had her own practice.

For his sins, Owen was still in the capital.

When he was put through to Miranda and she listened to his request for a consultation, she said, "No Owen, not the office. Come to my home. You aren't a stranger."

CHAPTER 22

Miranda's oldest daughter answered the door, opening it before Owen could knock. Chloe was a six-year-old version of her mother, with a perpetual cheeky grin, frizzy brown hair, and large brown eyes to match. She looked tiny in the doorway, bright lights from the hallway silhouetting her childish figure.

"Good evening, Owen," she said. "Mummy's been preparing all day."

Before he was able to respond, she beckoned him to enter, leading the way down a corridor decorated with family pictures of holidays, weddings and christenings in a mix match of frames with no apparent order. A chaotic montage of smiling people. He followed the skipping Chloe as she turned right at the end of a short passage into a home office, where she ordered him to sit.

"He's in Mummy's private room," she shouted, withdrawing to the corridor.

Owen could hear the voices of at least three other people, two adults and a younger child, all laughing and joking, in seemingly domestic bliss. The smell of food in the air was Thai. Making a mental note on his way in, he noted a photograph of two people, one Miranda, the other, he assumed, her husband, maybe boyfriend at the time, standing in front of a giant-sized Buddha perched on a hillside dominating a seafront town. In the distance was a thin strip of golden beach, visible over the rooftops, and beyond, an endless expanse of turquoise water. He imagined shared culinary lessons in some beachfront shack with ocean-facing views, as the two learnt to master Asian cuisine. An experience he envisioned they shared with friends and family, now extended to ex-lovers.

A door opened somewhere along the corridor before two sets of footsteps padded across a wooden floor, one heavier than the other, the lighter approaching much faster. Seconds later, a smaller version of Chloe peered around the door, smiling the same warmly grin.

Then a voice he recognised as Miranda's.

"Samantha, back to the kitchen. Now, darling. You'll get to meet our guest over dinner."

Owen stood to greet her, saying with mock concern, "I could've been anyone. I'm already inside your private space, having met both your children."

"Look," she said, pointing to a Polaroid of the two of them lying on her desk.

"Oh my God, Harry's Bar," he said, before she hugged and kissed him on both cheeks and then hugged him again.

She was still attractive in her patented, forthright way.

"So, what brings you to London?" Miranda asked after they both provided a brief synopsis of their lives since York.

"Sent over from Paris. Some trivial proofreading any lowly clerk could manage."

"Proofreading?"

"Checking various documents, supposedly linked to the Belfast Agreement. Banishment, really. Anyway, it's done now. I told you on the phone, Catina, her family's links to the FCO. Her father calls his contacts, who call my boss, who asks questions around the office, and so I'm red-inking documents, memos, emails. That's my version anyway. She's back now, in Paris. Apparently, I'm a bad man with too much time on my hands. I'd like to see the skeletons in their cupboards. Happy when it's someone else in the firing line. I'm calling it short-term memory syndrome."

"You mean the Good Friday Agreement?' Miranda asked, choosing not to loiter on his most recent breakup.

"Same thing. Signed on that day. It's upset a lot of people across both communities and, of course, those not even mentioned in its pages, soldiers who were there from the beginning. The Judas effect, some have called it."

"What do you mean by that?"

As Owen was about to answer, there was a light tap at the door, followed by a thin and slightly balding man in a thick knitted jumper, carrying two large glasses of red wine, peering into the room. Robert Tudor, who Miranda met while skiing in the Austrian Tyrol, was a partner in a law firm with offices in London and Vienna. Fifteen years older than his wife, his face was pink and shiny, like a drinker's. When he spoke, his speech was slow and measured, not fast and furious like his wife's. Perhaps the years in court, defending family trusts, had rubbed off on him. Robert looked nothing like the spouse Owen expected for his one-time drinking fuck buddy. Handing a glass to each of them, Robert backed out of the room, smiling as if he was in the presence of a celebrity, informing them dinner would soon be on the table.

Owen watched him leave before turning his attention back to Miranda, who was happily sipping her wine, looking at him over the rim of her glass.

"He's ardent when it comes to my investments. Free too," Miranda said, having read his thoughts.

"Accelerated programme for the release of prisoners," Owen said. "Killers really, all of them, but referred to as qualifying under the agreement. Would've angered Billy, but everything did in the end."

"And you, does it bother you?"

"No, it doesn't, but I'd never share my opinions on the issue with people like Billy. I don't mean any disrespect. The place seriously needs some peace. Deserves it. There are many sections to the agreement. I'm sure the ignorant will comment anyway without bothering to read it in its entirety."

The pressure of her questions was threatening to overwhelm him. He willed Miranda to contribute, to say something of worth, but she continued sipping and waiting.

"I keep going over our final meeting and Billy's accusation. Blaming me for the path life placed us on."

"Why would he blame you?"

"Because I stopped him throwing a stone. A stone, can you believe? When we were fourteen. Why leave me with such guilt?"

Owen explained what the three of them had been through when they were children: the train station, the road, and what they witnessed, and their shock at seeing Jimmy through the window, even Emri's intervention at the police station.

"Growing up, my grandfather was a huge part of my life. When I joined the army, he didn't approve, which caused a rift between us. His death came as a blow. It didn't come at a good time, never does. Work got in the way of my mourning, leaving Mum, still grieving. I hope it didn't hurt him too much, our falling out, because that would be unbearable to carry. Anyway, here I am."

"Did your grandfather know how much you loved him?"

"We were best friends. I worshipped him. My love for him was obvious, especially when I was young, living at home."

"And your friend, Billy, did he know how much you cared about his wellbeing?"

"I don't know. I hope he did. His wife was aware. We've all been friends since junior school. It was me who got them together."

"You introduced them?"

"Not introduced. We were already acquainted. Ruth knew I was Billy's best friend. Rarely did anyone else get close to him in school. She asked, as I was walking home one day, if she could hang around with me, to get at him. Great idea. Get him his first girlfriend. I had plenty of girls hanging around in those days, wasn't interested in most. That was before I even understood what *it* was I enjoyed about girls so much. Anyway, I let Ruth join our little group, eventually handing her over to Billy."

"Handing her over, Owen."

"I got the same response from my grandfather, disgusted with me. But he wasn't aware of the arrangement. There was nothing between me and Ruth, nothing romantic anyway."

"Did either of you ever tell Billy?"

"Not that I'm aware."

Owen looked back at the polaroid, bringing it alive: the smell of fags, beer and sweat, all mingling together, and the fading colours and sticky carpets, dirty glasses and drunken voices all fighting to be heard over a bawdy crowd.

"I never did get those fancy sunglasses," Owen said, continuing to stare at the photograph.

"There's still time."

"Yes, there's time. A crack at redemption, too, maybe."

"That's not what I meant. You have no reason to redeem anything. Change is fine, *good even*, but not because of some misguided sense of guilt. I'm not going to tell you how to see your future or provide the answers, but you have no place looking for redemption."

The remaining evening with Robert and Miranda was a memorable pleasure for Owen. His first impression of these two, any perceived oddities, were soon dispelled. What he envied as they sat around the table, laughing, joking, filling in the gaps of the life these two shared, was their bond, something he never experienced with Catina.

When Robert led the girls to their beds, it gave them time on their own to discuss their university days. Miranda manoeuvred Owen away from his earlier self-punishment, preferring to save such conversations for another day.

Just after midnight, he rose to leave, catching his reflection in a large ornate mirror. What he saw was the foreign office's most recent hope of success, a prodigy, now a disappointment, facing exile to some far-flung outpost.

"We must keep in touch," Miranda said, leading him down some steps to a waiting cab. "This evening was only the start."

"I'd like that."

"You'd do well to remember, Owen, we aren't models of virtue, and we were never meant to be."

No, we weren't, he thought, *and I'm not.*

She kissed him before watching him cross the road where his taxi was waiting.

Opposite the crescent was a park, where streetlights illuminated sections of its dark interior. A favourite spot for occupants of the affluent neighbourhood. The garden's flower beds had retreated, hibernating during the grey months, but the assured warmth of spring would soon be approaching. How many times had Miranda and Robert sat contemplating, under the shade of a copper beech, watching the seasons come and go?

Earlier in the evening, sharing dinner, all of them sat around the family table, Owen started to put the words together for his resignation letter. Imagining new opportunities, he no longer wished to be part of an official side of life anymore. The idea of going it alone gave him a renewed confidence.

Miranda had seen many cases like his, legions of clients struggling to escape their past. Self-inflicted sorrow, she called it behind closed doors. Why intelligent human beings could not just live and stop fighting against themselves fascinated her. Life was chaos, it always had been and always would be. She discussed such views with Robert many times. "People need to learn how to deal with their turmoil because one day it just won't matter anymore." It had been her philosophy from as far back as she could remember, Robert's too, an attribute attracting her to him when they first met. Even in York, she suspected Owen would never be able to grasp such a simple idea. He needed to be careful because guilt would consume him, like it had his friend, but that was a conversation for another time.

As she waved him off, Miranda thought he looked lost and adrift, that once witty and beautiful man.

CHAPTER 23

Owen's change of direction came with the acceptance of his resignation letter and then employment with a UK-based NGO, DRATSG (Disaster Relief Assets Training and Support Group). Their CEO saw in Owen someone with the ideas and experience to evolve the charity's waning vision. As head of operations, Owen would be second only to this man.

"Someone with your talents could be running the whole show in a few years," Ed Jenson explained to his newly appointed operations officer.

Jenson was an ageing entrepreneur who, in his mid-fifties, gave up chasing profit in reaction to the 1980s Ethiopian famine. He needed to fill the post, and on paper, Owen looked ideal.

"He's a decorated army officer with diplomatic experience and a first-class education in an area we need. What have we got to lose?" Ed said, convincing the charity's board of trustees.

DRATSG made a name for itself during the Rwandan crisis in ninety-four. While the rest of the Western world was looking in a different direction, Ed responded decisively to what was happening in central Africa. In the aftermath, he deployed relief teams to the Great Lakes region, learning lessons from his time in Ethiopia, and in the process cemented the charity's reputation.

It gained royal patronage, ultimately winning contracts to train national and international aid workers across several developing countries. By the time Owen joined the team, the not-for-profit organisation had gained worldwide recognition. Yet, as the millennium approached, the charity was becoming stagnant in a world saturated with non-governmental groups vying for business.

***

It was late in the afternoon when Owen arrived at North Manchester General Hospital. There to deliver a presentation aimed at recruiting medical professionals, he was shown into an ageing lecture hall with a damaged and dated projector to match.

"It's Friday afternoon, and IT has already left," said a first-year junior doctor tasked to deliver him to the venue. "I'm assuming you have notes?" she asked, reading the concern spreading across his face.

"It's all on disc," he said, holding it out for inspection. "I need that thing working."

Reacting to Owen's panic, his host climbed on a chair to remove the blown bulb, a procedure he watched with anticipation. Reaching, she stretched the full length of her slim body, allowing him to appreciate her sylph-like figure. Then, balancing precariously, she started to unscrew the lens, giving access to the dead bulb. Seeing the potential for an accident, Owen rushed forward, stabilising the chair, at the same time finding himself looking into her concave bellybutton. Once the bulb was removed, she climbed back down, handing it to him like it was the forbidden fruit.

Her eyes gleamed with mischief as she watched him inspect its burnt circumference.

"It wouldn't have helped your cause had I fallen," she said, "not with you being the disaster relief specialist. You get started. I'll go see what I can do."

Before he could thank her, she rushed out the door in search of a replacement.

"Give me five minutes," she said, shouting over her shoulder. "And it's Ellen, by the way. Can't wait to hear what you've got to say."

After watching her go, Owen noticed others had started to arrive, something he failed to acknowledge in all the excitement. A few early advents were already sitting, having been entertained by the show the two of them unwittingly performed. The realisation they had an audience was unsettling, as if the pair had shared something intimate with the gathering crowd.

Standing behind a lectern, looking at his computer screen while flicking through notes, Owen tried to make the best of what was turning into a poor job. Fifteen minutes into his wordy presentation, Ellen returned, bursting through the door with enthusiasm, something that had been lacking. The event had turned into what he feared, a bland and patronising sermon to twenty or so disengaged medical staff.

"Our vision," he was saying, "is to generate teams with the capacity and capability to respond to humanitarian needs, through, but not exclusively, one of our emergency response units."

"Just keep speaking," she said, "and I'll get on with screwing it in."

The auditorium filled with an explosion of appreciative applause at Ellen's erotic assertion.

Owen had all but given up, resigning himself to the notion technology had beaten him. Considering how to bring it to an honourable conclusion, he did what Ellen demanded and continued, while she got to work on the projector.

"DRATSG is actively recruiting doctors who are willing to place themselves on call to deploy wherever disaster strikes. Usually for a minimum of two months…"

A beam of light shot across the room, striking the wall behind him, mirroring what he was viewing on the computer. The image was of a doctor, a red cross adorned on her sleeve, administering an injection into the stick-thin arm of an emaciated child while its mother sat watching. Flies could be seen feeding from the little amount of moisture clinging to their mouths and eyes. In the background, a line of similar-looking couples queued, waiting their turn. Lying on the desert's floor was the carcass of a cow, its sun-bleached bones exposed through rotting skin. Above, where the parched and cracked land met a cloudless horizon, was a helicopter, brown in colour with black letters stencilled on its side, DRATSG. The image brought an immediate cease to the laughter as the audience's eyes moved from the descending Ellen to the skeletal-like figures inhabiting a desolate land.

A picture paints a thousand words, Owen thought, looking into the eyes of his saviour.

Taking her seat, Ellen looked back at him with a smile full of warmth.

He gave a small nod of appreciation.

***

"What about adopting quick-reaction groups, small teams deployable at short notice?" Owen asked within days of being appointed to his new role. "Task-dependent, of course." It was a system he experienced during his military days. With some adjustment to concepts and procedures, he could see how it would work in the world of disaster relief. "When the governmental types *finally* arrive, we hand over and move on. Go where we're most needed. Look at it like a triage. We assist the vulnerable at their most critical stage."

"Some of our donors will argue governmental organisations should be allowed to lead," Ed said. "Our resources slotting in where they want us, not the other way around. It's a model we've successfully used many times."

"Bangladesh, last year," Owen said, "a slow response that

cost lives. It takes time for governments to react, even to put in place pre-planned options. What I'm suggesting, Ed, is to close the time gap. You saw for yourself how the UN responded in the Great Lakes. Like giant snails crossing a road, sometimes not even arriving, crushed by their own bureaucracy. We'll need to recruit other professionals: doctors, logisticians, engineers, security specialists."

"Normally it's only medical staff on our books," Ed said.

"What use is normal? We need a multi-asset response. If we go for such an option and invest only in limited deployments, going where we're needed, not where we're told, then we make a difference. If normal is an issue, then let's make it our new normal."

"Present a detailed report, everything covered," Ed said, "and I'll get you an answer."

"It's already in your inbox," Owen said.

***

Clicking into his final slide, Owen looked around the room, before taking questions.

"Shouldn't we let them solve their own problems?" a doctor sitting in the front row asked.

There was a spattering of derisive laughter from some of the audience, while the comment provided the cue for others to leave.

"Can I ask your name?" Owen said, as he watched the disaffected readying themselves to start their weekend early.

"It's James. Before you answer, my point is international responses are normally centred on interests of investor gains. Not necessarily our concern."

Inside, Owen sighed, camouflaging his reaction.

"In any case," James said, unperturbed by the audience's dwindling interest, "we have the United Nations. Why should more money be pumped into another non-governmental?"

"That's assuming the UN shows up at all," an unidentified whisper came from the back of the room.

"Firstly, I'm not here to generate money," Owen said. "I'm here to appeal for your direct support. Get you involved in a new and exciting humanitarian initiative. Second, while we at DRATSG see the UN as a force for good, we also accept they have limitations. A top-heavy organisation. Take Somalia, internationals outperformed by NGOs. How's that possible?"

"Competence and dedication," shouted a middle-aged lady from the middle of the audience while jotting down the web address on Owen's final slide. "I've seen it. Experienced it too," she said. "Operations controlled from desks. What these guys are offering is a very different concept. Maybe even groundbreaking."

Before waiting for a response, she stood to leave, giving Owen a thumbs-up. Her seal of approval, perhaps, or an offer of her services. Whatever it was, he was grateful for the support. Within the few remaining members of the audience, a debate ensued, nothing of interest to Owen, just superficial arguments.

"I'm sure donors have policies dictating how much autonomy a charity is allowed," James said, countering the low grumblings of the few who remained. "Religious backers, for example. Not to mention suspicion and a lack of transparency that exist within the world of humanitarianism."

Throughout, Ellen observed, a self-assured smile attached to her face, as if to say, *I'm sure you weren't expecting that response.*

***

Later in the evening, Owen rang Ed, informing him he would be staying in Manchester for the night, using the excuse that the meeting ran over. "Always a good sign when that happens," Ed said, congratulating him. "See you back in London, first thing Monday."

Less than thirty minutes before, Ellen waited for the last of the stragglers to leave before asking Owen to take her to dinner.

"Let's call it payback for the bulb, if it helps," she said, wide-eyed and smiling.

She took him to Bury Old Road, where they ate Turkish food and drank red wine.

Ellen took control of the conversation, while Owen listened, happy to be carried along. He noted her personal history, one of privilege: boarding school, foreign holidays, gap year, medical school, before following her parents into the profession. Ellen described to him early in the evening her vision of a world full of equality, where there was no need for intervention. Had he not been absorbed in her beauty, then maybe he would have told her the world was not equal because those who inhabited it were all different. What Owen recalled from their first meal together was her wide, inquisitive eyes, not her idealist views.

As the final sweet course was delivered, *firin sutlac*, presented in its traditional form, Ellen asked, "What now, for your weekend?"

"The last train back to London," Owen said.

"Show me your ticket."

As he had done in the lecture hall, Owen followed her command, surrendering willingly.

Ellen noted it was first class to Euston. She tore it in half, placing the two pieces in her pocket.

"And now?" she said, with a defiant look of triumph.

"Looks like I'm stranded."

Forty minutes later, in her apartment, they sat drinking more wine, their bodies only inches apart. It was Ellen who made the first move, kissing him, and then again, more adventurously and forcefully. Each time he opened his mouth, probing with his tongue, and each time she reciprocated. Initially she held on to her glass, even when he brushed his hand across her waist, hovering over the metal button, before unclipping. Placing his hand inside the bottom of her shirt, he felt the warmth of her skin. Leaning forward, she placed her glass on the floor before leaning back again, inviting him to push his hand deeper. The pressure forced her zip down, revealing the silky material of her pants. Ellen closed her eyes, enjoying the moment, a small noise rising from deep inside her body. Putting one hand on the nape of his neck, she pulled him towards her, giving a simple direction. "The bedroom." Once inside the darkened interior, they removed their clothes, watching each other as each piece was discarded. Collapsing on the bed, their flesh became one as excitedly they continued to explore each other's bodies. Then, as she drew her fingernails across his back, he entered her.

It was a pursuit that kept them busy throughout the weekend. After each heated period of lovemaking, he fell into her arms, waiting for his heartbeat to calm. It had never been like this before: different, fast, mutually insistent.

Standing on the platform on a quiet Sunday morning, Ellen passed him the two pieces of his vandalised ticket.

"One day I'd like to marry you," she said.

For reasons he could not quite grasp, he answered in kind, going along with it all. After those first days together, Owen saw Ellen at every opportunity, even though he told himself on the first run back to London, a journey he would repeat many times, it was all folly. Six months later, thinking one of them would extricate from the relationship, they married. Ellen joined him in London, promising her parents she would continue her training in the capital.

Her father detested Owen from the moment he heard of their short engagement, pleading with his daughter to reconsider.

The news of their imminent marriage amused Ed enormously.

"You go to Manchester to find a medical practitioner and come back with a wife," he said. "Marvellous, just bloody marvellous."

Since Catina, Owen had grown used to being alone, imagining it would remain that way, for a while anyway. There were women, several, but nothing serious. Fending for himself came naturally, but the marital harmony between Miranda and Robert seemed to have inspired him. Maybe he had conveniently forgotten the Catina experiment, those life-affirming lessons. It was something he discussed with Miranda during one of their consultations, admitting they only dared to live together because of the pregnancy.

"It was a child," she said. "You're allowed to say it, rather than 'pregnancy', a child. Saying isn't an affirmation of guilt, rather an acceptance of a life."

"You don't need anyone judging you like that!" Ellen said, caught in a hormonal bout of morning sickness.

CHAPTER 24

Owen was sitting in a hotel's marbled gallery, sipping coffee with Ed and some of the delegates from the Disaster Relief Management Conference in central London. "A key networking opportunity for us," Ed told him. "With lots of non-governmental and governmental organisations in attendance. Let's not waste it." For Owen, the regular networking breaks were an opportunity to fine-tune his speech, but he had been distracted, a phone call that morning, whirling through his mind.

A familiar name thrown down the line.

Owen was the third speaker over a three-day period, his slot being the penultimate on the first day of the convention. The agenda for Owen was to present lessons learnt from the deployment of the charity's ERUs. "Don't give them too much detail," Ed said, "otherwise they'll all be following suit." From Owen's perspective, giving the whole story was the best option, an opinion bringing him into conflict with Ed for the second time in their working relationship. The first came when Owen requested to deploy with one of their teams into Mozambique in the early months of the new millennium, when the Limpopo River burst its banks during intense rainfall in the region. "I can't allow that," Ed said. "I want my operations officer by my side." Even though

Owen argued how crucial lessons could be learnt from such an undertaking, the answer always remained the same.

The second major deployment was underway by the time Owen was invited to speak at the 2001 conference. At the beginning of the year, DRATSG sent teams to Gujarat, providing disaster relief to the many thousands caught in a devastating earthquake.

***

Prior to leaving home, Owen found himself rushing breakfast, while Ellen, Lucy on hip, was trying to convince him how they should be working harder to mend bridges with her parents.

Mid-argument, the phone rang.

"Someone saying they're from the UN," Ellen said, shouting across the room, eyebrows raised. She passed him the phone while hitting the loudspeaker, keen to know why her husband was receiving calls from such an organisation.

Owen, who wanted to spend his precious time skimming through his speech, finishing his coffee and cramming in some much-needed sustenance, the priority being in that order, snatched the handset from his wife.

"Hello, Owen speaking…"

Their conversation over breakfast had been a topical one in the Morgan household, chiefly Ellen's parents continued frustration regarding their daughter's stalled career, reignited after the birth of Lucy.

"When will you ever get around to kickstarting what you began?" her father would ask, trying to goad his daughter into action.

"You'd think I'd robbed them of the jewel of Sparta," Owen often joked, a response to the continued hatred her parents held for him.

"Try and see it from their angle, my career—"

"—and their dreams."

"I love being with Lucy, but I'm going back to work, and soon."

"We have plans in place, as they know. Maybe you could remind them," was Owen's answer to what was becoming a regular dispute.

***

Before taking his slot on stage, Ed whispered into his ear, "Afterwards, once you've finished, and this place has calmed down, do you fancy a drink? Before we head for the suburbs."

Since the wedding, Ed had become a bit of a presence in the Morgan household. A widower and lonely, Ellen insisted. He was welcomed into the family unit, becoming a grandfather figure to Lucy, something Owen could not provide from his side. Unlike many of the other delegates, Ed's suggestion was not a desire to experience the delights of the capital, but rather a wish to spend time with Owen, like that of a father with his son.

"Afraid not," Owen said. "I have a meeting straight after. You head off, don't wait. I'll see you in the gallery in the morning."

"Meeting?" Ed asked. "Anything I should know about?"

Owen was rising to the sound of applause, welcoming him to the stage. There was no time to answer, which suited him. Not the right moment to discuss the phone call with so few details given.

The lady on the other end had claimed to be the PA to the UN's lead on humanitarian coordination in the Horn of Africa.

On stage, Owen did what Ed cautioned against, giving an in-depth account of how they funded and administered the charity. A do-it-yourself kit as far as Ed was concerned. Their working relationship was based on mutual respect, and for the most part, it had been a model example, each aware of what the other brought to the table. Owen drove operations, given the freedom to make decisions within reasonable boundaries, while Ed controlled the funds. In recent months, he had seen a restlessness in Owen's character, the Mozambique disagreement being an example. His wish to deploy to southeast Africa was not just about learning lessons on the coal face, Ed was not that naïve. It was an increasing frustration to want more, to experience being in the field with his creation.

"That's what draws a certain type to disaster relief, an instinctive need to do, rather than just talk about doing," Ed explained to the board.

He had grown fond of Owen, Ellen too, and now Lucy. But he was becoming increasingly aware he would not be able to tie this man down forever.

When change came, it was from a direction that surprised everyone.

The applause lifted Owen's spirits as he finished his speech, the noise an indication of the audience's enthusiasm for everything he said. Even so, it could have gone better, the upcoming appointment being a constant distraction. Standing at the back of the room, leaning against the wall, was someone he had known during his university days. The son of a powerful man, almost aristocracy some would argue, with more power to wield than Ed Jenson could ever wish. It was a presence preventing Owen from firing on all cylinders.

As Ed watched Owen leave the stage, he noticed a tall, athletic-looking man, suited and corporate in appearance, exiting through the rear door.

He was no stranger to Owen, but they were never close either. He too experienced extreme violence early in his life. A lover murdered in a crowded bar. Owen often played the incident in his mind's eye: a flashing blade under the arm of an unsuspecting victim, callous, but nothing personal, or a jealous brawl with an ex-paramour escalating out of control.

During his time on stage, presenting data, statistics, raw facts, offensive details to Ed's dispositions, Owen asked himself how Roland had become a humanitarian lead on anything.

***

"Mr Owen Morgan, operations officer for DRATSG?" a lady with an East African accent asked as confirmation.

"Yes, that's me…"

Bishara Mwangi, Roland's personal assistant, confirmed she had the right person before explaining on whose behalf she was calling. A name Owen would never have predicted coming back into his life.

"Roland? The son of Arthur Roden-West?" he asked. Even though he had been given the full name, his mind needed the double clarification to compute what he was hearing.

"Yes, that's correct. His late father, such a positive influence on his son."

Not from where I was standing, Owen thought, the quick dispatch of Jake to Spain flashing into memory.

What had Arthur known about the lakeside liaison with his daughter? A moment of madness and passion in the evening's summer heat. Of course, he knew everything. Had Owen become his big disappointment? All his potential, equating to nothing. "Not nothing," Miranda told him. All he achieved was part of a journey, the conditions met, even Paris, a voluntary resignation. It all contributed to where he was now, a guest speaker with a widening audience. He could hear her voice: "No looking back, Owen, it's the only way you'll manage to go forward." Still, these were memories, difficult to eradicate, shared experiences.

"And what can I do for Roland?" Owen asked, dragging himself away from his recollections.

"He's asked if you'd be willing to meet him, today, if possible. He'll come to you."

"Sorry, conference all day."

"We're aware, Mr Morgan. Thirty minutes only. I can book a table at the restaurant right across the road. The Hungry Hound. Immediately after your slot. Mr Roden-West is in London for one night only, and then he's heading back to Nairobi in the morning."

"And the agenda?"

"I've been instructed only to provide such information if you agree to meet. As you know, he can be very particular."

No, I don't know, thought Owen, *because you seem to be discussing a very different Roland from the arrogant twat I knew.*

"Yes, that'll be fine. Details, please," he said.

"Your employment. Hungry Hound it is then, across the road," she said. "Thank you for your time, Mr Morgan."

He was about to tell Bishara to call him Owen, dropping the formality, when the phone clicked silent. She was gone, her task complete, leaving no opportunity for further questions.

***

Walking out of the venue, Owen crossed a hectic Munster Road, envisioning Roland watching his every move as he navigated his way across the street, through the bustling traffic of Fulham. The morning rush hour seemed to have extended all the way into the afternoon's dash for home. Over the restaurant's door was a hanging sign reminding him of a scene from an Arthur Conan Doyle novel, something more suited to a country pub rather than the fine-dining establishment it was. He half expected a Jake-like figure to be standing guard, the restaurant's business name a forewarning, a pun, but there was no such person. Its dark glass doors matched the windows, denying a view of the diners inside, including Owen who wished he could see what was behind the building's mirrored windows. Entering, he was met by a man wearing an immaculate white shirt, open at the neck, and a black dinner jacket, not unlike a distant relative starting to relax at a wake, having removed the obligatory mourning tie.

"Mr Morgan, I presume?" the well-briefed maître d' asked. The greeting sounded like a pastiche of the coming together of Livingstone and Stanley in darkest Africa. "Follow me, sir, your guest is waiting. You're at the back, nice and quiet, as requested."

A misjudgement Owen admitted to himself. No prying eyes.

"Owen, such a long time," Roland said, rising from the table, clasping his hand in a firm grip. "Good to see you, and thank you for taking the invite. You can leave him with me now. He's in safe hands," Roland informed the host, who nodded at both gentlemen before returning to front of house. "Such a tight schedule, but always time for old friends."

"Yes, old friends," Owen said, unable to hide his surprise.

"Good, I have your attention. Such a big ask of me after a full day. You must be exhausted?"

"I'm fine. An interesting first day. Only two more to go."

"Great speech. Truly a game changer if you can generate the right support."

Owen noted Roland's innuendo as he took his seat gracefully.

While exchanging pleasantries, a waiter, wearing a purple cummerbund, otherwise dressed in the same style as the maître d', arrived with menus, handing one to each before proffering the wine list to Roland.

"Purple's obviously a symbol of his caste," Roland said.

"Oh, I see," Owen said, throwing a glance in the waiter's direction.

"A little rushed, but I believe Bishara told you about the offer?"

"She did, but working for who?"

Rather than answer, Roland turned his attention back to the waiter.

"We'll take the chilli miso salmon, with brown rice, not white," he said, before scanning the menu further, "and lemon butter broccolini."

"And drinks, sir?"

"Sparkling water will do."

"Yes, sir," the waiter confirmed, before collecting the menus.

"The UN," Roland said. "And why? Because my father saw something in you. Which says a lot to me and the people I work for."

"Aren't there procedures for this?" Owen asked.

"Leave the processes to me, Owen. I get what I want, and what I want is someone of your calibre in Nairobi, working on my team. You completed my father's conditions with distinction by all accounts. The more astute normally decline the third one, but not you. Your background, you really didn't have a choice. If it were up to my father, he would have brought back national service. Can you imagine? He was proud of what you did. It couldn't have been easy. 'Our special boy', he would say at every opportunity. He never forgot you, even at the end. If you hadn't resigned because of that little impropriety in Paris, who knows where you'd be now. Out of *my* reach, I'm sure."

"I didn't leave the service because of what people thought of my conduct. There were other reasons."

"Yes, your friend. My sincere condolences."

"And now, I work for DRATSG," Owen said, ignoring Roland's perceived knowledge of events.

"Ed Jenson, great guy. Commendable outfit too. We've thrown some work his way over the years. Problem for Ed is keeping the charity's big donors interested. Money's the only way you'll really get those ERUs off the ground."

Owen was aware of the constraints of working for Ed. Even though the charity was a respected NGO, it was still non-governmental, relying on generosity to survive. Having completed one major operation and with another ongoing, Owen had learnt such undertakings haemorrhaged money. His speech, giving away free advice, was a calculated gamble. He knew it would upset Ed, but he was hoping for other NGOs to come on board, bringing their donors with them. There were a few philanthropists in the audience, and maybe he could entice at least one of them.

"You know he'll never accept a merger," Roland said, as if reading Owen's mind. "He's been with DRATSG from the beginning. The concern for you is one day they'll revert to setting up refugee camps in high-risk areas, become bogged down, because once you do, you're there for the duration. When the funds dry up, helicopters being expensive to procure, let alone hire for months on end, you could find yourself fighting for the survival of the charity. After that, well, I can't imagine you sitting in a semi-circle discussing water purification with a bunch of peace corps hippies."

"Seems you've taken a keen interest in Ed's setup," Owen said.

"Your salmon okay? Maybe we should've had white rice?"

"What we have is fine with me."

"It's my job to know. To do my homework," Roland said. "People like you don't come to the market often. How many helicopters did you have in Mozambique? One I'm aware of. In India right now, two, three at most?"

Roland raised his hand to attract the waiter's attention, once again beckoning him to the table.

"Some wine with this salmon would help," he said, moving the fish with his fork. "A viognier. Two glasses," Roland said, passing back the wine list. "It goes well with oily fish," he said, addressing Owen, *"trust me."*

"And what would I be doing in Nairobi?"

"What you're struggling to do now."

"Response units?" Owen asked.

"Why not? We have all the assets you could ever need and, more importantly, the funds to make it work. Nairobi would be your base. I know your opinion when it comes to the UN, but that's why you're perfect. Africa is where it's all happening, again. Sierra Leone, for example, getting all the attention from us Brits. Amazing what a conscience can do."

"Your PA told me you work in the Horn of Africa?"

"I can go anywhere I wish, but yes, my area of responsibility is the Horn. An opportunity like this, Owen, and a salary to match. It's worth considering."

"And family?" Owen asked.

"Of course, you're married now. Belated congratulations. That was an interesting conversation with my sister. Penny's married, too, by the way. A German, and kids, awful mother, boy and girl, big place to the north of Munich."

"I'm pleased to hear she's doing well."

Laughing harshly, Roland said, "Married to a German, I said, not she's doing well. Never had an eye for a good man, my sister."

Owen looked at him with heartfelt astonishment, but Roland was too busy cutting his broccolini into small pieces to notice before he lathered it in salt and pepper ready for consumption.

"Bring them with you. Great place to raise a family: safaris, golden beaches, interesting ex-pat community. Perhaps not the place it was in Finch Hatton's day, but there are still opportunities for those who know how." Emptying his glass, Roland lightly patted the sides of his mouth with a napkin, one that had sat loyally on his knee throughout. "No need for an answer right now. But keep in mind these opportunities won't always come calling. Your evolutionary next step, perhaps."

"I'll give it some serious thought," Owen said, "and Roland, thanks for considering me."

"My father did that groundwork years ago."

Standing, Roland surveyed the table, searching its surface, readying himself to leave.

"I've paid the bill. Stay as long as you want."

Owen finished his food, going over the situation he found himself in: Roland offering him a job. As he left the restaurant, a bunch of delegates were entering, determined to get their night in London off to an early start. Recognising one, Owen said, "Don't get the salmon, bloody awful."

CHAPTER 25

Standing on the first floor of their new home in a gated complex in Westlands, Ellen surveyed her surroundings. They arrived in Nairobi in August, when the Kuzi winds were still blowing from the southeast, keeping the temperature cool and manageable for the newly arrived family. "You're going to love it, my dear, now the trees have finished drinking from the seasonal rains," Bishara told her weeks before they left London. "They're full and lush at Highgrove."

It was September, and Owen had already been gone for some days, ordered to Freetown in Sierra Leone. Ellen's mother demonstrated her angst at Owen abandoning his wife and daughter so soon after arriving. It was one of the few times, since leaving Manchester, Ellen agreed she had a point. The only people she knew were the hired help Bishara had arranged, a mixture of North African nationals escaping one war or another.

Roland was precise and insistent.

"Take care of her every need because I want Owen's wife settled as soon as possible. He has work to do and doesn't need distractions."

Bishara was right about the trees, Ellen found them a delight. They provided a protective dome enveloping the complex, giving some much-needed shade. Roland's PA described their new home as a small corner of England, her intention to enthuse the English lady. But when Ellen heard her statement, she physically cringed because it sounded nothing like the African adventure she was hoping for. This was Kenya, and that was the experience she desired. When Owen confirmed they were Nairobi-bound, she imagined it, her mind conjuring something not dissimilar to Blixen's romantic descriptions of her farm in the foothills of the Ngong Hills. What she got was one of fourteen luxury villas in a gated complex on the inappropriately named Highgrove Estate.

One of Ellen's favourite pastimes was staring in awe at the variety of trees that decked her view: acacia, eucalyptus, and African cypress. Their symbolic significance was described to her in detail by the estate's gardener, Kamau, a greying Kikuyu. His family had long since abandoned their ancestral homes and pastoral lifestyle on the slopes of Mount Kenya, seeking refuge in the capital. He told her how the Kikuyu once wandered the plains long before big hunters decimated the game that roamed through the bush in their millions. A time before their lands were sold by one white man to another.

On her first day, when he saw Ellen walking the estate, wide-eyed, drinking it all in, Kamau stopped his toiling with some stubborn weeds unwilling to release their grip deep in the garden's soil and stood, dripping with sweat in front of his audience, before explaining the characteristics of each tree.

"Madam, the fig is the queen of all African trees. The most revered by my people," he said. "We have three here, in the grounds. It's sacred to those who cling to our traditional beliefs. A place where our elders still worship, under its leaves."

Ellen was enthralled by the cultural lessons he gave, finding his passion refreshing. She had taken to watching Kamau from her vantage point, seeing him pray under the branches of one of the largest figs or in the hottest parts of the day, resting in its shade. It was possible to stand in her living room and peer between two of Highgrove's dwellings to where he sat at his altar. The tree he favoured grew against a razor-wired six-foot wall separating the residents from the frenetic bustle of Nairobi.

When her visitor pulled into the estate, she was looking in the other direction, towards the communal pool, visible between the thickening trunks of a group of acacias. Abeba, Lucy's Somali nanny, often entertained the child in its cool water, gliding through the midday heat, their skin protected from the sun's rays by the green canopy spread out in all its glory above. Lucy adored Abeba from the moment they met, drawn to the brilliant white of her emotionally charged eyes. She was tall, much taller than Kamau. Ellen often saw the two chatting in the gardens, Lucy placed perfectly on her hip.

She recognised a sadness in Abeba's expressive features, imagining some trauma had left its mark.

It was the noise of metal gates opening on the far side of the complex that disturbed Ellen's concentration.

The security gates had been an addition to Highgrove, implemented post-bombing of the US embassies in Nairobi and Dar es Salaam. "What if something should happen when trying to enter?" was the most urgent question asked at security briefings for newly arrived personnel and their dependents. "Just keep your engine throttled, doors locked and enter as soon as the gate opens," was the usual answer. Owen reassured Ellen they had the best security at Highgrove. Several of the houses on the estate were occupied by diplomats, key players in their country's missions, explaining the extra wall sensors and night lights and uniformed staffing of the complex. At number six, opposite, the largest residence by some measure, lived the family of the deputy ambassador to the Spanish Mission. Ellen was told they had a safe room on the top floor, with metal doors, able to separate them from intruders, even their own staff, if needed.

The rattle of closing gates subsided seconds before a Land Rover pulled into one of the parking spaces below. Ellen watched as Dr Oscar Reichlin emerged from the driver's side. Scanning the immediate buildings, he looked for the one where he was told a junior doctor could be found, fresh from the UK, willing to assist wherever she could. Checking his phone, he acknowledged he had the right address before looking up at its impressive frontage. Noticing a figure standing in the window above, Reichlin raised his hand in greeting. "You looked like Nairobi's own Lady of Shalott that first day," he later told her. "Serious and vulnerable." In truth, it was a fatuous comment because he was the one caught by Ellen's attraction, helplessly held in her spell. He would learn over time she was no maiden in need of a cavalier's protection and certainly not from one with debauchery in mind.

Walking towards the side door, where the houseboy was waiting, Oscar saw a beam of light breaking through the trees before it fell across the full length of the window in which Ellen stood. It pierced the glass before continuing its stellar journey, slicing through the cotton fabric of her skirt, exposing her slim waistline and thighs. Years later, when questioned about their first meeting, he felt guilty, embarrassed even, knowing she must have seen where his gaze fell. In response to their questions, he always gave the same answer. "For me it was love at first sight, or maybe lust followed by love, but love all the same. But I must stress, it was an emotion never reciprocated, even though I waited patiently."

Reichlin was visiting Highgrove because of a request Ellen made to Bishara, soliciting her help. She wanted to put her skills to good use, where they were needed, and where she could make a difference. It was an idea she had when still in London, insisting while she was willing to follow Owen to Kenya, there would have to be conditions.

"I'll need a purpose because without one I'll have nothing."

Owen agreed she had a point.

When Bishara contacted him in Freetown, explaining what his wife was asking, he gave his approval.

"Dr Reichlin," Bishara informed him, "works for a Swiss NGO, Medical Council of Switzerland in Kenya."

Owen knew who Reichlin was and of his reputation. The Saint of Mogadishu. A no-nonsense philanthropist, achieving what some called legendary status. Owen had seen him speak at several conferences, long before he met Roland in the Hungry Hound.

"MCSK is an advisory organisation that visits the slums of the country's big cities and refugee camps," Bishara said. "They provide support to hospitals and clinics struggling to administer their own communities, with outstations right across the region. An organisation that could put your wife's skills to good use, on an advisory level."

Oscar Reichlin was tall and tanned, a handsome looking man, known within certain circles for his charisma. Married with three children, he travelled alone, leaving his family in Bern. Often the subject of gossip, he worked the ex-pat circuit, known by wives in that community as the married bachelor. Always the last standing at a party.

All this Bishara knew but withheld from Owen.

"Good choice," Roland said. "A Lothario with a conscience. Perfect, my dear."

His praise was music to her ears.

"Nairobi's a city of contrasts, you'll see," Oscar told Ellen after listening to her first impressions of the capital. "Kibera, where you'll be best placed, is really a separate town within the city limits. An expanse of mud and rusting tin buildings standing out against the modernity of the capital. Diarrhoeal diseases, stillbirths, tuberculosis, the list goes on. And then there's HIV/AIDS, more prevalent than in other parts of the city due to sexual violence. The few staff running the clinics lack the fundamental skills to make a real impact, and that's where we come in."

Ellen found his enthusiasm infectious. What she could not have known in those early months was the pride Reichlin took in his ability to influence people, giving the impression he understood their needs and that he cared about them.

Once Ellen witnessed Kibera for herself, she understood

what he meant by contrasts. A stark distinction, to be more precise. It took time for her to adjust to its interior. The smell of human filth was everywhere, filling its open drains, causing disease, facilitated by an absence of basic systems. The experience helped to define her reason for defying her parents and following Owen out to Africa.

***

"I thought it'd be consultancy from a distance?" Owen asked on one of the occasions he managed to maintain a call from Freetown. "I'm not sure I want my wife frequenting places like Kibera. That's not what I had in mind."

"I could watch and do nothing if *you'd* prefer, which from where I'm standing would make me complicit now I've seen for myself."

"It's not just Kibera," he said, "the whole country is falling apart. Corruption, insecure borders, violent crime, too many problems for any of us to solve. Would you like me to go on?"

"We'll just have to take it one step at a time then," she said, not willing to give any more ground than his virtue signalling had already taken.

"This is Kibera we're talking about, not Manchester."

"There are procedures in place to keep me safe," she said.

"Ellen, it's my job to keep you safe."

"How can you? You're never going to be here."

"Work from home, surely that's enough?"

"Is that an order?"

"Of course not… What about Lucy?"

"Abeba," Ellen said. "She's almost her surrogate mother anyway, and you've seen her references, her experience. Personally recommended by Bishara. And Owen, it's fine to be concerned about me, but don't turn it into an obsession."

"Okay, you've obviously made your decision," he said,

vanquishing defeat. "I know you'll make a difference. I was thinking something a little more subtle, that's all."

Ellen was principled and strong-willed, what some called stubborn, but with the skills and knowledge to match. What more could Owen say when faced with such a determined partner? By the time he returned from his trip to Freetown, she had already been entrenched with MCSK for some time.

***

The old Kikuyu watched with amusement the comings and goings of the *mzungu*. During his years at Highgrove, the residents rarely acknowledged his presence, even though he toiled daily in the grounds, residing in a small shamba at the back of the compound. Growing irritated and then bored with the ways of white people, he turned away from them. But with Ellen, Lucy more so, he could sense a different force, one connected and in rhythm with their surroundings. His grandfather first talked about such things when Kamau was a child. Watching as Lucy grew, it astounded him how she really opened her eyes when looking up into the trees, her enquiring gaze full of understanding, as if she could see the ancestral spirits lingering there. Praying daily, he was eager to learn why his God favoured the white child.

He never received the answers he was looking for.

Taking it on himself to watch over her, Kamau, at every opportunity, whispered into Abeba's ear, giving direction, telling himself his concerns were for the child's wellbeing. Kamau knew he had to be vigilant with Abeba because Somali women were wise in their ways, with hidden intelligence and bewitching habits.

CHAPTER 26

Owen's first evening in Freetown was spent drinking cold beer in Alex's Bar with Roland, an establishment on the Aberdeen Peninsula. It was a haven of relative normality in a country torn apart by civil war. Grateful for the choice of venue, their table benefitted from a cool sea breeze blowing across the blue waters of Man of War Bay. A welcomed relief from the stifling heat and humidity.

"I'm sending you up to Bumbuna to spend some time with De Villiers," Roland said. "He's a bit rough around the edges, but it'll be an interesting introduction to the team. Perfect opportunity to show you what he brings to the table. He's following up on some CPC taskings."

"CPC?" Owen asked.

"Child Protection Committee," Roland said, while biting into freshly caught lobster washed down with cold beer. "Child combatants have long been used by both sides in this war."

Gidean De Villiers was an Afrikaner proud of his Boer roots. A man who liked very few people. He had worked for a large gold mining company outside Johannesburg, known for its efficiency, poor safety reputation, and low wages. Gidean had already been in Bumbuna for some days, a small town in the country's hinterland, one of a few not to have fallen into the hands of rebels.

A UN helicopter delivered Owen to the site of a defunct hydroelectric dam on the Rokel River, a World Bank project, abandoned midway through construction due to fighting that was consuming the country.

It only took a few hours in his company for Owen to learn Gidean paid scant attention to CPC mandates. A ruse to distract from his real interests. Days before, the South African briefed local authorities regarding his presence in town before delegating his responsibilities to certain officials, having first provided some dollars to make their work more palatable. It was an exchange that gave him time to pursue his favourite pastime, panning for gold, which could be found in the tributaries of the Rokel.

"Often you can find this stuff in streambeds and surface crevices," Gidean told Owen. "A one-man show. If you know how."

Owen would watch him work, placing his meagre findings into a brown leather satchel, one he rarely removed, unless sleeping, and then it remained within arm's reach. His enthusiasm never waned, even when he found nothing, which was most of the time. It never seemed to bother him. He just kept on panning, humming or whistling to himself, relaxed and cheerful. It was a disposition reserved only for those times he found himself engaged in such a favoured activity.

"Nothing else to do around here anyway," Gidean told Owen, trying to encourage him to join in, get his hands dirty. "In any case, it keeps me busy while we wait for the declaration of peace. When that happens, we can forget about being allowed to wander this far upriver. For now, let's abuse our UN privileges."

Fearing his first experience on the ground was turning into a Conradian-style excursion, Owen offered to head back into town to see what, if anything, was happening with CPC matters.

"Look, man, do what you want, but that stuff will sort itself out. They should learn to deal with their own problems anyway. All we need to do is give direction, which I've already done.

Our job isn't to hold their hands all the way. While they attend to business, I'm going to make the most of it while I have the opportunity. There's nothing of great value in these waters, but fuck, I'm enjoying myself, and you should too."

What Gidean De Villiers really brought to the table was not empathy for the local population or an enthusiasm for his role in a department whose aims were humanitarian, but expertise in the extraction of precious minerals.

Before its demise, Gidean was a staunch and uncompromising supporter of apartheid, an ideal influencing the segregated world in which he had grown. It surprised Owen that a man, who was clearly intelligent, could continue to live within an outdated idea of superiority. Yet he was no different from many of his peers who submitted to the prejudices born out of their childhoods.

"It's no accident the one holding the biggest gun always wins," he told Owen, smiling to himself, reminiscing, "and I want to be on his side."

It was a mantra he seemed to base his whole existence on, happy to reject any form of truth. Coming from a position of strength was all that mattered to men like Gidean.

"He has the staying power of an ox and the intellect of a Greek philosopher," Roland said when Owen voiced his concerns. "Don't let him get to you because that's *exactly* what he wants. In any case, he spends most of his time in the field, and when he's not out there, he'll find other ways to entertain himself. Keep in mind, though, he's your colleague and brings a certain expertise I want. I must ask you to respect that. For all his noxious traits, and I'll admit there are many, he has an acute sense of the way things work in this part of the world. Other than that, he's harmless. A relic best suited to a museum maybe, but not yet."

It was during one of many tropical downpours when Gidean accepted the river had become too dangerous to continue panning, forcing their retreat into the township for refuge. Their short relocation came the day after a handful of fundamentalists changed the modern world forever. An event the two were blissfully unaware of. The reason for their ignorance was simple geography. The steep river valley made communications with Freetown impossible the further upriver they ventured.

Gidean noticed it first. The slightest of differences the uninitiated could easily miss.

"Something's not right," he said, eyes fixed on the market stalls across the road.

They were sipping warm beer from a can on a veranda covered with thatch, watching the rains turn the town's roads into streams. The plan was simple: sit it out, then, when the rains ceased, check how many child combatants the authorities were willing to admit they had in the surrounding area. It was a concession Gidean allowed himself to appease his associate. They were in town anyway. Then head back to the muddy waters and see if anything further of interest could be found.

"What's not right?" Owen asked, seeing nothing of concern.

"Over there," Gidean said, gesturing with a nod, not wanting to point.

Owen followed his gaze across the road, but all he saw were local fishermen, their stalls set out, hoping to sell what they plucked from the river to the few vendors wandering around the market.

"Locals doing what they always do," Owen said.

"I don't know why the British love this continent so much," Gidean said, with a quizzical look in Owen's direction. "Should've just left it to us Boers. People who really know Africa's rhythm."

"What is it?" Owen asked, surprised he was no longer being kept within the boundaries of ignorance.

"Now really look."

There was something.

Merchants and customers gathered around the few people carrying small transistor radios, pushed tight against their ears. Those short-wave devices, ones cheaply manufactured by the Chinese, were a common sight. A status symbol to some. Whatever was being broadcast seemed to arouse the attention of the locals, enough to interrupt their best price negotiations.

"You mean the silence?" Owen asked.

"There's always something not right about this place," Gidean said, wiping beer from his lips. "Just like that dam upriver. If only someone could work out how to turn it on. It'd provide power to half the country. Instead, these people prefer to remain in the Stone Age, waging their wars."

It was another of his wistful comments, one Owen had heard numerous times in the few days they spent together. A longing for something lost amongst the wreckage of what was once Gidean's life.

In town that day, they were the last to learn the Twin Towers, those bastions of freedom, were no longer standing.

That evening, some hours after the rains abated, they sat on the abandoned structure of the dam, looking into the gathering waters of the Rokel. The unpolluted darkness made it seem like there was no demarcation between the river and its banks.

Any further excursions were forgotten.

"Now the rebels have seen how easy it is to make the West bleed, they'll come for us," Gidean said, his voice coming out of the tropical darkness that was engulfing them.

"What should we do?" Owen asked.

"We better head back to Freetown."

As he spoke, the wind rushed up the valley, rustling through the trees on either side of its steep banks. In the far distance, the rumble of thunder could be heard, bringing with it the smell of moisture in the air.

"More fucking rain," Gidean said, sounding exhausted.

***

Squeezed between piles of white grain bags stamped with WFP in large black letters, they had been strapped into their seats for the one-hour flight from Bumbuna to Freetown. Other than the rice bags and crew, Owen and Gidean were the only passengers. The noise of rotor-blades and screaming engines made any attempt at conversation impossible. For the Afrikaner, it was not such an inconvenience because sleep always came easy, his constitution impervious to the rattling of the helicopter's body. Owen watched his colleague's head jolting to every lurch and shudder, yet his eyes remained closed, arms wrapped around his satchel like a loving child.

Owen was surprised at the organisation's reaction to Gidean's request for an aircraft.

It picked them up from a potholed football pitch on the edge of Bumbuna. Its goalposts were made from thin branches local children cut from the bush, tied together with malleable strips of green bark.

"Priority boarding every time," Gidean said, as they ran towards the open door, his grin evidence of the pleasure he took from the authority he wielded.

The loadmaster was shouting above the noise of engines, indicating for them to approach in a way that avoided the spinning tail blades. The pilot preferred not to shut down, instead remaining ready to generate the thrust necessary for a quick exit. Flaming red dust and debris were flung in all directions by the violent downdraft, spreading like a three-hundred-and-sixty-degree sandstorm in a perfect circle with the helicopter's body at its epicentre.

To be heard, Owen had to yell above the deafening racket.

"Why're we such a priority? Surely, there are more pressing needs out here than our return."

Gidean was in front as they entered the danger zone below the rotor blades. Lowering his gait, he approached running at a crouch, an unnecessary reaction brought on by the lethal whirling above.

"Roland's the reason. Working for him makes it so," he said, as he climbed the steps into the belly of the helicopter.

Both fell into their seats, strapping themselves in because the pilot was already lifting from the ground. The nose dipped as the machine was pushed towards mud dwellings lining the perimeter of the pitch, causing cargo to strain under its netting. Children had already started to kick a ball of white hessian sacking filled with leaves back towards the centre of the makeshift football field. Moments earlier, they had been eating boiled groundnuts while they waited patiently.

Moving low over the town, the pilot sought out the banks of the Rokel, avoiding hills hemming in the township. The upturned faces of the few inhabitants walking the streets stared at the helicopter's undercarriage, watching the expensive machine depart, having brought nothing of value into their lives.

Owen observed the changing topography below, his head peering out of a bulbous window protruding from the side of the wafer-thin carriage. Using the steep river valley to gain height, the pilot manoeuvred along its twists and turns before clearing mountains creeping in from the northeast, their summits seeming dangerously close. Once over the peaks, they veered west across wooded hill country and on towards the coast. Below, Owen could make out the major towns of the hinterland, brown smudges disturbing the brilliant greenery of secondary jungle.

Once the noise of the helicopter faded into the distance, UN peacekeepers, ordered into the area for the duration of Gidean's stay, mounted their vehicles, readying themselves for the journey back to their headquarters. They remained out of sight, some distance from the dam, away from prying eyes. "A platoon at your disposal should you need," Roland informed Gidean. "They'll remain in the shadows, but they'll be there." With their silent departure, Bumbuna was once again left in the hands of a few government troops, the populace less of a priority than the white African spending most of his time foraging upriver. Lacking modern equipment and poorly trained, those few Sierra Leonian soldiers managed, against all expectations, to keep the town out of rebel hands. An exercise in survival rather than tactical genius. They roamed the streets with outdated weapons, once mothballed then dusted off before being gifted by old colonial masters. Why the UN never had a permanent presence baffled Owen, a stifling consequence of impartiality, he assumed.

"Write a report when you get back, but if you do, I know where it'll end up," Gidean said. "I've been up here many times. There's nothing here for the likes of us."

What had they achieved in those few days together?

Nothing Owen could see.

***

The heliport on the Aberdeen Peninsula was a frenetic operation, with its comings and goings of aircraft non-stop. Long lines of white trucks added to the disorder, revving their engines and sounding their horns, wanting to off-load cargo. The smell of aviation fuel, diesel and whirling rotor blades, mixed with engine noise, disturbed the recreation of those who frequented Lumley Beach across the road. It was a meeting place for aid workers, contractors and military types looking to purge their appetites in hastily built shacks passing as bars scattered along the seafront. Once the sun set, the place was frequented by hordes of night fighters, female prostitutes roaming the waterfront taking dollars from those seeking solace in their services.

A whole community of desperate people spawned by years of civil war.

Exiting the helicopter, Gidean shouted greetings above the sound of slowing rotors, heaving his satchel in Roland's direction.

"For you, my friend. Meagre pickings."

Roland shook the satchel, his arms wide in disbelief. Then, rather than pass it back to Gidean, he gave it to the man standing next to him.

The colour of Moussa's skin was much lighter than seen in this part of Africa, more like Abeba's. North African, Owen guessed.

It was a mutual inspection of character, not a one-sided affair. Moussa made his own deductions based on a visual scrutiny of the Englishman exiting the aircraft. Why was he the missing link in their quartet, as Roland had explained?

Owen guessed right, Moussa was of the Tuareg people, North African, a descendant of Berbers from the northern deserts.

"It's not worth the effort," Gidean said. "Leave the shithole to the Chinese. Somewhere else maybe, but not in that district."

After perusing the satchel's contents, Moussa returned it to its owner, flashing a contemptuous grin in the Boer's direction.

"He did warn you there'd be limited pickings," Roland said.

"Needed to see for myself. In any case, I got the chance to do what I enjoy. Peaceful too. For a while anyway."

Ignoring the innuendo, Roland introduced Moussa, Owen's newest colleague.

"Our interpreter and walking textbook on everything in this part of the continent, and your guide in the immediate term."

Hearing the compliment, Gidean made a disdainful laugh, saying something in Afrikaans. His words were drowned by the siren of an ambulance dashing across the helipad, racing to meet an incoming helicopter with a fading red cross embossed on its side. While he never saw Moussa as a direct threat, his respect faltered between reverence for the man's worth in North Africa and outright scorn. What he feared most was Roland's faith in the Malian.

"A helicopter and team at your disposal," Roland said, before pointing to a far-flung corner of the airfield. "That one, actually. A chance for the two of you to write a job description for those response teams. Then, when you've ironed out any anomalies, back to Nairobi, where you'll have the whole of the Horn to further develop the concept. First though, I want you and Moussa to drop Gidean in Kenema, first thing tomorrow. Once that's done, it'll be up to the two of you to come up with your own ideas how best to use those assets. Picking up child combatants in the Tonkolili district may be a good place to start."

"I'm the first priority, though," Gidean said, leather satchel back in his possession, its shoulder strap securing it to his body.

"You three take my vehicle and head to Alex's tonight," Roland said. "I'm booked on a flight back to Nairobi and then on to Geneva."

"Not for me, I'm heading to Lumley across the road," Gidean said, before nodding in Moussa's direction. "Much better than staring into those eyes all evening."

"But it's brown eyes you'll be staring into anyway," Moussa said.

"Touché and *gaan naai joself*," laughed the South African.

"It seems the only person copulating tonight will be you," Moussa said, responding to the expletive, judging Gidean's morality.

"You all have a room at UNOPs," Roland said, ignoring the insults being thrown between the two. "Not the most comfortable but close to this place. We'll be able to speak more when we get there."

At Roland's request, they had the top floor of a UN building turned into a makeshift dormitory. From the balcony, the views were spectacular looking over the turquoise waters of White Man's Bay, interrupted only by helicopters ferrying passengers to the airfield in Lungi.

***

Over the years, Owen would get to know Moussa like a brother, while others who tried to read him learnt nothing, unless it was something he wanted them to know. Outwardly, he came across as a calm individual, often instilling the feature in others. But Owen knew there was another side, a sharp contempt Moussa tried to camouflage. It was a quality he reserved for those who pushed his patience to its limits. Long after their friendship had grown, there was an altercation in the foyer of a hotel in Mombasa, a valuable lesson providing insight into Moussa's durability.

It all started with a routine pick-up of a client.

"He's a Belgian businessman in the employ of Ugandan Gold Industries," Roland told them. "Once you've finished in Lokichogio, get yourselves down to Mombasa. I want him flying back to Nairobi for a meeting. As far as you two are concerned, he's *royalty*."

When they arrived, the client's overly confident and loud pontifications demonstrated to anyone in earshot he was painfully unaware of his surroundings.

"A colleague of mine," the Belgian said, addressing his anecdote to Owen, "expat working in Kampala, passes his time with a *kaffir* he picked up in a casino. I've heard he's fathered a couple of bronzed illegitimates with her. Gone totally native. I can tell you that concubine and their little bastards have ruined his career."

At first, Owen paid scant interest to Moussa's movements as he lowered his cup, placing it back on its saucer before standing. Not until he saw the direction he was walking, making a beeline towards the client, did Owen become alarmed. Standing in front of the man, Moussa leaned forward, placing both hands on the arms of the lavish chair in which the entrepreneur sat, close enough to see the inflamed veins of his nose.

"Sir, how do you even know that?" Moussa asked, almost shouting, alarming Owen with the sharpness of his voice. There were a few hotel guests within earshot, enjoying their breakfast tea, who paused, looking gingerly in the direction of the raised voice.

Watching in disbelief, Owen could see large droplets of sweat gaining in density across the Belgian's reddening face. Doubt, surprise and then fear were all evident in the client's expression as he looked for support in Owen's direction.

"Because… that's what I've been told," he said.

"Men like you don't know anything," Moussa said, his face almost touching the Belgian's, "other than what you listen to with those large ears of yours pushed up against closed doors."

Owen explained to Ellen that Moussa's violation of discipline was due to a recently failed operation in the south of Sudan.

"We just couldn't get to them in time, not before those madmen from the north arrived. Six days we searched across the border. A column of refugees heading for the camps, mainly women and children. Moussa reminded me every day that if we couldn't locate them, they'd be lost to us. It was as if they'd simply vanished. He was distraught with possibilities. But, Ellen, I didn't expect such a response, not after Roland's warning."

"And you couldn't stop him?"

"No time. He caught me off-guard. We've listened to such bigotry before, many times. I thought we'd drink our tea. Humour him. Rebuke the comments later. He knows the rules. If Roland refers to them as clients, we treat them delicately because the context is already sensitive, but *royalty*."

"It was an insult," Ellen said, "born out of prejudice. One he couldn't overlook."

"Even so, Moussa should have ignored the comments, as offensive as they were. The Belgian blankly refused to travel with us. Wasn't even willing to meet Roland."

"There's a limit to what we can endure, what one is willing to bear," Ellen said. "With the memory of that column still fresh, he reached his breaking point. We all have one. He reached his. Not in the Sudan searching but sat across from a patronising impresario drinking tea in a luxury hotel in Mombasa."

There was something else, an observation Owen kept from Ellen. A look in Moussa's eyes, one full of violence, daring the Belgian to respond.

CHAPTER 27

Owen was drinking cold Heineken, while Moussa chose water, his religion not allowing him to take the alcohol on offer.

"Muslim," Gidean told him, minutes before leaving for his excursion to Lumley, "but not one you'll ever catch at prayer. Far from fundamentalist, but he's spent time in their company. Ask Roland, he'll tell you."

Taking Gidean's advice, Owen walked with Roland down concrete steps leading from their quarters into a small forecourt where a metal gate separated the compound from the bustle of Wilkinson Road. In the background, the building's generators hummed constantly, providing power for an army of air conditioning units bringing relief from the tropical heat.

"He came out of the desert where he spent his time mapping, looking for gold, somewhere north of Kidal," Roland said. "He knows the northern regions. Its people. His own tribesmen. Some insist he found what he was looking for, but all he brought back, all he told the authorities anyway, was rumours, nothing more. But there were those who didn't believe him. They'd heard talk about large gold deposits. His numerous expeditions brought him into contact with Islamic extremists, fighters, encroaching ever further into the Sahel. For some reason, probably survival, he guided a small group across the Tigharghar Mountains, from Algeria into Mali. If he hadn't, I suppose they'd have killed him. That's what he said when the group was captured. Seemed they were on a fact-finding mission. When they entered Kidal, the authorities were waiting. Brought them back to Bamako. Threw them in jail, Moussa too."

"Why put him in jail with the rest?"

"They said he was a spy, working for Islamists. They've long had ambitions for a West-African jihad. He was off-grid for a long time, Owen, before turning up in Kidal. Suspicions grew. Where had he been and who with? His father has a reputation, believing in an independent state for his people. Not linked to Islamists, but still anti-government. If they were to join forces… It's an idea keeping people awake at night. There's talk up there of an Islamic state of the Sahel with the introduction of Shariah law and it's gaining momentum. So, two and two together puts Moussa and his father in the same ballpark as the Islamists. But the Tuareg would never allow the northern deserts to be radicalised. They'd lose everything. Those first fighters, the ones who crossed with Moussa, they've become a huge talking point across the security world. Including the UN's Security Council. For now, northern Mali remains out of bounds to us. All that's going to change, and soon."

"And your interest?" Owen asked. "I don't see the significance."

"I'd heard stories. A Malian. One of the Tuareg, with knowledge of gold. I went to Bamako. Found him in a prison cell before the French got to him, crammed in with others. It was like looking into a slave ship."

"And you got him out?"

"Moussa had malaria with no access to a doctor, chained to a wall, rotting."

"You employed him because of what you think he knows?"

"It's there and lots of it. It's the reason he was gone for so long. Dwarfs other Malian mines into insignificance. Such large deposits have the potential to turn Mali into an economic powerhouse, right across North Africa. The big question is whether they can control it."

"Why's that of interest to the UN?" Owen asked.

"Where we are right now. What's the real reason this country is in the grip of a civil war?"

"Diamonds," Owen said.

"Blood diamonds, there for the taking. To fund the war machine of those strong enough to take what they want. No controls. Anything the army tried to enforce, long gone. They shed their uniforms like snakes and took up shovels and pickaxes. The government too corrupt to put the brakes on. Hands in every pocket anyway. By the time anyone did anything, the rebels were already amputating limbs and slaughtering at will."

"And the Malian gold?"

"Same idea. Once it becomes common knowledge, gives the extremists even more reason to venture into the Sahel, maybe all the way to the Niger. Further even."

The two men stood in the fading light, a white 4x4 visible by the gate, gently idling, waiting for Roland.

"My transport," he said, placing a soft hand on Owen's shoulder, an indication it was time to go. "If the UN moved units into those diamond fields, protected resources rather than people, cut off funds paying for this conflict, then maybe we wouldn't still be here, and maybe those atrocities could've been avoided."

As they spoke, three UN employees approached, heading for the entrance. All were known to Roland: a white Kenyan called Malisa, a Swede by the name of Klara and a ponytailed aging Scot named Wallace. All wore identical T-shirts decorated with the slogan, *Be part of the solution*, and on the reverse, *Internships with the UN*. In brackets, a web address. Owen noted the absurdity. Walking billboards offering free advertising. But who in this country had access to a computer, not the poor souls roaming across the Aberdeen Peninsula. Even if they did, they would have no hope of an internship with the organisation.

"You two heading to Alex's?" the white Kenyan asked.

"Not me tonight," Roland said," but two of the boys are."

"Not that vulgar Boer again, I hope?" she asked, before leaning into Wallace, whispering. Both laughed hard at the private joke.

"Entertaining himself elsewhere, you'll be pleased to hear," Roland said.

"And your handsome friend?" Klara asked, solicitously pointing.

Owen responded before Roland could, raising his left hand, showing his wedding band.

"That's a pity, but the night is young," she said.

"He's yet to learn no one has a history here," Roland said, joining with Klara's joking.

"It's the law in these parts," she said, imitating the voice of a western cowboy.

The three hurried out the gates, where a taxi was waiting, hailed by one of the guards.

"Later maybe," Klara shouted from the taxi's window as it disappeared into a crowded street.

"That's why I'm dropping Gidean in Kenema?" Owen asked once they were alone.

"Dropping and picking up when he's finished. If there are diamonds left up there to mine, and I get authority from Geneva, UNOPs will be tasked to move units in, secure the resources. All Gidean's doing is having a good look around with that satchel of his."

"But the horse has bolted," Owen said. "This war will be over soon."

"Hmm, maybe. It matters little anyway. This is the United Nations. The horse always needs to bolt first."

"And Mali?"

"If what Moussa said proves to be true, and extremists

move further south, not if, but when, especially after what's just happened in New York, then we stand a chance of doing what wasn't possible here. It's not just Mali. This whole continent is mineral rich."

"That's why you have Gidean. His knowledge of mining."

"Not forgetting his connections to that world," Roland said.

"And the humanitarian aspect?"

"If managed properly, Mali could pay its own way, eventually. This is humanitarianism, just from a different angle. Those sitting behind their desks in their plush offices in Nairobi, Geneva and New York, paid movie-star wages for writing endless reports, unwilling to put themselves in harm's way, aren't interested in humanitarianism, just self-preservation."

"And my role in all this?" Owen asked.

"ERUs, of course, and using your initiative when I need it."

"Moving Gidean around, you mean?"

"Something like that. For now, all you need to do is drop him off, complete the CPC task, pick him up again, and then, like I said, you have the whole of the Horn of Africa to play with. Sierra Leone is as good a place as any to make a start with your initiative. We don't need to wait for a disaster. Plenty of work to keep you busy across this region, all the way to the Indian Ocean. We'll talk more about what comes next when we're both back in Nairobi."

While Roland walked towards his waiting vehicle, Owen considered the opportunities already starting to present themselves.

In anticipation of Roland's exit, a guard opened the gates.

Out on the road, vehicles, carts, people and stray dogs hurried back and forth, a frenzied rush of life into which the vehicle started to inch itself. Two further guards rushed out, stopping traffic in both directions, allowing Roland's driver to exit unmolested. As the gates started to close, Owen noticed a woman on the far side of the road, a child strapped to her back and a heavy bundle wrapped in cloth balancing on her head. The child was sleeping, head tilted to one side, maize mulch smeared across its cheeks. The mother stared into the compound until the gates closed, looking in Owen's direction. What did she see in her fleeting glimpse into his world? He must have appeared ghost-like, barely visible in the yellowing lights of the inner compound.

Once Roland was gone, Owen stood listening once again to the humming of the generator, considering why he had been trusted with such sensitive information. Turning, he saw Moussa standing in the shadows, silent in the darkness.

***

"Roland sees me as an expert on culture and languages in this part of the world," Moussa said, pointing his steak knife in Owen's direction. "But for now, we have an important job to do. I suggest we collect as many child combatants as we can in the limited time we have. When we get that call to Kenema, our job here will be over. Let's make the most of it."

"What kind of numbers can we expect?" Owen asked, eager to be heading back upcountry with such an enthusiastic companion.

"Many," Moussa said. "When the rebels entered villages, whole communities were dispersed. Depending on which way you took to escape determined your fate. In those early days, parents spent time desperately looking for their children and children for parents. They'd have been better off just running. If female, the best you could hope for was rape or a quick death. Children were taken to boost numbers in rebel units, ordered to carry weapons, given amphetamine stimulants to encourage them to take part. Then the amputations, now an infamous trademark of this war."

Owen lowered his knife and fork, placing them neatly on the edge of his plate, appetite gone. Picking up his glass, he took a long drink, wetting his hand on the condensation forming on the glass's surface before rubbing its moisture through his hair.

"Christ!" he said.

"The ones we bring back, we'll get into the programme. Once we do that, they'll be safe. We'll have a few weeks, but even in that time it'll only be the tip of the iceberg."

"Roland told me about your time in jail," Owen said, changing the subject, determined to fill in any remaining gaps.

"There have been great injustices across this continent. My experience in those dungeons was a pain shared. If you stay here long enough, you'll learn what I mean because Africa touches everything and everyone, there's no escaping.

"What really happened in those mountains?"

"Pretty much what Roland told you. I was making my way back, having found what I was looking for. Coming south from Boghessa. In all my excitement, I crashed the vehicle I was driving. Bedouin picked me up and took me in. But there were others among them. People I didn't recognise."

"Others?" Owen asked.

"They saw me as a threat. I'd seen them. Their weapons, not the old rusting Kalashnikovs common up there, more modern. Prior to the accident, days before I decided to leave, I'd been noticed speaking to an old spice trader. A French spy, they said. I knew nothing about that or even if it was true. Since then, I've learnt the French have people they pay, fearful Islamists will come south and wage war. They decided to take me north, into Algeria, safer for them. I couldn't say where I was kept. Eventually, I agreed to guide a small group across the border, into the mountains. They wanted me to take them all the way to Bamako, but our journey was tracked. Maybe the spice trader was a spy after all. My name was passed to the French, who wanted the group stopped."

"And you intended to take them all the way?"

"I'm a Tuareg," Moussa said. "We aren't known for our loyalties to Bamako, but an Islamic state of the Sahel. Goes against everything we want to achieve."

"But you brought them south anyway," Owen said.

"Of course, through Kidal. I knew if we were going to be

stopped anywhere, it'd be there. But it seems I was guilty by association. Maybe the authorities would've seen it differently had I been decapitated by my captors. It seems we'd have been killed long before Bamako anyway. Lucky I took that route. Doesn't matter now," Moussa said, leaning back in his chair. "Roland managed to convince them otherwise or, more likely, bribed someone. Either way, he saved me from that place."

"What made you the perfect guide?" Owen asked, not allowing the subject to be changed.

"As a child, my father insisted I walk with the herdsmen, moving from one guetla to another. 'All part of your education', he would say. I simply followed a route I knew, through the Adrar des Ifoghas, weaving between the valleys and granite blocks, using waterholes to guide the group. I fear the nomadic herdsmen who once drank from those places will now be replaced by insurgents. If that happens, it'll be a great injustice for my people, swallowing our history. The Tuareg say that one day a great sandstorm will come, fiercer than any other, erasing all our enemies. Those winds have already started to gather."

CHAPTER 28

Dr Reichlin was scanning the *East African Herald*, his daily ritual, sat across from Ellen having breakfast in a German-style café in the Village Market. It was a routine they adopted prior to their visits to Kibera's clinics. The preferred meeting place for expats, tourists and Kenya's wealthier citizens able to pay the high prices demanded in its western-style boutiques and restaurants. Located in the pristine suburb of Gigiri, the place was a simulacrum, not to be mistaken for the bustling market of the same name in the centre of Nairobi, an error that could prove dangerous to the unaware. It had been some months since Owen returned from Freetown, and the Morgan family was settling into their surroundings, having spent an explorative Christmas and New Year in Kenya. Oscar was drawn to a report in the newspaper, one he read in its entirety, unusual for his temperament. Sliding the *Herald* across the table, he drew Ellen's attention to it, tapping his finger on the column holding his interest.

"That's your husband, isn't it?"

Ellen read the main heading at the top of the page, *UN News, Global Perspectives*. Underneath was a series of individual articles. The one of interest, the one his index finger was placed squarely in the centre of, was titled *New Concept Using Aviation*

Sees Children in Conflict Zone Lifted to Safety. Below was a picture of Owen and Moussa exiting a helicopter with its cargo doors open wide. Inside could be seen children of all ages. Some were still strapped in, while others were unbuckling, and a few, the more confident, were already standing, waiting to exit. The common denominator attached to each child was evident in their expressions of confusion and fear.

Ellen read, absorbing every word:

UN personnel fly into conflict zone to test its latest concept in the use of rapidly deployable aviation assets. A team led by Owen Morgan (United Kingdom), seconded to the United Nations Child Protection Committee (CPC), extracted child combatants from rebel strongholds in central Sierra Leone. The in-country chief of mission, Erland Fosse (Norway), said: "This humanitarian deployment demonstrates our commitment and resourcefulness through the courage and compassion demonstrated by my colleague and his team."

The recent mission employed a concept previously used in disaster relief operations, modified to suit what has become a critical need. The deployment of aviation assets, known as Emergency Response Units (ERU), proved to be decisive in meeting some of the CPC's promised mandates…

"Quite the hero," Oscar said, attempting to draw her attention away from the piece.

Ignoring his comment, Ellen finished reading before fixing her eyes on the editorial photo. Owen's tall figure was central and in the forefront of the picture, the camera's focus seeking him out. Scrutinising the image, she sensed what could only be described as excitement. Even in a photograph, she found her husband's sexuality alluring. Since their arrival in Nairobi, she had experienced an epiphany, a realisation that Kenya was bringing them closer together, something London failed to achieve.

When Owen returned from Sierra Leone, at Ellen's insistence, the three of them sat down to dinner together at Highgrove. "It'll give us a chance to break the ice," she encouraged. It was the only time she could recall Oscar making his excuses and leaving early. Having grown bored, he distracted himself by gazing at objects around the room, behaving like an unemployed voyeur. The two were immersed in each other's company all evening, a behaviour Oscar found vulgar and insulting. Giving his excuses, he fled, but not before making the shocking realisation Owen and Ellen were one of those rare married couples still embroiled in an intense love affair. It was not the first time a beautiful woman had made him feel like a lovestruck schoolboy.

Ellen lifted her gaze, dragging herself away from the pages.

"I'm sure he doesn't even know this was written. He would have said."

"Where is he now?" Oscar asked.

"Lokichogio, sent up there by Roland. Apparently, it's well-positioned for quick access across the border."

"Many borders," Oscar said.

"They're looking at setting up a permanent base. Some kind of staging post."

"I don't know why he leaves you for such long periods," Oscar said, hoping to uncover some weakness in Ellen's character, anything he could manipulate to his advantage.

"My fault, not Owen's. I followed him here, not the other way around."

"I've said this before, Ellen, but which branch within the organisation does your husband work?"

"It's Roland Roden-West who employed him. An old friend from his university days. Humanitarian head of something or other. I suppose we've all benefitted from a little nepotism in our time."

"HCR, WFP, Children's Fund?" Oscar asked, searching for an answer.

Ellen turned her attention back to the column, uncertain whether Oscar's persistence had good intentions. Rather than answer, she sipped her coffee, staring at the image, a brazen smile on her face, one matching her desires.

Such an easy person to read, Oscar thought, bringing on a fit of jealousy.

It had been some time since he imagined his own wife in any other way. With Ellen, though, he could evoke any aspect of her physical being: her waistline, thin wrists, and long athletic legs. Even when he went to the Jockey Club at the Intercontinental to seek pleasure, he would always visualise her during the sex that followed.

For some time, Oscar concluded Roland must be someone of importance working out of Geneva because all he managed to pick up from his associates at UN Headquarters were rumours, nothing more. The few times he was invited behind the wire and into the heart of the organisation, a meeting, conference, or drinks to make it seem like a joint effort, he never met anyone who knew Roland personally. It crossed his mind he could go back, after breakfast, enquire again. It was only a stone's throw from the Village Market. The sprawling grounds housing the headquarters was situated near several embassies, seeking safety in numbers. The place reminded him of a military base, like ones he had come across in Mogadishu, designed to withstand the harshest of blockades because those inside feared what was beyond their walls.

But Roland had Ellen's husband operating in a very different way.

"You know," Oscar said, testing the water, "Kakuma isn't a million miles from Loki. We have an office and personnel there. If you fancied a field trip, it could be arranged."

"Kakuma, the north-western refugee camp?" Ellen asked.

"Several camps. Maybe you'd get to see your husband at the same time. The Lodwar-Lokichogio Road runs straight through."

"Done," she said, immediately sold on the prospect.

Owen made no promises, but he saw the potential. He had visited the camps, dropping and picking up personnel and material and, on occasion, delivering refugees out of Sudan and Ethiopia. What he saw in Kakuma was a displacement of people on a biblical scale. He told Ellen it had to be witnessed to stand any chance of grasping the sheer size of it all. An endless vista of impoverished people living in shacks and tents, stretching as far as the eye could see. All fleeing persecution of some sort.

"These," Moussa told him, "are the ones who made it out."

***

Flying into Kakuma on a UN flight from Wilson, Ellen witnessed the scale of the operation as they approached. Her bird's-eye view made it seem like an autonomous city occupying large swathes of drought-infested desert and scrub. As the plane came in low, she noticed on its fringes, beyond the relative order of shacks and tents, were other dwellings, nothing more than makeshift tukuls built from branches, plastic and rubbish of various types.

"They really are Africa's forlorn," Oscar said, following her gaze. "They aren't refugees but Turkana people. Kenyans, not supported by the programmes, trying to hack out an existence."

Exiting the plane, they were met by Brian, a young doctor from New Zealand, wearing a dirty T-shirt advertising whitewater rafting on the Zambezi. He exchanged it for some woollen socks with a roadside vendor while on rest and recuperation in Livingstone. Next to him, a cluster of people gathered to welcome a colleague, a young Canadian hoping to strengthen her CV by spending time with Médecins Sans Frontières. Ellen spoke to her while they queued at Wilson. It was her third trip upcountry, but this time she was heading to the border with Ethiopia. "A real field trip, finally," she said. Her waiting friends screamed their greeting before jumping into a truck and disappearing into the dust.

The plane's cargo was offloaded using local porters directed by an old man with a shrivelled back, leaning forward on a decorated walking stick, once an instrument of battle, now an emblem of nobility. He shouted instructions while waving his sceptre, his every order carried out with speed.

Brian welcomed his two visitors, first shaking Oscar's hand before they embraced like old friends. Ellen got the impression the newly arrived, of any sort, were welcomed with celebrity status, visitors being rare. He escorted them to a waiting Toyota twin cab, its flat cargo area full of cardboard boxes.

"Finally, medical supplies," Brian said. "Hopefully some morale parcels too."

The smell of aviation fuel and diesel was so overwhelming Ellen pressed her floppy hat over her mouth, ignoring the penetrating rays of a late-afternoon sun.

"I've booked two rooms at the IOM Hilton (International Organisation for Migration)," Brian said, laughing at the comparison. "Hope you've both brought Kenyan shillings. Only thing they'll take in the canteen."

"I've been here before, you know," Oscar said, not wanting to be cast as the amateur.

"Then you'll remember we have five levels of security. Right now, it's level two, minimal risk to personnel. Evermore won't allow you outside the confines of the camps anyway, so don't try."

After a short drive, they arrived at a low building with a large sign on a picketed board advertising MCSK, Kakuma. The building was made of breeze blocks, painted yellow, and capped with a tin roof. Its most promising feature was a thrust veranda on which sat six plastic chairs, set in a semicircle.

"Best spot in town," Brian said as they walked across the porch, pointing towards the horizon.

Ellen turned to look.

From the small rise on which the building sat, she could see across a multitude of corrugated tin roofs. Dust and smoke were cast upwards from the camps, creating a brilliant orange haze in the sky, turning the sun into a red-tinged fireball. In the air was the smell of burnt oil wafting from the nearest dwellings. Dogs barked, competing with the shrill shouts of excited children and the clatter of utensils. A donkey and cart passed by, carrying what looked like brush, material used to line the boundaries of allotted plots. Those borders facilitated some kind of claim, an imagined ownership. A glimmer of autonomy perhaps, for those living within the camp's confines. But for many of the displaced, it was a prison. A life lived in exile. What she saw, looking towards the horizon, was truly beautiful, sublime when viewed in context.

As she entered the building, Oscar was handing a bunch of flowers to a rotund lady wearing a yellow T-shirt advertising Tusker beer. "Picked fresh this morning from the Naivasha farms," he explained before they boarded their plane. Ellen saw how he cradled them in his arms as the aircraft heaved itself into the air, climbing with its heavy cargo.

"Meet Evermore," Oscar said. "One of the original lost children of the Sudan. She's been with us from the beginning. MCSK's administrator for the whole of our Turkana setup."

Oscar told Ellen how, in 1987, when Evermore was twelve, she walked across the south of Sudan, joining long lines of children marching into Ethiopia, before she fled once again, crossing into Kenya, finding her way to Kakuma. "She was lucky," Oscar had said, "passing herself off as a boy to deter the interest of soldiers and bandits looking for a bride."

Still holding the flowers, Evermore embraced Ellen.

The sweet scent of rose and jasmine reminded her of the garden centres her parents dragged her around when she was a child.

"Keep these visible wherever you go," Evermore said, passing ID cards to her visitors, "and please don't get caught without them. And you," she said to Brian, "had better get going. Another plane to meet."

Oscar threw a quizzical look in Brian's direction.

"Plane?" he asked.

"Need to be in Lodwar. Relief nurses coming in from Nairobi."

"Will you be staying the night?" Oscar asked.

"Probably. Don't want to be on that road after dark."

"Why not?" Ellen asked, searching their faces for an answer.

"It's fine, by Kenyan standards," Oscar said. "It's the people out there once the sun goes down, not the road."

"I'll see you both in the canteen for breakfast, early," Brian said, before rushing out, slamming the screen door hard against its wooden frame, much to Evermore's annoyance.

"That boy will be the death of me if he doesn't kill himself first. Slow down!" she said, screaming across the room. "Not that he's listening. He's probably halfway there already."

"Now you're here, best you get orientated," Oscar said, guiding Ellen to a map on the wall. "Look where we are: Uganda to the west, Sudan north, and Ethiopia northeast, all with refugees here in the camps."

"Mainly from the Sudan, like me," Evermore said.

"There's a lot of banditry across Turkana," Oscar said, "but cross-border incursions from the south of Sudan are the main concern. Cattle raiding is the major reason, but violence over food and water is also common, reprisal killings an outcome."

"Then there's famine," Evermore said. "Not a seven-year one for us but a never-ending food crisis. Civil war the main reason. Khartoum fighting the rebels. Aid agencies in the middle. A quagmire, as I've heard it called."

"Brian's heading south," Ellen said, pointing to Lodwar on the map, "so I'm assuming safer?"

"Even so, after dark, we wouldn't advise travel," Evermore said.

"Why didn't they just fly in with us?" Ellen asked, the simplicity of her suggestion apparent in her voice.

"They're in-country staff," Oscar said. "We can't afford to fly them directly, not at four-hundred US a seat. Much cheaper to use a local flight. It's the difference between bringing all the medicine we had on board. Local airlines are fine, just takes longer. I've used them myself when the UN cancels."

"Brian likes to meet them off the aircraft," Evermore said. "Makes them feel valued. That's what he says. I say, why can't they get a *matatu*, even a *boda-boda*, but that's Brian for you."

Oscar pointed out other key locations as Ellen continued to scrutinise the map.

"I'll be on the porch when you two have finished," Evermore said, taking three cold Tuskers from the fridge. "The sun will be setting soon, which makes this place better than any NGO bar you'll find around here."

Carrying the cold beers, Evermore made her way to the door, continuing to listen, interested to know how far Oscar's infatuation had set in.

By the time they joined her, the sun was dropping fast, and yellow lights were springing up across the camps, a mixture of fires, paraffin lamps and torches.

"Tell me, Ellen," Evermore asked, once the three of them had settled, "how was Christmas in Kenya?"

Looking at ever-brightening lights across the road, Ellen was reminded of the tree she decorated with Lucy and Abeba. It was a shaming comparison. Weeks earlier, Ellen decorated the family tree, a custom Kamau found entertaining, watching as a plastic imitation was planted in the first-floor window where Ellen placed and replaced decorations across its branches. Before turning on the lights, she arranged a small house event to which Kamau was invited.

"We spent time in Mombasa and the Maasai Mara," Ellen said, pausing, uncertain whether she should be sharing stories bathed in luxury while sitting on a veranda in the impoverished midst of Kakuma.

"Go on," Evermore said, hearing hesitation in her voice. "I want all the details. Brian and I love a good story. Keeps us entertained during long nights. What did you like most about Mombasa?" she asked, trying to encourage Ellen to share.

"For me, it was eating seafood on a dhow in the bay. We watched the old town's lights reflecting off the water Christmas Eve. Just the two of us. An early gift from my husband."

Evermore pulled up a second chair, kicked off her flip-flops and stretched out her round legs, placing them on warm plastic, before folding her arms across a heavy chest, as if readying herself to watch a movie she had waited a long time to come to screen. Not looking at the narrator, she peered into the wooden timbers supporting the veranda's roof, visualising every word Ellen uttered. Although she was sweating profusely, her facial expression was the personification of a welcomed distraction.

"And your daughter, what was her favourite excursion?" Evermore asked, eager for detail.

"The simple things. Fooling around in the sea. Anything to do with water fascinates her. Christmas Day, she swam with turtles, we all did, which she adored. Then we ate fresh crab on Wasini Island. In the evening, we opened gifts back at the hotel."

She left out sex in the splash pool once Lucy and Abeba had gone to bed and walking barefoot in the surf into the early hours. Such things she locked away, reserved only for her own private viewing. Sex had become passionate once again, like in Manchester, with bouts of intense ferocity. On one such occasion, she whispered into Owen's ear, "We should have another child, a whole bunch of them," to which they burst into fits of laughter. They discovered each other in her apartment, but then, in London, something was lost, only to be found again in Kenya, a fresh blossoming of their relationship, with an invigorated intensity. Ellen could have given many accounts of her girlfriend's love affairs souring over time, the lovemaking dwindling into those odd occasions. She had experienced it herself. How lucky they survived.

"And then we flew into the Maasai Mara for new year," Ellen said. "We celebrated with sundowners on a viewing platform while giraffes paced across the savannah. But for Lucy it was the antelopes that entertained her the most, drinking from a waterhole, right in front of our balcony. She was enthralled. It was all over far too soon. Then back to Nairobi for a couple of days before Owen left for Lokichogio, again."

Oscar had heard all this before, sitting through all the amusing and affectionate anecdotes, romanticising their encounters. It had irritated him then, but even more so the second time.

"Those antelope you mention," Oscar said, "just one is worth more than ten of Kibera's residents to Kenya's government."

"And why is that?" Ellen asked, alarmed at the displeasure she recognised in his voice.

"Because lions feed off them, and that's what plastic tourists pay to see. Not the real Kenya at all, Ellen."

"Oh, Dr Reichlin," Evermore said.

Ellen was aware such comments were part of his continued agenda to move their relationship beyond the professional. She had hoped his return from Switzerland would have exercised those unsolicited desires. Africa had brought about a renaissance, and if it offended Oscar, then she would have to find some way of distancing herself.

Prior to the interruption, she was about to describe their visit to Karen Blixen's, an excursion she had been meaning to make since their arrival in Nairobi. A visit to the farmhouse from where the Danish entrepreneur once managed her coffee plantation. Ever since reading *Out of Africa* as a child, Ellen dreamed of one day standing in the grounds and looking up into the lush Ngong Hills, as she imagined Karen had done all those years before. On the day they visited, low grey clouds obscured the knuckles of the hilltops from view, shattering her vision.

"You know, Ellen," Evermore said, breaking the silence, "with Brian going off rafting one river or another across the continent, you could always stand in for him, on the odd occasion. It's perfectly placed for visits from your husband. Loki's just up the road. And then there's the work," she concluded, pointing towards the camps.

"Really—" Ellen started to say, already forming an idea.

She was interrupted by a vehicle appearing out of the dark, its headlights falling across the veranda, blinding the three of them.

"Is that Brian?" Ellen asked, shielding her eyes from the light.

"No, not Brian," Evermore said, beaming with delight now that her secret was about to reveal itself.

A white Land Cruiser with UN painted in black letters on its doors pulled in front of the veranda, causing a light dusting to shroud the vehicle in what appeared to be a transparent mist. As the driver's window lowered, Owen looked across at his wife before waving at Evermore, that larger-than-life lady whom he had spoken to for the first time only days before.

It was a bizarre experience for Ellen, her first night in the camps. Meeting Brian and Evermore was a pleasure, but then Owen, an unexpected rendezvous, and a double room at the IOM. It was the first of many such nights they came to value. But each time, when the sun rose in the morning, the veil would be lifted and the spell broken, revealing the reality of Kakuma, a place Ellen and Owen would return to many times.

CHAPTER 29

There were some who questioned Ellen's employment with MCSK, linking it to Oscar's obsessive behaviour. For those who knew him, there was truth in the accusation. But such allegations were difficult to substantiate during the inquest into Ellen's death, killed out on the Lodwar-Lokichogio Road. The illegal roadblock into which her taxi had driven was set where the road enters Kakuma. A couple more kilometres and she would have been inside the confines of the camps.

It was Evermore who called him.

"Owen, where's Ellen?"

He could hear panic in her voice and answered sharply.

"Right now, on your veranda admiring the view! Why?"

"We're getting reports of a white lady killed outside the camps. And… Owen, she isn't with me."

Evermore's words, and the details of the inquest became the themes plaguing his dreams: her UN flight cancelled, the decision to take a local one to Lodwar, and then a taxi to Kakuma. Then there were delays: thirty minutes at Wilson and the taxi's puncture. The driver had driven into an illegal checkpoint within sight of the camp's lights glistening in the distance. The robbery, the rape, and the nature of the killing, he sat through it all, as had Moussa.

Claims of poor parenting and details of Lucy's premature return to England were all details the press added to a variety of conspiracy theories. The tragedy came together in an uncanny collaboration, timed to coincide with the moment when they were both realising the full potential of their marriage.

Moussa flew back to Nairobi with Owen once Ellen's body had been identified and statements written.

Having stood at his friend's side in the morgue, he saw the crust clinging to her body, red blood having turned black and congealed, no longer fresh or recognisable as the elixir running through our veins. The two of them endured the stench together as well as the flies clinging to Turkana's victims lined up in rows, covered in soiled sheets, lying in a variety of grotesque shapes. Many were on metal trays, while others had been placed on the tiled floor.

There was no differentiation, not even for the white woman.

While Owen was completing paperwork, officially verifying Ellen's identification, a police officer, two yellow pips on his shoulder, took Moussa to one side, manoeuvring him away from the desk at which Owen sat.

"For a price, we can solve this case tonight. For your friend," he said, leaning close into his potential client and nodding in Owen's direction.

Moussa looked around, checking to see if anyone was in earshot before daring to answer the proposition.

"You know who did this?" he asked.

Once the question was out, Moussa noticed how quiet it was inside the building, less the humming of a fan dispersing the already stifling heat around the room and the movement of a pencil Owen was using, its tip scribbling away on cheap paper. In a corner, he sat with two other officers, filling in blank spaces on a form.

There was only one entrance Moussa could see, a wooden door with a glass window, its surface dissected by reinforced squares of wire. Looking like a map, the years of dirt provided topographical detail. Through the window, he could see a distorted version of their vehicle parked on the far side of a sparsely gravelled car park. As they crossed it earlier, an old lady with a small face, a blue glaze in her eyes, was sitting in the dust, a makeshift walking stick lying at her side. In her lap was a pile of miniature Bibles. She was selling her wares to grieving relatives as they came and went, hoping to make a few shillings. Moussa gave her little attention, but Owen stopped, dug deep into his pockets, handing over what he had, tapping her shoulder to indicate nothing was needed in return.

"We can go out on that road," the officer said, "and we'll find any number of bandits illegally stopping cars. Maybe some of them are policemen, soldiers. For a price, we'll bring someone in, put them in there with the rest," he said, pointing down the corridor towards the morgue. "No need for prison cells or lengthy proceedings, just revenge for your man."

"Just anyone?" Moussa asked.

"They're all guilty of something. Don't forget this happens every night out there, to *our* people…"

After a long pause, intended to give the impression he was considering the proposition, Moussa responded.

"I'll pass your suggestion to my friend," was the safest answer he could come up with.

It was a sensitive situation, one in which insults, a loss of control more so, would only exacerbate the situation with the corrupt official. The stench of death was still in his nostrils, a reminder of what lay at the end of the corridor into which the policeman pointed. Earlier, he fought the urge to vomit, fighting it as much for Owen as himself, but a new nausea started to overpower him, one driven by memory and fear. Standing close to the policeman, it was overwhelming Moussa's senses, something like rotten onions emanating from the man's body. It was like the stench of his cell in Bamako.

As the two exited into brilliant sunshine, the policeman shouted from behind.

"For a price. Come back anytime. Bring some tea, and we'll sit down together."

Moussa turned, threw him a smile, and gave a thumbs-up before guiding Owen across the car park.

"A price, for what?" Owen asked.

"Ignore it. He's trying to sell something we don't want."

The vendor was still sitting in the same position, arm raised, Bible in hand, looking up at the sky, hoping whoever was in the vehicle would make a purchase. She blended perfectly with her surroundings, everything dry and burnt. The colours of her clothes matched the thorny bushes, clinging to life at the edge of the car park's border. How people endured with such fortitude in this country never failed to amaze Owen.

Such bravery.

Moussa once told him, devoid of courage to continually face their fears, their pain, their dangers, what else did they have? Without endurance, nothing could be accomplished in such places.

Before heading back to Lokichogio, where a helicopter was waiting to fly them to Nairobi, they tried to locate Evermore, now in sole charge until Oscar arrived. Brian was on leave, probably rafting another of the continent's rivers, having fun, blissfully unaware. There was no sign of her, not in the office or in the camps. Hours earlier she had taken the truck, throttling its V6 engine, speeding off into the flaming dust. While Owen and Moussa were in the morgue, she went in search of the taxi driver's wife, knowing nobody else would have the resources or inclination to assist the bereaved widow. It was what she had in common with Ellen, a shared fear of becoming a bystander.

Arriving at MCSK's office, both men recognised the boy sitting on the veranda, a teenage Sudanese refugee called Faheem. Owen had grown fond of him during the occasions he managed to join his wife. The teenager was on one of the plastic chairs, panga laying across his lap, standing guard.

"Madam is gone," Faheem said, smiling in recognition of the two men. "Not back until morning. I need to remain here until Dr Reichlin comes from Nairobi."

Once the message had been passed, using the exact words Evermore instructed, Faheem noticed dark patches forming under the white man's eyes.

"Thank you, Faheem," Owen said. "You're a good guard, and you look strong and brave sat out here. Please tell Madam we called."

Hours earlier, not knowing he was being observed, Evermore saw Faheem wipe away tears. The lady who treated him like family was now dead. He always knew when she had been in the office, the smell of her perfume invading his senses. It lingered for days, weeks even, and he could still smell it. In his prayers, Faheem asked it to remain, if not in the air, then at least in his memories. Owen's comments failed to make him feel brave, though he knew it was the intention. It shocked him to see the *mzungu* like this, defeat evident in all his aspects. From experience, Faheem was aware that overwhelming grief, an urge for revenge, and a sense of powerlessness could all incapacitate the soul.

***

The news spread from house to house at Highgrove much quicker than the bushfires Kamau remembered as a boy. Once he confirmed the rumour with Abeba, he retreated to the fig tree, praying for direction. It was through these meditations he convinced himself someone was coming for Lucy, people he should trust. His troubled imagination assured him the child would be safer if she could be handed over before her absent father returned. When her grandparents arrived from England, he saw they were the ones for whom he had been told to wait. Within hours of their arrival, they were driving out of Highgrove back towards Jomo Kenyatta International Airport, granddaughter delivered into their arms.

The lasting memory haunting Ellen's parents was the unsettling wailing of Abeba as Kamau wrenched the child out of her arms, a sorrowful sound they hoped never to witness again.

The old Kikuyu knew nothing of the rift raging between Ellen and her parents or the continued pressure they placed her under. As hard as he prayed, his appeals failed to reveal that divide. The *mzungu* told him nothing, and neither did his gods. By the time Owen arrived at Highgrove, having left his wife's defiled body in a stinking room, Lucy was gone and Kamau could not be found, having walked out the gates hours before. The money Ellen's parents proffered was a necessary gift, his lifeline now that he had no gardens to tend.

CHAPTER 30

"Remain with us," Anne said. "Jimmy and his family, they'll make you happy again. I'll make you happy."

"The real reason she died was because she loved me," Owen said. "It's that simple. I told her we'd meet on that veranda, as we'd done many times. She was trying to get to me."

Ignoring his mother's appeals to stay and fight for Lucy, Owen returned to Kenya once Ellen had been buried. Her petitions were hopeless because he convinced himself the grief was his alone to carry.

Moussa was alarmed when he returned so soon. It shocked him how sallow he looked, matching the onset of a greying hairline. No longer was there a confident stride, his gait hunched, giving the impression his stature had shrunk. He had witnessed it before, in the cells, a withdrawing into oneself, usually followed by despair leading to a slow wasting away.

"He's becoming one of those wandering vagrants of the Sub-Sahara," was how Moussa described him to Roland.

Deciding to remain at his side, Moussa proved to be the only real friend Owen had, determined to help him shape the immediate future. Roland reminded him on more than one occasion not to care so much.

"I don't want it becoming a diversion," Roland said, keeping his opinion on the matter transparent.

He had that quality, Roland, apathy when faced with catastrophe.

"If Africa is where you choose to mourn, then so be it. But let's get back out there, Lokichogio, as difficult as it may sound," Moussa said, trying to be the guide Owen needed.

"I'm not sure I can. The camps, always there. Maybe we could remain here, mount operations from Nairobi."

"To stay in this house, even this city, will turn it into a prison."

"I'm sure Roland will agree," Owen said.

"Of course he will, but it's not the right thing to do. Lokichogio is. It'll take courage, but together, Owen…"

Both knew Roland would never question where they stationed themselves, so long as they did his bidding. Neither did he care about the lost columns of refugees out in the wastelands or plucking children from conflict zones. Those feats were for Owen and Moussa alone. To Roland, such exploits were nothing more than smoke screens, good press if managed properly.

Unlike Owen, Moussa was aware of the bigger picture when it came to Roland's purpose. His obsession with minerals. It was something he had always known. Fully informed from the beginning. A condition of his release. It united Roland and Moussa, a secret, one they never shared with Owen. Even during the years after Ellen, while he remained by Owen's side, Moussa thought it prudent not to change anything, there being too much at stake.

"In time," Owen said, "we'll go back up there, but for now let me do my grieving here, where we made our home."

"Then I'll stay with you. Wait for you to get strong again. God willing, that'll be soon," Moussa said, accepting his new role with the usual equanimity.

He refused to abandon him, not with the press camped outside the gates of Highgrove. Marooned within the situation, they both became prisoners, unable to escape unnoticed, not even by a back gate. The hounds were everywhere, baying for a story, spurred on by a white aid worker raped and murdered. The various versions in the press paid scant attention to the taxi driver, his demise being just as brutal. But then he was Kenyan and black, nothing newsworthy there, just another victim of banditry in Turkana County.

***

The day Owen and Gidean shared a warm beer on a thatched veranda in Bumbuna was the beginning of what Moussa called the perfect storm. It provided a reason for Roland to argue the case for the UN to increase its presence in the north. While Ellen and Owen were settling into their new life, and the ERU concept was being adapted, the first victim of that tempest was Afghanistan. The invasion came with a hollow promise of justice and peace delivered to the world by an enraged president. The initial successes of Operation Enduring Freedom seemed to provide the momentum and confidence to justify a frantic scramble for WMD in Iraq.

Moussa's interest had nothing to do with the overreaching ambitions of the US, or its hubris, but with what he expected would follow soon after. Everything was falling into place, providing the conditions Roland said would one day present themselves, allowing him to return to Bamako.

Only a fool would ignore the impact those wars would have on extremism in North Africa.

The conflicts following 9/11 entertained Gidean immensely. He took every opportunity, up until Ellen's death, to goad Owen, as if those hurried invasions were his personal responsibility. Repeatedly, he mocked the West's wish to democratise the world while secretly admiring such ambitions. "How little you people seem to remember of your own history," became his new refrain. In the spring of 2003, they picked the South African up in the border town of Malaba, on the Kenyan-Ugandan border. Entering the helicopter, Gidean placed his mouth up close to Owen's ear, shouting, "You've crossed into southern Iraq now, on a wild goose chase. Hilariously fucking entertaining."

In those early days, watching the unfolding show as armoured vehicles once again raced across deserts, Owen absorbed the cynicism thrown at him, aware of the circular nature of the narrative. Privately, though, he watched with a heavy heart as an ever-greater delivery of coffins draped in Union Jacks was repatriated by C130 cargo planes, followed by a procession of never-ending hearses through quaint English villages. As the two conflicts protracted beyond any anticipated timelines, Owen started to search the casualty lists for names he recognised.

After Ellen's murder, even though the two wars still raged, he became numb to the continued sacrifices, having his own inner battles to fight. In one of his regular conversations with Anne, Owen pointed out that had he stayed with Ed, she would still be alive. It was a torturous idea, but one he allowed himself. Under such pressures, the ERU concept was discarded, put to one side like a child losing interest in complex guidelines. Operations were scaled back. Their role became little more than servicing Roland's needs. In January of 2007, he made the decision to move the operation from Kenya to Mali, using increased insurgency in the region for his reasoning.

Only days before, Saddam Hussein had been hanged, while the term WMD, an acronym taking a whole coalition to war, was conveniently pushed to one side. In the UK, certain circles called for its prime minister to be charged with war crimes, ending the promise of New Labour.

For Moussa, it all meant he was going home, taking Owen with him, believing the move would provide the distraction his friend needed. Their earlier successes in the Sub-Sahara became a memory. Any reputation they had collapsed inwards quicker than it had been built, but it no longer mattered.

CHAPTER 31

Owen checked the text, not wanting to be late for the flight coming in from London. *I land at 6:30pm. If you can pick me up, great. If not, I'll take a taxi.* He recalled the last time he was meant to meet Mel at an airport and was determined not to make the same mistake. Once he confirmed the details, he went back to his mother's original message, the one resulting in a frenzy of more emails, texts, and then a face-call with Mel to confirm.

Hi Owen, Mum here,

I hope you're more settled in Bamako. Jimmy and family send their love and asked when you intend coming home. I said, and I hope you don't mind, you still need more time.

The hearing went well. Looks like I'll be having Lucy at least two weekends a month. It was a ferocious fight her grandparents put up, but I never backed down, never would. We could have sole custody if you decided to return. Just saying and hoping.

We're all pleased you decided to relocate Abeba. Has she settled? Must be strange moving from Nairobi to Bamako and her new place, but I suppose she's been moving all her life.

Can't imagine how it must feel. She mustn't blame herself. I know you've done a lot of work on that front.

Mel said, maybe, when you decide to come home, Abeba could apply for asylum here in the UK. There's plenty of room in your grandfather's house for all of us.

I'm happier since I made that decision. Pontypridd is where I need to be now, with Jimmy and his family.

Talking of Mel, she said she may be out your way soon, something about an article she's writing for the New York magazine she works for. Humbling to think she insists on visiting every time she's back this way. Loves the hills and mountains. A fit lady.

I've attached a copy of the article she wrote for the association I've set up. Worked a treat. Great exposure from the outdoor pursuit's aspect. So many enquiries. Sadly, there's a real need. Some ex-military struggling with PTSD being referred to us, local lads and lasses, but others from further afield getting involved.

Take care and stay safe. Remember, you have a daughter waiting.

Mum xxx

Mel out his *way soon*. Did she mean Africa, West Africa or Mali? He often needed to read between the lines when dealing with his mother's communications. On this occasion, there was no delay picking up the phone.

"Mum, please… Where? When? Oh, before I forget, there's no attachment to your email. Try again maybe."

"I'm sure she said Mali. Other places too. You'd need to speak to her. Now tell me, how's Abeba? Lucy's always asking."

"You're changing the subject," Owen said, annoyed at the slow progress.

"Something about AIDS, poverty too. Ask her yourself. Now Abeba, tell me how she's managing."

Anne knew about the violent struggle at Highgrove, Abeba refusing to let go of Lucy, something Ellen's parents vehemently denied. But it was all there, on the security video.

Abeba was in Mali because of Owen's UN passport. He had an allowance to fund his household staff, and while he managed to procure an apartment for her, she was, in effect, his housemaid. Should he return to the UK and stop working for the organisation, then there was every possibility she would be returned to Kenya, Somalia even.

"That's not exactly what I said," Mel told him. "What I meant was we'd need to explore every channel because an asylum request might not work. My research? HIV/AIDS across Africa and its link to poorer communities. Nothing new or groundbreaking."

From what Owen read about her career, and there was plenty on the web, Mel was not the type of journalist to go chasing old news. Mali leading on the spread of AIDS, not something that resonated with Owen, but poverty, absolutely.

"Not for my employer. A private client," Mel told him. "A promise I made some time ago. I'll tell you all about it when we meet. And yes, your place will be fine. I won't be staying long."

It must have been fifteen years since they last saw each other, at Emri's funeral, and then they only exchanged pleasantries after the briefest of hugs. Being bereft at the mention of her name had long since abandoned him, but he was intrigued. By his own calculations, it had been some time since he had thought of Mel, certainly not since meeting Ellen. She popped up in conversations with his mother over the years. Anne never missed an opportunity to advertise her numerous promotions and awards. Mel invited her to an awards ceremony in London in 2006. Something to do with investigative journalism, but the finer details failed him.

Before heading to the airport, Owen searched online, finding what he was looking for. Given by some journalistic trust for exposing secret talks between the Taliban and one of the coalition nations. It gained her international recognition and a place with a New York magazine. He also found mention of further investigative work, mainly exposing deceit and contradiction on a wider scale. It seemed her career had gone from exposing hare coursing syndicates in South Yorkshire to shaking the foundations of government. Her *uncompromising and relentless pursuit of the truth* was the wording of one of the more liberal broadsheets when acknowledging her work. While another more popular newspaper referred to her as *a rat willing to wriggle inside drainpipes*.

Owen texted the link to Anne, who took offence that Mel should be referred to as vermin, misinterpreting the honour of such an accolade.

It surprised Owen to learn Mel would only be in the country for some hours, her next flight on her whirlwind tour leaving for Kinshasa the following morning. Even more surprising was her confession.

***

Watching her emerge out of arrivals, the bright lights gave him the opportunity to look for changes the ravages of time inflict with an air of impartiality. From a distance, she seemed youthful and sprightly, not an observation he expected to be reciprocated. One of her hands was swinging back and forth as if on a parade ground, walking at light infantry pace, while the other held the strap of a small daypack hanging from her shoulder. She really was only planning a quick visit, something Owen found difficult to grasp, along with the fact Mel was here at all. She waved the moment she saw him, yet her face remained solemn, detached even, a reminder she was here on business.

Once she was through, Mel instigated the embrace.

"Finally, you make it to the airport," she said, hugging him tightly.

"Yes, finally," he said, hoping the comment was meant to be light-hearted.

Once out of the airport, they headed north towards Martyrs Bridge, turning left before the road crossed the river. They drove west along the southern bank of the Niger, where Owen rented two apartments in a guarded complex. It was a comfortable home but not extravagantly so, unlike Highgrove. Abeba had prepared food, placing wine and water on the table before retiring for the night to her place two floors below.

She had no wish to disturb them.

Owen explained how his visitor was quite a celebrity in the journalistic world. It was an honour that failed to impress Abeba, if that was the intention. She had read the cruel conspiracy theories in many of Nairobi's newspapers regarding Ellen's murder, and it worried her Owen would willingly bring a reporter into his home.

Sitting in her darkened apartment, she watched them arrive.

In the car, they caught up on the years of blank spaces missing in their knowledge of each other's wanderings and exploits, including Owen's loss and Lucy's love for Angharad. Mel never married because no one managed to come close to her expectations. She took most of the blame, explaining her all-consuming workload in a profession she loved and loathed simultaneously.

"AIDS?" Owen asked as they readied themselves to consume the mini feast. "Much more prevalent in other African countries than here. I'm not sure I'm going to be the expert you hoped for. Having read some of your recent work, I don't see how, with everything else going on in the world right now, you're going to generate interest. Not in an obvious way. I'm guessing you have some new angle. Something that's going to hurt someone somewhere. No offence intended."

"None taken," she said, noting a seriousness in his voice she recognised.

"It must be something big because, let's face it, America is losing two wars out east, and you, a journalistic celebrity, are sitting here with me. Far removed from what's happening at the end of the Persian Gulf."

"It's not removed, though," Mel said, refilling their glasses. "The consequence of what's happening out there is already being felt right here."

"In what way?" Owen asked.

"Jihadists appearing in greater numbers in North Africa."

"You sound like one of my colleagues."

"You mean Moussa?"

As she asked, he saw a look of attentive purpose cross her face. It was an expression he had seen before, masking fear and hesitation, or both, but he doubted such traits existed in Mel's repertoire.

"Look Owen, I'll get to the point. AIDS isn't the reason I'm here. I know that's the impression I gave and what I told Anne. Sorry, I made it up. I doubt you'd have met me if you knew the real reason."

"There's a real reason?" Owen asked.

"Corruption. That's the story I'm chasing."

The heavy warmth of the room swamped over him. For the first time, he noticed the aromas filling the air. The smell of fried fish and peanut sauce was the more potent, a clear sign his adrenaline was heightening his senses. The thrum of music he could hear coming from across the corridor was something he had grown used to, having two young French NGOs living next door. But their music had never sounded so intrusive. Apart from Abeba, they were the only fellow dwellers he took time to speak to. The rest of the block remained foreign to him. That was the new Owen, one no longer needing a tribe to call his own.

When he responded, his voice was low as he fought to steady himself.

"So, you lied?"

"Yes, but for good reason. I'm not going to lie to you now I'm here."

"You're here because of Moussa?"

Even as he asked, Owen had already guessed her motive.

"Not entirely. Roland Roden-West and how he uses his position for his own gains."

"That's my boss," Owen said.

"A team of four."

Her tone was matter-of-fact, an observation that irritated him.

"The South African," she said, "your other colleague. The fourth name I have. Used to work for the Gold and Diamond Foundation when he was fronting operations in Johannesburg. Awful company. Modern-day slavery in action. Not that it seems to mean anything down there."

"You know Roland?" Owen asked.

"Not personally, but I've met his father. Like I said, a private client."

"But his father's dead."

"We met a long time ago. He sought me out. A rising star in a journalistic world. Wanted my help, but only once he was no longer around. All his money dragged out the inevitable. I've been busy with other projects recently, but once I got started, the story became too big to ignore, even when I found out it involved you. It's taken some time to gather enough evidence to make it all worthwhile. To fulfil the remit, so to speak."

"Why would Arthur need your help to investigate his son?"

"Owen, I need your assistance, and you need mine."

"Do I?"

"Yes, you do," she said, and for the first time since sharing an embrace at the airport, he saw warmth in her expression. "You're involved in what I'm investigating. I really do apologise for the intrusion, but I don't know a better way of telling you. There simply is no good way to hear such things, which is why I've come to speak to you personally."

"And why would I help you?" he asked. "Is it because of our past?"

A confused expression crossed her face, and then it was gone.

"For Lucy and your mother. And yourself, of course. Call it redemption, whatever, but please believe me, I mean you no harm. One of my main priorities is to get you out of Bamako. Tonight, if necessary, but I'd like your assistance before you leave if it's possible. It won't be safe for you here, even if you decide not to help."

Redemption, he thought, *too late for that.*

If he was part of some wider conspiracy, a notion he started to suspect some time ago, then he should at least listen to what she had to say.

***

On the way back to the airport, there was silence in the car, their reticence matched only by quiet streets. The first light of morning was starting to show, and soon the city would be alive with the intense bustle of another African capital. Having considered her evidence, he decided to do what she asked. A simple look in a satchel, then report back. Even so, agreeing brought about a profound sense of guilt. If her findings were accurate, then right was on her side, regardless of methods. More importantly, from Mel's reasoning, she was offering him a way out.

It was the only reason Bamako was on her itinerary.

"You know," Owen said, breaking the silence, "when you arrived last night, it brought back memories of hiding in those bushes on Balaclava Street. I suppose it was the light in the airport and the fact you don't seem to have aged one bit."

"I'll take that as a compliment," she said. "At least we can talk about that day now, which is better than the last time we tried."

"A lot has happened since then. A whole life, more even."

"What's the light got to do with anything?" she asked. "From what I recall, the place was filthy, all dust, dirt and shadows. It was hot in there, and with all the testosterone flying around, bloody uncomfortable."

"I mean the dust balls, dancing in the sunshine, through the leaves."

For the second time, she threw a quizzical smile in his direction.

"That's not my recollection," she said.

Mel saw his wounded acknowledgement, a slight tightening of the lips. Reaching across, she touched his arm: to give him her strength, to show she understood, or just to feel him, to see if he felt different, the man she knew best as a boy.

"It was chaotic in there. That's what I remember," Mel said.

As a journalist, she knew how trauma can distort memory, with no real order or logic to it, exasperated further when multiple witnesses are involved.

"Yes, it was," Owen said, calling on his own recollections.

"I mean before the real madness started. My clothes, how filthy they were. Billy shouting, desperately seeking your approval. That's what sticks in my mind."

"Billy didn't shout. Not that I recall."

"Hmm, you'll find he did," she said. "He asked you over and over if he could throw his stone."

"No... he just decided that's what he was going to do. Trying to impress you."

"The only person I recall trying to impress anyone was you, overly concerned for my earrings," she said. "We had the whole convoy bearing down on us, and all you were worried about were my cheap imitations and escorting me back to the train station. Charming, but the timing wasn't great."

They both retreated once again into silence and their own personal memories, trying and failing to see the other's point of view. An impossible task after all those years.

"Billy was shouting?" Owen asked as he pulled into the airport's drop zone.

"Yes, at you. He wanted your consent. Billy always looked to you for support in everything he did, eager to gain your praise."

"What did he say?"

"Appealed for your permission. He must have asked twice, three times even. But you ignored him. When he went to throw anyway, you went berserk and really lost your shit."

"Billy said something similar when I last saw him, but I don't recall. Not like that anyway."

Once he was driving back towards the Niger, a return trip he dreaded now that the streets had woken, he had time to go over events. For years he had interpreted Billy's actions as defiant, constructing his own story. He held him accountable for what he considered his overenthusiastic need to impress Mel. All three marched out of the past before business was concluded, going innocently into the future, their friendships tainted, forever.

"I tried to flap my wings, and you stopped me," Billy said.

It seems I did. How stupid of me.

It was easy to ignore Billy in the confined space. Owen was only fourteen, and for the first time, he experienced the power of a girl's presence. An intense pleasure. The brush of Mel's jeans against his body aroused him like he had never known. Her soft face, never demanding makeup, unlike many of the others he knew. Then there was her summer tan. It all became a distraction. Everything changed in an instant, with long shadows turning the brilliant day into darkness.

CHAPTER 32

It had been a long night: the food and wine, the effort to absorb all the evidence, and the runs back and forth to the airport. An irritable tiredness had crept in. Nothing an anticipated quiet day would not resolve. Owen turned the ignition off and sat quietly contemplating. Trying to shape Mel's memories was a futile exercise. Maybe his recollections of the past enabled his own fantasies, a notion he was starting to accept.

Getting out of the car, he noticed a shift in the weather. The stillness of the night hours before was replaced with a light wind whispering through the date palms. Moussa had taken him on an excursion up the Niger towards Ségou some months after arriving. They stayed in a chalet on the edge of a group of palms, owned by one of his acquaintances. Owen recalled watching as the harvesters removed white muslin bags from the pods before gathering the fruits.

"A gift from the Persians," Moussa told him. "What other people can claim to have developed such delicacies?"

Owen recalled looking through the foliage at clear blue skies, happy to be sharing the moment with his friend. The decorative palms growing out of the concrete entrance to his apartment block looked like vagrants compared to the ones upriver, miserable and haggard, with months of dust on their stunted leaves. The seasonal winds blowing in from the north, rushing towards the Atlantic Ocean, would soon pick up sand and throw it across the courtyard. When mixed with rain, the sky would seem like it was bleeding, the redness sticking to everything like glue.

Opening the door to his apartment, the smell of the previous night's dinner was gone, replaced by an aroma of fresh coffee and voices, two of them, laughing and joking as they always did in each other's company. Ali Farka Touré was playing on the speaker. The mix of Malian music with African-American blues informed Owen of the identity of his visitor. Entering the kitchen, all hopes of a day of liberty faded. Here was Moussa, steam rising from a mug in his hand, and there was Abeba, eyes locked on her visitor, leaning back against the table, absorbing his every word.

The remains of their shared dinner had already been cleared away.

"The wanderer returns," Moussa said. "No rest for you. We need to pick up Gidean. Roland wants him back in Bamako before he returns."

***

"My knowledge of Moussa is limited," Mel told him. "But I have people working on it, and when I find anything more, I'll let you know."

The facts, as she presented them, were too strong to claim ignorance. He had seen it in Bumbuna all those years before but viewed it as poor strategy. Corruption never entered his mind. Not then anyway.

"Arthur was dying, and he knew it," Mel said. "You could argue it was the rants of an old man or the conscience of a guilty parent. Whatever view you take, he decided to trust me with what he knew."

"From what I've learnt about Arthur, he had lots of secrets,"

Owen said, as if his statement undermined Mel's knowledge of the man.

"Look, this is highly confidential, and by telling you, I'm breaking all sorts of agreements, promises."

Yet here you are, he thought.

"Roland may have… no… most certainly did kill a man. An ex-lover in Barcelona. A young Spaniard."

"You mean Juan?"

"You knew him?" Mel asked.

"Met him briefly in York. My uni days. We moved in different circles, except for a few alcohol-induced events at the end of my first year. And Roland didn't kill him. It was some random scuffle in a bar. Another tragedy of knife crime. No more sinister than it needs to be."

"And Arthur told you this?"

"Penelope, Roland's sister. Can't remember her exact words. It was a long time ago. But I do know the man sent to Spain to investigate, Jake Withers. I worked with him in Northern Ireland. He's thorough."

"Jake shared his findings with you?"

"No, and I never asked him to. At the time I was nobody to Jake, and when our paths crossed again, there were other more pressing matters. The Jake I knew would never have shared anyway, wouldn't have betrayed Arthur's trust."

"I've seen the evidence," Mel said, "and investigated the incident myself. In my own way. With people *I trust*. There's every possibility he did kill Juan. The motive, jealousy, frustration, both probably. Juan tried to end their relationship. Could no longer deal with Roland. The control and violent behaviour. He had a succession of other boyfriends behind Roland's back, multiple affairs. It backfired on him. Six wounds in total. Not random, fury more like. Roland's 'enveloping obsession' was how his father described it. Arthur got him out quickly, worried whoever killed Juan was really trying to kill his son. At first, they convinced themselves it was mistaken identity, but that quickly changed to talk of a vendetta. Such ideas were fuelled by Roland, trying to manipulate his father, and for a while it worked."

"So why wasn't this taken to the authorities?" Owen asked.

"The way Jake Withers gathered evidence would've landed him in jail for his methods. He used what we now call enhanced techniques. And then there's the irreparable damage it would've caused to Arthur's reputation. Not that it matters now. Jake was killed eighteen months ago in Afghanistan."

"Jake Withers, dead?" Owen asked, unable to hide his shock.

"Didn't you know? An IED. Travelling with a convoy from the Green Zone in Kabul to Bagram Air Base."

Of course, it had to end that way. Inevitable. Jake's lucky run finished. Owen was saddened by the news, not because another ex-colleague paid the ultimate price but because he stopped checking casualty lists some time ago. A consequence of his long period of mourning. There would have been no public recognition for Jake's repatriation, no televised flag-draped coffin, just family in a small chapel, if he had anyone. His name would never be added to a wall in the centre of landscaped gardens, among all the other tributes to our war dead.

The insanity of it all, thought Owen.

"As far as I'm aware, other than Roland," Mel said, "there are only two people left who know what he did. Me, and now you. It's not my intention to open old wounds, besides, nothing could be gained after all this time. And that's not why I was hired. My story's premise is simple, corruption at the highest levels in the United Nations. Roland the example. What Arthur wanted was for me to ruin his son's reputation, in a way he'll never be given responsibility again."

Owen could see it clearly, Arthur reaching out from the past and into the present, Mel his conduit. Chosen for her relentless pursuit of truth or, more likely, her ability to crawl inside drainpipes.

"But why would Arthur want to expose his son?" Owen asked.

"The business in Barcelona wasn't dealt with effectively. Roland literally got away with murder," Mel said. "A sociopath and his father knew it. He watched him climb to a position of authority within the highest echelons, using his genealogy to get there."

"You're going to use your influence to stop him doing what?" Owen asked.

"He's a corrupt UN official."

"I can provide you with any number of them," Owen said, irritated by such a patent response.

"His methodology, Owen."

"I'm assuming you've been paid for your services?" he said, going on the offensive.

"There are some funds sitting in a trust. Money I can use in whatever capacity I see fit. That's if I meet some simple guidelines. I have a charity in mind, but I'm not going to discuss that now. That's my redemption. It won't harm my reputation either. Exclusives don't always fall into one's lap. I agree with you, corruption doesn't necessarily make Roland stand out, but his unorthodox practices do. By exposing him, we get to bigger people. Those powerful corporations stripping this land of everything of value. Roland can see what's happening in Mali, right across North Africa. The French see it too. He's readying himself. Trying to get a head start."

"I don't see the big story. Locate the natural resources, protect them for the people they belong to. That's Roland's way. Maybe he takes some of the minerals for himself. Which only makes him a petty thief. Not necessarily big news."

"It's a disguise, Owen. Deception to deflect from who he really is. An international fraudster."

Owen stared hard at the floor, observing nothing. Then he looked up, searching her face.

Mel looked back, acknowledging he had changed. She could see it in his appearance. Much older and less passionate, aged beyond his years, the greying of his hair, and the crow's feet extending beyond the immediate limits of his eyes the evidence. He was thin, not in the athletic way she remembered, more emaciated around the cheekbones. Underneath those changes, he was still handsome and recognisable, but not for long.

"What I'm being told," Mel said, "is huge deposits of gold in the north. I also know Roland sent the South African up there recently to verify what Moussa knows."

"Wait," Owen said, interrupting her flow. "Who's telling you all this?"

"It's what I do."

"A profession in which you've excelled," he said, his counter-offensive losing its momentum under such pressure.

"It's clear Roland will use his influence to protect whatever's there," she said, ignoring his facetious comment. "Like he did in Sierra Leone, the DRC, and any other number of examples I could provide. Not for humanitarian reasons, but profit. The people who need the UN's protection getting nothing. You were in Sierra Leone, carnage for those left to fend for themselves. That's fine for the corporates, who have freedom to look the other way. Everyone getting fatter on the riches. Gold, salt, kaolin, phosphate and limestone, even petroleum, are all out there, Owen. These materials should've been their salvation, not their demise. The powerful, as always, taking what they want. With those areas in the north secured, and with UN backing based on Roland's recommendations, there'll be a rush to start blasting, and he has his favourites. The triumph of capitalism. We're talking billions, *more*, and some will do anything to get there first, beat the Islamists, and, of course, the Tuareg. That's where Moussa comes in, his influence. Roland's a dangerous entrepreneur, not a humanitarian, and he's readying himself to sell the rights of access."

"You're not expecting me to single-handedly take on the mining companies?" Owen asked.

"Nothing so complex," she said, acknowledging his blithe mockery. "You'd end up in the desert with your throat cut."

"So, what is it you want me to do?"

"Go and pick up the gold prospector, as you always do. Make it look normal, which it is. Find some way of looking into his satchel. The one he guards so well. Then tell me what's inside. You must keep in touch, if only to let me know you're safe."

"And that's it?" Owen asked.

After everything she presented, this was all she wanted.

"Leave Mali as soon as you get back to Bamako. I'll quote you in my column. Your exact words. Even use your name. Whatever's in the satchel, I'll include it in my findings. Nothing will be published until you're out. Then by the time you land in London, or wherever you decide to go, the whole world will know you played a part in exposing corruption. My report is all but written. I just need a quotation to defend you."

"Become a whistleblower, that's what you're asking?"

"A way out, Owen. It's why I'm here. To offer you this chance. The wonderful thing about life is we can change, take back control."

"Sounds too simple—"

"—yet dangerous, even more so when my findings are published. Vindicates you, making your position here untenable. Become the hero of the story, Owen, and then get out because if you remain, you'll be their antagonist. If you don't want any part in it, fine, but you'll still need to leave."

"And if I agree, will it be enough to ruin Roland?"

"Not just him. It'll expose corruption at the highest levels. UN, African Union, governments giving away their country's wealth. The mining industry too. Those promoting their own interests with their campaigns. But the catalyst for all this, Roland. It'll destroy him."

"Two birds, one stone," Owen said.

"Many birds. Let's crucify the fucking lot. Let the world know the service Roland provides at their expense and who benefits."

***

Sitting with Moussa discussing Roland's most recent request, a tepid mug of coffee in hand, Owen considered the few details Mel had on him. His time in jail seemed as far as her knowledge stretched. Moussa had stood at his side through all his grief, while others acted like it was business as usual. Treachery never ended well, but he would do all he could to protect Moussa, even if it meant bringing him into his confidence. But that depended on what else Mel could uncover.

There were good reasons to make this his final trip, Lucy being the top of his list. The thought of her and what he must do before seeing her again gave him a yearning for what could be. Not since Ellen had he experienced such optimism about future possibilities. There was reason enough to be grateful, not because of Mel's guarded promise of absolution, nothing so grand, but because he had been waiting for his life to start again. And, just like that, there was hope.

"You want me to arrange a helicopter to Mopti?" Owen said, looking between Moussa and Abeba. "Why not all the way to Raz El Ma?"

"Have you seen the forecast? Sandstorm, a big one, spreading right across the Cercle of Goundam. Predictions suggest it could reach as far as Burkina Faso."

"Then let's wait for it to clear."

"Owen, he wants Gidean back. Not next week but now. He's been gone far too long as it is."

"He's probably enjoying himself. Have you even told him?"

"I haven't heard from Gidean for days, but I have people who know where he is. North of Raz El Ma. I've told them to bring him in, regardless of excuses. We'll meet him there. You'll need to arrange a vehicle. Load it on the helicopter. From Mopti we'll have to proceed with wheels."

"We can't go north of Mopti on our own," Owen said, "and certainly not in a vehicle."

"Mopti's as far as we can safely take an aircraft to avoid the storm," Moussa said. "We won't be on our own. We're picking up an escort once we land. They'll take us the rest of the way. It was all arranged in Geneva. Roland tried to argue it wasn't necessary, but it's a quarrel he lost."

"No way am I taking a UN escort into that inhospitable place. Sanctioned or not. We both know it's asking for trouble, even with you by my side."

Moussa laughed at Owen's assumptions.

"Not UN, French military," he said. "They politely insisted. Roland said they put on the pressure, arguing there were no suitable alternatives. They adamantly refused to accept the organisation could look after itself anywhere north of Mopti. Hopefully, that goes some way in reassuring you."

"Hmm, slightly better, I suppose, but not by much," Owen said.

"We leave tonight. While you're getting everything sorted, I'm taking Abeba to brunch. I see you ate well last night, which gives you more time to make a start. I'll see you at the heliport, 8pm. No need for a team this time. Just a pilot."

Abeba and Moussa were in love. The revelation came when the three of them were resting outside a mountain village: Siby, a rural commune southwest of Bamako. They were relaxing on a rocky summit, where they spent some time observing the views across the plains, looking for a place to set up camp. It was late afternoon, and Owen was tracking a hawk hovering above. Moussa told him it was tame and somewhere out on the plains would be a hawker, waiting for its return. Having fallen asleep, the buzz of flies woke him. Opening his eyes, Owen found himself alone. The other two were sharing the shade of a rocky arch shrouded in thorny bush, somewhere below Owen's resting place. The muffled sound of voices gave away their position.

"I lost a baby some years ago," he heard Abeba say, "but it was a blessing. No, not in Nairobi, in Somalia. He was a rebel, and I didn't belong to him… Yes, it was a blessing."

As the two men pitched tents, he caught Moussa watching her as she lay curled in the shade, head resting on a small rock, her hand, palm upwards, pillowing her cheek, eyes twitching, locked in a dream.

It had been a hard day's trek for them all.

Moussa watched Abeba as she slept, as if trying to interpret what she was seeing. When she woke, he was still looking. She smiled back, acknowledging his affection.

Owen never wanted to return to Bamako, wishing to remain where friends could fall helplessly in love. A place surrounded with lush green forests and rocky outcrops, where water flowed over cliffs into perfectly formed pools.

A space where life was simple.

***

Once the two of them had left, heading for their favourite Malian restaurant, Owen opened the French doors before stepping onto his balcony. He could see through a gap between buildings to an exposed stretch of the Niger. Pirogues were making their way backward and forward, painted in reds, blues and yellows. It was a setting epitomising the pastoral until a tug came chugging by, diesel spewing from a single stack. Maybe it was going all the way to the Niger Delta, following the brown current, an idea not entertained for long because a vessel like that would never survive such a colossal journey. Soon though, Owen would be heading in that direction with Moussa, following the flow upstream.

Leaning into the railing, he felt the vibrations of the building responding to the increasing strength of the wind. There was no sign of dust, but it would come. He could sense it in the air. From his position on the seventh floor, he recalled another time when he looked out from his eyrie, waiting for a man to cross a border. Since that day, it seemed he had always been waiting to pick up somebody, somewhere, for someone. Going back inside, he heard music once again coming from across the corridor. It seemed the NGOs were spending another day indoors, entertaining themselves.

Before he started planning, Owen recalled Mel's advice, doubting if he knew what normal was anymore.

Working late into the day, he listened to the BBC's World Service reporting on the British army's withdrawal from Basra, a town to be left under the control of Iranian-backed militias. Gordon Brown said openly it was pre-planned and organised, not a defeat.

At least, Owen thought, *I just need to load one vehicle and fly it to Mopti. Not organise a full-scale retreat.*

Yet, like the prime minister, he would need to be liberal with the truth during the next few days.

CHAPTER 33

Moussa pressed hard on the brake, causing them both to be thrown forward, seatbelts digging deep into the flesh of their shoulders, while the vehicle's tyres struggled to grip the soft sand. They slid across the desert's floor before coming to an uncomfortable stop. Both looked through the windscreen at swirling granules thrown up by the vehicle in front.

"Why do you suppose he's stopped?" Moussa asked, as if the answer was etched in glass.

"Ask me one I know," Owen said, reaching for the handset dangling from a hook above his head. "But I'll find out."

The satnav, its triangular vehicle symbol flashing orange, informed them they were still some distance from their destination. Before he could press the send button to seek clarification, the radio crackled into life.

"We need to speak…"

The voice coming across the airwaves was Bastien Toussaint, a French army officer tasked to escort them to their rendezvous outside of Raz El Ma, at the western edge of Lake Faguibine. The lake's dry bed was a reminder of the droughts plaguing the region. Once an annual occurrence, the flooding of its tributaries from the Niger was a rarity.

"Centuries ago, Arab writers wrote about this rich land, its fertile soil, and fresh fish," Moussa told him. "Now nothing grows or changes, and people argue among themselves, holding us back."

The prospect of spending any more time than was necessary outside the air-conditioned cabin in the midday heat filled Owen with dread, but he could hear trepidation in Bastien's voice.

"You stay behind the wheel. I'll go see what the problem is," Owen said.

"Good plan. I'll keep the air-con blasting for your welcomed return."

Knowing it was reaching fifty degrees outside, Owen hoped Bastien would keep the conversation to a minimum. Opening the door, he was hit by a wall of heat, warming the cornea of his eyes, a testament to the intensity of the environment. Taking a sandy-coloured *shemagh* from around his neck, Owen covered his nose and mouth.

Climbing out of his seat, he noticed how the desert's surface shifted, building against his boots, as if some menacing force was in motion.

"Here, take the sat phone," Moussa said, shouting over the engine noise of the vehicle pulling up from behind. "Just in case you need to contact Roland."

"You're unusually keen to keep this convoy moving," Owen said.

"It's not every day we're tasked directly from Geneva."

Whilst it was true, he still questioned Moussa's suggestion. He had moved from an earlier passive approach, joking he was only there to drive, to a more active one.

"For pity's sake, close the door," Moussa said. "It's getting warm in here."

As the door closed, Owen noticed the donkey shit dead centre of the United Nations badge on his side of the vehicle. The excrement was splattered across the map of the world, ruining the intended equidistant projection. Owen smiled at the entertainment it must have provided those stone-throwing children. It had been some hours since then, and there was little sign of life this far out.

The further north they went, the safer it was to head across open ground, away from roads, a decision made by Bastien.

The vehicles had stopped in an exhausted wadi, with nothing but open desert on all sides. The occasional dusty swirl of sand could be seen rising in the distance, forming mini tornados. It was difficult to tell what was making such eruptions, the harmattan winds or other vehicles moving out there in the baking heat.

Up ahead, Owen could see Bastien climbing down from his vehicle.

The second escort was sat idling at the rear, its turret moving left and right, surveying deep into the desert.

Steel to their front and rear was a reassuring sign of the importance placed by the French on their escort duties. Or, as Moussa suggested, they were using him as a free guide into the northern regions. A reconnaissance opportunity.

Owen pushed against the wind grateful the officer chose the lee side for the impromptu meeting.

"What's the hold-up?" Owen asked.

"My HQ's telling me we no longer have clearance to go any further north today. We'll try again tomorrow. They want me to turn this convoy around. Head back to Mopti. I've requested a safe route so we don't retrace our steps."

There was no need for a reminder of the potential danger this far out, but Owen tried not to comment on the minutiae of Bastien's decisions. Roland would never support going back, not with Gidean still out there on his own.

"Did they give you a reason for the sudden change of plan?" Owen asked.

"Suspicious activity somewhere to our north, in this area here."

Bastien pointed to a place on his map so Owen could see the proximity of the potential threat. With some relief, he noted the disturbances he saw earlier came from a different area. It reassured him it was indeed sand devils dancing to the tune of the storm's erratic behaviour.

"Anything more specific, Bastien? It's not enough to authorise a turnaround. I have a colleague out there waiting for us."

"Sorry to say this, but my command informed me you don't have the authority here. I do."

Bastien was right, Owen was not authorised to undermine the decisions of a military escort, not on his own say. At least there was no need to go back and collect the phone. A good judgement by Moussa after all.

"Okay, you have your orders. What I'm going to do is put you on to my boss, the person who tells your people what to do. Once you've spoken, we either go on or we turn around."

Taking the phone from his pocket, Owen rotated the bulbous antenna to point it upwards into its call position, ready to pick up available satellites. Then he dialled. After speaking briefly, he passed it to Bastien.

Owen saw concern on his face and regretted having to do this to the soldier, knowing all he wanted was to impress his own people.

Before he spoke, Bastien asked, "What's your boss's name?"

"Roland, just call him Roland."

Once he had spoken, Bastien pushed the antenna back into its housing and looked at Owen.

"Well… what're we doing?" Owen asked.

"We go on," Bastien said, handing the phone back. "It seems my HQ has been overridden."

As Owen was about to return to his vehicle, the thump of gunfire erupted in the far distance, causing the Frenchman to jump at the aggressive sound. Owen assumed it was the first time the young officer had heard the discharge of weapons outside training. He wanted to reassure him, tell him they must keep moving forward, regardless, if only to atone for past sins. But how could he share such personal thoughts with a stranger?

CHAPTER 34

Hidden by walls of sand in the darkness of a cooling desert night, the three vehicles sat in a dry riverbed, a short distance south of Raz El Ma. Stars shone undisturbed in a brilliance rarely seen in the urban sprawls of city dwellers. A light show with a celestial context, making these men seem insignificant in the endless sands. The undulating surface gave the impression of a frozen sea in all directions.

Moussa told them while the storm had weakened, it was not over, and they should prepare for the night ahead.

"My men will pick up any movement long before it reaches us," Bastien said, in an outward attempt to reassure.

His words were served to comfort himself as much as convince Owen or Moussa, who both knew saying and believing were two different things.

"And if you detect anything out there?" Moussa asked while proffering dates picked up in the souk before leaving Bamako.

"We have options."

Three to be precise, thought Owen, *fight, flight, or freeze.*

Not wishing to add to Bastien's woes, he kept such ideas to himself, especially as they had been ordered to remain south of the village until morning.

They were sat around a dwindling fire, drinking lukewarm coffee one of the French soldiers had prepared some hours before, the blackened pot left warming on the dying embers.

"Gidean won't be in Raz El Ma until first light tomorrow," Roland informed Owen, calling back less than an hour after Bastien had been ordered to keep moving north. "It looks like a night in the desert," he said, with no acknowledgement that such an order came with risks.

"They won't like it," Owen said. "They're already outside their comfort zone. Me also."

"They insisted on taking the task, Owen. We never asked them to. Didn't want them. One night. A few more hours than planned. The French have a responsibility to this country, one going way back. And we can't just leave Gidean to find his own way home…"

"Time for a shovel patrol," Owen said, once the last drops of coffee were finished.

Rising, he spat a hard-coated seed from one of Moussa's dates into the fire. On impact, small sparks rose into the night sky, accentuating the shadows on their faces.

"More than we need to know," Moussa said, as he watched Owen wander across to the vehicles. "Maybe it's my fruit moving you in such a way?"

"Maybe," Owen said, "but it's more likely your driving and the thought of getting back in the cab with you that moves my bowels so."

"Don't go too far out," Bastien said.

Bastien's advice was far from Owen's reasoning as he opened the door to retrieve the sat phone and find a shovel.

What he sensed more than anything was Moussa's eyes boring into his back.

Walking out of the depression, he disappeared into a shrouding darkness. Finding a suitable mound, he threw the shovel to one side, its purpose served. All about was silence, as if he was the only person within a thousand miles. But a short distance away were three vehicles and a small group of men, all dependent on each other.

To the north was their destination, at the tip of a sand lake.

Dialling, he heard a low mumble of voices, indistinguishable, drifting on the air, mixed with the faint tang of smoke. In other circumstances, Owen would have enjoyed the experience, but he no longer had any love for the desert. It was unlike the fertile lands Moussa introduced him to on their excursions beyond the limits of Bamako.

"Hello," answered a familiar voice.

"It's Owen."

"Owen! Finally, you ring. Please tell me you're back in Bamako," Mel said.

"No, delayed."

"For God's sake, why?"

"Gidean's not where he's supposed to be—"

"Never mind him now, you need to leave."

"—but he'll be there in the morning."

"I'll have to manage without, if necessary."

"I can't turn this around. Too late. Roland wouldn't allow it anyway."

"I thought you'd be back by now," she said in desperation.

"And Moussa?" he asked, almost pleading, wishing he could shape her answer. "What more did you find out about him?"

Owen stopped talking, tilting his head to one side, listening.

He heard the faint voice of Mel as he lowered the phone, her words muffled. Panicked, he pressed the red button. What he heard was footsteps walking in his direction, coming from the camp. Looking up, he saw the dark figure of a man standing on a dune above, rifle in hand, peering into the night.

"*Monsieur, vous devez revenir, ce n'est pas sûr ici seul.*"

"Yes, I know it's not safe. I was taking a *shit!*" Owen said, feigning anger. After stuffing the phone down the front of his shirt, he searched frantically for the shovel.

Walking back to the laager, he noticed the wind had increased in strength, strong enough to rekindle the dying embers of the fire. Before rejoining the pair, he returned the phone, placing it on the back seat, confident Moussa had not seen him take it with him.

Moussa was busy delivering one of his lectures to his most recent advocate. The awkward silence when they were drinking coffee and eating dates was gone, late-night stories taking its place.

"Fifty miles east of here," Moussa was saying to Bastien, "on the great bend in the Niger, is Timbuktu. Caravans once met in its flourishing centre to trade gold, salt, ivory, even slaves, long before any westerners arrived. When Mansa Musa made his great pilgrimage to Mecca, passing through Egypt, his grandiose exploits rocked the economic foundations of that nation. Seeing such wealth drew the West's appetite towards this land, and its gold. But it wasn't until the nineteenth century your people managed to find their way across the desert. Centuries before, a more civilised and progressive people beat you to it. The greatest of cities, once renowned for its Islamic university, became a celebrated centre of learning."

They both listened, Bastien transfixed and fascinated, and Owen because that was what he always did when Moussa told stories. In the darkness he became one of those nomads he often spoke about, wandering from oasis to oasis, sharing stories across a fire. A role he fitted into perfectly.

The dates kept on coming, sweet and juicy, a welcomed fruit introduced so far back in time that some considered them native to these lands, but Owen knew the truth.

"The city rises out of a sand sea. You French eventually found it and then conquered it... Did your mastery of modern warfare make you more intelligent, more legitimate? And now you're here again. Not because of us but the Sahel jihadists, who come to destroy our history, with their eyes fixed on yours. Maybe it's time you all started to respect what we've always known, this desert, like any other, can't be tamed."

Yet here we are, thought Owen, *we three men of different nations.*

"It's a matter of honour, born out of responsibility," Bastien said, appearing flustered at Moussa's accusation.

"This is Mali. For you there is no honour here. As for responsibility, it's a sickness endemic in your world. All that'll come of it is unrest."

Owen watched the Frenchman listening like an eager student.

Be careful, Bastien, because all he knows could be dangerous, he wanted to say.

It was late, and a tightness in his stomach reminded him how close they were to their destination, a short drive across the sand, making him more certain of the outcome he desired.

CHAPTER 35

"Bastien, you need to remain on the outskirts with your men," Moussa said, as the three stood around a lifeless fire.

"Not something I'm going to do," the officer said.

"If you take those vehicles into the village, it'll cause panic, maybe even a response. Some of the men in there will be armed."

"More reason for us to go with you."

"Their weapons are for self-defence only, and you don't look as if you come in peace. They're expecting us, UN representatives, to pick up one of our observers. Unarmed. The last thing they want to see are French soldiers. It's best you remain on the outside. We'll only be a couple of streets in. Once we have our colleague, then we'll leave. No more than fifteen, twenty minutes at most. We can take one of your hand-held radios to call for assistance if it helps."

Bastien tried to object, but Moussa cut him off.

"These are my people. They trust me. I spoke to them before we left Bamako and again from Mopti for reassurance. Let's not give them reason to doubt my trust."

Moussa glanced in Owen's direction, looking for a reaction. While Owen managed to hold his stoical expression, there was a puzzled look in his eyes, but this was Moussa's world and his people, a notion making his suggestion perfectly reasonable.

The Frenchman pulled an aerial photograph from a map pocket sewn into the side of his desert trousers. Laying it on the ground, he indicated the other two should squat beside him, take a closer look. It was a village, but not one Owen recognised. There were various tactical markings across its surface, with other crosses and circles. No order to it that Owen could see.

Scrutinising the detail, Moussa took his time to take it all in.

"Raz El Ma," he said, looking at Owen.

"Show me," Bastien said, with a newfound confidence, "where you intend to pick up your colleague. *Exactly.*"

Moussa studied the photograph, moving it into a position of orientation before brushing off sand gathering on its surface.

"There," he said, pointing, "a couple of streets in. And you'll be just here. Not far away."

Bastien took a pen from his breast pocket, circling the house where Moussa had indicated. Then he did the same with the place where he would be waiting. Owen could see a street that led directly from point A to point B.

"It'll take minutes to get to us, if needed," Moussa said. "Let's not make this any more difficult than it needs to be."

"But I'm with you," Bastien said, "and I was tasked as your escort."

"Don't turn them into an enemy. It won't suit anyone's purpose, including those who sent you."

"Okay, two streets in. No more than twenty minutes," Bastien said.

The soldier stood, securing the photograph back in his pocket. Walking away from the pair, he spat into his goggles before clearing away sand with his scarf. Then he climbed the side of his vehicle, indicating with a thumbs-up it was time to start moving.

There was a noticeable change in Bastien's approach. The way he demanded the location was different from the naïve soldier sitting by the fire listening attentively. Perhaps both of Owen's travel companions were moving through different personas, diverse forms of disguise, each intended to confuse. Now they were only a short distance from Raz El Ma, it mattered little because Owen knew he was dependent on both, regardless of any façade. He had his own secret to maintain, hiding his own guilt, something he imagined was written all over his face.

"Where did that come from?" Moussa asked, once more looking through the windscreen, trying to maintain a safe distance. "The air photograph, pre-marked and deliberate."

"He's military. Of course he's going to have such things."

"But we didn't reveal our destination until Mopti."

"Maybe Roland or Geneva."

"Not Roland. We spoke, and he left it to me to decide when I should proffer such information. You're ex-army. What're all those symbols?"

"I don't get why we need to withhold information," Owen said.

"This is much more sensitive than usual. The Tuareg can be territorial in this part of the world. Who can blame them? And now they have the aspirations of Islamists to deal with. If they know what Roland wants to achieve before we've had the opportunity to speak to them, explain how they'd benefit, then all could be lost. We don't want to be responsible for all that knocking on our door."

"Is there something I'm not aware of, Moussa? Anything you haven't shared?"

"Those symbols?" Moussa asked, ignoring the question.

"Helicopter landing site. Key locations. Routes in and out. The rest I'm not sure. Look, he's had many chances to mark the photograph since Mopti."

"Making all those decisions himself? For what purpose?"

"That's what comes of all this fucking secrecy."

Owen was becoming angry, yet he knew such a response would achieve nothing. All he needed to do was look inside a satchel. Even though he was aware of this, he still found it difficult to settle and accept the simplicity of his role.

With no warning, Moussa started to brake, responding to the movements of Bastien's vehicle. They both watched as it manoeuvred, veering to their left, allowing room for them to pass.

Buildings started to appear out of the storm, revealing the entrance to a street.

Point A, Owen acknowledged.

Coming alongside Bastien, Moussa slowed, but then, like an afterthought, accelerated once again, driving into the village.

Owen calculated they were no more than a few hundred metres from the building where Gidean would be waiting. Looking through his wing-mirror, he could see the rear vehicle pulling into the right, reversing against a low wall, pointing its turret back in the direction from where they came.

"You need to stop," Owen said. "We didn't pick up the handset."

"Leave it," Moussa said. "We're almost there. Let's maintain the momentum."

The two escort vehicles became nothing more than impressions of themselves in the rearview mirror. Then they were gone, the dust engulfing their steel structures. Owen noticed the building from the photograph and imagined Gidean waiting inside. Surely, he would be smarting at having to surrender his foraging duties, mustering some abusive welcome to celebrate their arrival. For the first time, since their meeting on the Rokel, Owen was keen to see the South African. Not because of any kind of friendship they shared, that had never been possible. It was more a wish to be away from this place, back in the open desert, where he felt safer. Twenty minutes, and then they would be heading back towards Mopti.

To Owen's surprise, they drove on, deeper into the village.

"Wasn't that the building?" Owen said, looking over his shoulder.

"I must have lost my bearings. Same road, just a little further in."

Owen reached for the handset above his head, finding Moussa's navigational embarrassment difficult to accept. His intention was to inform Bastien and allow him to decide his own next move.

"It's not working," Moussa said. "Not when I checked this morning."

Owen pressed and spoke. Nothing. The radio was dead. Turning, he looked along the back seat, telling himself the sat phone would have to do. Even though it would take longer to make the connection, Bastien would be able to react to the change of plan.

"Where is it?" he said, staring at an empty space.

"Where's what?"

"The phone, Moussa. It was on the back seat."

"You were the last to use it. Last night, out in the desert," Moussa said, bringing the vehicle to a stop. "We're here now anyway. We can find it later."

Getting out, Moussa walked around the bonnet before stopping in front of a wooden door, a weathered entrance leading into a two-storey building. Its exterior blended effortlessly with the landscape, like the rest of the monochrome dwellings.

Rather than enter, Moussa waited for Owen to follow.

Stepping down from the passenger seat, he noticed how deserted the village appeared. Somewhere in the near distance, he could hear a loud bellowing, an alien and unnerving sound.

"Camels," Moussa said. "Feeding time. They're excited."

Pushing the door inwards, Moussa lowered his head below the lintel and entered.

Hours before, they were sleeping in a depression, their presence unknown to the village a short distance away. Now they were inside Raz El Ma, their arrival announced when their vehicles emerged out of the storm. It was a place nature seemed to be doing its utmost to choke out of all existence, drowning it in sand. How had this become Owen's fate, the son of a simple coal miner? In recent times, he had experienced many moments of inadequacy, but outside the building it was much stronger, like something stabbing at his pride now Moussa seemed to be the one controlling the narrative.

Following his friend, Owen stepped inside, his heart pumping much too loudly for what was meant to be routine. The reason for his apprehension was obvious. He no longer knew who was deceiving whom.

All this betrayal was born out of human weakness, in that point he was certain, making them all vulnerable.

CHAPTER 36

Moussa was talking to a Tuareg when Owen entered, recognisable from his turban and veil, its iridescent indigo a trademark of the people from the region. It was open at the face, exposing a weather-beaten and ageing man with a greying beard. Around his waist he wore a thick belt with a jambiya attached, the dagger's sheath decorated in gold. One of the blue men of the desert. Owen estimated he was in his late sixties, possibly older.

Voices could be heard in a back room using a language Moussa had spoken for the first time when he shouted at children the day before.

The Tuareg gestured they sit, his hand, palm raised, indicating where each should place themselves on the carpeted floor. The intricacy of the pattern and its exceptional beauty demonstrated its material worth. At the edges, a dried mud floor formed a margined gap between the carpet's extremities and the room's walls. Scattered around the floor were patterned cushions aimed at comforting guests.

In the centre of the decorative arrangement, contrasting with the setting, was a brown leather satchel.

Owen remained standing, taking in his surroundings.

"Take a seat," Moussa said, his earlier authoritative tone gone.

"Where's Gidean?" Owen asked, trying to affect a calm composure.

"It's been a long journey. Please sit, and then we'll talk."

Owen took his place, the cushions providing an element of luxury his body appreciated after a night on the desert's floor. Their host positioned himself opposite, both hands on the hilt of his dagger. Off to one side was a prayer mat rolled up neatly. Lying next to it was a rifle, a reminder of the present danger they all faced. It was a sensation not experienced since their excursions across Kenya's northern borders.

In that moment it seemed like those emotions had been with him for most of his life.

Two more Tuareg appeared, both with rifles slung over their shoulders, carrying food and drink. From the smell, Owen knew it was Arabic coffee, *gahwa*, contained in an ornamented *dallah*. He had drunk it many times with Moussa and Abeba during their frequent visits to the souks, sitting in narrow alleyways sharing stories and people watching. It was a spicy, bitter coffee. Owen never claimed to enjoy the taste, but he always chose to drink it anyway, not wanting to appear ungrateful. The food was simple: *tiguadege na*, a meat dish in peanut butter sauce, with *ngome*, a flatbread, and some dates. One of the men placed the food in the middle of the group on a silver tray while the other poured coffee into small cups.

During formalities, Moussa remained deep in conversation with the man opposite.

Once the offerings were served, he stopped talking and addressed Owen.

"This is my father, Wararni Mohammed."

"Your father," Owen said, the unexpected announcement threatening his composure.

Owen stared at Wararni, searching for evidence they were indeed related. Through the ravages of time, he could see a resemblance. Was this really the artisan Moussa had mentioned?

He wore a permanent smile, not mocking or malign, but benevolent and welcoming. There was a contentment about him too, one permeating his whole being.

"Why is he here?" Owen asked.

"He wants to bring the clans together, discuss an independent state for the Tuareg. Because of such dreams, he's considered an enemy by those who sit in government."

Owen offered nothing in response, absorbing the introduction, trying to work out where Moussa's father fitted into Roland's plan.

Father and son took the food and drink while continuing to converse, enjoying their reunion. What Owen noticed most was a softness in their voices, demonstrating respect and sincerity. It reminded him of the times he shared similar delicacies prepared by Abeba back in the apartment, when all three would sit at the table together like family, talking into the early hours. It was obvious the meeting had been pre-arranged, shaped to fit their needs long before Moussa had directed him to make the arrangements for their flight to Mopti.

"My father wants to know what you thought of the winds last night," Moussa said. "And, Owen, please, eat something. We have very little time."

Owen leaned forward, taking one of the dates, the sweetness a luxuriant distraction. Removing the fruit from its seed, he sucked on it before placing it on a small saucer.

Wararni watched, interested in the way the westerner secured all the juices from the fruit, like a man of the desert, one who understood the scarcity of moisture.

"An uncomfortable night," Owen said, struggling to make sense of proceedings.

"He asked if it's true this dust can be carried all the way to Europe?" Moussa said, continuing to interpret for his father.

"Yes, it can, and it does. On occasion," Owen said. "The heat too."

The old man laughed at the possibility that anything from his world could travel so far, affecting others.

"He says at least the wind wasn't cold, something we Berbers feel in our bones. Even more now he's old. He wants to know if you smelt the sweet scent it carried?"

Owen contemplated the statement before glancing back at Moussa's father.

"No, I didn't," he said.

"You should learn to manipulate such winds," Moussa translated. "It allows one to take advantage of his foe, moving unnoticed within the dust. Our people know how to become part of the desert when the wind lifts the sand. To outsiders, we can seem like ghosts among our enemies when adversaries hide in the folds of the ground outside our villages. Many an army has been outmanoeuvred in such conditions."

"He saw us?" Owen asked.

"They didn't arrive until early this morning. Maybe the villagers were watching. My father no longer spends time this far south, concerned these places are being watched."

"Watched, Moussa?"

"There are many eyes looking this way. Bastien, for example."

"Because of gold, that's why," Owen said, glancing at the satchel.

"My father is concerned the desert will take this village, like it has others. You know, Owen, there are places you can dig to find buildings where it's possible to shelter undetected. Ancient sites, long forgotten."

As they spoke, the two guards returned, clearing away the refreshments, taking with them the prayer mat, and placing the rifle by Wararni's side.

"He says you should take the bag," Moussa said.

"Gidean, where is he?" Owen asked, making no attempt to retrieve the satchel.

"Take a look, Owen. That's what you came for. Then your job is done."

Moussa took the bag and placed it closer, within arm's reach.

"How did you know?"

"I was told when your friend arrived, when she left, and that she's now safely in Kinshasa. I also know what you discussed. Come, look inside," Moussa said, a hint of impatience creeping into his voice.

"You spied on me?"

"Sometimes for your own safety, but more recently, for mine."

"And Roland, he sanctioned it?"

"I don't need Roland's approval anymore. His purpose is served."

"Does he know about my visitor?"

"If he does, then not from me. I've never said anything to Roland that would compromise you. I'm not sure your journalist will bring him down, though. He's one of the world's survivors. Let's hope she's the iconoclast her profile suggests. Now take the bag, or they will."

The two Tuareg guards watched, making Owen uneasy, the sweat running down his spine an indicator of his discomfort.

Leaning forward, he sat the satchel upright, its two buckles facing him. The fading leather was not so different from the exposed faces of the Tuareg, sunburnt and creased. Unbuckling the two straps, he lifted the flap before pushing it to the rear. It fell easily, the old leather no longer able to resist such a manoeuvre.

Four sets of eyes watched as he tilted the bag forward to look inside...

It was empty.

Peering into the void, he wondered if he had ever really known Moussa. Was it all just stories? Owen was no stranger to betrayal, having taken a man's life because of subversion. The man he killed had similar aspirations to Moussa's father.

"Why is it empty?" Owen asked, returning the satchel to an upright position.

"There is no gold."

Owen nodded in agitated disbelief.

"So why are we here?"

"The tale of Labtayt. Do you recall?" Moussa asked.

"I remember."

"Then you'll know without that rumour, I would never have made it out of jail alive. I created a story to bait someone, and Roland was the first to bite. Labtayt was his dream, Gidean's too. The deal to end all deals. I knew the reality and hid it from him, then waited. Roland wanted to use me, my people too, to get what he always desires, wealth. He wants to sell what he thinks are untapped resources. To the corporates. In return, they'd get the rights along with guaranteed security. All provided by the UN, along with the Tuareg's blessing."

"You do realise jail, once again, is the best you can hope for when all this is revealed," Owen said. "There are powerful people investing heavily on that lie."

"You mean the despots calling the shots? Making their own rules. Like your politicians who lie openly, never facing the consequences of their actions. The West no longer knows the difference between what is real and what is fake, or even cares. That's what makes them vulnerable, like Roland."

"It must have been a shock when you were told the French were coming along?" Owen asked.

"Nothing I could do, not with this storm building. As Roland pointed out, we didn't have any viable alternatives. 'Let's turn it to our advantage', he told me."

"I'm sure it would be easier for the French to give their support once they had tangible evidence," Owen said, glancing at the satchel.

"Of course, that's Roland. If they saw for themselves, then he knows it would be easier to convince the UN to provide the security needed in this region. Although I didn't like the arrangement, I had no choice but to work within it."

"How can you possibly go back to Bamako now?"

While they spoke, the two guards carefully assisted Moussa's father to his feet, a clear sign the meeting was over. Moussa and Owen rose too, as if in the presence of a king.

"I'm not going back."

"Of course not," Owen said. "And Gidean, is he?"

"He was found some days ago by Bedouin, wandering out there on his own. My father's people saw his bag in the possession of a trader selling camels. Shortly after we dropped him in Bourem, he was taken north and given escorts. His guides taunted him, saying there was nothing out there but sand. They will pay for their indiscretion. Such a revelation crazed him. He started arguments, became violent, wandering off during darkness. Search parties were formed."

"Because of what you told him," Owen said. "That's why he went looking. It's his obsession."

"He shouldn't have gone off on his own. Not out there."

"Where is he now?"

"They were too late."

"What do you mean, *late*?"

"The Bedouin found him first. Took him across the border. Sold him."

"*What?*" Owen asked, unable to comprehend Moussa's words.

"He was theirs to do as they wished, having plucked him from the desert. They brought him back from the dead, making it their right. Don't weep for him, Owen. He doesn't deserve your empathy."

"And what will happen to him now?"

"By tradition, sold into slavery. But I suspect he'll end up in the hands of Islamists. Maybe they'll pay for him or, more likely, take him by force. They won't kill him. He's old-school South African, not an idealist."

"And me, Moussa, what's my fate, the same?"

The sound of engines could be heard on the other side of

the village, a revving followed by idling, indicating a start-stop movement.

"They've entered," Moussa said.

With a sense of urgency, he spoke to his father. During their hurried conversation, Wararni removed his dagger from his belt, presenting it to his son. To Owen, it seemed he was witnessing something private between the two. The passing of some great responsibility. Once the ritual was complete, Moussa kissed his father on both cheeks before embracing him gently. Then one of the guards took Wararni's elbow, guiding him out of the room. As he left, the old man raised a hand to them both in a farewell gesture. Owen noticed how frail he looked, imagining a cold desert wind would indeed penetrate his thinning skin. The other Tuareg rolled up the carpet, collected the cushions, and followed them out, removing all traces of their presence.

A quietness settled in the room, interrupted only by the faint noise of engines stopping and starting, an indication Bastien was searching.

"You're free to go," Moussa said. "Wherever you wish. But I agree with your journalist friend. Leave this country, even this continent."

"Why don't you come with me?" Owen asked.

"I'm going north, where I'm needed. My people finally accept the only way they'll achieve independence is by taking it. When Bastien arrives, which won't be long, tell him this house is being watched, for a short while anyway. No harm is intended towards the French. But it's important *you* remain here for thirty minutes. Then you can leave."

"If I go before?"

"You'll be shot," Moussa said. "That's the best I could negotiate with my father in the time I had. He wanted to take you with him."

"Perhaps they'll leave me here, pursue you?"

"Maybe, but I wouldn't recommend it."

"So that's it?"

"There are two exits to this house, both with eyes on them. So please, heed my warning."

"Maybe I should come with you?"

"Go home, Owen. You're lucky to have been given this chance. Please, *my friend*, you must learn to protect yourself from the sadness that's engulfing you."

Their shared struggle, to find a way back unmolested, bonded these two men. It was an aspiration neither could claim to have achieved because each had suffered on those journeys.

Moussa opened the door, turning to face him.

"Remember, thirty minutes. Be liberal with your timing because they don't have watches," he said, "and I'm taking the vehicle." The humour evident in his tone was the Moussa Owen wanted to remember. "Accept the way things are, and one day, God willing, we'll both rejoice in the child that holds our hand and the woman that embraces us."

If anyone had asked Owen if he had learnt anything from his life so far, the answer, until that last lesson, would have been, nothing. But after all his travels, he understood what was needed to mend his own broken world. It was time to stop stumbling into other people's realms and find his own peace. We all have those personal files stored away in the main frame of our minds, the ones containing evidence of the times we failed to do the right thing, followed someone else, became directionless. If only it were possible to wash away our sins in one final act. Standing in a deserted house in a strange land where he didn't belong, Owen was beginning to imagine he was redeemable.

All he had to do was go home.

"God be with you, my friend," Moussa said, for one last time.

"Go with peace," Owen said, as he watched him slip through the door.

He hoped Moussa heard his farewell above the door scraping and the wind howling. The only answer he received was a whispering on the air, followed by the sound of vehicles. Owen contemplated running out into the road to call after him, join him in whatever lay ahead, but he was held by Moussa's warning. Maybe there was no one watching, just a deterrence, his way of protecting Owen from making such a foolish decision.

There was no escaping the loss he felt watching his friend depart. But there was something else too, like a weight of burden removed. It was the last Owen saw of Moussa, the man he loved like a brother.

CHAPTER 37

"Where are they?" Bastien demanded.

"Moussa's gone. They've all left."

"Gone where?"

I suspect he's going somewhere above Kidal, Owen said to himself, *where, as a child, his father sent him to learn. A place where he wandered between waterholes to experience a nomadic lifestyle. He once told me if you search hard enough, you can find evidence of long-forgotten battles among rocks and sand. It's the place where he found his history, among his own people, listening to stories around campfires. That's where he'll be.*

"He went east," Owen said, not wishing to share such comforting stories with anyone intending to harm his friend.

"Mauritania?" Bastien asked.

"Yes, that's where they must have gone," Owen said, grateful Bastien had planted the seed of misinformation.

"And the South African?"

"All of them, together."

"All?"

"Some Tuareg. No one of significance."

"They're all significant," Bastien said, nodding to one of his men, who immediately stepped outside.

"Why are they so important to you? They're Tuareg, doing what they've always done, wandering across this land."

"*Donnez-moi putain de patience!*" Bastien said, the expletive evidence of his growing frustration. "Your colleague helped jihadists cross the desert, and now their numbers are multiplying. He was thrown in jail for those services."

"You're wrong," Owen said, refusing to accept the Frenchman's story.

"We know he spent some years here in the north, mapping the land, learning the languages. On his last journey, when he was stopped in Kidal, he'd already made many crossings over the Algerian border. Rumours grew of a wealthy Tuareg with ambitions of helping Islamic fundamentalists expand their influence and access untapped resources. That's Moussa. He was tracked on his last crossing by people loyal to us. They lost him south of the oasis at Dijomel. The next we hear, he's being released from prison, working for the UN. Untouchable."

"And you can prove all this?"

"French intelligence," Bastien said.

Owen considered the story and whether the spice trader was one of those loyal people Bastien mentioned.

"It was Tuareg we met with today, not Islamic fundamentalists."

"How do you know who they were?"

"Because I saw them. We drank coffee together. That's all there was to it."

"I know what's in the satchel," Bastien said. "It's the reason I'm here."

"You're going to be disappointed," Owen said, lifting the flap, allowing the officer to take a step forward to look inside.

Once Moussa had gone, Owen took the bag, placing it over his shoulder, a memento of a phase in his life that ended in a dusty room in a place called Raz El Ma. On closer inspection, he found an inscription carved into the leather:

Presented to Gidean De Villiers, from The Gold and Diamond Foundation of Johannesburg, in recognition of your loyal service to the company. May God bless you with many happy years of foraging.

Reading it, Owen thought God had indeed delivered on the blessing.

"You see," Owen said, keeping the satchel open, as if the truth was in the empty space.

Bastien's look of disappointment was palpable, his agitation flowing into his expression.

"Out the door, turn left, and get in the first vehicle," he said. "We're leaving."

"We need to wait a little longer," Owen said, explaining Moussa's warning.

"There's no one out there. It's just another one of his feints to slow us down. Once you're battened down, you'll be safe."

"A few more minutes. What harm can it do?"

"You either go now or we'll leave you here. From where I'm standing, you're no use to me anymore," Bastien said, with an obvious air of clarity.

Once out the door, Owen noticed the storm was starting to subside, revealing the village in its entirety. To his left was one of the armoured cars, its hydraulic door wide open. Looking across the road, he noticed two of Bastien's men exiting one of the houses, searching perhaps, or maybe looking for support in their quest. Owen fought the urge to shout, advise them it was unlikely they would find any Francophiles. Removing the satchel, he threw it into the bowels of the steel structure before allowing himself one last look over his shoulder. In the dust were tyre marks and two sets of footprints. If Moussa was all story and myth, an idea Owen reviled, then he was glad those grand tales provided him with a place to hide in the most difficult of times.

Stepping on the support hanging from the vehicle's

undercarriage, Owen gripped the warm metal of the door's aperture, readying himself to climb inside. As he pushed against the step while pulling with his hands to take the weight, a single shot rang out.

The bullet slammed into his lower thigh, tearing at his flesh as it passed through. Its sledgehammer force threw him forward, arms thrown outwards, like the caricature of a crucifixion victim. Landing on the vehicle's floor, his first thought was he had been manhandled, punched hard from the rear. In shocked astonishment, he touched the dampness, blood running over his fingers. Its warmth surprised him. The pain was excruciating and immediate, an extreme burning sensation, as if a red-hot poker was thrust into his thigh. Then nausea, followed by darkness. It threatened to engulf him as his body took control, drawing him downwards into unconsciousness.

The first thing Owen noticed as he drifted back was a soldier threading a tourniquet above the wound. He watched as the man tightened the strap, turning a pencil-shaped piece of plastic to arrest the bleeding. Everything moved in slow motion, his mind not working, senses dulled. Then there was more pain, caused by another wrench of the tourniquet. They were racing across the desert, each bump sending yet another agonising pulse into his groin. Telling himself to lie still, he hoped a lack of movement would reduce his suffering as he anticipated the next rush of agony. It came when they drove into a small depression, causing the vehicle to lift as it accelerated across and out of the dip. The torture it brought dragged him once more into an unconscious darkness.

It was sometime later when he woke, gradually floating back. Crouching next to him, blood smeared across his face, was Bastien.

"You're injured," Owen said.

"It's your blood. We're trying to stop the bleeding, but it's proving difficult."

"I need something for the pain."

"We've already given you morphine."

"I told you I needed more time."

"Yes, you did, but we didn't have any to give."

"How bad?" Owen asked.

"We already have a helicopter in the air, crossing from Burkina Faso. There's a medical team on board."

"Why are we moving? Chasing the Tuareg?"

"We're heading south. It'll lessen the fly time if we can reduce the distance."

Making the decision to head back frustrated Bastien, who wanted to pursue Moussa. When he saw Owen lying in the rear of the vehicle, blood starting to pool on the floor, he knew he had no choice.

"Do I have much time?" Owen asked.

"We already had the helicopter on standby. Now the winds have abated, it won't be long," Bastien said.

Although he tried to reassure Owen, he had his concerns. One hour, and there was a chance. Longer would only be guessing. The profuse blood loss was his biggest fear, and while the flow had slowed, it had not stopped.

***

The French were determined to join the expedition, insisting they were the only ones able to protect such an undertaking. The approaching storm and restricted helicopter movement provided an opportunity to apply even more pressure in support of their request. They heard rumours about gold and Moussa's involvement, the son of a known dissident. French intelligence would later claim they had been aware of him for some time. One of their spies even claimed to have met Moussa. Like Roland, they chased the stories and listened to the spread of lies. A deception, circulated to cause confusion, clearing the way for Moussa's return. The French wanted confirmation, their concerns verging on hysteria at the idea insurgents would be able to fund their aspirations with the wealth under their feet. It was Bastien's specified task to prove the intelligence. If Owen was right, then it was all a lie, allowing Moussa to cut his umbilical cord and return to the northern tribes. Not to support Islamist ambitions, but to reignite domestic subversion from within the Tuareg.

From the moment he was chosen, Bastien found the unorthodox approach of it all appealing, stimulating even. Like those who sent him, he was oblivious to history's plan to draw France into another protracted war in North Africa. His small venture from Mopti to Raz El Ma was the first move in a game that would drag his nation into something far bigger.

When he heard the shot, Bastien froze, staring at the door. The shock was acute, and the urge to do nothing, remain inside, was powerful. The clearest bodily response he recalled was a dryness in his mouth, followed by an overwhelming need to drink water. Another sound, one coming after, worried him even more. A rotating turret. If those mounted weapons were used in the village, they would obliterate the buildings in an instant, including everything and everyone inside.

Exiting the door, he roared his command.

"Hold your fire!"

The village remained silent while Bastien and his men waited.

"*L'observateur de l'ONU il a été touché!*" someone shouted out of the deafening silence. "The UN observer was hit!"

***

Owen was waking, groaning, trying to speak, his words unintelligible. He was shivering too, cold in the dark confines of the vehicle's hull. In the stillness, there was no longer a constant vibration or a rattling of equipment.

They were no longer moving.

The intense pain had become nothing more than a dull throbbing. Willing himself into wakefulness, he tried to adopt a sitting position.

The person sitting next to him was smiling, a gesture Owen found reassuring.

"Just relax," he heard the figure say.

Owen struggled to place that youthful tone.

"You need to remain calm," he was told, not recognising Bastien's voice. "Put your head back and rest."

Owen welcomed the softness of a jacket placed under his neck for comfort. The dampness down below was embarrassing, so much so he was concerned the other two in there with him would think he had wet himself.

"Uh-huh," he said, trying to speak, his words not coming together.

Exhausted and confused, Owen was drifting, imagining other places, other times. At one point, he was running across a road, sprinting towards the confines of a den on the far side, fear making him hurry. Not because of the approaching convoy, but something much more sinister.

I've been shot, he thought.

Touching his mashed flesh, Owen considered the notion he was going to die, fighting against the terror such a premonition brought. It gave him some comfort knowing his mother would be in Lucy's life.

Then a shadow crossed his face. Someone moving above perhaps, or an object falling. Once it passed, all his fear slipped away.

Opening his eyes, he noticed Bastien had returned, staring down at him, looking serious.

"Ghosts in the desert," Owen said, barely audible. "I tried to tell you."

"They're almost here. I can hear them."

The relief in the Frenchman's voice was intense.

Owen listened, recognising the telltale sounds of chopping rotors getting louder by the second.

"Yes, I can hear it," Owen whispered, worried he might be making too much noise in the confined space. "Why are there three of us in here," he giggled, "when there's only room for two?"

"Don't worry, everything's going to plan," Bastien said.

"Let's not worry anymore about plans."

Bastien leaned forward, positioning himself closer to Owen's mouth, trying to catch his words because he was making no sense.

As the hydraulic door started to open, a sliver of light entered through the widening gap, exposing thousands of dancing dust mites.

"A plan can change," Owen said, into the ear hovering inches from his mouth.

"I can't hear you," Bastien shouted above the noise of the helicopter's engines and debris crashing against the vehicle.

Opened to its full extent, the door revealed an emergency response team sprinting, bent double, laden with heavy packs containing everything they needed to start working on the wounded man.

A brilliant white light rushed inside, consuming everything. Owen absorbed the beauty and calmness of it all. In those last moments, he used every bit of strength to place a hand behind Bastien's neck, twisting hard so he could see his old friend's face. Billy stared back, smiling and shouting, like the happy fourteen-year-old he once was.

The dust danced a golden jig for them both.

"Speak louder," Bastien said, one last time.

Owen laughed, having been flung back to a hot summer's day.

"Just throw, Billy," he said, looking into the Frenchman's face. "Throw, and let's see what happens."

About the Author

Alan D. M. Garner was born and raised in South Yorkshire. *Causes of Consequences* is his debut novel. Alan's family worked in the coal mining industry, but due to its demise, he chose other interests. Initially pursuing a career in the army, he subsequently attended university and worked in the field of education. Having travelled extensively across Africa, he was honoured with an MBE for services to Sierra Leone. After eight years living and working in the Middle East, he now resides and writes in the East Midlands.